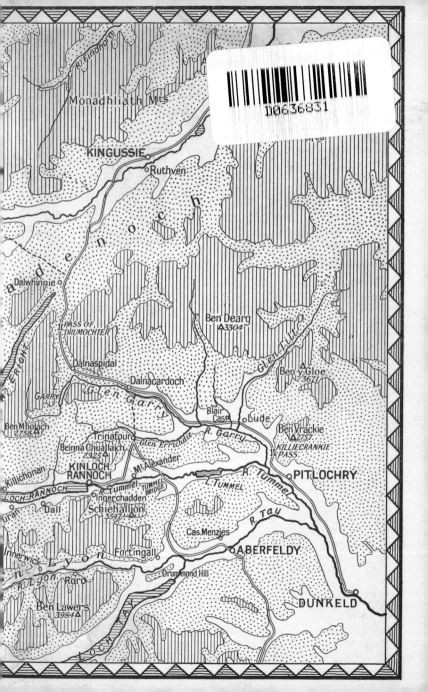

£10

Almond, Wild Almond

Almond, Wild Almond

by

D. K. Broster

London - William Heinemann Ltd.

First Published 1933

Printed in Great Britain at
The Windmill Press, Kingswood, Surrey

TO
FRANK AND ELIZABETH EMSLIE
FORMERLY OF KINLOCH RANNOCH
IN MEMORY OF MUCH KINDNESS RECEIVED THERE
AND ELSEWHERE

Almond, wild almond,
  Give counsel to me,
And hush thy fierce lover
  The wind in the tree!

Along the night pasture
  I've come through the dew
To tell thee, wild almond,
  The old songs are true!

I too have a lover. . . . . .
  . . . .
O had he entreated
  I could have said nay,
But he, he says nothing,
  And then goes away!

Ah, loves he for ever?
  And loves me alone?
These things that men say not
  How can they be known?

He may, but he may not—
  And I would be free:—
Now play not, now sway not,
  Thou little black tree,
Almond, wild almond,
  Give counsel to me!

                    Herbert Trench.

CONTENTS

CONTENTS

CHAPTER I

SEVEN o'clock of the dark, furious March evening, seven o'clock on the second day of the second storm. "Unless," thought the young French officer standing with one hand upon the high, yellowing mantelpiece, "unless we should reckon this week's tornado as but a prolongation of last week's. God, what weather!"

A fiercer blast than before pounded at the windows of the Intendance de la Marine at Dunkirk, and a vicious puff of black smoke came volleying out between the impassive caryatids of the fireplace. "Forty thousand devils!" exclaimed Lieutenant the Vicomte Marie-Cyprien d'Ornières de Lancize, as he sprang back, amid some derisive laughter from the other end of the room, and, whipping forth his pocket-handkerchief, clapped it for a second or so to his nose. Out of range of the odious discharge from the chimney, he next made a movement as if to flick his boots, those long cavalry boots which came halfway up his thighs, but cut the action short, remembering that the boots in question, usually so immaculate, were already spattered with mud, and sticky with sea-water nearly to their tops. Sea-water had stained and discoloured the wide full skirts of his brilliant uniform coat as well. Dandy though he was, officer in Dauphin-Dragons, and acting aide-de-camp to the Comte de Saxe, M. de Lancize's attire, like that of many another soldier and sailor in Dunkirk to-day, bore speaking traces of the two closely succeeding tempests, the second of which was raging there now.

They were peculiarly disastrous tempests—save from the point of view of Hanoverian England—because they had wrecked and driven on shore about one quarter of the large flotilla of transports assembled at Dunkirk in

I

this year of 1744 for the purpose of landing ten thousand Frenchmen upon English soil, in support of the claims of the House of Stuart—in support also of King Louis XV's desire to pay out George II for the defeat inflicted last June on old Maréchal de Noailles at Dettingen. It had seemed to His Most Christian Majesty and his advisers that even if they did not succeed in bringing about an actual revolution in England, they might at least stir up civil war, and in either case the English and Hanoverian troops would have to be withdrawn from the Continent and their inconvenient succour of the cause of the Empress Maria Theresa in this present war over the Austrian succession.

The orders for the concentration of merchant and fishing vessels at this port of French Flanders had been given as early as the previous November, but there had been delays of various kinds, not a few of them caused by the difficulty of wresting definite information about support from the English Jacobites; and even of getting any information at all. Pilots, for instance, were promised by them, but never sent, and it was intimated from across the Channel that January was too cold a month in which to expect English noblemen and country squires to assist in a revolution. By February, indeed, much of the enthusiasm of the French for the project had waned, but preparations had gone too far to be dropped. On the 28th of the month, after delays and misfortunes at sea, appeared the convoying squadron, under M. de Barreilh; next day (it was leap year) arrived that famous soldier Maurice, Comte de Saxe, who was in supreme command of the expedition; outgoing vessels were forbidden to leave and the work of embarkation began.

Meanwhile, sixteen miles away at Gravelines, there waited an ardent young man of four-and-twenty, who had made a romantic incognito dash from Rome to join it. But since it was given out, in the hopes of deluding the English, that the expedition was intended for the Low Countries, Prince Charles Edward Stuart's presence in the neighbourhood was so sedulously concealed that though correspondence had passed, no personal meeting had taken place between him and the Comte de Saxe. Yet, particularly as a number of Jacobites had flocked to Dunkirk, the news of his being at Gravelines was no longer in reality a secret, indeed the Vicomte de Lancize, during some hours of leisure at the beginning of the previous week, had ridden over to see if he could get a glimpse of the princely adventurer for whom his own sovereign was nominally doing so much. But he had not succeeded.

And then, during the night of Friday, the 6th of March, there had arisen a tremendous equinoctial gale from the north and north-east. Of the unfortunate transports, crammed with troops, out in the unsheltered open road of Dunkirk, no less than eleven were driven on shore, and two of them, the *St. Raymond* and the *Barentin,* packed with soldiers, were in considerable danger of becoming total losses, since they had grounded too far from low-water mark for assistance to reach them from the shore, and the breakers were too furious to permit of any boat putting out.

Vivid, indeed, were M. Marie-Cyprien de Lancize's recollections of last Saturday morning, from which his boots would probably never recover. Summoned at seven o'clock to attend the Comte de Saxe to the scene of disaster, he had ridden with him to that wild, flat, surf-beset shore, and also, like his leader, had ridden into the angry sea, then beginning to ebb. And he had personally grabbed by hair or uniform a couple of half drowning wretches who were trying to swim ashore. In that grey and white sea, against that livid grey sky, he had caught glimpses of other transports in like distress, and learnt that for a vessel to be called the *Reine des Anges* or the *Victorieux* was no safeguard against a lee shore in a gale. By low tide, however, nearly all the troops had been saved, many of them probably to fall ill from having to endure long periods of waiting in the bitter wind after being drenched to the skin. But all the tents, arms and baggage were lost.

Next day, when the wind was somewhat abated, it transpired that the vessels in the road which had been fortunate enough to ride out the storm were entirely destitute of provisions, though they should have been victualled for a considerable period. Even the bread which they had was uneatable through being soaked with sea-water. Nor would it be possible to refloat the stranded vessels before the next spring-tide, a week hence.

All this was bad enough, but almost as bad was to follow. Hardly had the great gale of Friday and Saturday blown itself out, and the reckoning of damages and licking of wounds begun in earnest, when there arose another tempest of almost equal violence, coming up this time from the west and south-west. This was the storm which, having begun about one o'clock the previous morning, Tuesday, was now raging round the Intendance, where the Comte de Saxe had his headquarters. It had already done enough damage to render it a serious rival to the first hurricane. Of the thirteen vessels which, in accordance with orders, should have come from the road into harbour, only one had succeeded in doing so, and she had left her anchors and cables behind. At ten o'clock to-day a transport had gone ashore with four companies of Royal-Corse on board, though in the event only two lives were lost. When the contrary wind permitted, could be heard this afternoon the melancholy booming of signal guns from three more vessels who were in difficulties off the coast. Marie-Cyprien de Lancize, who had a friend in the Régiment de Diesbach, embarked in the *Hareng Couronné*, felt however that he had some grounds for hope that a vessel with such a name might have remained afloat.

But what was going to happen to the twice-maimed expedition? That was what everyone connected with it was asking; it was the question now engaging the group of subaltern officers at the other end of the long room, where, if they had no fire to warm them, they were at any rate not menaced by smoke. The young dragoon, who could at least congratulate himself that his regiment, the only cavalry going with the flotilla, was still safe on shore, strolled towards them. A naval officer from M. de Barreilh's own vessel, the *Dauphin Royal,* who had come ashore with a despatch to go off to M. de Maurepas, the Minister of Marine, was holding forth in an annoyed voice about the conditions on board.

"Quite a third of the crew are ill, and the rest are worn out with work. As for the ship herself, everything rattles and bangs about as if it would carry away. Moreover," he sank his voice a little, "M. de Barreilh is apprehensive that Admiral Norris may suddenly appear and burn all the ships in the road."

("Added to which," said the young aide-de-camp to himself, "I have heard M. de Saxe give it as his opinion of the sailors of the convoy that they would be more at home in a farm-cart than in a boat.") But as it would not have been prudent to announce this fact he merely observed cheerfully, "I hazard a guess, monsieur, that what your commodore is really praying for now is the receipt of orders for the transports to go back to the various ports whence they came, and for himself to return with his own ships to Brest?"

"Monsieur le dragon," said the sailor, "I think you are not far wrong."

"I have heard," remarked a lieutenant in the black and white of Royal-Corse, who had suffered shipwreck in the first storm, "that the Jacobites gathered here in Dunkirk would on the contrary have M. de Barreilh seek out and attack Admiral Norris."

"When he has only five ships and Admiral Norris is said to have twenty!"

"These Jacobites!" exclaimed the naval officer. "They ask the impossible from us and stir not a finger themselves! What are they doing to prepare for us in England? And, messieurs, do you realise, that when we reach the mouth of the river of Thames—if we ever do—even though there be not a force sufficiently strong to prevent our sailing up it, the English have only to remove the beacons which mark the channel, and every pilot we have will be useless!"

"I do not think we need trouble our heads about that," said the subaltern of Royal-Corse. "We shall certes never reach the river of Thames. Listen to that!"

A fresh blast shook the windows; again the smoke bellied forth between the marble nymphs, but this time there was no one in front of them.

"Congratulations, Vicomte," observed someone, "on not receiving that discharge!"

"Sad, however, that a dragoon cannot stand fire!"

"At any rate he is not afraid of water! Did he not save two men of the Régiment de Monaco from the *St. Raymond* on Saturday?"

"Yes, but only by nearly scalping them!"

But the Vicomte de Lancize, with a wave of the hand, was removing himself from these pleasantries. An officer in the scarlet and blue of Cour au Chantre had just come through one of the doors which faced each other in the sides of the long room, and was crossing in haste to the other, as one going upon an errand. But he was looking about him for someone as he did so. He was the aide-de-camp previously on duty; the someone was M. de Lancize, who would now take his place outside M. de Saxe's apartment, to be ready for the next order.

And that young gentleman, as he went briskly along the corridor towards his post at no great distance, saw to his surprise that the Comte de Saxe's door had been left half open—presumably but unaccountably by the just-departed aide-de-camp. Light streamed out from it, and voices were audible in the passage, though a great stamped leather screen, which stood just inside, concealed the speakers, and indeed the whole room—concealed too from those speakers the fact that their deliberations were no longer as private as they probably imagined. Yet, reflected M. de Lancize, as he approached the portal, it was no business of his to shut it. For all he knew the Comte de Saxe might have commanded it to be opened for some reason or other, to let out, for instance, some such horrible on-slaught of smoke as he himself had recently experienced. So, with a shrug of the shoulders, he took up his post at precisely the distance from the doorway which he would have selected in any case. Since his eavesdropping was unavoidable he might as well take what heaven sent him; it would while away the time of waiting.

Whose, he wondered, was that deep voice now resound-ing in the room? Not, certainly, that of M. de Saxe him-self, nor of M. de Ségent, the *commissaire des guerres,* who was said to be closeted with him there. It sounded more like that of M. Bart, the commandant of the port of Dunkirk.

". . . hard at work from six o'clock yesterday morning, Monseigneur, furnishing different captains with such things as anchors and cables, and necessities for the un-fortunate troops who have suffered so much. I could not undertake——"

"Monsieur Bart," interrupted the voice which the Vicomte de Lancize knew best, clear, rapid and forceful, "I will relieve your anxieties. There is no need for you to undertake anything further. I cannot interpret M. d'Argenson's letter to me as anything but a formal order to abandon the expedition entirely and without further delay."

If Marie-Cyprien de Lancize had had the faculty of moving his ears he would certainly have pricked them for-ward at this. Yet he did not advance his person a step nearer.

"To abandon it entirely!" exclaimed another voice— presumably M. de Ségent's.

"In truth," growled out M. Bart, "I am glad to hear it— even though hostility with England comes natural to a man of my name. But—with a second tempest! Is it per-mitted to ask for M. d'Argenson's reasons? The bad weather, I presume."

"Here is the actual letter from the Minister of War," said the Comte de Saxe. M. de Lancize heard the rustle

B

of paper, and a moment later the deep voice began to read something over. Alert though he was and straining every nerve to hear, the listening aide-de-camp could not catch every word.

"'... *bad weather* ... *Admiral Norris* ... *precautions which the English have had time* ... *lack of news* ... *promised to support* ... *reasons more than sufficient* ... *meet with more success* ... *led His Majesty to order me*' (here the voice became louder) '*to send you instructions that on receipt of my letter you should give the necessary orders for the disembarkation of our troops*'—Ah! this, then, Monseigneur, is the real reason of the orders to that effect which you have already given! But I myself received a letter from M. de Maurepas informing me that though the troops were to disembark the vessels were to remain where they were!"

"Not the first time, perhaps," said the voice of M. de Ségent, with some acridity, "that the Minister of Marine and the Minister of War have not understood their orders in quite the same sense!"

"It's a pity, though," said the commandant of the port as though to himself. "All those men embarked, all those preparations——"

"It is clear that the winds are not Jacobite," observed Maurice de Saxe. "Count Alberoni learnt the same thing in 1719. And at court I think the weathervane has been turned in a fresh direction by some breeze or other of intrigue. The expedition, as you know, has always had its enemies. One good purpose, however, will be served by these two storms. They make it much easier for me to convince that poor prince without a kingdom of the impossibility of setting out. I wrote to him three days ago to tell him that M. de Roquefeuil had not succeeded in blockading Admiral Norris in Portsmouth, and that the latter had slipped away into the Downs.—Girardot, is that door by any chance open? There is a damnable cold air from somewhere!"

In all history no door was probably more swiftly and

silently closed than was then M. de Saxe's in the Intendance de la Marine at Dunkirk. And the closer knew that it must have been well and truly shut by the time that M. Girardot, the Comte's secretary, got round the screen, otherwise he would certainly have made investigations.

So, quite definitely, the great expedition was knocked on the head! M. de Lancize was not really surprised. But those poor, disappointed devils of Jacobites—and the Prince Charles Edouard himself! Well, in his situation he had probably learnt philosophy by now.

Standing there, cut off from hearing any more interesting and as yet unpublished news, yawning, rather tired, Marie-Cyprien de Lancize invoked philosophy to his own assistance. He did not know when he was likely to be dismissed; not for hours, perhaps, and his desires were just now turning strongly to a certain wine-shop on the quays, though indeed it was not for the sake of the less than passable Bordeaux to be had there that he proposed, if he could, to fight his way to the sign of the *Trois Navires*. It was he who had discovered the *fillette* . . . that fair Flemish type, when it was not too heavy, possessed its attractions . . . he had always inclined to fair hair in a woman. But the *Trois Navires* might have been blown down in the night for all he knew.

After all, he was not to go to England! Well, more glory was probably to be won by following the Comte de Saxe to the Low Countries and Germany—for it was believed that he was to command the army of the Moselle. He, Marie-Cyprien de Lancize, would be able to fight against the English in some pitched battle, which would really be preferable to scrambling encounters on beaches after a seasick voyage across the Channel in some craft not much bigger than a herring-boat. All was for the best.

All was certainly for the best! The door was opening already. Girardot looked out, saw him standing there at attention and beckoned to him. He was going to get his orders sooner than he had hoped—perhaps his dismissal for the night also. He went past the leather screen, saluted and stood waiting.

Behind the vast, shabby table, whose mother-of-pearl inlay was stained with ink from the labours of many intendants, the son of Augustus of Saxony and Poland and of Aurora von Königsmarck sat writing. Tall and imposing, the victor of Prague (who was not yet the victor of Fontenoy and Raucoux) was now in his forty-eighth year; his eyes under his beetling brows were very blue, but his complexion was swarthy and his hair dark; he seldom wore powder. Fate, in denying Maurice de Saxe his great ambition, a territory to rule (since the ducal throne of Courland to which, at thirty, he was elected, remained his for only nine months), and in allowing him only an intermittent display of his brilliant military gifts, had driven him, always impatient of inactivity, to occupations much less austere. Adrienne Lecouvreur had now been dead for fourteen years, but upon how many ladies of the stage or the opera had he not fixed his fancy since then? Prospects of dazzling marriages had not been wanting in his younger days; he was semi-royal and very attractive. There had been question of two princesses of Peter the Great's family, each of whom afterwards ascended the imperial throne of Russia in her own right. One of them reigned there at this moment. But he had not married either, and his Lutheranism, purely nominal though it was, debarred him from being created a marshal of France, for all that he had rendered his adopted country such signal services. To Marie-Cyprien de Lancize, who admired him enormously, this seemed a crying scandal— since he could not know that in less than a month the coveted baton was nevertheless to be placed in that strong and elegant hand.

The young man stood respectfully waiting, his eyes upon his commander, yet not unaware that Monsieur François Cornil Bart, looking as a man would look who bore that name of which Dunkirk was so proud—and indeed the famous corsair Jean Bart was no other than his father—

was standing with his back turned on the *commissaire des guerres*. He seemed to be studying the painting of the furious naval battle over the hearth, wherein the sea was scarcely visible for the quantity of floating spars and drowning but attitudinising sailors which it contained. Perhaps, as a naval officer of distinction, he was thinking resentfully of that uneatable bread of M. de Ségent's providing.

At last the Comte de Saxe dusted over his letter, whose recipient would probably have difficulty with his fantastically bad spelling, folded, sealed and addressed it. Then the blue eyes were lifted and looked straight at the aide-de-camp. The latter at once came forward.

"Take this letter, if you please, Monsieur de Lancize, to the Bailli de Givry at the Gouvernement. After that I shall not require your services further to-night." And with those last words there was a glimpse of the smile which was reputed irresistible.

A moment later Lieutenant the Vicomte de Lancize had closed the door of Monsieur de Saxe's room for the second time. He could guess at the information which he was conveying to the Governor of the town of Dunkirk in this letter sealed with the arms of the House of Wettin traversed by the bend sinister; it was to tell him that the enterprise was as dead as a doornail. But for himself, he was more concerned with the knowledge that his evening's pleasure was now secured.

Although there were occasional lulls, it was still blowing very hard in the Parc de la Marine, where the Intendance was situated, and when the young dragoon, bearing to his right, crossed the bridge over the Canal de Furnes into the town, he staggered for a second against the parapet, bent nearly double as he was, and clutching his hat with one hand, his wildly beating cloak with the other. In the Place Royale, which he then skirted, there was not a soul to be seen, but as he passed along between the parish church of St. Eloi and its separate-standing tower he met a couple of priests with unruly cassocks, and after that a small squad of soldiers of the Régiment d'Eu. High above the roof-tops a pale, astonished ghost of a moon struggled to fend off the masses of scudding blackness. She looked, he thought, like a drowned face among seaweed. It was marvellous that there had not been more drowned faces out there in the *rade*. How unfortunate was the House of Stuart; that poor young prince at Gravelines, all ignorant of the orders recently received from Versailles, must be almost out of his mind with anxiety! With this sympathetic reflection M. de Lancize arrived at the building known as the Gouvernement.

By the time that he had discharged his mission rain had been added to the discomforts of the night. Undismayed, he set his face now in the direction of the water-side. The sight of Nicolle's golden hair would compensate for much, and that the *Trois Navires* lay in such close proximity to those masts which even in harbour were to-night swaying and straining wildly, to those creaking hulls, would only make its interior the more attractive. Even though he would be wet as well as muddy, he did not anticipate the wench objecting on that score to sit upon his knee. Since the expedition was not now to sail, he would be unable to pursue any studies with regard to Nicolle's counterparts in England. Well, the Low Countries were full of girls with fair skins and golden hair; he would probably be sick of them before long.

The rain-lashed streets seemed even more deserted than when he had left the Intendance. The young dragoon found himself plunging into one of whose name he was not sure, though he believed it to be the Rue des Minimes. It led, at any rate, in the right direction, and he pursued it whistling a little air which the wind slew on his lips. Borne in snatches on the blast came the tinkle and clang of various bells ringing for compline from the numerous religious houses of Dunkirk, the Conceptionnistes in his immediate vicinity or the Clarisses, the Pénitentes or the Dames Anglaises—or even the Minimes ahead of him. In this *ruelle*—for it was hardly more, so narrow was it and short—two lights only were visible; one at the further end, affixed for the guidance of the public to the wall of a house, and one of a different nature which streamed out from the uncurtained ground-floor window of some dwelling at the nearer. By the more distant light, which leapt violently at every fresh gust, something like the arm of a semaphore could be seen, though indistinctly, to swing to and fro.

The young officer's immediate attention, however, was caught by this low, lighted window on his right hand, and as he neared it a quite purposeless curiosity prompted him to glance in. For the window was open—an unusual phenomenon on so wet and boisterous a night—and a man was standing at it, a tall man and a young, as far as could be guessed. Looking for the arrival of someone, perhaps. . . .

"She will not come, monsieur, in such weather," remarked M. de Lancize, slackening his pace as he passed. "You would do better to go to bed!"

There was no answer, or none that reached his ears, and with this piece of impertinence the Comte de Saxe's aide-de-camp passed on to what was awaiting him at the end of the street. It leapt down upon him, the smile still round his lips, with a noise like the clatter of several iron pots, with an astonishing souse of water and a simultaneous blow on head and shoulder that sent him reeling, astounded and indignant, into the rain-filled gutter in the middle of the *ruelle*, where, slipping in the slime of it, he fell his length.

Not without cause had the retired notary who dwelt in the corner house with the lantern feared that the whole of his already rickety gutter would carry away one of these nights if the gale continued.

CHAPTER II

WHEN Mr. Ranald Maclean, younger of Fasnapoll in Askay, had opened the window of his lodging in the Rue des Minimes, it had only been because of the unconscious pressure of his thoughts. Were the elements never going to relent? A Jacobite by upbringing and conviction, he had nevertheless no more come to Dunkirk in order to join Prince Charles Edward and the French expedition than he had unfastened his casement through impatience of the advent of a lady, as that impudent French officer just passing in the rain had suggested. It was chance which had brought him, all unknowing, to Dunkirk on his way back to Scotland from the wine country of the Gironde— only to find Dunkirk a hive of war-like preparations, and all outgoing vessels forbidden to leave. In less than an hour he had discovered why; in less than two, finding that the Earl Marischal was among the Scottish Jacobites gathered there to accompany the expedition, he had waited upon him and placed his sword at the disposal of King James III and VIII.

That was last Thursday, before the first tempest; and this was Wednesday. What of the condition of the French flotilla now, what of all those brave hopes? "The wind blew and they were scattered." Mr. Maclean did not know whence these words came to torment him; he thought from some English medal struck to commemorate the destruction of the Spanish Armada. Yes, the winds always fought for England; had they not wrecked the hopes of the Jacobite attempt of 1719 by scattering the Spanish fleet which was to bring such solid assistance to the Cause? He turned away from his contemplation of the streaming, howling dusk outside with something between a curse and a sigh, and, forgetting to close the inward opening casement, moved away, a tall, lean, muscular Highlander of eight-and-twenty or so, not ill-looking, rather grave of aspect, dark of complexion, grey-eyed and wearing his own dark hair. But after a moment, realising that the rain was coming in, he turned back to shut the window, and was just pushing it to when there came to his ears from without a sort of clattering and a cry. Pulling the casement wide again, he thrust out his head. The vacillating light at the end of the little street showed him a cloaked and falling figure. Ranald Maclean swung a leg over the low sill and vaulted out into the rain.

"Are you much hurt, sir?" asked a voice in Marie-Cyprien de Lancize's ear, a voice which that young officer, a quarter stunned though he was, realised to be other than French, though it was using that language. Its owner was assisting him to rise.

"Parbleu, I hardly know!" Once upon his feet, the Vicomte carried a hand to his hatless head. His elegant white wig was askew and soiled in one place with the mud of the unsavoury channel in which lay his galooned and cockaded tricorne, upside down. His helper picked it up.

"May I offer you, sir," he said, "the hospitality of my little room along there to put yourself to rights, and to repose yourself awhile if you wish?"

With thanks the Frenchman accepted the hat and the offer, too. "But I should like to know," he added, looking up at the unbetraying, blank wall, "what enemy I can have in this little street, of whose name I am not even sure!"

"It is called the Rue des Minimes."

"Eh bien, never have I serenaded any fair bourgeoise in the Rue des Minimes—yet to receive an iron cauldron full of water . . . by the way, I hope it *was* only water?"

The Highlander pointed to a twisted length of metal sprawling across the gutter.

"There lies the instrument which smote you, monsieur—a piece of guttering from the house, I think—and as to the hand which wielded it, you must accuse the tempest which has so much to answer for. Will you take my arm?"

Mr. Ranald Maclean's little apartment, entered in a more conventional manner than he had left it, was almost illumined by the presence of the handsome and uniformed new-comer, wet and a trifle dishevelled though he was. He threw his dripping cloak with a word of apology on to a chair, and going straight to the mirror over the hearth investigated closely a smear on his right cheek. Ranald, clapping to the casement, hurried out and returned with water and a towel.

"Nothing!" pronounced the young soldier in a tone of relief after a moment's dabbing. "Nothing but a scratch, fortunately!"

"But your head, monsieur?"

The Frenchman carefully straightened his wig and then shrugged his shoulders. Mr. Maclean had a strong conviction that it was only the possibility of damage to his looks which had caused him concern. "That devil of a gutter fell principally on to my shoulder. I am none the worse—but no less grateful to you, monsieur, for coming to my assistance," he added politely, "than if you had saved me from an earthquake. Especially," and here he had the grace to redden a little, "especially as I was sufficiently ill-bred to perpetrate a foolish pleasantry when I passed your window just before. I hope you will accept my sincere apologies for that."

The eyes which looked at him were a trifle cold, and the tone, too. "What I caught of your remark, sir, was entirely beside the point. But, naturally, I accept your apology." The voice became less stiff. "You will take a glass of wine with me, I hope?"

"Most willingly. Allow me first to present myself—the Vicomte de Lancize of Dauphin-Dragons. You, I think, monsieur, are an Englishman?" ("And not only from your accent!" he thought, with interior amusement.)

Ranald had bowed slightly. "I am not English; I am a Scot. My name is Maclean." Going to a cupboard he produced a bottle of Bordeaux and a couple of glasses. "I regret that I have no eau-de-vie to offer you after your accident; it would perhaps be better." He filled and held out a glass of claret.

"A thousand thanks," said M. de Lancize, accepting it. "You are a Scot, Monsieur Maclean? Then I drink to the success of the cause to which I am probably not indiscreet in guessing you pledged!"

But the Highlander did not drink, did not even fill his glass. "Of what avail is that toast now?" he asked bitterly, flinging out a long arm towards the little window against which the storm-driven rain was at that moment hissing hard. "It is true that I follow that most unfortunate of causes, against which even the elements are leagued. You, too, sir, from your uniform, are of those who were lending it assistance. But how can you help us now? Many of your ships are badly crippled, if what I hear on all sides is true?"

His dark grey eyes searched the face of M. de Saxe's aide-de-camp as if hoping against hope for some reassurance. The Vicomte de Lancize set down his emptied glass upon the table without replying. It was embarrassing to know as much as he knew and to be uncertain how much of this unauthorised knowledge should be allowed to appear. These poor devils of Jacobites. . . . On the whole, he shared his commander's opinion of them in the mass—inept conspirators, unready allies. But this tall, lean young man looked neither inept nor unready, and his words, his very refusal to toss off the easy glass, showed that he was better prepared to face facts than most of his infatuated fellow-partisans.

"You were about to say, Monsieur de Lancize . . ."

What was Monsieur de Lancize about to say? To proffer him the naked truth, unpalatable though it were—the truth which perhaps he owed him in return for his assistance and the Bordeaux—or to bring out some soothing evasion? As the young officer hesitated there was distinctly audible, in a lull of the torment outside, the sound of rumbling wheels and of horses' hoofs clattering on the cobbles. Both ceased, and not because the tempest had outvied them, for next moment a knocking of some urgency was assaulting the outer door of the house.

The Vicomte de Lancize reached out his hand for his wet cloak. "You have a visitor, I think, Monsieur Maclean" (and some recollection of his ribald comment of a while ago went again through his mind). "Allow me to depart."

"No, no," said the Highlander, listening with a puzzled air. "The knocking cannot be for me. I have but one acquaintance in all Dunkirk. Pray sit down again, monsieur, and give me some light upon the chances of the expedition."

But M. de Lancize had hardly complied when the door of the sitting-room opened and the voice of Mr. Maclean's landlord was heard announcing that there were two gentlemen to wait upon him. The young Frenchman sprang up again, Ranald stared in surprise, and one of the gentlemen in question came forward, a cloak round the lower part of his face. His eyes could be seen to go quickly from Ranald to his visitor.

"I understood that you were alone, Mr. Maclean," he said in a somewhat aggrieved tone, and in English.

"Sir," put in the Vicomte de Lancize pleasantly, in the same tongue, "in one moment Monsieur Maclean is alone. I take my leave."

But the new-comer made a gesture as though to stay him. "On the contrary, sir, I'll be asking you to remain, if you will have the goodness. It is, I believe, a piece of good fortune which allows me to find you here, since I see by your uniform that you are an officer of His Most Christian Majesty's, and are therefore of our friends—I speak as a Jacobite."

"I have certainly the honour to be both," returned M. de Lancize politely, observing—as did Ranald Maclean—how the second visitor, even more closely muffled, kept in the background out of the light.

The Jacobite uncloaked himself. "My name is . . . Malloch. It is my privilege to be in the intimate confidence of the Prince of Wales."

"Malloch!" exclaimed both the young men together. But it was the Frenchman who first found speech. "Then are you not, monsieur, the gentleman who was the sole companion of the Prince Charles Edouard on his adventurous journey from Rome? A daring enterprise! Is it possible that I can be of any service to you?"

"Indeed, monsieur, you can," promptly replied Mr. "Malloch" (whose real name happened to be MacGregor of Balhaldie). "His Royal Highness desires particularly to see the Comte de Saxe without delay. You can doubtless inform me how he may best be come at—to whom application should be made?"

But at that the young officer looked embarrassed. "You must be aware, monsieur," he replied, returning to his native tongue, while one hand fidgeted with his sword-knot, "that M. de Saxe, solely for reasons of State, has never permitted himself the honour of an interview with His Royal Highness the Prince of Wales, and that His Royal Highness, for the same sufficient cause, has perfectly concurred in this arrangement."

"But he concurs no more!" said a voice from behind, a young, strained, impatient voice with the faintest trace of some other accent in its French. "My God, it can be borne no longer! I am but flesh and blood, and reasons of State must go! I must know—I must know to-night what M. de Saxe intends! I must see him in person!"

Balhaldie sprang round, Ranald Maclean recoiled, and Cyprien de Lancize, astounded beyond words, did the same, as into the middle of the shabby little room there strode, uncloaking himself as he came, a good-looking, fair-complexioned young man, beautifully proportioned, with an oval face, bright brown eyes, a rather small but imperious mouth, and an air charged with the will to command.

"Your Royal Highness," remonstrated his companion, "I thought you had not intended——"

"To reveal myself until you had prepared Mr. Maclean for my arrival? But there is surely no need of that! The roof which shelters one Highland heart can surely shelter me! Is that not so, Mr. Maclean?"

His eyes flashed; he held out his hand, and Ranald, thus beholding for the first time his lawful prince, dropped on one knee and reverently pressed the hand to his lips.

"And this gentleman," went on Charles Edward, "who wears, I see, the uniform of my royal cousin——"

"Monseigneur," said Cyprien de Lancize, with great deference, "deign to behold in me also one whose sword has been most willingly put at your Royal Highness's service." He bowed deeply. "I have the honour to name myself to your Royal Highness—the Vicomte de Lancize, of Dauphin-Dragons, aide-de-camp to the Comte de Saxe."

"Aide-de-camp to the Comte de Saxe!" exclaimed the Prince, his face lighting up. *"Che buona ventura!* Monsieur de Lancize, will you do me a favour?"

"It will be for me a favour to receive your commands, *mon prince!*"

"Merci, monsieur. Then I pray you to go and enquire of M. de Saxe—he is lodged at the Intendance de la Marine, is he not—whether he will receive me?"

The Vicomte de Lancize was not expecting this.

"To-night, monseigneur?" he asked, hesitating.

"Yes, to-night," returned the Prince firmly. "It is imperative that I should learn from his own lips what are his intentions, his instructions from Paris. 'Tis with that purpose that I have come from Gravelines. How can I continue to remain there inactive, hearing of disasters to the fleet, but ignorant of their extent and their consequences! I propose to stay awhile with Mr. Maclean, if he permits——"

"Your Royal Highness!" ejaculated Ranald, somewhat overwhelmed.

"—while Mr. Malloch goes to ask whether M. de Saxe

will receive me." He turned to Ranald. "Mr. Malloch conceived the idea of asking a brief hospitality for me, Mr. Maclean, from something which Lord Keith let fall about your having no other acquaintances in Dunkirk, so that my presence was unlikely to be noised abroad.—You see, Monsieur de Lancize, that I am desirous of embarrassing M. de Saxe as little as may be!"

That was quite possible, but he was embarrassing M. de Saxe's aide-de-camp a good deal, and all because that young gentleman knew too much. The last thing the Lieutenant-General of King Louis' forces would do was to receive the Prince of Wales now.

"Monseigneur," he said, with a shade of deprecation, "I would willingly do your Royal Highness's behest, but——"

"But you conceive that I shall ask in vain?" finished Charles Edward, his brown eyes flashing. "Is that what you wish to convey?"

"I think, monseigneur," said the young Frenchman, "that your Royal Highness—if I may venture to say so with the greatest deference—would do better not to make the request. The Comte de Saxe is entirely devoted to your Royal Highness's interests, but, for that very reason, he may think those interests are better served——"

"By keeping me waiting at his door?" broke in the Prince hotly. "I'll not believe it! If you prefer not to escort Mr. Malloch, he shall seek M. de Saxe alone—or, per Dio, I myself will go in person and knock at his door in the Intendance!"

"No, no, your Royal Highness!" exclaimed all three men together, and Balhaldie, shocked, but a little, too, in the tone of one expostulating with a mutinous child, said: "We agreed, sir, that it would be totally unbecoming for you even to remain in the coach outside the Intendance while I approached the Comte de Saxe. Do you stay here with Mr. Maclean, as we devised; then, should M. de Saxe feel unable to receive you, no one need know that you ever came to Dunkirk to-night."

"Indeed, your Royal Highness," said Ranald Maclean earnestly, "that is the better way, unworthy though my poor room be to shelter you."

As for the Vicomte de Lancize (who was aware that whether M. de Saxe agreed to receive the Prince or no, the result, as far as the expedition was concerned, would be exactly the same, and who sincerely wished that the Prince had not taken this step, bound to end in his discomfiture), he hastened to declare that he would conduct M. Malloch to the presence of the lieutenant-general, assured the Prince of Wales of his respectful devotion, asked leave to kiss his hand, and on that left the room to which the notary's loose guttering had conducted him, and drove off with Mr. MacGregor of Balhaldie in the waiting coach.

So Ranald Maclean found himself alone with that impetuous, fascinating young man of four-and-twenty over whose bright head hovered the shadow of a crown made more visionary still by the double tempest, and (though neither of them, naturally, knew this) by those instructions from Versailles, which lay upon the ink-bespattered inlay of the table in the Intendance. It was a half-hour which the Highlander was to remember all his life.

"Cruel, cruel!" the Prince would reiterate, swinging round the room. "Just when all looked so promising— weather of this violence! It was more than flesh and blood could stand, to wait like a stock, sixteen miles away at Gravelines! God knows I have done enough of it already! . . . Do *you* think, Mr. Maclean, that M. de Saxe will see me? He must, he must! I'll not take 'no.' 'Tis absurd to keep up any further this farce of concealing my presence in the neighbourhood, of announcing another destination for the transports!" Then he would fling himself down in a chair, toss off another glass of Ranald's rapidly dwindling claret, and talk of his royal father's gratification when Balhaldie had arrived in Rome in mid-December with news of the impending expedition, and of his own dash in January incognito from Rome to Genoa and Antibes and thence across France. Nor did he omit to enquire of Ranald's own circumstances.

"And so, Mr. Maclean, it was chance which brought you here at this juncture? You were on your way back to the island of Askay from the wine country of the south-west? Then surely a vessel of the Bordeaux and Glasgow wine trade had served your purpose better?"

"My uncle at Girolac," explained Ranald, "not only wished to send a greeting by me to his old friend Mr. Alexander Robertson of Struan in Perthshire, whose name will be familiar to your Royal Highness, but had some business which he was anxious to transact through my agency at Lille. 'Twas for those two reasons that I chose Dunkirk as my port of departure, all ignorant of what was toward there—and of what an opportunity was to be given me to put my sword at your Royal Highness's service."

A fresh blast beat screaming against the little casement. "Your sword, sir, might as well be . . . at the bottom of the sea!" replied the Prince gloomily, glancing towards the window. "Heaven itself arms against me, it is clear." He poured himself out another glass of claret. "But I will not bow my head to Fate! Seeing that King Louis has espoused my father's cause—and after all the Comte de Saxe, great soldier though he be, is but an instrument in his hand—even if the transports are too badly damaged for so large a body of men to be sent to England at the moment, he will despatch them later. He could not allow such great preparations to issue in nothing! And as for M. de Saxe himself, I am assured by the tone of his letters to me that he is as devoted to my interests as his aide-de-camp has just asserted. . . . I have finished your wine, I declare, Mr. Maclean. I apologise! But we will yet crack a bottle together in Scotland, and laugh at the remembrance of this dismal night!"

"Indeed, sir, I hope so with all my heart," said Ranald.

"You perhaps know," went on the Prince, twirling round the empty wine-glass as he sat there, "that there

c

was earlier some talk—and I believe the Earl Marischal himself was one of those who gave it credence—of a separate expedition to Scotland. That is abandoned now; the descent will take place in the south-east of England. But conceive, Mr. Maclean, that it was not until quite recently that I was made aware of the fact that Admiral Norris had slipped away from Portsmouth, where M. de Roquefeuil had orders to blockade him, into the Downs, where, as I need hardly point out to you, he may be infinitely dangerous."

"I had not heard that, your Royal Highness," said Ranald in a tone of concern. "Yet perhaps the stormy weather may have affected his fleet also, and——" He broke off, listened a second, and then sprang to his feet.

"Yes," said the Prince, imitating him, "it is the coach; I hear it, too."

Ranald hurried out to the door of the house and opened it. Somewhat to his surprise he saw a figure in uniform swing out from its interior and, before the lackey could dismount to do it, let down the step for Mr. Malloch. A good sign, surely, that the Comte de Saxe's elegant aide-de-camp should return and show such politeness to the Prince's envoy.

The two passed him so quickly, without word or look, that he could gather nothing. He stayed a moment to secure the door against the bluster and rain; but the moment he re-entered the living-room he knew that his deduction went for nothing, and that the Prince's request for an interview had been refused.

"—charged me with this letter to your Royal Highness," he heard the aide-de-camp saying.

The Prince was standing motionless, his back to the window, with a flush across his face as though he had received a physical blow. He made no movement whatever to take the letter which the Vicomte de Lancize was respectfully tendering.

"Read it, Balhaldie!" There was more rage than disappointment in his voice; but he was keeping it under control, perhaps because of the presence of the French officer.

Mr. MacGregor, with a face of storm, took the missive and opened it.

"The King my master"—his voice was as hoarse as a crow's, his French accent indifferent; he tried again: *"The King my master orders me to make known to your Royal Highness that the untoward circumstances which have arisen oblige him to suspend at this moment the execution of the enterprise and to defer it to a more favourable opportunity.*

"The bad weather, the contrary winds, the position of Admiral Norris and the uncertainty as to that of M. de Roquefeuil, and above all the damage done by the last storm to our transport vessels, nearly all of which have lost boats, anchors, cables or other furnishings which it is impossible or difficult to replace at this juncture, are so many misfortunes which justify the order given me by His Majesty to disembark the troops and bring them into Dunkirk.

"The King commands me at the same time, monseigneur, to assure your Highness that he will not lose sight of the interests of your august house, and that His Majesty delays the execution of the project only in the hope of resuming it at the first favourable opportunity which may present itself."

There was a dead silence. MacGregor of Balhaldie slowly raised his eyes and looked at the Prince; they all looked at him. He was extremely pale, and his hands were clenched on the back of a chair.

"So—I am to say Amen!" he said in a stifled voice. "'The first favourable opportunity'—there will never be another so favourable." Then he broke out, with dilating nostrils: "If I must needs go in a fishing-boat, I will go! Though King Louis abandon me, though not a ship accompany me, I will go! In the Highlands there are still faithful hearts—I have proof of that here—in the Highlands I shall not have to wait upon the intrigues of Versailles——"

"Your Royal Highness!" interposed Balhaldie, with a warning glance at the French officer.

"—nor, once there, will ill-weather be allowed to break men's hearts and a spell of wind keep my father from his crown. Before God I swear it, here and now: though I go with but six, with but three followers, though I go alone!" And with his words fire seemed to run round the room.

"*Mon prince,*" said Marie-Cyprien de Lancize, approaching him, "if ever you go thus, I pray Fate she give me leave to accompany you, though she deny it to-day!" And seizing Prince Charles's hand, he bent his knee almost to the floor and kissed it.

("An easy vow to make," thought Ranald Maclean, more sadly than sardonically, "since he knows that he will never be at liberty to carry it out!")

But the spontaneity of the declaration, mere gesture though it might be, seemed to touch the young man from whose grasp so much had just been dashed. "I thank you sincerely, Monsieur de Lancize. I shall need all the good-will I can reckon upon.—Come, Balhaldie, let us begone."

"Your Royal Highness," began Ranald, deeply troubled, "when the day comes . . . there are claymores in the Highlands—and mine will be among them. . . ."

The Prince tried to smile at him. "I know that, Mr. Maclean, and I am convinced that I shall see the glitter of them before long.—Balhaldie, the sooner we return to our obscurity at Gravelines the better. No, gentlemen, I will not have you attend me to the coach; I wish to go, as I came, without attracting attention."

So, since his commands were precise, the two young men were left in the humble little room to listen to the sound of wheels grinding away along the Rue des Minimes until it was swallowed up in the clamour of the storm.

"Le malheureux!" said the Vicomte de Lancize under his breath. But the Highlander resented pity for his Prince.

"The more unfortunate, surely, are those who have undertaken a great enterprise which they have failed to carry out!" Glance, tone and words alike were challenging.

Surprisingly, the young French officer did not pick up the glove. "I agree with you entirely, monsieur. We also are the losers by this decision. But . . . how can one argue with *le bon Dieu* when He is so inconsiderate? Even Versailles has no ambassador *là-haut*"—he waved a hand towards the ceiling—"who can influence the celestial Minister of Weather! But my personal regret is sincere, now that I have had the honour of seeing His Royal Highness, and I beg you to believe it. Moreover, who can read the future, or the minds of His Majesty's advisers? We may yet meet in some hamlet of the county of Kent when you march south from Scotland to support a French landing! I shall look for you there. For the present, then, if you permit, I will take my leave—with a thousand thanks for your hospitality!"

With him Ranald Maclean went to the street door, though he might not show this courtesy to his Prince. It was still raining hard, but the wind appeared to have dropped a little. "To our next meeting—over the sea!" said the young dragoon as he gave the end of his cloak a swing over his shoulder and jammed his hat firmly on his head. Then with a last salute he was gone.

When the Highlander returned to his empty little room he stared round that transitory habitation as if he could hardly believe that it had enshrined to-night the young idol of so many Scottish hearts, and that within it the final disastrous blow had been dealt him. For Ranald himself the evening had been an astonishing one. He alone of all the Jacobites in Dunkirk had been singled out to shelter the Prince in a black and bitter hour, he first had heard the final doom of the expedition pronounced. It was small wonder that he sat late by his dead fire, sat and heard the wind rise once more to shrieking point, as though to announce that it had not yet finished with the ships which presumed to cross the Channel on a Jacobite errand—as indeed it was to prove to-morrow that it had not.

But after an hour or so the thoughts of this particular Jacobite reverted, in spite of himself, to his own affairs and to that warm vine country of the south where he had just been spending eight months on the modest estate among the vineyards which his dead mother's brother, old David Fraser, a Jacobite exile of the Fifteen, had inherited from his French wife. Mr. Fraser, a childless man, believing his end not far off, had sent to Fasnapoll for Ranald last summer, desiring to make his acquaintance with a view to leaving him his property, and Ranald had been at Girolac all through the vintage, his uncle initiating him into the mysteries of the production of the claret which was so plentifully and so cheaply to be had in Scotland. And in those days of labour under a cloudless sky the young man had been tempted to accept this inheritance if, when the time came, the choice was in his power.

For he was poor, and he dreaded always being a burden on his half-brother Norman, the laird (though they were excellent friends); he dreaded it the more since Norman's wife was about to present him with a second child. The bitter lot of the consistent Jacobite was Ranald Maclean's, for the army, the law and all Government posts were closed to him unless he could bring himself to take the oath to the house of Hanover. No profession was left but that of medicine, which had no attractions for a young man who, if his lot had been cast in less difficult times, would have chosen to be a soldier.

But to carry on Girolac and its vineyards as this should be done would mean exile, or practical exile, from the Highlands. He would have at the least to spend a good portion of each year in France, and the annual change of residence, the long journey, would be very costly. He was not sure that his uncle did not intend to make it a condition of his legacy that his heir should reside entirely at Girolac, and that Ranald did not know if he could bear. However, the decision was not yet to make.

The grey skies and the cold green water of his home were beginning to call him directly the autumn was over, but Mr. Fraser's entreaties and a short but alarming illness which overtook the old man delayed the Highlander until well into January. At last, the great question still undecided, Ranald left Girolac in February, transacted Mr. Fraser's business at Lille, and came to Dunkirk to find—this.

And now, after all, when the weather permitted, he would carry out his original intention, find a passage to Leith or Dundee and, on his way to the West and the shores of Isle Askay, deliver the letter with which his uncle had charged him to that old comrade in arms of his, twice exiled, but now suffered in his declining years to reside on his Perthshire estate, the old poet chief Alexander Robertson of Struan. After that, and as soon as possible, Fasnapoll, the house on the bay, the gulls crying and dipping, and mist over Askival. There was no mist at Girolac.

CHAPTER III

(1)

MUCH whiter than the wool she was spinning, the snow-flakes floated past the window, but Bride did not see them, for she was too intent upon her task. And as the wheel went round she crooned to herself a song in a sweet little voice which matched her stature, her almost childish air of innocence and her hair of pure, pale gold, itself spun upon same faery loom and for ever slipping out of place beneath her snood, so soft were the loose silken waves.

In the bed-chamber where she sat spinning this after-noon—bed-chambers being put to so many uses in Scot-land—the firelight seemed to please itself by drawing a sudden gleam from those bright locks of hers, and the dull green hangings of the bed, inwoven with a faded scroll pattern of mulberry, by making a not ineffective back-ground for them. There were those in Bunrannoch who called Miss Bride Stewart, of Inchrannoch House, *Bride an Oir,* "Bride of the Gold."

Had the whirr of the treadle ceased you might have heard the river hurrying past at the back of the house, strong and wide, though shallow, with the late March full-ness drawn from Loch Rannoch but a quarter of a mile away; and might have looked out upon it, too, from the little window rather oddly squeezed in near the fireplace. The room, the whole house might well be damp in winter from this close proximity to the Tummel, but such a thought had never troubled Bride's uncle or aunt, nor would indeed be likely to occur to anyone living in the Perthshire Highlands in the middle of the eighteenth century. Inchrannoch House being conveniently near the ferry, its situation was most proper.

And Bride had a very different view from her main window on the other side of the room, and one, too, which she loved better, for thence every morning and evening she could greet *Sidh Chailleann*—Schiehallion, the beautiful and shapely mountain dominating all Strath Tummel. From Kinloch Rannoch village, from all along the loch, from the distant Moor of Rannoch itself Schiehallion showed a perfect cone—the ideal peak; but dwellers along the Tummel further east saw it otherwise, for the long ridge behind came into view. Bride esteemed them much less fortunate.

There was a knock at the door, and the head of an elderly woman was thrust in. "Mr. Malcolm Robertson's below," it announced.

Bride continued to spin.

"Do ye no' hear me?" enquired the head.

Bride nodded. "But I'm busy."

The tall angular body which was topped by this head now came in entirely. "Are ye no' gangin' doun, then? There's a strange gentleman wi' Mr. Robertson."

The wheel stopped. "O Phemie, why do you come fashing me?" exclaimed the spinner. "Now I have broken the thread!"

"Then gang ye doun!" counselled Phemie starkly. "There's Mistress Stewart in her bed, and the laird no' hame yet. Ye canna leave puir Mr. Robertson by his lane."

Bride made a tiny gesture, perhaps called forth by the mention of that name, perhaps not. "But you say that he is not alone! However, if Uncle Walter is out. . . ." She rose resignedly. "Why, I declare 'tis snowing!"

"Aye, and as I gaed across the ha' I heard the gentleman that's come wi' Mr. Robertson say he hadna aft seen snow upon the ground."

"Then where can he be from—the tropics belike! I think," said Bride, "that I will go down.—The gentleman's not black, I suppose?"

"Now would young Mr. Robertson bring a black man

to wait upon your uncle and auntie, Miss Bride! Sometimes I declare ye have not the sense of a whaup!"

"Sometimes," retorted Bride, with an elfin smile, "you have not the sense of a joke, Phemie! But I will go down. We see enough snow and to spare in Rannoch. Ah, never mind the wool; I'll soon be back."

Standing before the dim, discoloured little mirror on her modest toilet table, which gave back her dazzling fairness transfigured to a singularly unflattering, greenish tint— but Bride looked little at her reflection in any glass—she hastily tucked a rebel lock or two more firmly into place under her snood and left the room.

Downstairs by the generous fire, in the room dark with panelling, old furniture and old portraits, under the great stag's head, noble and threatening, with crossed claymores resting on its tines, two gentlemen, both young, were waiting. That Mrs. Stewart was abed indisposed had just been conveyed to them, rather in the way of an afterthought, by the middle-aged manservant, bearded and lame, who had ushered them in.

"Is Miss Stewart at least at home?"

"Ay, Mr. Robertson, Miss Bride's to whoam. Phemie will tell her yo're here, sir. But t'laird hissel' 'll soon be back, by what he said."

"That man is surely English!" exclaimed Mr. Robertson's companion as the door closed.

"Yes, he is English, a Lancashire man. He was a sailor once, Jonas Worrall; he has been at Inchrannoch, however, these seventeen or eighteen years."

"Is there but the one daughter, Mr. Robertson?"

"Miss Bride Stewart," answered Malcolm Robertson, turning away as he spoke, "is not a daughter; she is a niece—and ward. The laird's own children are scattered or dead. Bride"—he so palpably lingered over the brief name, as though he wished it not so soon gone from his lips, that the other man glanced at him—"Bride—she's a sort of cousin of mine—is an orphan with a tragic history. Her parents——" He stopped short. "Here she is!"

The visitor whom he had brought with him turned and saw that there had come into the sombre, firelit room a golden-haired little figure with no faintest hint of tragedy about it, as one usually reads that word. This girl belonged surely to the race which lives feasting for ever in the fairy *duns,* where the only tragedy is not mortality but the lack of a soul. The young man was quite startled; the colour deepened in his lean cheek. A curtsey in response to their bows, and she who was "Bride" to his companion came forward, and he heard himself being formally presented: Mr. Ranald Maclean of Fasnapoll in Isle Askay.

(2)

The snow had ceased when the two visitors left Inchrannoch House; it had indeed little more than laid a fine carpet upon the ground. But against a livid sky rose up the white cone of Schiehallion, so near, though in appearance so inaccessible, a shape of ethereal purity. The short winter's daylight was almost spent, yet away in the southwest lingered a fading wound of rose-colour. Ranald Maclean was curiously silent as he and Malcolm Robertson were ferried over the Tummel. He would carry away with him from Perthshire a companion picture to hang beside those canvases of storm and disappointment painted at Dunkirk. Out of them also stood a vivid young figure, a young, never-to-be-forgotten face—but it was a man's.

It was nearly a week since he had presented himself at Mount Alexander, the seat of Robertson of Struan, with that letter from his uncle which was the cause of his being in Perthshire. He was royally welcomed at the romantically situated house by the old poet-chief of Clan Donnachaidh, who had fought as a youth at Killicrankie fifty-five years before, and, being subsequently captured, had spent an enforced exile of thirteen years on the Continent in sowing a good many wild oats and in writing poems whose tenor was such that in these his reformed and septuagenarian days he was not likely to publish them. On Queen Anne's accession his sister Margaret had personally obtained from her a pardon for Struan and the return of his confiscated estates. Unfortunately this pardon never passed the Great Seal, and no sooner was Queen Anne in her coffin than he was promptly expelled from them again. It was scarcely wonderful, therefore, that he joined the Earl of Mar's rising in 1715, when he was once more taken prisoner, rescued by a gentleman of the clan, recaptured, taken to Edinburgh Castle, re-rescued by a party headed, so it was said, by the dauntless Margaret, and for the second time driven to seek refuge abroad.

This second exile, most of which Struan spent in French service, lasted for eight years, and was terminated by his sister's again interceding personally with royalty on his behalf, her chief plea being that his health was breaking down. In 1723 George I allowed him to return, giving his estates, however, to his sister. Nursed by her, Alexander Robertson went to Bath, put himself in the hands of the celebrated Dr. Cheyne, and, returning with a resolution to lead a more regular life, swung to the other extreme and took a step worthy of St. Anthony, for he expelled from his "hermitage" or "earthly paradise," as he liked to call it, every woman not of his own kin, and inscribed a poem to that effect over the door, winning by this behaviour the title of "The Great Solitaire" from the ladies of the neighbourhood.

But Struan was an old man of seventy-six now, the inscription, no longer needed, was fading, his sister Margaret was long dead. He remained, nevertheless, intensely Jacobite, still employed his excellent education and ready pen in writing verse (now, however, exemplary and even edifying in tone), and was, as Ranald discovered, a "character." Indeed when the Chief found that his guest, anxious to get home to Askay after so long an absence, would not accept his hospitality for more than four days, he declared that at least his last night should be one to be remembered, and with the assistance of seven or eight neighbouring lairds, Robertsons, Stewarts, or Menzies, proceeded to carry out his boast.

Towards the end of the feast, when all the Jacobite toasts had been honoured, and the most inflammatory anti-Hanoverian sentiments sent echoing round the table, under which one of the guests had already subsided, and when their host had without too much difficulty been persuaded to recite some of the less scurrilous verses of his youth, a fair, pleasant-looking young man rose suddenly from his seat and came, perhaps the least trifle unsteadily, to Ranald's chair.

"Sir," he said, "I hold myself to blame for not having realised sooner who you were. Are you not the son of the late Mr. Angus Maclean of Fasnapoll, in the island of Askay?"

"I am," answered Ranald, faintly surprised.

"Then it behoves you, sir, being his son, to allow my father—who is not here to-night—the pleasure of repaying the hospitality which Mr. Maclean extended to him in the year 1738, when the vessel in which he was returning from the Lews went aground in Camus a' Chaisteil. Indeed, sir, I'll take no denial! My father will be grieved to the heart if you refuse!"

So next day Ranald, instead of starting for home, had almost willy-nilly to transfer himself to the neighbouring and lesser domain of the Robertsons of Auchendrie, where, among a family of daughters, Malcolm, his acquaintance of the banquet, was the only surviving son. Having so recently met the Prince, having, indeed, entertained him, and having first-hand experience of the storm which had wrecked such high hopes, Ranald Maclean was, as he had already discovered, a prize to be exhibited in local Jacobite society; and thus he had found himself this afternoon being borne off by Malcolm Robertson to Inchrannoch House.

And certainly they had listened eagerly enough, old Mr. Walter Stewart and the girl from fairyland, to what he had to tell them. Miss Stewart had produced a little

engraving of Prince Charles Edward as a boy which someone had brought her from Rome, and had asked if it were
like him now. In the candid child's eyes with which she
had gazed at Mr. Maclean of Fasnapoll—eyes of the hue
of sea-water, neither blue nor green, it seemed to him—
there was a light which might have dizzied him could he
have flattered himself that he had lit it. But he knew
that he had not; it burnt for that young Desire of all true
Scottish hearts, whom now, perhaps, they would never
see. . . .

"You were going to tell me Miss Stewart's history, I
think," said Ranald suddenly, a minute or two after they
had got out of the ferry-boat on the further side of the
river. "I am sorry to hear that it is a tragic one."

"Fortunately," replied young Robertson, "my cousin
does not remember her parents nor the catastrophe which
robbed her of them both. They were drowned coming
over from the West Indies, where her father had established himself as a planter. Bride was a child of two—
their only child, for they were young, and not long
married—and she had a narrow escape of sharing the
same fate. They were on their way from Jamaica to Liverpool; Mrs. Stewart was delicate and the West Indian
climate did not agree with her constitution, so she was
returning for a while to Perthshire with her little girl;
her husband was merely escorting her thither. Their
vessel was wrecked in a fog off the Calf of the Isle of
Man, and went down so suddenly that no boats could be
launched. Only those who were able to swim and to
clamber up the surf-beaten rocks survived, and there were
not many of these. Mr. and Mrs. Stewart both perished;
their bodies were cast up later in Castletown Bay."

"And the child?"

"A sailor from Lancashire who had played with her on
the voyage snatched her from her mother's arms and
swore that he would save her. He did, although in protecting his charge he himself received injuries from the

rocks which eventually resulted in the loss of a leg—as
you may have observed when he admitted us this
afternoon."

"The lame English servant?"

"Yes, Jonas Worrall. He has been at Inchrannoch ever
since; he has never been separated from Bride. I believe
he feels that he has more claim to her than her uncle,
Mr. Walter Stewart, has!"

So it was not from a fairy *dun,* but out of the waves that
she had come to Perthshire! "I hope Miss Stewart does
not have occasion often to think of this very sad story of
hers," observed Ranald Maclean. "Perhaps it is as well
that she does not live by the sea."

"Perhaps so; though our loch here is sometimes so
agitated as to resemble it. Yet I speak from hearsay,"
added Malcolm, smiling, "for I have never seen the sea."

(3)

At Inchrannoch House meanwhile they talked of what
they had just heard.

"And that young man," said Mr. Stewart reflectively,
passing his hand over his high, pale forehead, "that
young man, only about two weeks since, saw and spoke
in Dunkirk with our Prince, whom we thought to be in
Rome! Does it not seem well-nigh miraculous, Bride?"

Bride nodded her little head gravely.

"A great pity that your aunt was not well enough to
receive him. I must go to her presently and tell her this
news."

"I will go and see if she is awake now, Uncle Walter,"
said Bride, and slipped from the room, noiselessly, as she
did most things.

But upstairs, between the half-drawn curtains of the
bed, she could see Mrs. Stewart's nightcap motionless;
stealing a little nearer she verified that she was asleep,
and thought how old and frail she looked. She was not

very old in reality, but she had never known good health, poor Aunt Rachel! And, having reported to her uncle, Bride went back to her room, to the silent wheel and the half-spun wool, and sat down to them.

Five minutes later she was still sitting there, her hands idle in her lap. She was thinking of all that she had been told—what more natural? But she was thinking not only of the substance of it, but also of the manner of its telling; for she heard still in her ears the voice of the narrator, a pleasant, deep, strong voice, and grave, as befitted the subject. A Highland gentleman who had so recently held intimate speech with the Prince passing this way, like a vessel with great tidings! Bride was aware of a faint but distinct regret that she was never likely to see him again.

With a sigh—no doubt for the hopes which the storm had wrecked—she began to press the treadle of the spinning-wheel—and then remembered that the thread was broken. The light was gone too; she would not spin any more to-day. So she rose, and going to the window, stood with her elbow on the high sill, looking out at Schiehallion, now only dimly visible, despite the snow upon its crest, and wondering whether Mr. Maclean, from the Isle of Askay, had admired her dear mountain.

CHAPTER IV

"Yes, this northern side of the loch is known as the Sliosmin, the smooth slope," said Malcolm Robertson. "The other is the Sliosgarbh, the rough slope. As you see, it is steeper and much more thickly wooded; the famous Black Wood of Rannoch is over there. And on the far side of those heights runs Glen Lyon, the longest glen in Scotland."

"And this side of the loch, I think you told me, is Menzies territory, and the other Robertson?" commented Ranald Maclean, as the two young men went briskly next morning up the easy sloping track through the birch and hazel.

"Yes, this is Menzies territory—though no Menzies live here. Rannoch, Mr. Maclean, is a district of strange anomalies, peopled by many clans. There are, for instance, many MacGregors on this side, but no MacGregor chief; and though if you were to count heads in Rannoch you would probably find the majority to be Camerons, yet no Cameron chief has ever owned land here. And though the southern side is Robertson territory, we of Clan Donnachaidh are not so numerous there as others. Moreover, there are the Stewarts, whose especial territory is Bunrannoch, the district at the eastern end of the loch, where we were yesterday."

Young Robertson was going, upon business for his father, up to the clachan of Annat, on the northern slope, about a mile from the end of Loch Rannoch, and his guest was accompanying him. There was the slightest sprinkling of snow here and there upon the dead and brittle bracken, and little pockets of it stowed away in the crooks of the birch trees, but the sky was clear, the air exhilarating, and before they had started their ascent

D

they had seen, away at the far end of the loch, the sugar-loaf shapes of the mountains at the entrance of Glencoe, the Watchers of Etive, showing blue and clear, as though ten miles of water and fifteen more of desolate waste did not lie between. As they mounted, Malcolm continued his remarks upon the history and landmarks of Rannoch; and fierce enough some of the former was, since for many years that inaccessible district had been a haunt of broken men. After a while the talk came round to the Stewarts again.

"Did I understand you to say, Mr. Robertson," asked his listener, "that the Stewarts at the end of the loch are Stewarts of the royal line?"

"Yes, descendants of Alexander Stewart, the son of King Robert II—the Wolf of Badenoch. Yet, even so, not all of them," said Malcolm, laughing, "for the Stewarts of Innerchadden are from Appin, offshoots of the Stewarts of Invernahyle. 'Tis always said that you will know the two strains apart by the colour of their eyes; the Wolf's descendants—*Siol a' Chuilein Churta*—having them usually blue." And he embarked upon some rather complicated family history to which, as it was addressed to another Highlander, he had an outwardly attentive listener, though actually Ranald was pondering over the question as to whether those eyes he had seen yesterday in the firelight could be called blue.

"But, talking of Stewarts," broke off Malcolm suddenly, "look who is ahead of us!"

And further on, between the trees, Ranald saw a little female figure with a small basket. She was by her dress a gentlewoman and by her step young, but from the rear he could not assign to her any especial identity, more especially as the usual tartan "screen" was thrown about her head and shoulders.

" 'Tis my cousin Bride," announced Malcolm; and again the little name came caressingly from his lips. "I think she must be on her way to visit that very old woman, her father's nurse, who lives up here. Shall we overtake her and offer our escort for the short way that remains?"

They quickened their pace, and just before they came to an old stone wall of some height which crossed the track, allowing it however an uninterrupted passage between two half-crumbling and gateless pillars, they overtook the young lady of Inchrannoch House. After greetings had passed young Robertson possessed himself gently of the basket.

"Why do you come up on foot with this, Cousin Bride?" he asked. " 'Tis no very light weight. What has become of your pony, and your man?"

"Mist has gone lame, I know not how, and Jonas is busy digging in the garden," she answered.

"And the deerhound?"

Her little laugh at that was enchanting; it sounded to Ranald like the note of a stream in summer, liquid and gay. "Fiona would not consent to carry a basket, cousin! Or do you mean that I should have brought her as a protection? Do you think I'm like to be run away with, just stepping up to Annat? If that is in your mind, I fancy you must have been telling Mr. Maclean the story of the beautiful Rachel MacGregor who walked in the birch wood at Dunan and was carried off by her suitor and a band from Lochaber.—But you know that it turned out to be a very happy marriage!"

"Ay; but *you* know, Cousin Bride, that she did not marry the man who planned the outrage," retorted Malcolm. "She married one of his companions, a Cameron."

"At any rate, good came out of evil," remarked Miss Stewart, smiling up at her kinsman from the folds of tartan. "Now give me the basket, if you please, for here is old Eilidh's cottage, and you will not be wishing to come in."

They had, indeed, arrived at a little stone and thatch cottage, an outpost of a collection of similar ones higher up the mountain slope. So they took leave of Miss Bride Stewart, who entered on her errand of mercy while the two young men continued their way towards the clachan.

Malcolm Robertson's business with his father's tacksman was not, however, as summarily despatched as Ranald had anticipated, for the latter was out upon the hillside and had to be sought for. After some twenty minutes of fruitless waiting Malcolm suggested that his guest might prefer to start downwards again, escorting Miss Stewart perhaps, if he cared to wait a little for her. To this suggestion Ranald was far from offering any objection; but when he tapped at the cottage door a young girl appeared, and in response to his query told him that Miss Stewart had just left.

Ranald reflected that if that were so he could probably overtake her, and hurried down the snow-sprinkled track between the bare, unstirring trees. And after a moment or two he did indeed catch sight of her little figure, but to his surprise she was not alone; there was a man with her. It could not be Malcolm Robertson, whom he had left behind at the clachan; nor was it probable (to his mind at least) that Malcolm would walk beside Miss Stewart, admirer and kinsman though he was, in that half-masterful way, bending so closely over her as they went. And they were going quickly too; he had a half impression that it was Miss Stewart who was setting the pace. No, it was certainly not Malcolm.

His own intention of escorting the young lady home was now frustrated; nor was there any reason why he should follow behind the couple all the way down to the loch—indeed, every reason why he should not, since there was something about this unknown man which suggested a loverlike interest in Miss Bride Stewart, of which Ranald Maclean had no desire to be witness. He must then either stop for a little and wait until the two were out of sight, or walk yet faster and pass them. Ranald elected for the former course; but, though he stayed his steps, he could not keep his eyes from following them nor from observing something indefinable about the way in which Miss Stewart was walking, which seemed to testify that the proximity of her companion was not welcome to her.

Within the limits of the narrow path she seemed to be keeping as far as possible from him; while he, for his part, appeared determined to walk as close to her as he could. And once, perhaps under pretext of helping her over some inequality, he caught her arm, but from the way she turned her head Miss Stewart plainly asked him at once to release it. Yet he was a little while before complying.

And at that Ranald changed his mind and once more started onwards. He would walk at some distance behind, but he would keep them in sight, so that if Miss Stewart were going to be offered any unwelcome attentions by this admirer—if he were an admirer—he could, by merely overtaking the couple, cut these attentions short. The two gave no sign of hearing his footfalls behind them; these were deadened, perhaps, by the thin layer of snow on the track. Here already was the wall running downhill, with the unfenced gap between the tumbledown gateposts. The instant they reached it the couple disappeared abruptly to the right, behind the wall.

Now, as Ranald knew, the path itself went straight ahead. He was sure that the man at her side had taken Miss Stewart's arm again and forced her out of the path . . . Unless, of course, there was a track running down the further side of the wall which he had not noticed. He quickened his pace almost to a run.

As he arrived at the gap he heard their voices upraised together: hers protesting, "I cannot listen to you now . . . pray let me go on!" and the man's, fired with passion, "You must, you shall listen, Miss Stewart! If you can listen to that dullard, young Robertson of Auchendrie——"

Ranald advanced through the gateposts. Yes, Miss Stewart's companion had her by both hands, had her pressed up against the wall all among the snowladen brambles, her empty basket upside down on the ground. As Mr. Maclean's indignant eyes took in this fact, however, it became a fact no longer, for the intemperate admirer instantly loosened his hold and faced round; his glance was as hot as a blow. The very evident relief in Miss Stewart's face made Ranald glad indeed that he had come up.

Restraining himself with a good deal of difficulty, he raised his hat. "If this gentleman is escorting you home, madam," he said, much more coolly than he felt, "I think he has mistaken the right path. May I assist you back to it?" And he offered his arm.

But it was struck aside, and he looked into a dark face lit by a pair of blazing eyes—a Highland face, too, no doubt of it, though its owner wore no tartan. "By what right do you interfere, sir? As you say, the path goes on—go you on with it! I am quite capable of escorting this lady."

"I doubt that!" retorted Ranald. "And if you ask Miss Stewart herself, I think she will prefer the direct path to this patch of brambles, and, if not my escort, at least that of her kinsman, Mr. Robertson, who will shortly be returning this way."

"Take yourself off!" shouted the other, as he would have shouted to a dog, his right hand going instinctively to his right hip—another proof of his race.

"Not until you do!" replied Ranald with equal animosity. "Miss Stewart——" But the girl had slipped behind them and was doing the best thing, perhaps, that she could have done by starting to walk away down the path. When he realised it her admirer made to follow her, but Ranald gripped him by the shoulder.

"No!" he exclaimed in the height of indignation, "no, not if you know so little how to behave to a lady!"

"Who are you that presume to teach a Griogarach manners?" flashed out the other; but before he could strike Ranald had closed with him. The veneer of good breeding and respect for the proximity of a lady ripped off in an instant, they struggled like two wildcats. Although Ranald looked the stronger and had slightly the advantage in height, the MacGregor was extraordin-

arily wiry and beside himself with fury; it was therefore
doubtful how the encounter might have ended had it been
carried further. But a man's voice calling, "Bride, Bride—
is that you, Bride?" all at once announced the approach
of Malcolm Robertson, who could, apparently, see his
kinswoman on the path ahead, though not the two men
at grips behind the wall. The MacGregor, on that, made
a final effort, tore himself free, sending Ranald staggering, dashed at the wall, was over it like a stoat, and was
running down the farther side when Malcolm Robertson
came through the gateposts to perceive his guest recovering his balance with difficulty.

"*Dhia gleidh sinn!*" he exclaimed, catching him by the
arm. "What have you been at, Mr. Maclean, and who
was it that jumped the wall just now?"

The panting Ranald put a hand to his throat and hastily
rearranged his cravat. "Some unmannerly fellow who was
molesting Miss Stewart—a MacGregor, by what he said."

Malcolm's placid brow grew black. "It will be Gregor
MacGregor—Gregor Murray—from Glen Lyon, maledic-
tion on him! He is mad after her . . . and he does not
always comport himself like a gentleman. I am glad you
came by when you did. Was she much alarmed?—Let
us go to her."

Miss Bride Stewart, hearing his voice, had come to a
stop. He hurried down the path to her.

"Oh, Bride, my dear"—there was all the distress and
tenderness in his voice of one speaking to a beloved child
—"I wish I had not left you to return alone! But who
could guess——"

She slipped her hand into his arm and smiled up at
him. "There's naught to be perturbed at, Malcolm," she
answered, and her voice, sweet and cool as rain in spring,
was steady, though she was paler than her wont. "I was
a trifle startled, that was all. We all know that Mr. Gregor
Murray is somewhat . . . impetuous.—But that is not
to say that I do not thank you, Mr. Maclean, a thousand
times, for your intervention."

But Ranald Maclean was not so cool. His deep-buried but volcanic temper was fermenting. He had seen what Malcolm Robertson had not—this girl, who seemed to him of an elfin fragility, helpless before that unmannerly brute. He looked back. "I have a mind to go after Mr. Gregor Murray or MacGregor," he said between his teeth, "and teach him a lesson he will not soon forget. Small wonder that the very name of his clan has been proscribed these hundred and forty years!"

"Oh pray, pray do not think of doing such a thing!" exclaimed Miss Stewart, evidently really alarmed at this prospect. "Mr. Gregor Murray will, I am sure, be sorry for his conduct and ask my pardon when next we meet."

"If I had my will," declared Malcolm Robertson with a vehemence which he had not yet shown, "he should never see you again. He is not of the Dunan or the Ardlarich MacGregors, here in Rannoch," he explained to Ranald. "He lives at Roro, in Glen Lyon—a kinsman of the chief's."

"He goes back to Glen Lyon to-day," said Bride. "That is why, I think, he particularly desired speech with me." She coloured a little. "I ought to be going on home now, Malcolm, I think—and indeed 'tis not over-warm up here."

Atmospherically it might not be so, but mentally, for one at least of the three, it was torrid. Yet Ranald had perforce cooled a little by the time that he and Malcolm Robertson bade farewell to Miss Stewart at the ferry over the little river on which she lived, to which they both escorted her. He did not suppose that he should see her a third time before his departure two days later; nor did he. And since nothing was likely ever to bring him into the land of Schiehallion again, he knew that, as far as he was concerned, Bride Stewart might have vanished into that enchanted country forbidden to mortals, which, to his thinking, was her true home. But he would not soon forget her.

CHAPTER V

(1)

At Fasnapoll, in Isle Askay, summer brought many a
treasure dear to a child and left them for her on the white
sands, or, better still, hid them in the shallow rock-pools
of Camus a' Chaisteil, among the sea anemones or the
moss-green water-weeds. On this July morning of 1745,
therefore, a sunburnt little girl of five or so, her homespun
skirts kilted above her bare, wet sandy legs, was absorb-
edly dredging with her fingers in one such pool, the ends
of her fair hair, which had come unbraided, dipping now
and then into the clear water over which she stooped.
Delightful and serious work; for one had to lay all one
found of shells and coloured stones and small crabs in a
neat pattern on the sand round the large starfish . . . only
the crabs would not stay there. The child could not
imagine why Uncle Ranald should prefer to sit over yonder
on a rock, staring out to sea and not saying a word, even
when she called out to him, testifying to her successes.

And in truth Uncle Ranald was, for once, paying Miss
Helen Maclean scant attention, though he was conscious
of her presence among the pools—the child who would
wake for years yet with the sound of the waves in her
ears, and see from her window the great island peaks of
Rum rising all blue and purple from the sea, and was so
far from guessing that her existence was a part of the
reason that he himself would wake thus and see them no
more.

In the year and four months since the great storm at
Dunkirk which had shattered Jacobite hopes, Ranald's
circumstances had entirely changed. His uncle at Girolac
was recently dead and had left him the estate—on condi-

tion that he settled there. The news had come but eight days ago, and since then the young man had been through the most tormented week of his life. Yet there was nothing for it but to accept this inheritance, to try, indeed, to feel overjoyed at his good fortune, since it would not only relieve him of his dependence upon his half-brother's hospitality and of the idleness which irked Ranald himself so deeply, but would give him a chance of repaying Norman's unfailing hospitality by supplementing his scanty budget. For in a good season, as he had learnt when he was there, the vineyards of Girolac should bring in a very comfortable sum.

So his sister-in-law had started looking over his clothes and the old shoemaker at the tiny clachan was frowning as he considered the worn corners of a valise which needed more than the one strip of hairy cowhide to make it really serviceable again. Ranald was to set off for his French heritage the day after to-morrow; and at this moment he was almost wishing that to-morrow would never dawn.

Small Helen, the skirt of her little gown weighed down with some treasure or other, came and plumped herself down on the sand at the side of his rock. Fond as he was of the child, Ranald paid her no attention. A gull was complacently riding on the dance of the waves close inshore—happy bird! Aye, and happy bird even in those drear days of winter, when the great grey rollers thundered in with the noise of battle, and the spindrift would fling itself up against the lichens of the ruined tower on the low headland, where the first Maclean of the Askay branch had lived and died a hundred and seventy years ago.

A hand tugged at his coat. "Look, Uncle Ranald, look at my feet!" shrilled Helen.

The young man looked down. On most of the toes of those small, fat feet was perched, like a hat, a tiny shell.

"To keep them dry if it should rain," explained Helen, glowing with pride, and shaking back her loosened hair, she lifted a sunburnt face to him.

Ranald smiled and put a hand on her head. "Vastly

ingenious, *mo chridhe!*" How yellow the child's hair was, partly bleached by sun and sea. But it was not of that pure, pale gold, silk-fine . . .

It was most foolish of him, he knew, to intend passing through Western Perthshire on his road to the coast, retracing thus the route he had taken on his homeward way in the spring of last year, instead of setting out for France by way of Glasgow, more usual for dwellers in the West. But, devil take it all, though he was poor enough still, he would be tolerably prosperous this autumn, and what were riches meant for but to enable one to indulge one's whims? Above all, when riches were purchased so dear as his would be.—But he had not so far told Norman of his intention.

Yet Bride Stewart was by now, quite probably, married to Malcolm Robertson. He would no doubt make an excellent husband, though a thought dull for that bright creature. Not that Bride had shown especial wit or sparkle in Ranald's two encounters with her; but she was like no other girl whom he had ever seen, and that first impression of her in the dark room at Inchrannoch would always live with him, effacing even the second, less conventional meeting. She was of the blood of the *sidhe;* she had been cradled in a fairy *dun,* been lulled to sleep by the fairy songs. That was no doubt why he had so vehement a wish to see her once again, married or no— and meant to indulge it.

A step behind him made him look round, and Helen's welcoming shriek told him whose it was.

"Dinner's all but ready, Ranald," announced his brother, "or so I'm told. So get you in, Helen, and put yourself to rights a little—faith, you look like a tinker's child!"

"No, no," protested Ranald, "she's only a stranded mermaid! And some day, Helen, I will send you from Paris a blue silk gown, with a fine snood for Sundays!"

Jumping with joy, Helen ran off towards the house on the verge of the bay behind them. But Norman's face was dark. "Ranald, as God sees me, I'd liefer she wore a beggar's clothes all her life than that I should seem to push you out of Fasnapoll! I'd liefer——"

"Stop, or in another moment you'll be believing that you *are* pushing me out, and never was a falser notion in the world than that! Am I not the lucky man to be coming into so fine an inheritance, and ought not I to be counting the hours until I set eyes on it? . . . If I do not, 'tis mere foolishness."

Norman's hand was on his shoulder, gripping it hard. After a moment he said, rather huskily: "I were as foolish in your place, I know well," and the two of them looked in silence at the bright, plunging water.

The call of a woman's voice came to them, and turning, they could see the mistress of Fasnapoll standing in the doorway of the low weatherbeaten house, the year-old heir in her arms.

"That will be dinner," said her husband. "Ranald"—he paused a second, glancing at his brother's face as if to see how he would take it—"Ranald, I hope . . . that is, of course you will follow your own bidding in the matter . . . but 'twould like us better, you'll well understand, if you did not wed with a French lass."

Ranald's expression was inscrutable. He stopped and picked up one of the child Helen's discarded shells. "Then it would seem that I am not like to wed at all! Would you have me force a Highland girl into exile too?"

"You'd not be saying that if you had set your heart on one—nor would she!"

"Then, by all the rules of logic," riposted his brother, "'tis clear that I have not so set my heart! I doubt I'll die unwed, like my uncle."

"Unwed he was not, but childless."

"Ay, I had forgot. But he made a French marriage—'twas that which brought him Girolac . . . Well, find me a wife then, Norman, a wife as good as your own, if such an one is to be found, and I'll make shift to come home and marry her."

(2)

It was but natural that this scrap of conversation should ring again in Ranald Maclean's head when some days later he rode along Loch Rannoch side. As he had foreseen, his brother had been surprised at his electing to take ship for Bordeaux from the east coast, which involved so much longer a sea voyage; but Ranald said that having come from France last year by that route he would return the same way; moreover he had a fancy to see Struan again and to tell him that he himself was now the possessor of his old friend's inheritance. And since he had never mentioned Bride Stewart's name at Fasnapoll, and had just thrown cold water on the idea of marrying a Scottish girl, Norman could have no suspicion of the real motive underlying, not only his preference for Leith over Glasgow, but his preference for the roundabout approach to Leith by Perth, instead of by Stirling.

Ranald Maclean was always inclined to reserve over his own affairs—some might have called him secretive—and those few who knew him well were quite aware of this trait, as of the proud and passionate temper which lay, usually unstirring, beneath his self-contained demeanour; a temper which (like a wise young man) he had struggled, and with fair success, to bit and bridle. But one is not always wise at nine-and-twenty, nor, at any age, is one always consistent. For in conjunction with what in a Lowlander would be termed dourness, Ranald possessed a strong vein of the startling impetuosity of the Celt.

And he was, he knew it himself, giving rein to something a little unbridled and impulsive now, coming this long way to indulge a whim. He had journeyed very slowly, giving himself as long as possible to feed his eyes on the last glimpses of his native Highlands, on the sweeps of heather or scree, the flash of the narrow mountain torrent or the mist stealing from the mountain crag. And even as he crossed the upper end of Rannoch Moor, that great tract of mortal desolation, all quagmire and stones, he had said to himself, "What will the vineyards of the Gironde have to show as dear . . . to me?"

And what like this, he thought now? He had already seen, before ever he got to Loch Rannoch, the pointed peak of Schiehallion lifting itself in perfect symmetry twenty miles away. Now, much nearer, and more lovely still, it welcomed him across the lazy sunlit water, between the birch trees—*her* mountain.

This fine afternoon the old Chief of Clan Donnachaidh was in his garden, sitting near the beloved spring which he had enshrined in his verse under the name of Fons Argentinus. Among the flowers hummed the bees, three pints of whose honey was the rent he paid every Martinmas to the Duke of Atholl for the right of fishing in Loch Rannoch. He welcomed the traveller warmly and gave orders for a bedchamber to be prepared for him.

"Exile!" he exclaimed that evening over the wine. "Faith, I have known enough of that to have no wish to see France again! Too many years have I spent there! But *your* absence will not be exile, for there's no Government ban on you, Mr. Maclean. You'll soon be coming back to the Highlands with your pockets full of louis d'ors to pick yourself a châtelaine for Girolac."

Why would everybody harp upon this question of marriage? Ranald turned the conversation; yet it was not long before he asked after his late hosts at Auchendrie— as a preliminary to another enquiry—saying in a sufficiently unconcerned tone that he supposed Mr. Malcolm Robertson was a married man now.

There was a twinkle in old Struan's eye. "Nay, and I doubt if he ever will be. The young lady would not take him—I know not why—but I wager he will ask her again. Did you meet the nymph in question when you were a guest at Auchendrie last year?"

"If you mean Miss Stewart of Inchrannoch, yes, I had the honour of making her acquaintance," replied his visitor with a most curious feeling, as though someone else were answering for him. "A good lass, and a very fair one," commented the "Great Solitaire," thus revealing that his title had become somewhat outmoded. "You might do worse than try your own luck with her, Mr. Maclean!"

Outwardly quite unmoved, Ranald smiled. "I think, sir, that I should have small chance of success, seeing that I must needs ask my wife to forsake her own kindred and come with me into a foreign land."

"Well, there's no knowing but that she'd do that, and willingly. Bride Stewart was gotten in a foreign land herself, and she's the lass, I believe, to sail the seven seas with the man she loved—if such an one came her way. Little and saint-like she may be to look at, Mr. Maclean; but the heart in her, unless I'm vastly mistaken, is that of a lion.—However, these are no days for wooing and wedding." The old Jacobite dropped his voice and lent forward with a light in his eyes. "You are newly come from the West, and the Inner Isles; tell me, does not a wind from France blow strong there now?"

Ranald took his meaning without difficulty. He shook his head. "I doubt it never will."

The old Chief drew back a little. "You need not play so close with *me*, Mr. Maclean," he said, good-humouredly, but with an accent of reproach. "So much circumspection is uncalled for, since I assure you I am pretty well posted up in the plans of a Certain Young Man. We are at the beginning of August; unless there has been some miscarriage, the day has already arrived."

Ranald stared at him in amazement. That smile had knowledge behind it.

"I assure you, sir, that I should not dream of using reserve towards you if I had anything to communicate on that subject. But I have not; I am completely ignorant. You will remember, for one thing, that our Chief was arrested and imprisoned last June."

"Ay, and that was an unchancy business for other people

besides himself," said Alexander Robertson, shaking his grey head. For Sir Hector Maclean of Maclean, the head of Ranald's clan, an officer in the French service, who had come to Scotland to enlist recruits, had been arrested in Edinburgh, and was now a prisoner in the Tower. The despatches which, in addition, he had been carrying to the Jacobite Duke of Perth and that very active Jacobite agent, Murray of Broughton, were nearly fatal to both those gentlemen, though the authorities did not dare openly to arrest the Duke at Drummond Castle, his seat, because he was so much beloved there, and an attempt to do so by a ruse failed. But both he and Murray had had to go into hiding. "*Dhé*, Mr. Maclean," went on Struan, "don't you know in Askay—for your brother's on the right side like yourself, surely!—that the Prince should have arrived in the Long Island or even possibly at the mainland by now?"

And now Ranald stared indeed. The old Jacobite was surely romancing, to speak of that vague possibility of the arrival of Prince Charles Edward as a matter cut and dried! He could not credit anything so definite. "Sir, on what grounds——" he began.

"On the grounds of his own letter to Murray of Broughton, Mr. Maclean! I heard it all from Mr. Murray's own lips, and not so very long ago neither. He was here awhile under another name, in his forced rambles after the discovery of those despatches. It seems there was a letter writ to the Prince last winter by the members of the 'Association' begging him not to come unless he brought some thousands of French troops, arms for still more, and plenty of louis d'ors. But the letter was delayed sending—by Lord Traquair, I know not why—for months; and when at last it was despatched it brought no answer. Mr. Murray, fearing that it had miscarried, began like a wise man to collect money and arms; they are hidden, what's more, here in Perthshire, at Leny House, near Callander. Meanwhile, he wrote another letter to His Royal Highness, and to that he had a reply more than a couple of months ago, informing him that the Prince had made all his dispositions, and would be in South Uist in July."

"But . . . but it is impossible!" exclaimed Ranald, more and more astounded.

"Why do you say that, lad? He may be there by now! When did you leave Askay, may I ask?"

Ranald told him. But he was still full of incredulity. The unquenchable old Jacobite might be correctly informed of what Murray of Broughton knew and expected, but the fulfilment of those expectations was another matter altogether. Had the Prince been coming with a considerable French force some whisper of the fact would surely have been blown on the winds to Fasnapoll; while without a considerable force he would not come (despite those brave words at Dunkirk), for what could he hope to accomplish? Scotland was quiet; Whig and Jacobite lived peaceably side by side. Here in Perthshire, for instance, Ranald had observed that their relations seemed almost cordial. And then he perceived, with a sting of shame, that in his inmost heart he was protesting against the idea of a fresh rising in favour of the White Rose at all—and hastened to excuse himself by the reflection that this lack of enthusiasm arose from the knowledge that before anything of the kind came to pass (if ever it did) he would no longer be on Scottish soil.

These uncomfortable thoughts all went through his mind while his host, having poured fresh wine for both of them, was rising from his chair preparatory to saying devoutly with lifted glass, "May we soon hear the good news!"

And Ranald, on his feet honouring that toast, was put to shame anew.

(3)

Next afternoon he went striding up by the Allt Mor, through the sheets of pink heath on the lower slopes of

E

Beinn a Chuallaich. He had felt the need of a walk, but instead of paying his respects at Auchendrie, as he had half intended, he had gone on past its gateposts, and after a while found himself ascending the mountainside over Kinloch Rannoch, half wondering why, when the mind is at odds with itself, the body also should wish for conflict.

His body at any rate was soon getting its desire, for the very considerable steepness up which he was urging it forced him to slacken his pace. The path now skirted the vehement mountain stream which, lower down, fell over the edge of the steep in a spraying waterfall edged with pines. Here it had carved for itself a miniature gorge, above which one or two small rowan trees dangled their green feathers. And as Ranald ascended beside it his eye caught sight of some brown objects ranged in a row on a narrow ledge of rock across the little gully. They were young hawks. He stopped to look at the birds, which sat there almost as motionless as jugs set by a housewife on a shelf.

After a moment Ranald sat down on a little mound which swelled up amid the pale waxy bells of the heath and the deeper carmine of the bell heather, and his thoughts winged instantly far from the Allt Mor. They were not in the least concerned, however, with last night's inner hesitancies over Struan's toast. He was once again among the heavy-fruited vines on the slopes round Girolac at vintage time. There was much for him to learn, he knew, but the estate had had a good overseer in his uncle's day, and he should remain. In time, yes, in time Girolac might come to seem home to him; in time he might plant his heart there, marry, hear the voices of children under that high-pitched French roof.

Whose children? He saw them with locks like spun gold, locks that the wind would lift with delight, that would slip at a touch, hair that a man could drown in, lying with his face buried in it . . .

Ranald pulled himself up short. This was, indeed, to weave fantasies! She would never consent to marry him,

she who dwelt under Schiehallion, who must leave Schiehallion's shadow if she did. And yet, unless he took her
to the warm land of the vine, he had no roof under which
he could shelter that bright, magic head.

The burn talked below him, talked of the mists it knew,
the deer which came to drink of it, the waterfall to which
it was hurrying, the river in which it met fulfilment.
"You'll hear nothing like me over the sea!" And the
heath by his foot, pink as a shell, the bold, tough sprays
of the July heather, the patch of stagmoss and the
mountain turf itself, they too said: "If you should light
upon us over there, we shall not look the same!"

The young man suddenly flung himself full length among
them and dug his fingers into the ground. The moss beneath the heather was wet—what hillside in the Highlands was not? and the vineyard slopes round Girolac
were dry . . . dry as his heart would become there. . . .
Mo thruaigh! What use to dwell upon it longer?—it had
to be! Ranald sprang to his feet and went on upwards.

An hour and a half later he was coming down the burn-
side again; but he had not left his heartache behind him.
To have seen on the heights of Beinn a Chuallaich what
must prove his last stag at gaze was not a panacea for
it . . .

Below the tiny ravine where he had gazed at the young
hawks it had pleased the Allt Mor to form a pool, before
slipping further. Ranald had noticed, as he passed upwards, the slab of flat rock above it and the noble Scots
pine which shaded both. There had been no one there
then, but now he saw that a black-clad figure was sitting
there—a woman, evidently, with a large dog by her side.
Both appeared to be gazing down at the burn below them.
Some widow, he supposed, come to indulge her grief in
solitude.

He continued to descend rapidly, and since he would
pass a little above the level where the woman was sitting,
would naturally have gone past without saluting her in
any way had not the dog, a large deerhound, got up and

begun to bark at him. Its mistress spoke to it, put out a hand to its collar; the hood of dark grey silk which she wore over her head slipped a little, and as she looked up to see the cause of the dog's behaviour, it fell completely back. To Ranald's surprise, and something more, he found himself gazing down upon the hair of his day-dreams. It was Bride Stewart in that sombre gown.

He uncovered. "Good-day, Miss Stewart. May I hope that you have not forgotten me?"

Plainly she had not—unless, indeed, with a skin so fair as hers even the most transient and ordinary blush was magnified to this lovely rosiness, or unless he had startled her. Choosing to assume the first explanation, Ranald leapt down the short descent on to the smooth flat slab of rock—to the increased perturbation of the deerhound.

And he was right. "It will be Mr. Maclean from Askay, will it not? Be quiet, Fiona!" Now upon her feet, Miss Stewart caught again at the big dog's collar. "We met last year, sir, when you were returning from Dunkirk."

Ranald assented. And postponing from ulterior motives the information that he was returning to France for good, he gave her to understand that, affairs taking him to Perthshire, he was happy to be able to pass through Kinloch Rannoch and to pay his respects to those who had shown him such hospitality on his former visit. He had, however, only arrived at Mount Alexander the previous day.

Standing there with him below the pine tree, above the clear and smiling pool, Bride Stewart listened, looking up at him with those eyes as limpid as the burn, but not of its colour. The mountain breeze fingered the tendrils of fine gold upon her brow, their pure glow enhanced by the black ribbon which confined them, and Ranald found himself almost eagerly hoping that she would continue to let that eclipsing hood lie idle, as now, upon her shoulders. But why was she in such sable attire?—though indeed there was a little bunch of pink heath thrust into the great mourning brooch, all funeral urn and weeping willow, which fastened her white kerchief. Struan had not told him of any death at Inchrannoch. He was discomposed.

"You have not, I trust, madam, suffered any recent bereavement? . . . Yet indeed I fear you must have done so!"

The tears came into Bride Stewart's eyes and she lowered them. "Yes, Mr. Maclean; we have lost my dear aunt—but not very recently. She died nearly a year ago. She had long been ailing."

"Indeed," said the young man gravely, "I am very sorry to hear it."

And the thought came at once, very much to increase his regret: "She is all the less likely to leave her widowed uncle. It may indeed be that Mrs. Stewart's death is the reason for her refusal of Malcolm Robertson. But perhaps she has only bidden him to wait." Well, *he* was not going to wait, save long enough to avoid appearing uncouth and abrupt.

And after enquiring how Mr. Stewart did, Ranald, divining that she was on the point of leaving this retreat overlooking the pool, asked whether he might have the privilege of escorting her down the brae.

Bride Stewart assented, accepting his hand up to the path, but was not, unfortunately for him, sufficiently incommoded by the steepness of the familiar descent to accept it again. Indeed, she flitted down before Ranald like an elf. He wished she had not been in black; she should have worn green, like all her fairy race.

All too soon, since the way was so short, they arrived at the little river, with Inchrannoch House standing on the further bank. While Bride Stewart waited for the old blue ferry-boat to come across for her, Ranald asked and obtained permission to escort her over in order to pay his respects to her uncle. He was debating whether this was a good opportunity to break the news of the change in his circumstances and observe how she took it, or whether it would be wiser to make a little headway with her first, before he told her that he must ask her to share the fortunes of an exile. But Miss Stewart herself settled the question for him by asking how soon he would be going back to his island. "You told us about it when you were here before, sir," she added.

"Alas, I am not returning to Askay at all," he answered. "I am on my way to France."

For a moment she looked surprised, but the look passed. "Oh, upon the affairs of . . ." She lowered her voice and did not complete the sentence; it was not necessary.

"No, not that, madam. On affairs of my own. I am now a French landed proprietor." And Ranald laughed, not very happily. "My uncle in the wine country has died and left me his small estate—a house and vineyards. You must allow me to send Mr. Stewart a cask of Girolac some day—though I suppose that with France and England at war that may be none too easy to do."

"Mr. Maclean, I hope you'll not get captured yourself by a French privateer on your way thither!"

"Would that distress you, Miss Stewart?"

"But naturally it would," replied Bride, smiling. "I would not wish to be thinking of a friend of mine in chains!"

Confound the old ferryman, he was half-way over! "I am glad to know you so compassionate, madam—nay, more, that you allow me the title of a friend. I assure you that I very greatly value it."

The words were not much; they might have conveyed little more than a formal politeness, but Ranald Maclean, perhaps in compensation for having little play of feature, was gifted with a very expressive voice. Bride's colour rose a trifle, and he saw it. And then and there, looking down at her, he felt with conviction that here was the one woman for him, that he must have her if he carried her off by force . . . and knew with equal certainty that he would never dare touch a finger of her unless she willed it.

Immediately there was further occasion silently to curse Donald the ferryman, for he gratuitously informed Miss

Stewart ere she stepped aboard his ancient vessel that he had recently put the laird across to this bank, thus rendering it useless for Ranald to escort her to the house on the pretext which he had found—and indeed impossible, for the young lady thereupon practically dismissed him. Yet she did not rebuff him when he said that he would wait upon her uncle on the morrow, though she returned a noncommittal reply when he expressed a hope that he might find her at home, too.

But as Bride Stewart, holding the deerhound by the collar, was borne away across the strip of water she smiled at him—that was something. It was at this very spot by the ferry that he had had his last glimpse of her a year ago last spring, he and Malcolm Robertson, after that unpleasant encounter of hers with the MacGregor from Glen Lyon in the wood on the slope. Naturally Miss Stewart had made no reference to that episode, and equally naturally Ranald would have been the very last to base upon it any claim to gratitude, having acted on that occasion merely as any man must have done. But had it in *her* mind the aspect of even a spider's thread of a link between them? He would probably never know.

(4)

The window was open that evening to the long July twilight; and it was an evening so quiet that the fall of a cone from the ranks of sentinel firs outside the front of Inchrannoch House had the importance of an event. It was light enough to read still, and, Uncle Walter being absorbed in his book, Bride's needle began to ply slower and slower until it ceased from its task altogether, and she was gazing abstractedly at some rosy feathers of cloud which the flushed west, invisible from this room, had sent to drift towards the summit of Schiehallion.

Was it possible that thinking of a person had some effect upon their movements? For a year and four months—she could not deny it to herself—the image of the dark, lean traveller from Dunkirk had remained as fresh as though she had possessed a picture of him—no, fresher, because it could move and speak in her memory. And she knew that was because she had often thought about him, though with no hope of seeing him again—just as a dweller on a remote sea-loch might recall, even to its spars and rigging, a chance ship which had put in there where ships seldom came. And now the same vessel had sailed once more into the uneventful waters of her life.

How was she to know whether he had meant anything particular by that little speech at the ferry about her friendship? Perhaps he was accustomed to say such things, with just that earnestness, to any young lady who took his fancy—though somehow one would not easily think that. Yet how could one know? He was an absolute stranger in Rannoch, even to Malcolm Robertson, who had first brought him to her uncle's house. But she would very much like to believe that he had meant what he had said.

Fiona got up from her place near Mr. Stewart's chair and came and put her muzzle on Bride's knee. "I wish *you* could tell me, Fiona," thought her mistress as she stroked it.

The deerhound's movement caused her uncle to look up and then lay down his book. "If you are not sewing any more, my dear, I should be obliged if you would read to me awhile—that is, if this light is good enough for you. I'd not have you try your young eyes to save mine."

Bride rose at once and took the book. "'Tis full light enough for me here by the window, Uncle Walter," she said, with her accustomed sweetness. "Is this the place?"

But it is quite possible to read aloud—read intelligently—and think of something else as well.

CHAPTER VI

It was very misty next afternoon when Ranald went to pay his respects at Inchrannoch—misty and cold. For Mr. Stewart's sake there was a fire. He had not been well of late, and the death of his wife, if not unexpected, had greatly shaken him. After about twenty minutes of talk he suddenly fell into a doze, though he was still sitting upright in his chair.

"You must excuse him, sir," said Bride in a low voice. "It happens thus at times. When he wakes he will be distressed at his discourtesy to a guest."

"Perhaps," hazarded Ranald, equally low, "he will not realise that he has slept."

It seemed to join them in a bond, this hushed colloquy in the firelight; the mist without also joined them, shutting them off together from the world. Miss Stewart glanced at the window.

"You will never experience haar like this at Girolac, Mr. Maclean."

"My sorrow that I shall not, madam!"

"You mean that you will regret it?" questioned she in a whisper. "But in its place you will have the sun, and I suppose much of it—more than we ever see here!"

He looked at her sitting there, nun-like, in a little sober grey gown—no, blend of nun and *sidhe*. "It will not be the sun of my own country."

Bride clasped her hands on her knee. "And yet you must go?"

"If I am to accept my uncle's legacy, Miss Stewart, I cannot continue to live in Scotland and leave the care of the estate to a deputy—not, at any rate, for many years yet."

"You expect then to be absent from Scotland for a long while?"

"For a long while."

"And you are going alone," she pursued in the same hushed voice, "taking no one with you—not even a servant?"

"Quite alone, Miss Stewart. It is exile; could I impose it on another who like myself loves the wind down the corrie and the burn in spate?"

There was a silence. The old man still slept, his head a little fallen forward; the fire flickered, the mist pressed on the window-panes, and Fiona, stretched at Bride's feet, gave a deep sigh. And Bride herself, though her eyes were fixed on the fire, knew that the guest was looking at her very intently.

At last he said slowly, with little pauses between the phrases: "When I have been in France a while, and have learnt how pleasant a land it is . . . and that indeed I know already, since I was there two years ago at vintage time—perhaps I may have gained a sufficiently persuasive tongue to paint its praises to . . . to the one person whom I would have share its sunlight with me. Nevertheless, even so, I fear that would be too much to ask . . . from a Highlander."

Still Bride looked into the fire, at the flames branching like a deer's antlers—the antlers of a stag thrusting horns of lightning all round the charred wood. Her thoughts went flickering with them, now here, now there. . . .

"You cannot tell that, sir, until you try." Had she really said that?

"But what if I am afraid to try?" he answered, almost inaudibly; and then was silent.

She stole a look at him again; but he, too, was gazing at the fire now. Yet she could see that he was frowning.

"Does your friend know of your intention?" she hazarded. One of them must say something; the silence was too difficult. Her heart was beating in a strange fashion—an unaccountable fashion, for what were Mr. Maclean's future plans to her?

But the answer to the question which she had put to him she was destined not to hear. Those lithe, twisting antlers of flame played her a sorry trick, for through their agency a piece of half-burnt log just then subsided with a crash sufficient to break Mr. Stewart's light slumber, impervious though it had been to the murmur of voices. He woke with a start, but seemed indeed not to know that he had been asleep.

"You were saying, Mr. Maclean, that in the district of Bordeaux the vines——"

The moment was gone; and none like it recurred during the brief remainder of Ranald Maclean's visit.

The mist seemed denser than ever when he left Inchrannoch House; old Donald was even inclined to grumble at having to ferry him across the river. It was not so thick, however, as to hinder progress if one knew the way, and Ranald set out eastwards on the four miles or so to Mount Alexander with the long stride habitual to him.

When could he contrive to see Miss Stewart again? If need be, he must extend his stay in Rannoch. After all, she hardly knew him; she was a little person with pride, he guessed, under all her sweetness—no girl to fling herself into the arms of the first stranger. And what had he to offer her more than another? He could not hope to sweep her off her feet; he must lay a certain amount of siege. He did not know whether he had been maladroit this afternoon, but he had been unfortunate. Yet he had approached the subject nearest his heart; she must surely have guessed. . . .

Dully through the fog, when he had got as far as Drumchastle, came the clop-clop of a horse's hoofs, not behind him, but in front. He was, in fact, overtaking the horseman. As man and beast began to loom up before him, Ranald could tell that both must be tired; the horse was but a shaggy pony—poor little beast! The man jogging along on him had a weary back; a rolled plaid strapped behind him suggested that he was a traveller. And the odd thing was that both rider and garron had a familiar look; yet surely that must be a trick of the mist. A few strides more and Ranald stopped dead with an exclamation—and immediately afterwards set forward still more rapidly, calling out: "MacVeagh, MacVeagh, is it you?"

The rider, startled, pulled up; Ranald, alongside, found himself indeed looking into the little wizened visage of Murdoch MacVeagh, his brother's factotum, sometimes dignified by the title of grieve.

"Indeed, Mr. Ranald, it is—at least, I'm thinking so, but I'm none too sure of it! *Mo thruaigh*, it might be that I was nothing but a piece of old board, so stiff as I am!"

Premonition of some disaster at Fasnapoll now swept surprise from Ranald's heart. "In God's name, what is it? You have come after me with ill news, I fear. My brother . . . the children . . . ?"

"Do not be troubling yourself now, Mr. Ranald," replied the little monkey-like man consolingly. "They are all well and hearty. But there was a bit of a letter come for you from France——"

"Well, give it me, man!"

"Wait now, Mr. Ranald; I've more for you than that, and when you hear what it is you'll maybe not open the letter . . . or maybe you'll open it the quicker. But let's be getting off the middle of the road!" Swearing under his breath, he creaked out of the saddle and pulled his shaggy mount to the side of the way, where the wooded slopes, shrouded and dripping, lifted above them. "Come closer now, Mr. Ranald, for there's no knowing who may be passing in this haar." And as Ranald, mystified, stooped his head the little man said in a penetrating whisper: *"He's come!"*

"Who has come?"

"You can ask that?" exclaimed MacVeagh in shocked tones. "Why, he that's waited for, to be sure—*Phrionnsa òg Tearlach mac Sheumais!* The French brig that brought him passed under Muick the very day you left—I mind marking a strange sail, but I was busy, and thought little of it at the time. And she put into Loch nan Uamh, and there he is, it seems, in the house of Angus MacDonald of Borradale!"

Ranald stared almost petrified at the bringer of such tidings out of the mist. There were beads of fog on the nap of his old hat, on his eyebrows. Then Struan was right! "Come! He has really come! . . . And what force has he brought with him?"

"Force, is it? Not a soldier, not a gun—just himself, blessings on him, and a few Scots gentlemen—or maybe Irish."

The young man ran his hand through and through the pony's tangled forelock. "This is likely some fantastic tale that's got about," he said after a moment. "Without men, without arms—it can't be true!" Then some words came back to him, ringing through a little room on a night of storm: *Though I go with but three followers . . . though I go alone!* By God, then the Prince *had* done as he swore he would! It was fine, extraordinary fine and spirited, but—what next?

"Has the laird written to me on this matter, Murdoch?"

MacVeagh shook his grizzled head. "He would not. And I was first to tell you this news for your private ear alone, in the case that you should wish—you'll be understanding, now?—to be off to France as though you had known nothing of it!"

Ranald tore at the patient garron's hair. "But—how can I? If this news be true one at least of us must follow the Prince!"

"Ay, 'tis so," agreed MacVeagh, wiping his face. "You will have talked about it with Fasnapoll; he said as much."

"If my brother goes out, Murdoch, and the business comes to naught, as well it may, then——"

"Ay," said old MacVeagh again. He was perfectly conversant with the situation; for him it was but a day since the Fifteen with its confiscations and attainders. "Ay. If it comes to naught, there's the estate will be taken by the Government and the weans dispossessed, not to speak of himself in danger, maybe, of Tyburn."

"But one of us must go! It must not be said that no Maclean of Askay fought for his Prince!"

"Forbye Maclean of Maclean will not be leading out the clan," MacVeagh, himself of a Maclean sept, reminded him.

"Only because he is a prisoner in the Tower of London. 'Tis I will have to go out, MacVeagh; last year when I came back from France we settled that, the laird and I." But in those days he had not had an inheritance waiting for him. . . . Well, the inheritance must wait a while longer. The young man of Dunkirk had come almost alone, almost in the fishing smack he had spoken of—for very shame another young man, a professed Jacobite, who only last night had drunk to his coming, could not slink out of Scotland just as he set foot on it, slink out to cultivate his vineyards and lie soft in a French bed when he might be belting on the claymore and lying with Prince Tearlach in the heather.

"You must start back to-morrow, Murdoch, and tell my brother I am going out. But come along now to Mount Alexander, and the Chief will give you a bed. I doubt, however, if this poor beast will carry you there."

Murdoch fumbled in a pouch. "And here's the French letter."

Ranald broke the seal and glanced at the beginning and signature with preoccupied eyes. The letter was from M. Marcelin, his late uncle's lawyer, requesting to know when he might expect him at Girolac. When indeed? He read no further, but thrust the letter into his pocket and went forward in the mist with MacVeagh, the pony and the news. What would Struan, that inveterate old Jacobite, say to what he had to tell?

Ranald found at Mount Alexander much excitement and a number of Robertsons, Malcolm among them. For the tidings had already reached "the earthly paradise" by another channel, and Struan, brewing with his own hands a vast bowl of punch, and surrounded by arrack, brandy and lemons, was declaiming the combined Nunc Dimittis and Te Deum of an enthusiast who for all his seventy-seven years and past outlawries did not intend to sit quietly at home merely to observe the progress of the Lord's Anointed.

"Faith, we scarce know ourselves, from the Chief downwards," exclaimed Malcolm Robertson, wringing Ranald's hand. "(I heard you were here, Mr. Maclean, and have been looking to see you at Auchendrie.) If 'tis true, as they say, that Lord Tullibardine—Duke William—has come with the Prince, what a to-do there will shortly be at Blair!" And he laughed like a schoolboy at the prospect of mischief, his fair face quite flushed with excitement.

It was not until he was in his own bedchamber that night that Ranald had leisure to think coolly. It was late, and to mark the occasion he had been obliged to imbibe a certain quantity of claret as well as of punch—but he could put away a bottle and be none the worse of it. As he sat by the open window he was glad to exchange the heat and noise of festivity for the sound of the unseen Tummel pouring over its rock-pools between him and Schiehallion. The mist had completely vanished and the moon was coming up. What would this postponement of his taking possession of Girolac, his taking up, instead, arms for the Prince, what effect would this have upon his chances with Miss Stewart? Why, surely, it would increase them! She was, he had seen last year, heart and soul a Jacobite; she must approve his action. It was true that in the end he would still have to take her over the sea, because he had not the means of supporting a wife elsewhere . . . unless indeed with a Stuart once more upon the throne he could obtain suitable employment in Scotland. And it was true that if he was to join the Prince at once he must immediately turn back again to the west coast, giving up his plan of remaining here to woo. But he could not think that this conduct would impair his chances of winning her in the end.

Yet the venture was terribly precarious . . . no French help, no money, no arms! Even the fumes of punch had not entirely obscured that aspect from the excited throng downstairs. Ranald considered it. Would the country rise? Would the Hanoverians prove too strong? Only the gods knew; and all the more call was there that Fasnapoll should give a hostage to either side. Then, if the English won, Norman and his family were safe; on the other hand, the Prince, if he were successful, would never harm a man whose brother had drawn the sword for him immediately upon his landing. It was a not unusual arrangement. He must write and explain matters to M. Marcelin.

He drew the French lawyer's letter out of his pocket, pulled the candle nearer, and for the first time read it through; read it again with a changed countenance, and then sat very still, staring at the foreign handwriting. For the letter was not, as he had thought at the first hasty glance, a mere enquiry as to the date of his arrival at Girolac; it was an urgent appeal to come at once, to lose not a day. M. d'Ormeuil, the nephew of *feu Madame,* was claiming the estate on the ground that Madame's foreign husband had not the right to will away what had originally been her property, and unless the Scottish claimant made great haste the courts would have settled the matter and, the writer greatly feared, in M. d'Ormeuil's favour. This had been sprung upon M. Marcelin out of the blue; he had had no warning of such a procedure; but unless M. Maclean could be in Bordeaux before the end of August it might, the writer cried with pessimism, be useless his giving himself the trouble to come there at all.

The end of August! If he left for Perth to-morrow morning . . . yes, he might possibly reach Bordeaux in time . . . more than possibly, certainly. But then—what of his duty to the Cause, to his brother, to his own convictions? And what of Bride and his chance of her hand?

But Bride was lost if he did *not* go! For without means

and a home how could he ask her to be his wife; and
unless he set out instantly for France to fight his case, it
was abundantly clear that these would be taken from him
ere he had possessed them. Never in that case would he
walk among the hot alien vineyards, longing for the sands
and the heather of Askay, for the vineyards would never
be his. Nor Bride Stewart . . . nor Bride Stewart either!

Ranald stood leaning against the side of the open
window, deaf to the rush of the river, his senses chained
by the dumb clamour of an inner struggle where the
warring armies swayed now that way, now this . . .
though up till now in his life he had found little difficulty
in making up his mind. *"Deoch slàinte an righ!"* the cry
had gone round the board this evening, and like all there
he had swelled it and lifted an exultant glass. But there
would be more than that in following a Prince who had
come alone and unbefriended, more than merely drinking
the health of James III in Struan Robertson's punch!
Who knew where the road from Borradale would lead
them all in the end? And to tread it he at least must
forgo safety, possessions and her he had set his heart
upon. Nor could he wait: the decision must be taken to-
night, before he slept—the double decision. For he, a poor
man and in love, must choose not only between his duty—
if it were a duty—to the Jacobite cause, and his heritage;
but also between his duty to that cause, and Bride Stewart.
Two such weighty inducements in one side of the scales
against a claim so impalpable, so questionable even—how
could a sane man hesitate?

For some time now the moon had been mounting the
southern sky, but Ranald had not marked her progress to
serener heights. Now at last he realised that she had
topped Schiehallion, full-orbed, and both she and that
peak of peaks swam together in almost unimaginable glory.
The young man drew a long breath and stood gazing at
the sight. Then he turned away and began to make ready
for bed. His choice was made.

F

COULD any situation be more unpalatable, on this last evening of August, more worthy of real sympathy, than that of Mr. Thomas Bissett, the Duke of Atholl's commissary, a man of weight, of proved honesty and devotion, left in charge of the great Perthshire seat of Blair Castle, the Duke having prudently withdrawn himself farther south, first to his new mansion at Dunkeld, then to Edinburgh? The tribulations of the just steward are surely more sensibly felt than those of the unjust, and Mr. Bissett had been, and still was, suffering acute apprehension as to the damage which the approaching Jacobite invaders might inflict upon the castle and its surroundings. What, for instance, might not happen to those thousand treasured young larches—trees still new to the Highlands —which had been so successfully planted three years ago, to the trout in the new pond, to the Duke's English cattle, or even to the Temple of Fame, wherein the gilded bust of the Duke himself presided amid a circle of the philosophers and poets of antiquity?

When it could no longer be ignored that the whole "Highland army," in Mr. Bissett's eyes a half-naked and probably rapacious horde of reivers, was making for Blair in the wake of "the Pretender's son" and of that ghost from the past, William, Marquis of Tullibardine, the exiled elder brother who, but for his attainder, would have succeeded to the dukedom one-and-twenty years ago, Mr. Bissett had done the best he could in the emergency. Earlier on this ill-starred Saturday he had ridden out two or three miles to meet the rabble and their "Prince" on their way from Dalwhinnie, in order to make arrangements for their reception and their billeting round the castle. He had subsequently been forced to witness the castle being taken possession of (in a perfectly orderly manner, it was true) and to behold the reverent and ecstatic welcome of the "Prince" at the door by an imported Jacobite hostess, the Honourable Mrs. Robertson of Lude, "Lady Lude," whom Lord Tullibardine, her cousin, had summmoned thither for that purpose.

His wig awry, Mr. Bissett now sat writing to his master the Duke an account of the day's unprecedented events. His own room was quiet, but the castle was in a turmoil of occupation. Lights shone in its mounting rows of barred windows—for Blair Castle was five or six storeys high, and but for the irregularity of its design and its perching turrets, held a certain suggestion of a prison about it. But no prison was ever set in so green and spacious and well-watered a site, with pleasances and plantations and bowling-green, between the swiftly falling streams which the great mountains of Atholl at its back sent down to swell the River Garry below it.

The commissary's pen travelled feverishly, with now and then a pause as he groaned slightly and pushed his wig still further out of place. Yet he was a just man. He had, for instance, already recorded that the uninvited guests had so far behaved very civilly. For the rest, he reported that he had allowed the Highlanders to picket the few horses they had in the park where the hay was cut, immediately above the Wilderness and bewest Banavie, to prevent them from overrunning the other enclosures. He was more afraid of to-morrow night, when, so Lady Lude had told him, the Duke of Perth, Lord Nairne, and other "Low Country gentlemen" were to join with 800 men, and, necessarily, more horses.

Mr. Bissett read over what he had written, and then continued, with a twist of disgust on his visage:

"The Highlanders doe not yet exceed in number 2,000, and they'll scarce be so much, two thirds of which are the poorest naked-like Creatures imaginable, and verry in-

differently armed: I doe not think the one half of their guns will fire."

The scorn went, to be succeeded by a more tolerant expression, and the scribe penned these words:

"The young Gentleman himself seems to be good natured, but I doe not think that he hath verry much in him, and your brother is still the old man that he was; he looks as if he were of greater age by ten years than he is. There are with them five or six gentlemen, that came over in the ship with them, old aligrougus fellows as ever I saw."

Having thus set down his slight opinion of the young man whose advent was soon to assume for a brief space the fiery portentousness of a comet, and his unfavourable impression of that comet's tail—for by the word which he applied to it he meant "grim"—Mr. Bissett passed on to inform the absent Duke what chiefs and chieftains he had observed among the throng, Clanranald and Keppoch, Barisdale and Lochgarry, and how he had caused kill a cow and one of the large sheep for their sustenance. Proceeding, the chronicler came to the subject of fruit. *"I thought there had been pine-apples in Italy, but it seems not, for we hapened this day to get one up from Dunkeld, whereof the young Gentleman eat, and said it was the first he had ever seen"*—a feather, this, in the cap of the Duke's gardener at Dunkeld, who grew oranges and lemons, too, in the "stove" or hot-house.

And a little later, after reporting how His Grace's brother had enquired after the brass pieces which used to be there, and whether there were any arms in the house, Mr. Bissett came to a stop, and signed his name with due humility, as "one of your Grace's servants." Pursing his lips he reached out for the sand-box, deciding that he would send the letter by Maclaren, one of the garden-men; it was to be hoped that it would reach its destination without interception. And then, quite suddenly, he added a postscript, at high speed and with a quill which dug into the paper, so strong was the gust of indignant wrath which drove it.

"Lady Lude is here with them, and behaves like a

*light Giglet, and hath taken upon her to be sole mistress
of the house."*

(2)

"I take my text," announced the Reverend Duncan
Cameron next morning as he stood behind a table in the
dining-room of Innerchadden, "from the 23rd and 24th
verses of the 118th Psalm: *'This is the day which the
Lord hath made: we will rejoice and be glad in it,'* " and
the little Episcopalian and Jacobite congregation of Bunrannoch settled down for the sermon.

There was no Episcopalian chapel at Kinloch Rannoch
—no kirk even of the Established Church—and when Mr.
Cameron, the Episcopalian minister from Fortingall, came
the fifteen miles or so thence, service was usually held at
the house of the particular gentleman of that persuasion
who happened to be giving him hospitality for the night.
To-day it was the turn of Mr. Stewart of Innerchadden,
the house under that high green ridge west of Schiehallion,
to which Nature's graving tools had given the semblance
of the head and shoulders of a sleeping giant.

Technically Mr. Cameron might not minister to a congregation of more than eight at a time, but so easy-going
were relations between Jacobites and Whigs in that part
of Perthshire that no one had ever called the attention of
the authorities to the fact that his flock was always much
larger. Even Mr. Fergus Ferguson, the very zealous Presbyterian minister of Fortingall (of which immense parish
Kinloch Rannoch formed part), had never taken any steps
about it.

"It is going to be a sermon about the Lord's Day,"
thought Bride, with a sigh, settling the folds of her blue
dress (for she was no longer in mourning) over her Sunday
hoop. "How we ought to keep Sunday. Indeed, I do not
think we need it; Uncle Walter is nearly as strict as the
Presbyterians. Besides, *any* sermon would be difficult to
listen to to-day!"

Yet, if he proposed giving an admonitory discourse on these lines, the Rev. Duncan Cameron's air seemed singularly elated, and he had not gone far in his homily before the congregation, a little surprised, but by no means reluctant, discovered that their thoughts were being diverted from a brief contemplation of the seventh day of creation and the Temple services at Jerusalem to events much more contemporary and to a locality nearer and better known. They found themselves, indeed, at the end of a mere quarter of an hour, invited to regard Blair Castle as the Jews regarded Sion, and this particular Sunday as the beginning of the Return from the Captivity. And yet the preacher was guarded in his allusions, and no one ignorant of the wonderful news which had reached most of his hearers yesterday evening could have been sure that he was glorifying what to a congregation of a different persuasion would have been rank rebellion and blasphemy.

Later on, however, Mr. Cameron grew bolder, and, proceeding backwards in the same Psalm, followed up a brief exposition on the verse, *"This is the Lord's doing and it is marvellous in our eyes,"* by one on a still earlier statement, *"This is the gate of the Lord; the righteous shall enter into it,"* which drew a very different picture of the present condition of Blair Castle and its new occupants from that which Mr. Bissett had penned the previous evening to his master. And finally the congregation were reminded of the promise made by the Lord unto David: *"Of the fruit of thy body shall I set upon thy seat,"* though it was not the accession of Solomon which they were thereafter invited to contemplate.

Once outside, the Jacobite ladies of the congregation buzzed like bees. Was it really true that *He* was at Blair Castle? How long would he be there? Oh, if only it were a little nearer, and there were a driving road!

Young Mrs. Menzies, Malcolm Robertson's sister, as vivacious as her brother was quiet, came up to Bride and her uncle as they were going down the drive, and after greetings burst out: "Well, now that we have the Church's blessing I shall certainly do it!"

"Do what, pray, Mrs. Menzies?" asked Bride, drawn by her excited air.

"Ride over to Blair to-morrow!" responded she. "Mr. Stewart, will you allow Bride to accompany us? We shall not be the only ones, I'll warrant. My husband is too canny to go until he sees better the way the cat is likely to jump, but we shall have Malcolm to escort us. Will you come, Bride?"

"Oh, Cousin Catherine!" breathed Bride, her eyes sparkling. "To Blair, where the——"

"What is this?" enquired Mr. Stewart. "You are proposing, my dear madam, to ride to Blair Castle? But consider——"

"Oh, sir, can one allow anything to keep one away so long as one has the means of getting there! To see our rightful Prince in the flesh, to kiss his hand, to assure him——"

"Yes, yes," interrupted the old man, "and I hope I am as eager to show my devotion as any, but remember, my dear Mrs. Menzies, the sort of following that will have come with His Royal Highness—hordes of wild Highlanders from the West, many little better, no doubt, than cattle-thieves. There are sure to be many Camerons with him, and you remember the extremely high-handed conduct of those Lochaber Camerons who came into Rannoch a fortnight ago to force out those of their name. . . . And then the Duke is away, and the Duchess, too."

"You can call Lord James Murray Duke of Atholl, sir!" expostulated the ardent lady, "when the true and rightful Duke has returned after near thirty years of exile! And, Mr. Stewart, Lady Lude is hostess at Blair; in any case, as you know, the Duchess would not have been there, for the deed of separation was signed only a few weeks ago . . . you know 'tis said that when at Dunkeld she threw a leg of mutton at the Duke's head . . . and as I said, Lady Lude is there to receive for Duke

William, who wrote and desired her to act in that capacity. There can therefore be no irregularity in a visit so long as that is the case, more particularly as Lady Lude is the widow of a kinsman of ours. Let us put it that Mr. Malcolm Robertson is riding over to pay his respects to the Honourable Mrs. Robertson of Lude and carries with him his sister and his cousin! And if Someone Else happens to be at Blair. . . . Oh, pray, Mr. Stewart, give your niece leave to accompany us! We will start very early and proceed as leisurely as we please; 'tis still summer weather, and Bride is a good horsewoman. We shall take our night-clothes and sleep if need be at the inn. . . . Mr. Stewart, if you refuse I vow you'll be putting an affront on me, a married woman, and on my brother's qualifications as an escort for ladies!"

And before they reached the gate of Innerchadden Mr. Stewart had given a rather reluctant consent.

(3)

As Bride rode with her Robertson kin over the high, narrow little bridge above the Tilt, in the late afternoon of next day, she was feeling a trifle disappointed at the change in the goal of this pilgrimage. For at Milton of Invervack, just before crossing the Garry, the travellers had been told that the Prince was leaving Blair Castle for Lude House, and that Lady Lude had gone thither to prepare for him. So they resolved not to go to the castle at all, but to hurry on to Lude House, which was not a great deal further.

Their road had taken them round above the castle sitting majestically in the midst of its wide, green domain, the Prince's standard, as they could see, still flying, rather surprisingly, from the summit of Cumming's Tower. Bodies of Highlanders were camped untidily round about the castle—Camerons (in the majority), Stewarts of Appin, clansmen out of three of the four main branches of Clan Donald and, so it was believed, some Grants of

Glenmoriston. But Bride had wanted to see inside Blair Castle—though not, it was true, if the chief ornament was gone. Her uncle was too confirmed a Jacobite to be on visiting terms with Duke James; but to be received there, now that the rightful Duke was back, would be a different and a very pleasurable affair. However, the decision to go by had been taken, and they clattered over the little ravine, Mrs. Menzies talking hard as usual, and Malcolm rather silent; and presently were riding up the long, steep slope to Lude House, with its view over the narrow strath to the wall of hillside under which the River Garry, swollen by the waters of Tilt and Fender, swept onwards to that place of fierce and triumphant memories, the Pass of Killiecrankie.

Lude House, when, after passing between its low, flanking towers, they had entered its courtyard, seemed to be in a state of great animation, if not of confusion. The widowed Lady Lude, a daughter of that implacable old loyalist, the Baroness Nairne, was evidently turning it upside down to receive the princely guest, who had not yet arrived. Presently she came rushing along, flushed and voluble: she was delighted to see her visitors: no, His Royal Highness had not come yet, and she doubted if he intended to sleep at her house, but she was making all preparations; there would probably be dancing this evening when he and his officers came over, for there were other ladies expected, though none from so far away as Bunrannoch. The three of them must all lie there to-night— had she not heard Miss Bride Stewart of Bunrannoch spoken of as the White Rose of Rannoch . . . but she must not blush like that, or she would belie her name! The two ladies had nothing but riding-habits? No matter; she could furnish them with gowns, for her cousin Menzies and she were much of a height, and there was time—a couple of hours yet, probably—for a few stitches. She handed them over to a maid-servant and fled, issuing rapid orders.

"Mercy on us!" exclaimed Catherine Menzies when she

and Bride were alone in the bedchamber assigned to them. "Lady Lude is like a whirlwind; I verily believe that playing hostess at Blair has gone to her head! 'Tis true that she was always easily elevate. I'd fain know Duke William's opinion of her in that capacity!"

But she herself was scarcely less excited, practising curtsies to her own image in the mirror, taking minuet steps hither and thither with lifted riding-skirt, and adjuring her dear Bride to do the same.

"I fear," said Bride wistfully, "that I shall but watch the dancing from a distance. I cannot expect Lady Lude to have a gown of my small size."

But she had—a green gown, green as spring grass, made, it appeared, for some kinswoman of hers recently visiting her, who in the end had not sufficient courage to wear it because it was of the fairy colour, and had left it behind when she went. If Miss Stewart had no such superstitious fancies it was at her service.

Bride had not been a true Highland girl if she had been completely free from these; but who could have endured on this of all nights to be seen by a Prince—and perhaps by someone else also—in a dress which precluded taking part in a ball? In the hooped green gown with its paniers opening over a petticoat sown with silver daisies she looked like a fairy herself, and Mrs. Menzies, who had no jealousy in her composition, told her so.

"Truly, it might have been made for your shape, and sets you amazingly, Miss Stewart!" confirmed their hostess. "And when your hair is powdered—la, I must remember to send you my maid for that!" She swirled towards the door again.

"Oh, madam," exclaimed Bride imploringly, "what is he like?"

There was only one "he." A rapt expression came over Lady Lude's countenance. "The most ravishing young hero that you can conceive—the top of perfection and heaven's darling! Could you but see . . . but you will see!" And with that she was gone.

(4)

The great drawing-room at Lude House, cleared for dancing, brightly besconced and full of the gaiety of tartan and the sheen of silk, the latter material chiefly adorning the ladies, for the gentlemen, at least those who had come from the West with the Prince, had not brought with them festive attire—the drawing-room waited. Never in her life had Bride's usually unperturbed heart behaved like this. Actually to be in the same room with him for whose welfare and that of his father the rightful King she had prayed every day as long as she could remember! But one had always thought of him as so far away, in Rome, almost in another world.

The folding doors were flung open, and through them came the strains of the pipes, playing (to Bride's delight and pride) the Stewart march, *"Gabhaidh sinn an rathad mòr"*—"we will take the good old way." Was not her family, too, of the branch of the Royal Stuarts?

And then, leading the flushed and excited Lady Lude by the hand, came Prince Charles Edward Louis Philip Casimir Stuart in a coat of pale satin crossed by a tartan scarf which half concealed the star of St. Andrew on his breast, young, slender, handsome, smiling, encircled with the double aureole of his own personal fascination and of his birth. It was difficult to realise that he was newly arrived from a long march across wild hill country, for he might have stepped straight from the French court—or from Oberon's. Swooning with admiration and loyalty the row of ladies sank with bright, ballooning hoops to the floor, while behind their young leader the chiefs advanced into the room, Duke William of Atholl, Lochiel and Keppoch, young Clanranald, young Angus MacDonell of Glengarry and his elder kinsman Lochgarry, and several others. And before the ladies were up again from their deep and reverential curtsies every sword had left its sheath in glittering homage, so that the ballroom seemed pricked with a sudden harvest of steel.

An hour and a half later the candles were burnt more than half-way down in their sconces; the intoxicating evening, save for supper, was over. Intoxicating it had truly been for every lady of dancing age there, for, since there were so few of them, the Prince had danced with every one. Seldom, after this occasion, was he to dance at all, even in the greater gatherings of Holyrood House; but to-night he was in the mood for it, calling for the Highland tunes, equally at home in reel or minuet, moving with the ease and perfection which he brought to every physical feat, whether it demanded merely grace or endurance as well.

To Bride Stewart the great honour of being his partner —an honour which she had never for a moment expected— had cast a kind of unreality over the proceedings. And the wonderful moments were gone so quickly. But often after-wards—all her life, indeed—she would be able in memory to go through them again, to remember exactly what the Prince had said, for instance, when he had elicited the fact that she and Mrs. Menzies had that day ridden all the way from Kinloch Rannoch to see him. . . . Bride had danced with other gentlemen too, but not with that gentleman in particular whom she had hoped (against hope, as the evening went on) to see there in the Prince's train. Several times she fancied that she had caught sight of the still somewhat unfamiliar Maclean tartan, but once at least its supposed wearer proved to be a stranger, a Keppoch Mac-Donald. It must be as she feared; he had not come over from Blair Castle—supposing even that something had not intervened to prevent his joining the Prince at all, of which intention Malcolm had told her some three weeks ago. Nevertheless, after the last dance, when all the company had broken up into groups and were awaiting the announcement of supper, she turned to that faithful cavalier and asked him outright (though with some inner qualms as to her boldness) whether he had any information about "the Mr. Maclean from Askay" whom he had originally brought to Inchrannoch, avowing that she had half expected to see him at Lude House to-night. And Malcolm, saying that he thought he had actually seen Mr. Maclean that evening, volunteered with his usual amiability to go and see whether he could not get news of him somewhere or other.

If you suddenly and most unexpectedly behold once more what you desire most in the world, but have made up your mind you must forgo; if the lovely sight hurts you like a knife and yet draws you like a lodestone, what is the wisest course to take? Not to gaze too long, not to linger at all, lest the pull of the magnet prove irresistible, but to slip out of the ballroom, with its advancing and retiring figures, before the green gown, the beautifully-set little head—no longer pale golden, but snow-laden—makes you quite dizzy; and to go and stand at the furthest end of the adjoining room with your foot on the hearthstone and to fall into some kind of converse with a stalwart young Cameron aide-de-camp of the Prince's who happens to be there.

That, at least, is what Ranald Maclean did—he who had left Rannoch and Atholl for ever, as he thought, in order to join the Prince; and who in consequence of that very proceeding found himself back in Atholl once more. And it was thus engaged that Malcolm came upon him.

"I cannot think how I failed to see you before, Mr. Maclean!" observed the latter, as he shook hands with him. "Surely you have been in the ballroom dancing with the rest?"

"No," answered Ranald, and, to ward off possible questions as to the reason for this abstention, added, with truth: "I did not come over from Blair in the Prince's train; I followed later."

"There's a lady who has remarked your absence—my cousin, Miss Stewart," continued Malcolm, as Captain Ewen Cameron of Ardroy, the tall aide-de-camp, went off with a salute. "You'll remember her, no doubt? I think you had best come and make your bow. Had you been earlier you might have had the chance of standing up with her, though indeed she has been much beset."

The red mounted for a second or two to Ranald's lean cheek. "How came Miss Stewart here to-night?" he asked, with an accent of surprise, which was in itself disingenuous, even if the actual question was not, since he knew only too well that, by whatever enchantment brought, she was here.

And as Malcolm told him he followed, reluctant and overjoyed. However keen it proved, he would welcome the knife.

"Here's an acquaintance you did not know was at Lude House to-night, Cousin Bride," said Malcolm tactfully.

Bride, talking to Mrs. Menzies, had not seen the two approaching through the throng; on her face, too, the traitorous colour ran up a brief flag. Ranald had never seen her in powder before: adorable was a poor word for her thus transformed, for the winter upon her close-dressed hair lent a new delicacy to her features, a new and different purity to her milky complexion, a piquancy as of a nymph in masquerade to her whole being.

"Mr. Maclean puts us of these parts to shame," went on Malcolm Robertson. "His sword was drawn for the Cause some couple of weeks ago, while ours are yet to draw!"

Recovering herself, Bride gave the timely recruit her hand. "You have done what every honourable man must do," she said, with a smile so sweet that the knife went in deeper yet. "I am very glad to have the pleasure of seeing you once more, Mr. Maclean."

Ranald's eyes were on the little hand which might perhaps have been his for life. "Had I known that you were here, Miss Stewart . . . I have not long arrived . . . I might have asked for the privilege . . . but now it is too late."

"Nay, it is not too late!" broke in Malcolm, with animation. He had left the group for a moment and now returned with news. "It appears that there is to be one more reel, at the Prince's request. He has called the tune also."

"Then," said Ranald humbly, "would you have the

charity to stand up with me, Miss Stewart, late-comer
though I be?"

Surely—if the boon were granted—he might set this one
brief cup of happiness to his lips, though they should only
be the more parched hereafter? But perhaps she would
refuse? No, she was smiling. " 'Twould give me much
pleasure, Mr. Maclean.—But are you sure, Cousin
Malcolm, that you are not mistaken?" For no one was
yet leading out a partner, and away at the end of the
room the Prince could be seen in converse with Mac-
Donald of Keppoch.

Malcolm went off again to make fresh enquiries. Ranald
dared only utter commonplaces. "You must surely be
fatigued, Miss Stewart—though indeed you have no
appearance of it. It is a far day's journey for a lady from
Kinloch Rannoch!"

"I often ride some distance," answered Bride simply.
"And you need not ask whether I would not have ridden
till I fell from the saddle in order to see——" Her glance,
bright and soft, strayed to the end of the room again.

"And are you lying here to-night, you and Mrs.
Menzies?"

"—Good evening, Miss Stewart!" struck in a man's
voice behind Ranald. "I am late—a mishap on the road
to one of the small following that I am bringing to join
the Prince. But I hear there is to be a last reel. You'll
allow me, I hope, to claim it as some compensation for
my misfortune?"

Ranald saw the girl stiffen; her little teeth caught for a
second at her under-lip. "Miss Stewart has just done me
the honour of granting me this dance," he observed very
coldly, turning round. Who was this man who spoke
arrogantly of claims and compensations? And then he
saw, and wondered that he had not known at once.

Looking past Ranald as if he did not exist, Mr. Murray
MacGregor (or MacGregor Murray) tendered his hand
to Bride. "The sets are already forming," he observed,
with a hint of impatience in his voice.

It seemed, in the ensuing moment of tension, as though visible sparks would be struck out, as from the meeting of steel and flint. The situation could be handled, however, by no one but the young lady herself; and Ranald, suppressing with immense difficulty his passionate impulse to dash away the intruding arm, realised with fresh admiration that his lost love's spirit, if gentle, was not meek. He saw it in the lift of her little frosted head. She was not going to be disposed of like that.

"I am sorry, Mr. Murray, but I am already promised." And with a wonderful dignity she put her hand into Ranald's just as a single violin struck up in announcement the tune the Prince had asked for—the Jacobite air of "O, this is no' my ain hoose."

CHAPTER VIII

(1)

SUPPER, prolonged and vivacious, was over; the ladies had
withdrawn either to their homes or to their bedchambers
in Lude House, for there was now to be discussion of plans
by the Prince and his gentlemen. But the latter remained
at the long table, closing up the gaps left by the fair
absentees.

At this feast Ranald had not had the privilege of Miss
Stewart's society nor even of her nearness; he sat far
down the table where there were none of her sex. He had
been able therefore to devote all the more time to thinking about her—look at her he could not, since she was unfortunately on the same side of the table. That reel, then,
was to be his last remembrance of her, for he was returning to Blair Castle to-night and would be on the way to
Perth with the Prince to-morrow. Never, as long as he
lived, would he dance to that tune again; it should be
consecrated to an exquisite memory. . . . After the reel
was over, as he led her back to Mrs. Menzies, she had
shown some perturbation on his account (bless her!),
murmuring a hope that Mr. Gregor Murray had not recognised him. Ranald had been unable to keep from replying, with scarcely hidden scorn, that it was quite
immaterial to him whether that scion of Clan Alpin had
known him again or no, but that he rejoiced to think that,
as Mr. Murray had apparently joined the Prince's little
force, he would be removed from Miss Stewart's neighbourhood.

That gentleman, with whom he had been at actual grips
eighteen months ago in a hillside wood, was not visible
anywhere at the supper-table now; Ranald had not, in

fact, seen him at all since he himself had carried off Bride
Stewart from his insufferable arrogance. And indeed at
this moment Ranald's thoughts were occupied, not with
him at all, but with Duke William of Atholl, sitting on the
Prince's right hand at the head of the table, smiling a little
but silent. What was it like, Ranald wondered, when one
was over fifty, as the Duke was (and showed it), to return,
after nearly thirty years of exile and poverty, not merely
to one's native land and the home of one's boyhood, but
also to the great title of which Parliament had deprived
him for his share in the Fifteen? All this wide district over
which his younger brother ruled in his stead, all the fiefs
which Duke James held, the innumerable vassals he could
summon, the new mansion at Dunkeld, the great castle in
which hung the pictures of their common ancestors—how
did he feel about these, the returned proscript, to whom
had fallen the honour of planting the Prince's standard at
Glenfinnan? Over in France during those long years his
penury had not seldom been dire; for someone at Blair
had told Ranald yesterday that fifteen years or so ago
"Mr. Kateson," as Lord Tullibardine called himself (from
the circumstance of his mother's Christian name), had
been obliged to keep his lodging for more than a year from
lack of clothes to go abroad in, to sell his horse for a trifle
because he could not pay for fodder, occasionally even to
sleep without sheets. (It was true, however, added
Ranald's informant, who seemed to be well acquainted
with the affairs of the ducal family, that as soon as money
was sent over to him "Mr. Kateson" gave it away, and not
to worthy recipients.) . . . Yes, if ever a man had given
up everything for his convictions, that was the man whom
the law of England knew as the Marquis of Tullibardine
and all Jacobites as the Duke of Atholl.

But had even he given up the woman he wanted to
marry?

The punch was flowing more freely now, and men rose
from the table, Ranald among them, to cluster together
and talk of future plans, but without much semblance of

a council. And, in fact, it had already been decided that when the Prince started for Perth to-morrow Duke William should remain behind to raise the men of Atholl, vassals and tenants of his family, to whom he had already sent letters. And, though not all knew it, a very momentous letter had been despatched by the Prince also, the letter which was to bring the third brother of the house of Murray and the most able, Lord George, out of his happy and secure home life at Tullibardine to arm again (for the third time) on behalf of the Stuarts, to spend himself to the uttermost in their cause, to lose in it everything but life, and to win for all recompense Prince Charles Edward's undying resentment.

It was not long before Ranald suddenly became aware of the presence of Gregor MacGregor, who, with his back turned, was talking to a couple of MacDonald gentlemen near him. It seemed, too, almost as if Gregor were edging gradually towards him, but as he did not look in Ranald's direction, the latter came to the conclusion that chance alone and the vicissitudes of conversation had brought Mr. Murray in the end quite close to him, though apparently unconscious of the fact.

So close indeed that he heard MacGregor observe to another man how hot it was, and saw that he was unfastening the brooch of his plaid, as though to loosen or take off the garment. And the next moment, to Ranald's complete astonishment, he received the end of this plaid fairly hard across his face. It seemed possible that it was an accident, for Gregor still had his shoulder turned and was continuing his conversation. Yet about the corner of his mouth, which Ranald could just see, there was a curious curl. . . .

Ranald set his glass down upon the table and gripped hold of the plaid-flourisher's arm.

"May I ask, Mr. Murray, if you did that on purpose?"

"If I did what?" asked Gregor carelessly over his shoulder. "Ah, brush away a fly that was annoying me? Yes. Have you any objection to that, sir?"

"Are you aware," asked Ranald in a dangerous voice, "that you struck me across the face with your plaid? If it was pure mischance, then it is easy to apologise for it."

Gregor swung round. "Apologise?" said he. "I don't know the word! You should not have been so close to me, Mr. Maclean; 'tis better, you'll find, to keep out of the reach of a long arm like mine!"

He *had* done it on purpose! "You'll learn that mine is just as long!" retorted Ranald, fighting not to let his fury master him. He glanced up the table. "I cannot return the blow here, in the Prince's presence, but if you will come outside——"

"Gentlemen, gentlemen!" murmured one or two voices.

"Certainly I'll come," replied Gregor instantly, and began to make a way through the group. But he had gone no distance before a stentorian voice called for a health for His Royal Highness, and it was out of the question to leave the room before drinking it. For a moment the tide of wrath which had boiled up within Ranald Maclean subsided, and he almost forgot the MacGregor's just-offered affront, moved afresh as he was with wonder and enthusiasm at the sight of that inspiring young figure in satin and tartan at the head of the table, moved as when he had found him in mid-August at Kinloch Moidart in sober dress and with only a bodyguard of Clanranald's men. How different this evening from that black, tragic night at Dunkirk! Yes, the Prince had come home to his own, God bless him . . . and God be good to them also, starting out, so few, on this great adventure!

And, having lifted it high, Ranald drained his glass, set it quietly down, looked round to be sure that all were too intent to hinder him, and slipped quietly away to settle his score with Mr. Gregor Murray.

The man without a tartan or a name was already waiting in the passage at a little distance from the door; there was no one else there. Ranald wasted no time in words, but plucked out his handkerchief and slashed him across the face with it; and as the MacGregor's hand went convulsively to his dirk, said coolly: "Not here, sir! Outside, if we can find a quiet spot?"

"Without witnesses?" asked Gregor, a gleam in his eye.

"Certainly. We could find none, for they would stop us. Are you content without them?"

"I prefer it so," said his enemy. "Lead on; I'll follow you."

Ranald managed to find a door, and together they went out into the garden at the side of the house, which appeared fairly secluded, and was not on the slope like some other portions. And though there was no moon, it was quite light enough to kill each other by, near the pine tree with a great star hanging over its dark, unstirring crest. The grass of the lawn, dewed after the hot day, showed their footprints; and would perhaps show only one set coming away.

The duellists stopped under the pine and took off their plaids. Ranald looked back. The light was streaming out from a ground-floor window—probably one of those in the now deserted ballroom, and he realised that they were not as far from the house as he had imagined. Yet unless they left the garden altogether they must make do with this spot; they could not go further off on this side, since a little way off was a thick yew hedge to check them; and, as they both knew well enough that should they be long absent they would certainly be sought for, they took off their coats in haste, and out came Gregor's claymore. The star looked over the tree-top on the wide blade, and the steel glinted faintly.

But Ranald shook his head. "No," he said in a half-whisper, "the clash might be heard—that window is open. This is better." And drawing his dirk he held it between his teeth while he removed his broadsword, belt and all.

Gregor nodded. "For the one of us that's not going to march to Perth to-morrow the *biodag* will dig as deep a grave." And he leant his claymore against the pine stem.

(2)

"Captain Cameron," said the Prince to the tall aide-de-camp behind his chair, "find me, if you please, Mr. Ranald Maclean, who is, I think, at the other end of the room. In his lodging at Dunkirk on a night in March last year, when our hopes were broken, he shared a bottle of claret with me; and now that they are mended I wish to drink a glass of wine with him again."

Now Captain Cameron of Ardroy—whether because he had by nature a cool head or because it was set upon a six-foot body—was generally aware of what was passing around him, even when a good deal of punch or usque-baugh was flowing, and to this command he observed, "I believe that he is not in the room now, Your Royal Highness, but I will go and fetch him." For he had seen the incident of the plaid and a slight discussion there-after, though he was too far off to hear what was said, and to gather whether the contretemps were accident or no; and he had also observed Ranald Maclean quit the room directly the Prince's health was drunk. Now, before leaving his place behind the Prince's chair, Captain Ewen Cameron took a good look for the man who had flourished the end of a plaid about—the Murray tartan it was. He could not see him either. So it had not been an accident!

Instead of going to the other end of the room, therefore, and making enquiries, he slipped out by the door behind the Prince, which led into the empty ballroom. The fewer people who knew of what was probably going forward somewhere outside the house the better. But where *was* it going forward? By the one ballroom window left un-curtained and open Captain Cameron halted for a moment and listened. Then, by straining his eyes, he made out two figures against the dark of the yew hedge at the end of the lawn. And, as it was quicker to leave by the window, he left by it.

He came on the intending combatants just as Ranald had laid his sheathed claymore on the grass, and his coming was so quiet that it took them unaware.

"Gentlemen," said he, without any sign of haste or of surprise, "if one of you is Mr. Ranald Maclean, the Prince has sent me to fetch you."

Mr. Ranald Maclean snatched the long dirk from between his teeth and held it down his right side, out of sight. But Ewen Cameron had seen it.

"Present my loyal duty to His Royal Highness, if you please," said Ranald with as much coolness as he could muster, "and say that I will attend his pleasure in a few moments."

"Is that the reply that I am to carry back, sir—that His Royal Highness must await your convenience?"

"No!" broke in Gregor MacGregor. "Since you are here, sir—I do not know who you are—you had best take back no reply at all, but wait until this business is over. I suppose you are not so simple as not to know what we are about . . . and it is possible that Mr. Maclean may be unable to obey the Prince's command—so why take back a doubtful message?"

"Why, indeed?" echoed the Prince's emissary. "However, I must take back something." And before either of them guessed what he was about he had snatched up both the MacGregor's broadsword from the pine-stem and Ranald's from the turf, and was walking away with them.

With a stifled cry of anger Gregor swung round after him, but Ranald caught him by the sleeve. "Let him go!" he whispered. "He believes he has stopped us. If you keep him here parleying, or try to take back the claymores——"

"You are right," said his foe. "By the time he can get in and report we'll maybe have finished with each other. But we must find another spot, in case he returns. Who is the interfering fellow?"

"Cameron of Ardroy, one of the Prince's aides-de-camp, and cousin, I think, to Lochiel."

"He may be cousin to the devil for all I care—although, indeed, Clan Cameron and the Griogariach have usually been friends—except in Rannoch—— Here, behind the hedge . . . through this gap!"

A little before the Prince had sent his aide-de-camp in search of Ranald Maclean the latter's absence, and that of Gregor Murray, had been observed by Malcolm Robertson, whom it had made rather uneasy. He had not seen the incident of the plaid, but he had the incident in the ballroom to go upon. Yet—supposing they had gone away to fight—he could not stop them if they were really bent on cutting each other's throats, for though he really knew little of Ranald Maclean he knew more of the MacGregor. Mr. Maclean was his good friend . . . and Bride . . . Bride, he was sure, would not hear of his wounding, or worse, unmoved. But what could he do? Only one thing.

The Prince had just detached his aide-de-camp in search of someone, and Malcolm had the impression that he had previously heard him utter the word Dunkirk. At that his project crystallised into action. Making his way to the head of the table and approaching the smiling and debonair young man at the top, he asked whether His Royal Highness would have the extreme goodness to allow him to say something for his private ear.

Charles Edward's eyebrows went up, but he made a motion with his hand. Those near drew back, and Malcolm, stooping, whispered.

"What!" exclaimed the Prince. "Here—almost in my presence! That I cannot tolerate! I must go after them and stop it. Where are they?"

But this Malcolm did not know. He could only suggest respectfully, and still in a lowered voice, that he supposed they were gone into the garden.

The Prince was on his feet in a moment. "This is the shortest way, I think," he observed and, as his aide-de-camp had done, left the room by the door behind him,

Malcolm Robertson following, and hurried into the empty ballroom.

"*Per Dio,* what's that?" For over the low sill of a window giving on to the garden had just climbed a tall man with a couple of sheathed broadswords in his hand.

"I hoped they would have come after me," observed this intruder as he stood up, "but they still have their dirks. I think that if your Royal Highness were to go yourself it might have some effect."

"I shall take care that it does!" replied His Royal Highness in no pacific tone. "You Highlanders—fighting between yourselves already! Put down those claymores and take me to them instantly, Ardroy—yes, man, if you can use the window as a door so can I!"

It was possible to squeeze through the hedge in this particular place, as Gregor Murray had suddenly perceived. "Why did we not discover this sooner?" muttered Ranald, as he pressed through after him. For it was humiliating to be deprived of one's sword like a naughty child; and despite this partial disarming it was quite likely that further attempts would be made to stop their encounter, now that their purpose was known to the Prince's aide-de-camp.

The space behind the yew hedge was a kind of limbo, to which the Honourable Mrs. Robertson's gardeners evidently consigned their outworn tools, and where, too, dead leaves were amassed. But there was room for action in spite of these mounds of rotting vegetation, and the colony of broken rakes and the like piled against the derelict wheelbarrow. It was certainly more private, also, though darker. Gregor went to a little distance; Ranald took off his coat, wound his plaid round his left arm and once more gripped in his right hand that formidable weapon the *biodag*. He could barely distinguish Gregor a few yards away, yet he knew that he was about to gather himself together for a rush. His own pulse quickened; he made ready to receive his attack. He would stab upwards . . .

And then all at once there were hurried voices on the other side of the hedge. "Where are they gone to?" "This way, I think . . . no, *I* go first, sir!"

"Damnation!" said Ranald to himself. Impossible to continue. He relaxed his tense pose; Gregor did the same. Then the latter, throwing down his dirk and holding his right hand high in the starshine to show that it was empty, ran lightly over dead leaves to his foe.

"Say that we are reconciled—say that it is all over!" he whispered. "Another time! See, they have found the gap!" For a shadowy head and shoulders were visible over the hedge.

"Agreed!" murmured Ranald. "We can make another opportunity." He hurried to the hole in the yew screen. "No need to come through, Captain Cameron," he said quickly. "Mr. Murray and I have settled our difference— no, we have not fought, 'twas a misunderstanding between us."

"A very unfortunate one, then," observed Cameron of Ardroy dryly, "since it has brought the Prince himself to separate you."

A little way off a satin coat and a star glimmered palely under the pine. Ranald was completely taken aback. Curse the MacGregor for having forced this upon him! But he collected himself, left the hedge and going forward bent his knee to the dewy grass.

"I humbly ask your Royal Highness's pardon for having deranged you!"

"There is something more than that to ask pardon for," said the Prince sharply. "I had not thought this of you, Mr. Maclean. And you, Mr. MacGregor, what have you to say for yourself?"

"Nothing, sir," answered the voice of Gregor behind Ranald, "but equally to crave your pardon, and to assure your Royal Highness that our misunderstanding is at an end; we have settled our difference."

"Without recourse to cold steel?" asked the Prince, rather incredulously, looking at the two coatless figures.

"Yes, your Royal Highness," said both the would-be duellists.

"I am glad of that, gentlemen. But as a condition of pardon you must both pledge me your words never to revive your dispute."

But on that there was a silence so deep that Malcolm Robertson, standing at a little distance behind the Prince, heard the faint, far-away voice of a clock in the house beginning to strike the hour. It had not finished before Gregor Murray broke in boldly:

"Forgive me, your Royal Highness, but that is too much to exact! How can one foresee the future?"

The Prince gave an angry little laugh. "You are trying to fool me then, gentlemen, when you say your difference is settled, for plainly it is not. I think I have the right in that case to ask the subject of it."

"With the deepest respect," began Ranald quickly—but Gregor interposed.

"Mr. Maclean and I had an argument, sir, about the conduct of a party of his clan which came over to these parts in 1598 and ravaged Alastair MacGregor's lands along the Erochty water."

"What!" cried Charles Edward. "And this is the moment you choose to settle a petty squabble about a cattle raid of the century before last! I might as well disband my army at once were I to allow such conduct. If you wish to remain in my service, gentlemen, you will shake hands and swear that neither past nor future enmity shall lead you to another brawl like this!"

"There has been no brawl, sir," said Ranald stiffly, much disliking this word.

"Then shake hands, both of you!"

But neither of the adversaries moved. The Prince shrugged his shoulders with a foreign air.

"So much for your reconciliation and my wishes! I shall have no choice then . . ."

But Ranald did not wait to hear the threat. "If Mr. Murray is agreeable I am willing to swear that I will revive no dispute nor lift a hand against him while we both serve under your Royal Highness's banner."

"I suppose I must be content with that," said the young man. "Do you hear what Mr. Maclean says, Mr. MacGregor? Will you swear the same thing?"

"Yes, your Royal Highness. I will swear to that; and I am accustomed to observe an oath," said Gregor MacGregor with immense hauteur.

"I too have that habit," said Ranald scarcely less proudly, and he looked his late opponent full in the face. In the eyes of neither was there the slightest appearance of real desire for the reconciliation about which they had been so glibly speaking, but rather of an anticipation of the end of their forced truce.

And the real subject of dissension (who had not so much as been mentioned at all) having doffed her green gown, lay in bed with Catherine Menzies on the other side of Lude House, the two of them talking hard about this unforgettable evening, quite ignorant that five men, and one of them the Prince, were out in the garden under the stars because more than a year ago one of the five had tried to insist upon her listening to him when she did not wish to. No one would have been more horrified than Bride if she had known of this; but not all her Highland blood had warned her that the man who had rescued her from that embarrassing interview on the hillside was in danger of receiving a foot of cold dirk through his ribs in Lady Lude's shrubbery. When at last she slept she dreamt of dancing . . . with Uncle Walter on the bridge of Tilt!

(3)

As fleeting, as spectacular as some flushed sunrise, the Prince's stay in Atholl, with all its attendant rapture and excitement, was over. There remained glory and peril for the men who sprang to follow him, but for the women of the White Rose, who could not, only its memory to feed upon, and the burden of inaction. Bride was already beginning to feel the first slight pressure of that load when, two days after her return home, Malcolm Robertson came to take farewell of her. For Struan, as was to be expected, had called out Clan Donnachaidh, though, his age forbidding him to lead it in person, the command was given to Robertson of Woodsheal.

She was feeding her hens when the visitor was announced, for, rather than have her fetched into the house, the young man, who was well acquainted with the topography of Inchrannoch, had gone out to her. He was surer, thus, of finding her alone. She was there, bareheaded, a little flowered apron over her spreading lilac gown.

The assembled poultry scattered in all their customary hysteria as the young man approached, doffing his bonnet with the white cockade. Bride, approving her kinsman's martial appearance, or rather its purpose, dropped him a curtsy.

"Cousin Malcolm, I wish I too were a man! And so you are off with the rest. God go with you!"

"I thank you, my dear Bride; I hope He will," said Malcolm soberly. "Yes, we set out for Perth this afternoon. You'd not be minding, Bride, if I wrote to you once or twice, could I come by a post or a messenger?"

"I think I could thole it," answered Bride in a grave voice, yet with the half-impish look she had when she was teasing. "Indeed, Malcolm, I would welcome a letter or two very heartily, when you have the time to write."

Malcolm Robertson looked at her as if there were not much doubt about his finding the time.

"Yes, indeed," she went on, throwing a handful of meal to her returning subjects. "I would like well to hear how matters go, and what the Prince does, and what, without being indiscreet, you can tell me of his plans . . . O, I wish I could go to Perth too!"

"Catherine swears that should the Prince eventually march on Edinburgh, she will make shift to get there," answered Malcolm with eagerness. "If she does . . ."

"No, no; I could not leave my uncle. So be sure to write to me, Malcolm, and I will send you a letter with the news of Rannoch, if there is any."

"You will? Bless you!" Carried away by his feelings, the young man seized the platter of meal out of her hands without knowing that he had done so. "O Bride, if all goes well—could you not give me a spark of hope that when I return you might listen to me? I know I said (very foolishly) that I would never speak of the matter again . . . but then none knew that this would happen. Perhaps I shall never come back to pester you," he added with an apologetic smile, "but you do not know how much a little hope would hearten me while I am away!"

Bride looked at him, standing there in full martial attire, claymore, pistols, dirk, the red, green and blue of the Robertson tartan vivid in the sun, holding her platter, but plainly unconscious of the fact, with the expectant hens clucking indignantly round his feet. "Dear Malcolm, I don't want to marry . . . just yet . . . to marry anybody! What would Uncle Walter do?"

Malcolm offered no conjectures. But he set down the dish upon the ground—with disastrous results. "Bride," he ventured more insistently, "say that you will at least listen if I speak again if—when I return?"

"Malcolm," she said very gently, "I'm fearing it would not be any use. But you know that I will welcome you back."

The wind swooping suddenly from the river caught at a loose end of the ribbon which secured her little apron, and blew it against his breast. Malcolm started almost as if he had been struck, carried a hand up very quickly and caught the fluttering thing.

"Would you allow me to cut off a scrap of this?" he asked humbly. "Only a very wee scrap?"

Bride nodded. "If you wish, Malcolm." It must have

been that little gust of wind which had brought this smart-
ing feeling to her eyes. "I will hold it for you."

And when he had sliced off a little piece with his *sgian*,
he kissed the hands which held the ribbon taut for him
with a passion which she had never known in him before.

CHAPTER IX

(1)

ALTHOUGH Duke William of Atholl had been received with touching demonstrations of affection by the peasantry on the lands which should have been his, and although with so many Jacobite gentry in the district there was deep and genuine interest in the Cause and many displays of sentiment, it was not so easy actually to raise recruits, especially among the lower orders, when once the Prince had left for Perth. And this was but natural, seeing that Duke James, by far the largest landowner, was a convinced Whig. Many of the lesser sort had to be pressed out—and deserted afterwards. Duke William worked his hardest, and by the second week in September Lord Nairne, who was also recruiting, had raised a regiment of four hundred and fifty Athollmen, which reached Edinburgh in time for the victory of Prestonpans on the 21st; the Duke of Perth formed a regiment which included two companies of MacGregors, and Lord Strathallan raised a small troop of horse.

And when, next month, came the news that the Prince had resolved to invade England, fresh and stronger measures were taken in Perthshire to supply him with men. Menzies, led by Archibald Menzies of Shian, came from Weem; Campbell of Glen Lyon's second son, of schoolboy age—his elder brother was on the other side—brought a contingent from Breadalbane. Blair Castle was held for King James III by Robertson of Drumachine, but Perth, which had been a general rendezvous for the various levies, was left in the end without a garrison. Though a Jacobite stronghold, its inhabitants were not all well affected to the White Rose, for on the 30th of October,

King George's birthday, there was a disturbance in the Fair City and some casualties. Nearer Rannoch, Dunkeld was exceedingly Jacobite, and even the parish minister prayed publicly for King James—the only Presbyterian parish minister in Scotland to do so; yet on the other hand the Whig minister of Monzievaird, near Crieff, had the courage to preach on the text "Thy princes are rebellious, the companions of thieves," though Drummond Castle, the Duke of Perth's seat, was not far away, and there were hundreds of Highlanders in the neighbourhood.

By the second week in November the burden of waiting and wondering, hoping and fearing, had come down full upon Inchrannoch House—at least, upon Bride and her uncle. Mrs. Euphemia Reid, for instance, a Lowland woman, was if anything Whig in her inmost sympathies, and Worrall was not only an Englishman, but a Lancastrian, to whom the prospective invasion of his native county was not at all palatable. Mrs. MacRobbie in the kitchen, however, had her late husband's nephew "out," as befitted a member of a Robertson sept; but Mrs. MacRobbie herself, being by birth a Mackay, secretly rejoiced not at all in this vicarious wearing of the White Rose, though being devoted to her master and young mistress she let it be assumed that she shared the perfervid Jacobitism of Jeanie Macpherson, the kitchenmaid, to whom young MacRobbie was paying his addresses.

For Bride the hardest thing to bear now was the absence of news. Often she wished that Rannoch were nearer, if not to the Border or to Edinburgh, at least to Perth. She felt like someone gazing from a cliff, straining to follow with the eyes, through mist and distance, the fortunes of a ship gone forth into certain peril. But one could not see; one could only imagine.

Until the Prince's departure for the Border on the first of November she had tried to picture Edinburgh with tartans flaunting in and out of its narrow entries and Holyrood House stirred out of its sleep and its memories

H

of Queen Mary by the coming of this great-great-great-grandson of hers, who too was gifted with the Stuart charm. And in this exercise Malcolm's letters, though he had no turn for picturesque description, were fuel enough for her fancy. Twice there had been mention in them of Mr. Ranald Maclean of Fasnapoll, who was well, and "desired his duty" to her. It appeared that he was now attached in some manner to the Atholl contingent, so that Malcolm had not lost sight of him. Neither of them, she was thankful to learn, had received a scratch at the battle of Prestonpans, which had inaugurated the Prince's victorious career, for there, as Malcolm had written, the scratches were all receaved by the English, after their Dragoones had runn away."

But with November Malcolm's letters ceased, which was only natural, reflected Bride, since he must be constantly upon the march. The gratifying news of the surrender of Carlisle on the 15th of November was not conveyed by his pen. And often and often in the long, dark evenings, looking into the caverns of the fire, she would try to conjure up those two, the gentleman of her own countryside and blood, and him from the isles, marching triumphantly through some English town, whether it were ringing with welcome as to deliverers, or overawed, as before conquerors; and, broadsword in hand, storming some castle—Lancaster, perhaps. Of one of them—the islander—her last recollection had been in the ballroom at Lude House. His had been no leave-taking like Malcolm's; only, in words at least, a formal utterance of thanks for the honour she had done him in standing up with him. How unmaidenly, therefore, how ungrateful to her kind and devoted kinsman to allow herself to wish that it had been Mr. Ranald Maclean and not Malcolm who had come to bid her farewell in that less romantic but more private spot among the clucking poultry! Yet there had been something in Ranald Maclean's glance that night at Lude and in his tone which a woman's intuition could scarcely avoid speculating about . . . as there had been too in this very room, by this very hearth, on that misty day in August. But now, as then, the man from the isles had vanished with never a word. Well, God keep him wherever he was—and Malcolm and all from Rannochside! *She* could not risk her life for the heaven-sent young Hero . . . but was she giving her only hope of happiness?

(2)

In an army where the men of each district usually marched together, and every clan (as from time immemorial) was in itself a regiment, it was a great mortification to Ranald Maclean that his own was not as yet represented. The capture and imprisonment of his Chief had indeed been fatal in this respect, since there had been no one to call out Clan Gillean, so loyal and usually so early in arms, and though isolated groups of Macleans had attempted to join the Prince, their geographical position with regard to their implacable Whig neighbours and enemies, the Campbells, had made this very difficult; in fact, a body of Macleans, marching with intent to reach Edinburgh, had in October been attacked and dispersed by Colonel Campbell of Lord Loudoun's regiment. Yet Ranald himself had the satisfaction of knowing that he had been one of the earliest recruits from any clan, since when he tore himself away from Rannoch in early August, he had joined the Prince at Kinloch Moidart, even before the influx which took place at the raising of the standard at Glenfinnan on the nineteenth of that month.

It was as a gentleman volunteer that he attached himself (as later, the contingent of his own clan was to do) to the MacLachlans, who, under their chief, had joined at Edinburgh; and, since the MacLachlans were brigaded with the Athollmen, he found some compensation for his isolated position in occasional opportunities of intercourse with Malcolm Robertson, whom he liked for his own sake as well as for his connection with Inchrannoch. But the

girl far away in that old house on the Tummel, as she sat
and dreamed of them in the firelight, could not read in
the embers that, after the crossing of the Esk, there were
only two occasions on which they were actually in close
contact, nor what those two occasions were.

November had but one day more to run when the Highland army entered Manchester. After the usual period of
confusion—for billeting arrangements were very imper-
fect—Ranald, seeking quarters for the night, near the
market place, suddenly caught sight of Malcolm Robertson in parley at the door of a tiny milliner's shop in Toad
Lane, and guessing him to be on the same errand as himself, joined him. Together they concluded a bargain with
the timid little old seamstress who owned it, and went
off again. But, later on, entering the parlour on the upper
floor, which she had put at their disposal, Ranald found
Malcolm seated at the table quietly reading, and asked
what book had the fortune to interest him after their tiring
march from Wigan.

Smiling, Malcolm held up a small pocket Ovid. "You'll
think me fitter for a dominie than a soldier, I fear, Mr.
Maclean. But I have ever had a love for Ovid—for some
parts of him, that is—and when I wanted a little book
that would go along with me in my pocket, why, this came
to my hand; and for an idle hour the *Heroïdes* do well."

Ranald sat down on the other side of the table, his
chin propped in his hands. "Aye . . . I recollect . . . I
learnt Latin as a boy from an old schoolmaster in Moidart.
Some Ovid I must have read, I think; yes, the *Metamorphoses*. The *Heroïdes* I do not know; are they not
letters of the heroines of legend and mythology?"

Malcolm nodded. "I have just been reading the Second
Epistle, the letter of Phyllis to Demophoön."

"Phyllis? I have forgot her story. Was she not a
nymph turned into some tree or other when pursued by
a god?"

"Not precisely," answered Malcolm. "She was the

daughter of the King of Thrace, who fell in love with Demophoön, the son of Theseus as he returned from the Trojan war. They were betrothed, and he went home to settle his affairs. But as he tarried overlong, Phyllis believed herself deserted, and in her despair hanged herself. On Demophoön's return—for he did return—she was changed into an almond tree, and as he threw his arms in love and remorse about its stem, the tree budded and broke into blossom."

"A pretty tale—but a sad one. This Demophoön seems to have taken after his father—the affair of Ariadne, you remember?"

"Exactly the thought," said Malcolm smiling, "which occurred to the hapless Phyllis; and Ovid makes her give expression to it in this very 'Epistle.' "

Ranald turned and sat looking into the fire. It was very cold and had been raining. The old milliner peeped nervously in to ask at what hour the gentlemen would sup; like all the English of the lower classes she was frightened of the wearers of the tartan, for the most alarming reports preceded the Highland army, and she was as yet only partially reassured by the peaceable demeanour of her lodgers.

"The poor old soul," said Malcolm Robertson as she withdrew. "To be obliged to give us a lodging must be vastly disturbing after a life spent, I suppose, among lengths of paduasoy and reels of cotton! I imagine that after bodkins a claymore must seem exceedingly formidable; at any rate she gave a shriek when she saw mine lying on the table a while ago."

"Perhaps I had better put my pistols away before she brings in our supper," remarked Ranald.

"By the way," asked Malcolm, "did you observe her name—the name, at least, on the little sign which hangs out below. It is Worrall—the same as that of their Lancashire factotum at Inchrannoch House."

"A relative, perhaps? He himself may have come from Manchester."

Malcolm shook his head. "Jonas Worrall hailed from Liverpool before he became my cousin Bride's slave."

The mention of that name stirred them both. Ranald got up. He wanted to talk of her and yet he did not. Opening a drawer near him he took off his pistols and laid them within. Then he went to the window and stood looking down on the little dark, wet street, where two or three small boys were peeping out of an archway in half terrified, half joyful anticipation of the passing of some tartan-clad ogre with claymore and dirk.

"Yes," he said at last, "Miss Stewart owes that seaman much."

"And yet he's a lucky man."

"To have had the privilege of preserving her life, you mean."

"To have the privilege of being always near her. Often and often have I envied him and wished some fate would give us to change our lots, Worrall and I. For I'll never win to the one thing better than he possesses, I know that now."

Why was Malcolm Robertson talking of her—here in this alien English town? It was torture . . . and yet Ranald would not have the pulleys slacken. And Malcolm himself was on the rack, too; it could be heard in his voice. Yet he went on:

"You no doubt guessed long ago, Mr. Maclean, what my hope was. . . . But Bride is not for me. She has been too long acquainted with me, bless her! And there are many others in Rannoch, though, indeed, she gives none any encouragement." He looked rather measuringly at his companion. "I'm thinking that in the end 'twill be some stranger who has the luck to carry her off."

Ranald felt himself redden as the blood quickened about his heart. "That seems hard fortune for her admirers in Rannoch, who surely have the better right to that hope."

"Ay. There'll be little sun left on Sliosmin or Sliosgarbh for some of us when her golden head is gone away."

"Let us hope it will not go far," said Ranald rather

hoarsely, after a moment. "She has her uncle to consider."

"I have thought whiles," said Malcolm, opening and shutting the Ovid, "that it might be going a long way . . . crossing the seas . . . to a vineyard in France."

Ranald faced round quickly. The speaker was still sitting at the table, his face a pale blur in the dusk. "In God's name, what makes you say that?"

Malcolm got up. "Have you not hoped the same?"

There was a silence. Something of the nature of a constriction in Ranald's throat delayed his answer, but it came. "You may make your mind easy about that, Mr. Robertson. Miss Stewart will not leave Rannoch for any vineyard; there's none (that I know of) for her to go to. She will wed some home-biding Highlander; and I hope you may be he."

But Malcolm shook his head with a little smile. "I spoke of the matter again when I took leave of her. There's no chance for me, Maclean. And truly I have no certain notion neither whether 'tis you she cares for; perhaps her heart is entirely free. But I fancied—forgive me—that yours was not?"

Ranald turned to the window again. "Had I dared to let myself think long of her," he said with suppressed passion, "I believe I had deserted before we crossed the Esk. And for that reason I shall never see Rannoch again. How could I have asked her to wed a beggar? . . . I could almost wish that she had told you that she could not abide the sight of me!"

Before Malcolm could say anything in reply to this unusual aspiration the door opened and there was their landlady with a lamp in her hand.

"I was about to bring in your bit of supper, sirs," she said deprecatingly.

"Do so, pray, madam," said Ranald instantly, half relieved at the interruption. He had not meant to say so much to his companion. And he went to hold the door wider for the good woman and her lamp, while Malcolm returned the Ovid to his pocket.

But when, having put the lamp upon the table, Miss Worrall went to a drawer to take out a tablecloth, she started back with a moan of horror as though she had come upon a cockatrice's nest. Ranald had not selected a happy hiding-place for his pistols.

(3)

It was ten days later, the 9th of December—only ten days! Was it possible, thought Ranald, that the spirit of a place could be so changed! Was this really Manchester, the town which not much more than a week ago had actually yielded between two and three hundred recruits and where large crowds had cheered the Prince who went to claim his throne? . . . But between that day and this lay that "Black Friday," when at Derby he had been forced to turn his back upon it. And Ranald, with many another, was learning what different treatment can be meted out by the same populace when the wheel of fortune has revolved. Ten days ago the Highland army, with its face set south for London, had been a force to be reckoned with, to be placated; now, even though undefeated, it was trailing back to Scotland with one English army in its rear and another marching to intercept it. So those inhabitants of Manchester, who had cheered and waved them on, now gave the tired and dispirited Jacobites as they entered the town a very different reception of hoots and laughter and hostile cries.

With bitterness and disillusionment in his heart and weariness in his limbs, Ranald kept his eyes steadily fixed on the bold blue and scarlet of the MacLachlan plaid on the shoulder of the man in front of him, torn and discoloured though it was, partly because by so doing he was not obliged to see the angry, mocking faces which were occasionally stuck out of windows, or the upraised arms along the sides of the street which brandished fists or sticks, that, so far, they had not attempted to use. The jeers and abuse, however, it was not so easy to keep from one's ears.

It was difficult to realise that they were retreating, although they had never been beaten in fight. No, they had tramped through the rain and hail and snow of midwinter over hundreds of miles of bad roads, bleak moors and frozen fells, lured on by false hopes, by empty promises of aid from English Jacobites, by lying statements of the readiness there was in England to rise against the Hanoverian—of none of which had there been the slightest sign. So they must go back—thus their leaders had decreed in that day-long debate at Derby. A rumour went about that these counsels had been influenced towards retreat by the knowledge that there was in Scotland a new army to fall back upon, those very considerable reinforcements—some of them from France—which had massed at Perth during the Prince's absence, while in England, where—except in this very town, now so transformed—no recruits had joined them, there was Cumberland's army, of more than twice their numbers, coming up fast in their rear, and Wade hurrying from Newcastle in the hope of cutting them off. At any rate, for all the Prince's desperate resistance to it, the decision to retreat had been taken and, as all could see, his heart broken.

All at once the flow of Ranald's bitter and angry reflections was cut off. There were now sounds and cries ahead more ominous than mere hootings; and in addition some obstacle in front must be creating a stoppage, for the ranks of his companions were perforce halting. The head of the column—Athollmen under Mercer of Aldie—was evidently finding its passage obstructed. And almost instantly the MacLachlans, without waiting for orders, began to drive forward, spreading out from their formation of four abreast and sweeping aside the bystanders, as a broom sweeps dust, into doorways and side streets.

There followed a few moments of great confusion, but

no actual fighting, for MacLachlan of MacLachlan, in front, was shouting above the din to his clansmen not to draw their claymores. But ahead stones could be seen to fly and a missile or two came hurtling out of a window; Ranald saw a bare-armed woman throw a large iron frying-pan. Penned as they were in a narrower part of the street and with no enemy whom they could charge, the Athollmen could do little, but the affray, such as it was, ended as suddenly as it began, and the ranks began to march forward again. By that time the over-eager MacLachlans were somewhat mixed up with Mercer of Aldie's men in front; and that was how Ranald came without warning, on one of the latter, a Robertson by his tartan, lying stretched in the street with a comrade bending over him.

Ranald stopped perforce, for the prostrate man was almost under his feet in the press; indeed, the advancing MacLachlans had to exercise care to avoid stepping on him as they went. But when a little space had been cleared, Ranald found himself looking down at blood on the muddy cobblestones, blood soaking into fair hair, and a face he knew—Malcolm Robertson's—with a great gash on one temple.

"'Twas a stone did it—a curst great stone!" said Malcolm's fellow clansman furiously; and there was more than fury in his voice.

Dread awoke very sharply in Ranald's heart also. He knelt down in the mud, slipped an arm under that bleeding head and would have wiped away the blood with his plaid-end, but that something in Malcolm's face made the action seem altogether useless.

"Mr. Robertson—Malcolm!" he stammered, "I trust you are not gravely hurt?"

But, though Malcolm's eyes were open, he did not answer. He seemed to be looking into a great distance. Ranald felt for a wrist; no perceptible tide flowed there. Woodsheal, the Robertson commander, was also bending above them now.

"Malcolm," repeated Ranald, "don't you hear?" For surely he could not be unconscious with his eyes open!

And, indeed, a faint whisper did float from the scarcely-stirring lips, but of so ghostlike a texture that Ranald, stooping still nearer, could guess at no word save one that sounded like "dragoons." And then, not on the victorious field of Prestonpans, where he seemed to fancy himself, but in a dirty street of Manchester, all among the marching feet, Malcolm Robertson died.

Before he continued his march next day to Wigan, the Prince levied a fine of £2,500 upon the citizens for their behaviour in obstructing his passage. Had the whole of that large sum been in Ranald's possession he would have given it all for the friend whom no money could bring back. Malcolm's possessions, including the little Ovid, were taken charge of by John Menzies, his brother-in-law; the scrap of ribbon which was found sewn inside his coat went with him to his hasty grave. Ranald thought that he could guess from whose hand it came.

CHAPTER X

(1)

THE day of the Prince's birth, the 20th of December,
dawned bright and frosty in northern Perthshire, as
though to honour the occasion. It was always celebrated
at Inchrannoch House with a better dinner or supper
than ordinary, at which Mr. Stewart and his niece and
any guests who might be present drank that Royal
health with more than customary solemnity. And now,
since the news of the turning back at Derby was known,
there seemed more need than ever for such a proclamation
of devotion, and Mrs. Menzies, who, since her prudent
husband had taken the plunge and "gone out," had retired
to her father's house of Auchendie, was organising a
supper-party there for the purpose, to which Bride and
her uncle were duly bidden.

Not even the Jacobites of Perth, further south—who
were celebrating the occasion with a ball, paid for out of
public funds, since none of them had any money—knew
that this was the very day on which the little army, crossing the Border, had dragged itself back on to Scottish soil.

It was long since Mr. Walter Stewart had been bidden
to an entertainment, and when he was about to put on
his best embroidered silk waistcoat, drawn from its
wrappings for the occasion, he discovered a button in a
state of insecurity. Taking it to his niece's room to ask
her or Phemie to put a stitch to it, he knocked twice
without result, and was beginning to wonder whether this
meant that Bride had not yet begun to dress—though he
was sure that he heard sounds within—when the door
opened and Phemie came out with a countenance half
gloom, half anger.

"Ay, Miss Bride's within," she said, in response to Mr. Stewart's unspoken question. "Ye'd best gang intil her, sir, I'm thinkin'. I dinna ken what's wrang, but she's greetin' her heart oot ower a bit letter that's just come frae Auchendrie. Aiblins there's tae be nae junketin' there the nicht."

"But she would not cry her heart out for that!" thought Mr. Stewart, perturbed, and went in.

And there, in the midst of her preparations, sat Bride at her dressing-table, her hair all about her shoulders, her head down upon her arms, crying, indeed, as though her heart were breaking. An opened letter lay upon the floor.

"My dear child, what is it?" asked her uncle in some alarm, for she was not one who wept either easily or often.

She took no notice of him, so after a moment he stooped and picked up the letter. His eyes caught, above the signature of Catherine Menzies something about *"newes but just receaved . . . deare Malcolm . . . Manchester . . . buryed there . . . my poore father . . ."*

"Good God!" he exclaimed. "Bride, Bride, is this true?"

"I . . . suppose so!" sobbed Bride, without raising her head. "Oh, Malcolm, Malcolm . . ."

And yet the Prince's birthday was toasted at Inch-rannoch House that night, for, said Bride with still-swollen eyes, "Malcolm would have wished it so." And when just before saying good night she whispered earnestly, "Uncle Walter, I shall never forget him," the old man thought sadly that the poor lad would have wished for no better epitaph upon his nameless English grave.

(2)

To those waiting so anxiously for news from England, December had gone by slowly enough; now that, with the return of the Jacobite army on to Scottish soil, tidings of it came more freely, January, tense with alternating good fortune and bad, slipped away faster. The Prince's defeat of General Hawley at Falkirk, on an evening of bitter wind and tempest, profited him little, for he could not subdue Stirling Castle, and meanwhile Cumberland had been appointed commander-in-chief in Scotland. And on the 1st of February the Jacobite forces, weakened by desertion, began to retire northwards in what at times was almost a stampede. It was known that the Prince and the clans (as distinct from the Lowland regiments and the horse), were coming north from Crieff by Aberfeldy and Tummel Bridge, and since the latter spot was only seven miles from Kinloch Rannoch, some went thither to see them pass, but no one from Inchrannoch House. For three days the Prince was again at Blair Castle, then he left Perthshire for Inverness, never to come back.

But the White Rose had been withering in Perthshire before that. Ere the middle of January Atholl was so full of deserters that Robertson of Drumachine, in command at Blair Castle, declared himself not only ashamed, but quite unable to comply with his orders to arrest them, left as he was without money or men capable of being made officers. As he truly said, "Every man that knows the Highlanders might lay his account with their marching home after a scuffle;" yet no steps had been taken to counteract this propensity. Desperate efforts to get recruits were made by Duke William when he was again at Blair; he even had recourse to the Fiery Cross, but the men of Atholl would come out no more . . . of their own free will, though a couple of hundred were forced out by burning or threats of burning their houses. And so, in a few days after the Prince's departure, there was but one remaining Jacobite post in all Perthshire—for even Blair Castle had to be abandoned for want of men to hold it. This was at Dalnaspidal, where Cluny Macpherson, with his clansmen, guarded the gate to the North through which the Jacobite army had retired, the desolate and exposed pass of Drumochter.

Then a slow and hostile tide began to swallow up the

defenceless county. The Duke of Cumberland entered its borders on the 4th of February; two days later he was at Perth, and remained there with his army for a fortnight. Blair Castle was occupied by a large Hanoverian force on the 13th, and another was thrown into Castle Menzies, near Aberfeldy. Many Jacobite houses, Lude among them, were looted, and nonjuring Episcopal meeting-houses wrecked. When Cumberland went north his place was taken at Perth by a part of the division of five thousand Hessian troops, commanded by Prince Frederick of Hesse, King George II's brother-in-law, which, taken into English pay, had recently arrived at Leith from the Continent. In Perth also was Lieutenant-General Campbell, with several companies of his Argyllshire Militia, and at the beginning of March four companies of these arrived in Atholl and Rannoch to hold various houses and farms as outposts. Bunrannoch, with its "passage boat," was naturally a point marked for occupation, and as of all its dwellings of any size Inchrannoch House best commanded the river and this method of crossing it, Mr. Stewart was given to understand that it would be garrisoned by the enemy. There was nothing to do but to submit; yet, finding what a large number of intruders he was expected to house, he sent Bride off to the guardianship of Mrs. MacDonald at Dalchosnie, about a mile away. Take shelter there himself he would not. "How much would be left in my house," he demanded indignantly, "if I were away and all these cursed Campbells loose in it?" It was gall and wormwood to have the Whig Highlanders there; and the old man found it difficult to show a civil front to their officers. When he went over to see his banished niece at Dalchosnie he would never stay more than a few minutes, and Bride found Uncle Walter possessed of traits of fierceness she had never known in him.

"I could even wish, madam," he said to Mrs. MacDonald as he took his leave one mid-March afternoon, "that the loch or the river would rise in the night and drown the whole hypothec of them, even though I drowned too. 'Twould be the only way to sweeten the place after them. My own food chokes me when I must see that red-headed Campbell of Glenure at my table—I'm thankful to say that he has gone off to-day, to Aberfeldy I think, to procure meal; but there's always the other man, Ballachoil."

"I suppose," said Mrs. MacDonald with a sigh, thinking of her husband, brother-in-law and son up in the north with the Jacobite army, "that they will remain until——"

"Until one of two things, madam; until the Prince obtains a decisive victory over the Duke of Cumberland, or . . ." His heart evidently failed him to finish the sentence, but he made clear the ellipsis by adding, "In that case there would be no need of them."

(3)

But Mr. Stewart was wrong; it was neither of these two events which removed the Hanoverian garrisons from Kynachan and Blair and Bridge of Tilt and Struan and other places—including Inchrannoch House. The river did rise, metaphorically speaking, and on the very night after he had visited Dalchosnie.

When the noise first woke him out of a sleep into which his persistent but unavailing anger had pursued him even in dreams, Walter Stewart almost believed for a moment that his wish had come true, and that the Tummel at his back door had really overflowed its banks. What could be going on below stairs—what was all that trampling and talking? He struggled out of bed, and in his agitation knocked the tinderbox to the floor and could not find it in the darkness—sure, meanwhile, that the "Campbells" below, after the manner of devils, had taken to themselves other Campbells and were completely looting his house—as Lude had been looted and Fingask (though not by them). Torn with wrath and apprehension, but unable to find his clothes or his dressing-gown, he felt over the bed, snatched up the plaid which lay at its foot, and wrapping it round him, fumbled his way to the door, opening it just in time to see, by the light coming up from the hall, a tall fully-armed Highlander swing round from the top of the stairs, a small lantern in his hand. At sight of Mr. Stewart, with the plaid draped about his nightshirt, he snatched off his bonnet.

"I am come to tell you, sir——" he began.

"But who is it—why, 'tis not—*you* are not of the Argyll Militia!" The tartan alone, bright red and green, showed that.

"God forbid!" The newcomer thrust out his bonnet, holding up the lantern, so that Mr. Stewart could see upon it, not the red cross which distinguished the Hanoverian Highlander, but the white cockade of the Jacobite.

"But . . . but how——" stammered the old man incredulously.

"The garrison are all prisoners.—Indeed, sir, I am not jesting. Allow me to fetch you something warmer from your bedchamber, or"—as he saw the unlit room—"or take my lantern, Mr. Stewart."

"Pray bring your lantern in," said the old man, stepping back into his apartment, and conscious that he had heard this voice before. And now he took a good look at the strange Highlander. "Why, 'tis Mr. Maclean of Askay!"

"It is, and very much at your service, sir!" answered Ranald.

The avowal did not really much assuage Mr. Stewart's astonishment. "How in God's name did you come here?" he exclaimed. "There are no Jacobite forces in Atholl or Rannoch now!"

The young man laughed cheerfully. "There were not yesterday; there are to-night! No, I have not captured the garrison of Inchrannoch single-handed; I am not even in command of the party which has done so, merely a volunteer. But Lord George Murray has made a rapid forced march down from Inverness, and is engaged in surprising all the Hanoverian posts to-night. If the rest of the raiding parties are as successful as ours has been the district will be clear of the enemy to-morrow. Lord George means to have Blair Castle back again too."

"God be thanked!" said Walter Stewart, with great fervour. "I pray he succeeds!—You say you are not in command of the force which has delivered my house from these caterans?"

"No, for I am not an Atholl man, sir. It was only by Lord George's special permission that I was allowed to accompany it as a volunteer. Major Donald Robertson, from Dalcraigie, is in command."

"I must go down and thank him—thank everyone," said Mr. Stewart, looking round for his clothes. "I shall feel that I can breathe again, once I am rid of these Campbells. But I am afraid that their commander, Captain Campbell of Glenure, has slipped through your fingers, for he went off to Aberfeldy yesterday."

"Yes, so we discovered; it is unfortunate. Are you looking for the tinder-box, sir? Here it is. I will leave you to dress and inform Major Robertson that you are shortly coming downstairs."

It was many a day since the master of Inchrannoch had got into his clothes so quickly. When he opened his door it was to find Ranald Maclean outside again.

"I wished to say, sir," a complete change had come over his voice, "that I hope Miss Stewart has not suffered alarm? I fear she may have heard something of our proceedings, though as a matter of fact we were able to carry out the actual surprise very silently."

"No, no," replied Mr. Stewart, buttoning his waistcoat. "My niece cannot have heard anything, my dear Mr. Maclean, because she is not here at present."

Ranald Maclean stood very still. "Not here!" he said at last, in the tone of a man hearing something which he does not wish to believe.

"No. We were so crowded with this gang of Argyll-men that I sent her off to Mrs. MacDonald of Dalchosnie. She will be very sorry, I know, not to be able to thank you and the rest of our gallant rescuers; you may be sure that I shall tell her you were among them.—Lead the way, Mr. Maclean, and I will follow you."

Without a single word Ranald turned and preceded him down the wide and shallow staircase. Nothing was visible in his bearing of the elation which a few moments earlier had carried him up it three steps at a time. And once down in the hall, among the little group of Atholl officers there, he vanished.

But exultation was very visible in Mr. Walter Stewart, whose appearance was greeted by these gentlemen with acclamations. He at once proclaimed his desire of entertaining the victorious little force, but they would not accept more than a glass and a mouthful, which they took standing, for they must get their prisoners away before morning. The captured Argyll militia had been herded into the kitchen, strongly guarded. The surprise had been so complete that neither among them nor among the attackers had there been any killed, although a few of the defenders were wounded, and one or two of the Athollmen had minor injuries.

Major Donald Robertson of Dalcraigie was known to Mr. Stewart; they talked together a while. When the old man referred to Malcolm Robertson's untimely death and asked if he knew any details, Malcolm's kinsman, for such he was, replied that Captain Maclean was the man to ask about that, for Malcolm had died in his arms.

"But where has Captain Maclean got to?" asked the old man. "He was with me a while ago."

"I am here, sir," said a grave voice behind him. "I think I heard you mentioning Malcolm Robertson. I should be glad indeed if I might speak to you of him— but not here."

"No, not here," agreed Mr. Stewart; the wine going round, the laughter and the triumph assorted ill with the thought. He beckoned to Ranald and opened the door of a little room off the hall, rather grandiloquently known as the library, because it housed a high bookcase and nothing else of much importance, save the globe where Bride's childish fingers, from constant application to the spot, had almost worn away the West Indian island of her birth. Catching up a candle from the hall Ranald followed him in and shut the door.

"Poor Malcolm, poor lad!" said Walter Stewart in a moved voice. "He should have been here to-night—he should have shared in this success."

"It was he who first brought me to this house," said Ranald, in a dead voice, putting the candlestick on the projection of the bookcase.

"Ah, yes, I remember . . . My niece was very much grieved at his death. They were fourth cousins, you know. At one time I thought . . . I had half hoped . . ."

"Yes," said Ranald, fingering the candlestick, "I know. I guessed it from the first day. Later, he told me. It was at Manchester, that same accursed town, before the retreat . . ." Frowning, he stared beyond the candle-flame at the glass of the bookcase; but it was not the backs of the books there which he saw. After a moment, bringing himself back with a wrench to the present, he gave Mr. Stewart a brief account of how he had come on Malcolm lying in the muddy street, of how quickly he had died—gave it without any evidence of feeling in his manner. But the light fell betrayingly on the strained knuckles of his left hand, spread with a grip unnaturally tight over the top of the big basket hilt of his claymore.

"There was an end of ribbon sewn inside his coat," he finished. "I saw to it that it was buried with him."

"Poor lad!" said Mr. Stewart again, and he blew his nose. "I will tell Bride. If I had not sent her to Dal-chosnie . . ."

Ranald moved; his face now came into the light, and it struck Mr. Stewart that he looked almost ghastly.

"You have not received any hurt in this affair, Mr. Maclean?" he asked with a sudden anxiety.

"No, sir; I am untouched, I thank you. I am singularly lucky, it seems . . . in ways that do not matter. Will you"—he appeared to have difficulty in bringing out the words—"will you make my compliments to Miss Stewart?"

"I will, Mr. Maclean. As I say, I regret now, very much, that I sent her away!"

Something seemed to snap in the man before him. "That—from my point of view—was the worst day's work that you ever did in your life, Mr. Stewart," he said hoarsely and very abruptly. He turned to the door.

Walter Stewart was so staggered by his sudden vehemence that Ranald had got the door open before he interjected quickly: "Stop, Mr. Maclean; pray stop a moment! Shut the door, if you please!" And then, since there was no time to be other than blunt, he came out with it.

"Are you in love with my niece, Mr. Maclean?"

"I loved her, as I know now, from the first moment I saw her," replied Ranald almost savagely. He had shut the door, but still retained his hold of the handle.

Mr. Stewart gave this a second or two's consideration. "And—you must forgive the question—you were hoping to seize this opportunity to tell her so?"

"Far from it, sir! I can never tell her. I have forfeited the right to marry. I cannot now support a wife."

"Why, what do you mean?" asked the old man, not a little astonished. "You spoke once of a French inheritance——"

"Ay, but I let it go to another claimant in order to follow the Prince. It is for that reason that I have never addressed a word of love to Miss Stewart. I was upon the point of doing so when the news of the Prince's landing forbade it. When we met again at Blair I was dumb; I could be nothing else." He paused, looking over Mr. Stewart's shoulder into the half-lit little room just as though he saw someone standing there. "I do not know if Miss Stewart found my conduct strange. . . ."

"Then you came to-night . . ." began Mr. Stewart, puzzled—for why had he volunteered for the Bunrannoch party—"to tell us of poor Malcolm, I suppose."

Returning from his brief contemplation, Ranald shook his head. "No, not for that. Merely to get a glimpse of her for the last time. I had to scheme and pull strings enough at Inverness to come with Lord George, and yet not to be sent with any other party but this. But you have defeated me, sir. Perhaps it is as well . . . and I will be going now."

But the more he tried to depart the more Mr. Stewart felt impelled to stay him. For there was something in this confession which might possibly serve to explain certain unusual moods in Bride this last winter, a certain musing look which he had once or twice observed. "Nay, Mr. Maclean, Major Robertson is not leaving yet, and this is a matter of importance. Does my niece know anything of your feelings for her?"

Ranald shook his head. "I cannot say, sir, since I have not spoken explicitly—for the reason I have given you."

Mr. Stewart studied him a moment, backed against the door, a fine, grave young man, if a thought too lean. "But *why* were you forced to make so great a sacrifice as that of your French estate?"

"Because I could not go over to Girolac and contest this rival claim last August when the Prince needed every sword. . . . But *that* sacrifice was nothing in itself, for I was very reluctant to go and live in France. It is the other sacrifice which it entailed . . . though indeed I do not know why Miss Stewart should have accepted me had I asked her—it is the other that has cost me . . . all I have." His voice shook.

Mr. Stewart began to be moved in a direction he had never thought to travel. Yes, perhaps Bride *had* a leaning towards this stranger from the Isles, though he had never spoken. And young though she was, he could scarcely imagine that she would choose really amiss. "You speak," he said gravely, "of being unable now to support a wife. You are probably ignorant that Bride would not be dependent upon her husband. She is, in her own modest way, an heiress. You did not know that, Mr. Maclean?"

The information did not seem to give pleasure. "No, sir; I had no notion of it. But it makes no difference."

"Pardon me, Mr. Maclean, but I think it does! For she has the revenues from her parents' plantation in the West Indies; not a great sum yearly, but by accumulation sufficient to afford her a very substantial dowry and a good subsistence thereafter."

Ranald drew himself up; his hand went to rest again upon his hilt. "For her husband to live upon! No, Mr. Stewart, what you have told me sets the fulfilment of my desire even further from me than before, if that were possible. I could never tolerate being kept by my wife!"

" 'Twould never come to that, I am sure," said Mr. Stewart, with conviction. "But I appreciate your sensitiveness upon the point. Perchance if . . . if things go better for us this spring you may be able to travel to France to fight your claim anew."

Ranald had opened the door a little way. He shut it again. His face was that of a man confronting a foe. "In God's name, Mr. Stewart, why do you thus offer me encouragement? Is it because you have some notion that Miss Stewart——"

"No, no," broke in the old man hastily. "As to that, I know nothing whatever. She must speak for herself . . . even as I have always resolved that she should choose for herself, provided that I could perceive no actual objections to her choice."

And at that Ranald leant against the door as if he were seeking support from it. "Are you telling me," he said almost inaudibly, "that if only . . . if only I *could* ask her to be my wife you would at least not disapprove me as a suitor?"

Mr. Stewart looked at him and made up his mind.

"Yes, I am telling you that," he answered steadily.

The young man started upright. "Then—though I thank you, sir—you are merely torturing me!" The words, wildly spoken, were scarcely out of his mouth before he was through the door like a man fleeing from temptation.

CHAPTER XI

(1)

LORD GEORGE MURRAY, highly competent strategist that he was, had indeed brought off a dramatically successful coup. There was that to exult over, even for a man in Ranald's situation. Every one of the Hanoverian posts surprised, seven in all, had been captured without the loss of a single man on the Jacobite side. Now, having established himself anew in Atholl, sent off his three hundred prisoners to Ruthven, pushed his outposts as far as Dunkeld and secured the Pass of Killiecrankie, the only direct road for attack from the south, Lord George set to work with the scanty means at his disposal to invest his brother's seat of Blair, once more in the possession of Duke James—or rather, of the Government, for Duke James himself remained at Dunkeld. A Scottish soldier, the irascible Sir Andrew Agnew, occupied the castle with a reduced garrison of 300 men, without artillery and with not much in the way of stores save biscuits and cheese, since a siege was the last contingency of which the English military authorities had dreamed.

Lord George, bestowing himself and his staff at the inn of Blair, on the rising ground above the castle, and placing three hundred men in the little village under Cluny Macpherson (who had joined him on his way to surprise the Hanoverian posts) and another at the mains, the home farm, began by summoning Sir Andrew to surrender. The difficulty in this case was that Sir Andrew's temper was known to be of such violence and so incalculable that there was not a single Jacobite officer at all desirous of carrying the summons; and it was actually conveyed in a manner rare, if not unprecedented, in military history.

A handsome and obliging serving maid at the inn, now
Lord George's headquarters, who was on good terms with
the officers, offered to take it; and take it she did, delivering its contents by word of mouth to a group of the
younger ones mirthfully assembled at a lower window
of the castle. But not one of them would consent to bear
the document itself to their commander, until at last a
young subaltern, too far gone with wine to realise what
he was risking, undertook the enterprise. Sir Andrew
kicked him downstairs for his pains and threatened to
shoot any further messenger from Lord George Murray.

So the bombardment began, by means of the only
artillery which the besieging force possessed, two four-
pounders brought from Inverness. To Lady Lude was
assigned the privilege of firing the first shot. Ranald
privately thought that she might as well have continued
in her new rôle, for the French gunners proved singularly
inefficient, and frequently missed the castle altogether,
even at the distance of a musket-shot or less. Artillery
of this calibre was not indeed likely to make much impression on the enormously thick walls of Lord George's
ancestral mansion, as stout as Sir Andrew's heart and as
defiant as his temper. Discovering this, the gunners
attempted to set the roof on fire by heating the cannon-
balls red-hot. But (no doubt to Lord George's secret relief) these missiles never did much damage, the besieged
promptly picking them up on arrival in an iron kitchen
ladle and immersing them in a bucket of water.

Meanwhile Duke William, informed of what was going
on, despatched from Inverness a pained but patriotic
letter to "Brother George," observing that "since contrary
to the rules of right reason you was pleased to tell me a
sham story about the expedition to Blair, you may now
do what the gentlemen of the country think fit with the
castle. I am in no concern about it. Our great-great-
grandfather's and grandfather's and father's pictures will
be an irreparable loss on blowing up the house, but there
is no comparison to be made with these faint images of

our forefathers, and the more necessary public service."
He was even magnanimous enough to suggest a convenient spot at which mining might be undertaken.

In all this serio-comic business Ranald's mind was not
sufficiently engaged to keep his thoughts from winging continually to the house by Loch Rannoch, less than twenty
miles away. But even if he could have got leave to go
there, his declaration to Mr. Stewart stood in his path,
an insurmountable obstacle of his own making.

That interview with the old gentleman was nothing but
an added torment to him now. To have learnt that Bride
had her own fortune, that Mr. Stewart, surprisingly,
would have had no objection to his making his suit to
her—what were these but successive Tantalus draughts
held to his lips? Now he knew regrets for lost Girolac
such as he had never dreamt that he could feel. And he
had thrown away his heritage for . . . a dream? A fair
and hopeful dream at first—till that dark December day
at Derby, and still a dream which was not utterly shattered. Yet were last August and its choice to be given
him anew he could not have acted differently.

Ranald was rather fortunate in the quarters which he
occupied at Blair. The Presbyterian minister, the
Reverend Alexander Stewart, had been taken prisoner
by the Jacobites, but he had not been removed from his
manse, which was, with the inn, the only decent habitation among the peat-constructed little dwellings of the
village. The Highlanders quartered there, of whom
Ranald was one, served as the minister's gaolers. In this
species of honourable captivity Mr. Stewart was generally
to be found in his "book-room" or study, and once or
twice Ranald had borne him company there, despite the
reverend gentleman's somewhat acrid comments on the
situation in general and his own position as a captive of
"the Amalekites, Gibeonites and Moabitish men," as he
alternately called the Jacobite force. But one could not
bear him ill-will for these strictures.

At the end of nearly a fortnight little progress had been

made by those whom Mr. Stewart thus designated, although they were so close as to be right up to the castle walls in positions where they were safe from musket shot, as, for instance, round the new and unfinished construction at the east end, which was as yet little more than one storey high, and whose only communication with the main building was by a ladder. Here Sir Andrew had naturally planted a guard, and it was the amusement of the Highlanders to throw stones up at its members, accompanied by pleasantries against their commanding officer— who, in the castle itself, gave daily vent to his opinion of the loon who was so daft as to be knocking down his ain brother's hoose. But Lord George, ill-served by his two cannons, had by now given up this idea; to starve out the garrison was plainly the better plan, for he guessed them to be short of provisions and knew they must be short of water, since they were no longer able to use the brook which fed the pond, and had now only the draw-well in the castle itself to supply them.

But to starve out the defenders demanded time, and meanwhile, as Lord George was well aware, Hanoverian troops were massing in very much superior numbers at Dunkeld—by March 25th, after a week of the siege, 3,000 Hessians had arrived there, some of them hussars, with Lord Crawford in command of the cavalry. It was true that, though the Jacobite outposts had now retired on Pitlochry, there was still the dreaded Pass of Killiecrankie which any enemy force, however strong, must traverse before it could reach Blair, and nothing would induce the Hessians, or indeed any other soldiers, to risk meeting there at the hands of Highlanders the fate of Mackay's army in 1689. On the other hand, in Lord George's rear, away to the north-east at Aberdeen, lay Cumberland, with his staff and the second line of his army. The Jacobites could not therefore go on blockading Blair Castle for ever; their own position was perilous, and before long they would be needed elsewhere for the final throw.

(2)

Cold and windy, with now and then a burst of sun, the first day of April broke over Blair. By now it was clear to all the Jacobite officers that the blockade would very soon have to be abandoned. Lord George had, in fact, made all necessary dispositions to draw off at short notice, and that very morning had sent off his two unfruitful pieces of cannon. Ranald Maclean, returning about noon from a spell of blockade duty, heard with surprise that an express arrived from Inverness with despatches had been asking for him by name before going on to Pitlochry after Lord George, who had ridden over there, as he frequently did, to keep a watch on the movements of the Hessian cavalry and the St. George's Dragoons from Dunkeld, since they sometimes pushed up as far as the mouth of the pass. Since Ranald could not be produced at the moment, the messenger had said that he would seek him out on his return. To occupy his restless, wheeling thoughts until this should happen, Ranald went into the "book-room" of the manse.

The Rev. Alexander Stewart was seated at the table, and appeared to be composing a sermon against the time —very near now, whether he knew it or no—when he should be free to deliver one. He looked up as the Highlander entered, gave him a not unfriendly little nod and continued his labours. Ranald went straight to the bookcase in the corner, though he had really small hope of finding anything to occupy him but sermons, for he had surveyed those shelves before, and his eyes now ran with but tepid interest along a group of tomes which he had heard Mr. Stewart recommend as suitable reading for the Sabbath—Doolittle's *Call to Delaying Sinners,* Pearse's *Preparation for Death,* Guthrie's *Trial of a Saving Interest,* and *The Theatre of God's Judgments,* by one Beard, who had been connected in some way which Ranald had now forgotten with Oliver Cromwell. But on a higher shelf, tucked into a corner with very much the air of segregation from the rest of the pious company, were one or two books of a secular appearance which Ranald had not noticed before. He reached up and plucked out at random a thin, somewhat battered volume, which turned out to be briefly lettered "Poems," and, seeking more precise information from its title-page, could not suppress a little exclamation.

What had met Ranald's eye were these words: "Poems upon various of the Heroicall Epistles and Metamorphoses of P. Ovidius Naso, by a Young Gentleman of the Inner Temple." The place of publication was London, the date 1719. And Ranald for a moment was far away from the manse of Blair.

The Young Gentleman, as a cursory examination showed him, had not attempted to render Ovid into English verse; allowing his Pegasus a longer rein than strict translation would have afforded he had merely used the Latin original as fodder for that steed, and Ranald, turning instinctively to see whether he had tried his hand at the Second Epistle, found, not Phyllis's reproachful lament, but a narrative, continuing on to Demophoön's return and the blossoming of the almond tree into which, according to the Young Gentleman, the deserted daughter of Sithon had already been metamorphosed.

His eyes strayed down the page, taking in only a fragment here and there, since part of his mind was on the alert for sounds of the arrival of the messenger from Inverness, and part sadly occupied with the picture of poor Malcolm sitting at the table under the old mantua-maker's roof, his finger between the leaves of that story; and with the words they had spoken afterwards. Nevertheless, he was conscious of certain lines.

> " 'O false *Demophoön*, my Love, in vain
> Thy *Phyllis* scans the unrelenting Plain,
> No Traveller descries, nor from the Shore

Observes the Galley which from *Ilium* bore
Thee when thou first, in proven Arms array'd,
Vanquish'd the Heart of this fond *Thracian Maid,*
—Vanquish'd, possess'd, and at the last betray'd!' "

Mr. Stewart's voice broke in; he had turned round in
his chair.

"I trust, Mr. Maclean, that ye have found something
of edifying there? There is much very nourishing doctrine,
and purging likewise, on those shelves."

"I thank you, sir; I shall no doubt find something suitable," returned Ranald mechanically, his eyes glued to
the Young Gentleman.

"She spoke, and round her Throat the slipp'ry Noose
Affix'd——"

he turned a page and came on:

"But who is this that knocks at *Sithon's* Gate?
'Tis he, the Suitor, who now knocks too late!
'I come to wed, my plighted troth to keep!'
Alas, her Maidens hide their eyes and weep.
Enter yon Garden, view the mortal Spot,
See, laggard Lover, what thy Deed hath wrought!"

"I should recommend one of godly Mr. Wedderburn's
discourses from his *David's Testimony Opened in Forty
Sermons,* Mr. Maclean; ye'll find it on the midmost shelf."

"Thank you, sir."

"Demophoön paces through
Olive and Vine and Death-foreboding Yew
Until the fatal Mound stands in his View.
He hides his Face: Beneath that grassy Heap
By her own Hand destroy'd doth *Phyllis* sleep.
Yet he, the Truant, drove her to her Doom,
Too long delaying, *he* prepar'd the Tomb!

Groaning he casts him down upon the Earth,
Which at that Moment gives the Portent Birth;
For when at last he lifts his Streaming Eyes,
With tardy Penitence and useless Cries,
Lo! greets them o'er her Grave an Almond Tree
Uprisen flowerless and forlorn.—'Tis She!
The stricken Lover clasps it to his Breast,
Kisses upon its Stem hath weeping prest.
—Instant above him breaks the rosy Flood
Of Blossom from the metamorphos'd Wood,
Into his Ears a Whisper thin has sigh'd,
'Hadst thou but sooner come I had not died!
Now in the blessed Sun no more to live——' "

Ranald went no further along this alley of rhyme, stilted
yet barbed for him; indeed, he shut his eyes for a moment,
so keen was the pain. Despite her uncle's permission, he
could never claim *his* Phyllis. Not indeed that he had the
presumption to imagine that she was longing for his re-
appearance, much less that she was likely to die for want
of it—nor had he ever undertaken to return. None the
less, he could not but see himself, somehow, in the rôle of
Demophoön. . . .

"Ah, I observe that you have found somewhat to cause
you to reflect, young man," came once more the ministerial
voice, replete with satisfaction.

"Yes, sir." ("Though I cannot imagine how it came into
this company," added Ranald to himself.) Half against
his will he found himself turning back the leaves, and discovered that in this free version of the story Phyllis had
been made to prophesy her fate.

"And from my Tomb an Almond Tree shall spring,
Bright with slim Leaves, but never Fruit nor Flower;
One only Voice to summon them hath Power,
Those Arms alone——"

But some subtle spiritual instinct must by now have

informed the Reverend Mr. Stewart that it was not, after all, a sermon which was absorbing his visitor, for he startled the preoccupied reader by observing suspiciously:

"What's that book ye have there, Mr. Maclean? It has not the appearance of anything pertaining to good doctrine. I wonder ye do not take this opportunity of true edification and refreshment—the last ye'll have, maybe, before ye are summoned to meet your Maker!"

"I am not a great reader of the homiletics of the Established Church, Mr. Stewart," replied the young man, rather shortly.

Mr. Stewart pricked up his ears. "And why not? Do not tell me that ye are a Seceder, a schismatic, a follower after the Erskines and the Associate Synod! I had thought better of you than that!"

Ranald looked up. He knew that the minister was referring in this tone of reprobation to that scission—the first—which some nine years ago had taken place in the Presbyterian ranks over the vexed question of patronage and the right of presentations.

"Certainly not, sir, since I am——"

"Not, surely, a Papist!" exclaimed Mr. Stewart in horror, jumping to this blood-curdling conclusion without giving him time to finish.

Ranald closed the book. "I am, like most of my name, Mr. Stewart, an Episcopalian."

"An Episcopalian!" said Mr. Stewart, dragging out those numerous syllables with slow disgust. "A Prelatist! And why, may I ask, are ye not a member of the Church of your native land?"

"But that is just what I flatter myself I am. Why are not you, sir?"

The minister rose from the table, his face red. "You are scandalously impudent, Mr. Maclean! To suggest that the Solemn League and Covenant of our fathers is— that Presbyterianism is not the true and natural religion of Scotland! Never in my life. . . . Perhaps, however, you are but making an ill jest?"

K

"Jesting I certainly was not, sir. But let us not enter into dispute," said Ranald pacifically, "—though indeed it was not I who introduced the subject."

" 'Twas my duty as a minister of the Gospel to introduce it, Mr. Maclean. And glad I am that I did. Come now, tell me why, seeing that at least ye do not bow the knee to Antichrist upon the Seven Hills, ye belong to that stubborn and blind remnant which still seeks nourishment from those hireling shepherds the bishops, rejecting the pure milk of——"

"Of Calvin!" broke in Ranald, with sudden spirit. "Mr. Stewart, if I do not go to Rome for my religion, neither do I go to Geneva, like all your sermon-writers here, and your Pope, John Knox. 'The true and natural religion of Scotland,' you say! Will you tell me in what part of Scotland Calvin was born—or, for that matter, in what Scottish town the Westminster Confession was drawn up?"

"Come here!" ejaculated the minister, beckoning. "Come you here and sit down while I wrestle with ye! Ye poor straying sinner! I doubt Satan has a close eye on ye, Mr. Maclean, that he can put such awful speeches into your mouth! Nevertheless, it must have been the Most High who caused ye to be thrust upon me in this manse! Come here, and with God's assistance I'll bring ye to a sense of your condition before ye can utter more blasphemies! Godly and glorious John Knox a Pope! I'll Pope ye! Ye shall yet be snatched as a brand from the burning!"

But Satan (presumably) was quicker at snatching than he. Before Ranald had time either to excuse himself from this process or to comply there was a voice at the door announcing that Captain Maclean was waited for on the instant. And Ranald, stuffing back the Young Gentleman's embroidery of Ovid at random among the *Calls*, *Preparations* and *Alarms*, went with but a hasty word of apology from the room.

Outside, in the wind which was briskly displaying the

still defiant English flag upon the castle below, a horseman was waiting upon a splashed and weary mare. To
Ranald's surprise it was a gentleman of his own name
from Mull, whose acquaintance he had recently made at
Inverness—for the Macleans, a hundred and eighty
strong, under Maclean of Drimnin, had joined the Prince
during the retreat from Stirling, and, being without their
own Chief, had elected to serve, as Ranald had previously done, with the MacLachlans under theirs.

"Ah, I'm glad to find you this time, Captain Maclean,"
said the rider. "I have a letter for you, which came to
Inverness not long after your departure. I chanced to
know of it, for it was brought to me in error. Drimnin
took charge of it against your return, or until there was
an opportunity of sending it to Blair; so when I was
ordered to carry a despatch thither I went and asked him
for it. But, faith, had I known that the despatch was to
recall Lord George at once to Inverness, I own I might
not have troubled about your letter. However, here it
is; you get it the sooner."

"To recall us at once?" repeated Ranald, receiving the
letter without even glancing at it. "Is Cumberland
moving, then?"

" 'Tis believed so," said his fellow-clansman briefly, and
refusing Ranald's suggestion that he should dismount at
the manse and take some refreshment, went off to procure
himself a fresh horse as soon as he could.

Ranald retired to the manse doorway to read his letter,
which he had by this time realised was addressed in his
brother's handwriting. It only consisted, however, of a
few lines to say that all were well at Fasnapoll, and to
send him a copy of a letter which had come for him from
the lawyer at Girolac, the original of which, hoping that
Ranald would hold him justified, Norman had opened
and kept, lest it should miscarry; and he congratulated
Ranald with all his heart upon the intelligence conveyed
in it.

Wondering whether he were misreading Norman's

rather crabbed handwriting, Ranald hastily opened the enclosure. And it was not the wind which took his breath away for a space of seconds. M. Marcelin's letter, already two months old, was to the effect that the decision of the French courts about the counterclaim to the estate made by the late Mrs. Fraser's nephew, only reached last autumn after weeks of delays, pleadings and repleadings, had not, despite Ranald's absence, been given against him, as the lawyer so greatly feared; on the contrary, he had been declared the rightful owner under his uncle's will. This good news M. Marcelin had already written to his client last November, but, having learnt at the New Year that the privateer in which the letter had been sent had fallen into the hands of the English, he was writing a second time. And meanwhile, guessing that M. Maclean was in arms and not at liberty yet to come over to France, he had seen to it that all proper care was being bestowed on his property until his arrival.

Ranald leant heavily against the minister's doorway, and for a moment or two the stiff and wind-rustled ivy-leaves around it took on the semblance of a greener and more gracious foliage. . . . So he was not a landless adventurer any longer; he was what he had been last August before he threw away his heritage in honour's cause! The whole shield of life was turned again. There was nothing now to prevent him from going to Bride Stewart—to his Phyllis. He *had* something besides his heart to lay at her feet. David Maclean could never be sufficiently thanked for bringing this letter instead of leaving it to await him at Inverness.

Round the corner of the manse swung suddenly into Ranald's only half-attentive sight a little group of Macpherson tartans. A moment later he heard a voice addressing him, and coming out of his half trance found a Macpherson with three eagle's feathers in his bonnet standing before him. It was Cluny himself.

"Captain Maclean, is it not? I am wanting a messenger to carry an order from Lord George to the party at the mains, and I shall be obliged if you will go, sir. The siege is abandoned; we start north to-night. Lord George is drawing off the men from the Pass of Killicrankie at ten o'clock. Be good enough to tell the officer at the mains to hold himself in readiness."

Wholly and not at all pleasantly jerked out of his dream to the reality which he had quite overlooked since David Maclean went off, Ranald saluted the Chief and prepared to obey. Starting north to-night! Farewell to any smallest chance of riding over to Inchrannoch—save by means of desertion! The letter from France had not reached him just in time, but just too late. The disappointment was so bitter that he almost wished David Maclean had left it at Inverness.

He hurried away upon his errand. He must write to Bride—there would be time for that—and send the letter by some man of the district. He must write too, at once, before the commotion attendant upon withdrawal became too intense; there were signs of it already.

When, therefore, he came back from his errand he went into the book-room at the manse to beg a sheet of paper and the loan of a pen or pencil, and found to his discomposure the Rev. Mr. Stewart upon his knees. In a resonant voice he was congratulating his Maker—or so it seemed—upon having at last bestirred Himself to gird His sword upon His thigh and bend His bow against that son of Belial, George Murray, and his Amalekites. It was evident that he had heard the news. Ranald, snatching up what he wanted, stole out abashed, but this time resentful.

Save in that same book-room there was no chance now of quiet in his quarters for the writing of this, the most fateful letter of his life. Already the minister's little house was in a turmoil. It was absolutely necessary to find some secluded spot not too far distant. Ranald bethought him of the little old kirk among the yews of its graveyard, below which the Highland battery had at first been erected. He had often seen the door open when he passed.

Yes, it was open; indeed, from the drift of last autumn's leaves and rubbish inside it was plain that it was never closed, and to Ranald's surprise—for he knew that Mr. Stewart when at liberty preached here every Sunday—many of the pews were broken down and the whole interior lamentably neglected. It must be that the minister's zeal for God did not extend to the care of His house. This was an old chapel too, in use before the Reformation, as its architecture showed, and before the spell of Geneva came upon it must have looked very different. And beneath its old stones, as Ranald suddenly remembered, lay, fast sleeping of his mortal wound, one whom this hour and this cause so sorely needed—John Graham of Claverhouse, Viscount Dundee.

Ranald sat down in a pew, his claymore ringing on the untended floor, and laying his piece of paper on a dust-covered shelf, began to write to Bride Stewart the tale of his hardly suppressed love and longing, beseeching her, since he was presently ordered away, to send one word of hope to him at Inverness.

As he rose to leave he remembered, with a strange, warm feeling at the heart, something else which he had heard about this neglected little place. It was called St. Bride's Chapel. For a moment he almost regretted that he was not a Papist, so that he could put up a petition to St. Bride of the many and beautiful legends for her earthly namesake. It would not be a difficult thing to do, nor a wrong one, surely? . . . The pipes, Cluny's pipes, were shrilling outside as, after trying in vain to close the rust-stiffened door, he went to find a messenger for his letter.

And from two o'clock that night, when in the windy dark the withdrawal began up Glen Garry towards the wild hills of Badenoch and the valley of the Spey, Ranald thought of little else but of Bride's reception of his letter and of how many days he should have to wait for some word from her . . . and of what that word would be when it came.

But in Inverness, when, with his comrades, he reached

it and rejoined the rest of the little Highland army, those first days of April, 1746, ebbed and ebbed as that midmost day came nearer when it should be an army no longer, yet no word came to Ranald Maclean, nor had he any means of knowing why it did not.

CHAPTER XII

(1)

"I took thee from the sheepcote, from following the sheep, to be ruler over my people, over Israel; and I was with thee whithersoever thou wentest, and have cut off all thine enemies out of thy sight."

Bride Stewart was reading to her uncle, as her custom was before he retired, the evening lessons for the day, since Mr. Stewart saw but ill by candle or lamplight. For this, the 17th of April, the appointed portion was the seventh chapter of the second Book of Samuel. In his chair by the fire the old man sat listening intently, with Fiona at his feet, listening also, perhaps. Bride went on.

"And when thy days are fulfilled and thou shalt sleep with thy fathers I will set up thy seed after thee. . . . And thine house and thy kingdom shall be established for ever before thee."

Her voice shook a little. O, if only it might be so! Her uncle, with his eyes shut, nodded his head as if in affirmation; a single tear stole down his wrinkled cheek. Both of them were recalling the lesson for the previous evening; how the Lord had said unto David: *"Go up, for I will doubtless deliver the Philistines into thine hand"*; and how David and his men had thereafter smitten the Philistines at Baal-perazim, the "plain of breaches." That lesson had fallen on their ears with comfort, and almost in the guise of a prophecy of what might be taking place even then in northern Inverness-shire, where their Prince and his foe and kinsman Cumberland must so soon come to grips with each other. That was yesterday, but no news of such an encounter—no news of any sort—had reached Inchrannoch to-day.

It was wild, cold weather; since morning flurries of sleet had spat in the icy wind. Snow had fallen heavily on Schiehallion; Beinn a Chuallaich, too, wore a white mantle over his shoulders. Yet, as Bride finished the chapter and began to turn the leaves of the great Bible for the New Testament lesson, the thrifty old laird bent to pull apart the still burning logs upon the hearth. Inchrannoch House had settled down to its nightly quiet; and so there was no missing the hasty and unmistakable stump, stump of Worrall's wooden leg along the passage, and another much slower, stumbling tread behind. Then without warning or permission the ex-sailor burst into the room. Mr. Stewart, startled, dropped the heavy iron which he was holding.

Bride had sprung up from the table. "Is it news, Jonas? . . . O, what news?"

For all his haste in entering Worrall said nothing for a moment. He looked from one to the other, and drew the back of his hand in a curious gesture over his mouth. When he spoke his voice was harsh.

"They're reet smashed to bits," he said. "There's no army any more."

News at last! But Bride fought against accepting it. Worrall was himself no Jacobite, might he not mean . . . "Which . . . which army is smashed?" she asked faintly, a hand on the table for support.

"Eh, t' Highland army, God help 'em! T' yoong man's fled. 'Tis all ower and dun wi', Miss Bride lass!"

She knew that his stubborn English prejudice forbade him to give the Prince his title. Did not that somehow prove that his news was exaggerated? It must be—O God, it must be!

Her uncle had got up from his chair. "How did you hear this, Worrall?" he asked slowly and painfully. "How do you know that there's a word of truth in it?"

"Here's Jamie MacRobbie just coom ower Drumochter, fair clemmed, can tell yo' more, sir—if yo'n excuse t' muck on him?"

Mr. Stewart sat heavily down again. "Let him come in."

No more than Fiona, who growled at him, would Bride at once have recognised the trim youth who had been courting Jeanie Macpherson in the exhausted and shivering man who appeared behind Worrall then, with wild, tangled hair, congealed blood down his face, his kilt in tatters and one hand muffled up in a dirty rag. A few disjointed words were all that he was able to get out, but they were enough to make it clear that, at one o'clock yesterday on Drummossie Moor, utter disaster had overtaken the Jacobite army in the space of less than half an hour; and that the Atholl Brigade, on the right wing, had been almost cut to pieces. There was something not very intelligible about the broken walls of a park enclosure and dragoons—probably the fugitive himself scarcely knew what had happened. . . . Afterwards . . . yes, he had stumbled into a snow-drift under the Boar of Badenoch in his long flight through the mountains and had had great difficulty in extricating himself. . . .

He seemed indeed to have come to the limit of his endurance, and as he stood there blinking his sunken eyes, red-rimmed from wind and sleet, Bride whispered hastily to Worrall to take him at once to the kitchen and see that he was fed and given a bed of some kind. And after Jamie MacRobbie—or what the last eight-and-twenty hours had made of him—had followed the Englishman like an automaton from the room and the door was shut, a silence fell there that was more terrible than weeping.

It was the deerhound who broke it; padding restlessly about, snuffing as she went, she threw up her head at last and gave vent to a single long howl. Then she lay down. Afterwards Bride remembered this; at the time she did not hear it. But she heard her uncle after a little say to himself: "Baal-perazim . . . Baal-perazim . . . the plain of breaches," and saw him, later still, slip to his knees by the side of the table. He prayed in an audible voice: "Oh, Lord, if it be Thy will so heavily to afflict us, at least preserve the life of him, our hope, even as Thou didst preserve David in the midst of his enemies!"

He knelt there so long, his head on his clasped hands, that Bride became anxious and stooped over him. She helped him up, and then up the stairs, too; he seemed dazed. And having summoned Worrall from the kitchen and sent him up to the old man, she entered those regions herself, and found Mrs. MacRobbie crying over her half-famished nephew as he devoured broth and bread. Bride came in as quietly as a wraith, and the spent man did not see her until she was at his elbow.

"Jamie," she said in a composed voice, "do you chance to know aught of the fate of Mr. Ranald Maclean of Fasnapoll, who is a friend of ours?"

The fugitive set down his bowl and rose hastily, though she made a motion to stay him. "Nothing, Miss Stewart, nothing at all. We were not near the Macleans . . ."

"But have you heard how they fared?"

He looked at her and turned his eyes away. "I heard," he murmured reluctantly, "that the half of them were killed. . . . But that will very likely not be true."

And Bride remembered that the Macleans had the reputation of being the last to leave a stricken field. "Thank you, Jamie," she said quietly, feeling very cold. "Go on with your meal, pray. Mrs. MacRobbie, you'll make him up a bed here to-night; he cannot go on to his home in Carie Glen. I think we'll all do well to go to bed now . . ."

She found herself in her own room soon after that; but how *could* one get comfortably into a warm bed, when on Drummossie Moor, since yesterday afternoon—on Baal-perazim, where the Lord had shown Himself on the other side—in the bitter cold rain and wind, all she knew in Rannoch and Atholl, maybe, were lying dead . . . and one, too, who was not of either. Yet she could not weep, even for him; the shock of a disaster so complete had dried the source of tears. She could think, however, "poor Malcolm was spared this at least!" She walked about her little bedchamber not knowing what she was doing; finally, with a gesture as if she were pressing something out of sight, went and listened at her uncle's door.

After a moment she tapped gently. Worrall came out. "Ay, he's abed, Miss Bride, and drowsy-like. Aw was just thinkin' Aw'd leave him." She slipped in, saw the old man lying quiet, gave him a kiss and came out again. Worrall was waiting for her, and with one of his rare reversions to an earlier relationship, he seized her hand and held it tight in both of his rough palms. "Doan't be tormentin' thysel', ma little lass; there's mony comes through a fight, and owd Pegleg'll live to see thee happy yet!"

Bride gave him a sad little smile and a "Thank you, dear Jonas," and was back in her bedroom ere she wondered what he knew or guessed.

(2)

All next day, as more fugitives made their way back, the disastrous news poured in. Jamie MacRobbie had not exaggerated the extent of the catastrophe. Yet it appeared that some remnants of the broken army had made their way to a rendezvous at Ruthven in Badenoch in the faint hope of some reorganisation; but a message from the fleeing Charles Edward dispersed them, each man to seek his own safety. And then, besides contemplating what seemed, only too surely, the death-blow to the Cause, Atholl and Rannoch could take stock of their own private ruin. What young MacRobbie had stammered out about the park wall was explained now; the Atholl Brigade on the extreme right of the Jacobite army had this wall on their flank, but the Argyllshire Militia and some of Loudoun's Highlanders broke it down in order to make a passage for the dragoons and themselves to pour a fire thence which mowed down the Atholl men. . . . Quite half of the latter had been killed in the battle or in the subsequent slaughter, and there was a long list of officers dead or missing: Lord Strathallan killed, Mercer of Aldie left on the field, his young son too, Menzies of Shian burnt to death in a sheep-shelter with the other wounded who had taken refuge there, Major Stewart of Kynachan last seen defending himself with a broken broadsword against a couple of dragoons and probably perishing in the same manner; Robertsons of Balnacree, of Invervack, of Calvine, of Trinafour, of Wester Bohespick, Stewarts of Tempar, of Inchgarth, of Tullochcroisk, none of whom would return; and at Dalchosnie, which so recently had harboured Bride, Mrs. MacDonald was weeping for all she had seen go—her husband, his brother, and her son. It was a country-side of mourning.

Of Ranald Maclean no news was obtainable. But only too soon Bride learned that the Macleans, brigaded with the MacLachlans, had suffered as severely as the men of Atholl, although they were not on the right flank, but in the centre, next the Mackintoshes. Their colonel, MacLachlan of MacLachlan, had been killed, their major, Maclean of Drimnin, and his two sons also. Of the hundred and eighty that they were, it was said that barely eighty came away alive. She tried to reconcile herself to complete ignorance of Ranald's fate; for even if he had escaped, there seemed no reason why he should write and tell her so. He had never spoken a word of love to her; and from what Uncle Walter had told her of the hurried and inconclusive conversation between them on the night of the retaking of Inchrannoch House, it seemed unlikely that he ever intended to. Seeing that the loss of his inheritance—in her eyes, too, so nobly thrown away—was no real obstacle to their marriage since she had money of her own, Bride had difficulty in believing the love very deep which refused to declare itself on account of such a scruple. She could understand the scruple, and respect Ranald Maclean for possessing it; but if after the encouragement which Uncle Walter said he had given him, he still would not speak, it was surely a proof that his pride was more to him than she was. So, in the sea of sorrow and dismay which swept over almost every head in Rannoch, the full, cold tide of grief to which one woke every morning, there was for Bride Stewart a current colder and bitterer than the rest. The salt draught of it would have been less choking if she could only have learnt from Ranald himself, before he went to almost certain death, that he truly loved her. But she had not, nor did she know of the letter despatched from Blair, whose bearer, delaying to start until late the following day, had fallen into the hands of Lord Crawford's advance guard, as it hurried up from Dunkeld.

(3)

Four days passed. In that time one seemed to have attained a kind of stunned stoicism. Life, surprisingly, went on; one was forced to rise, to eat, to go about one's household duties. Soon, in addition, one tried to find all kinds of additional small activities to keep oneself from dwelling all day long on what one was beginning to hear now—horrible reports of wounded massacred on the field, shot in cold blood, huddled up without food or surgical care in cellars, paraded in all their misery before the victors. Read a book one could not. Even Schiehallion held no comfort now; it was too aloof in its snow-tipped purity. Bride had never been conscious of that before. Perhaps, she thought, it had known all the time what would be the end ever since that August day when the young Hero who was now a hunted fugitive came riding at the head of the clans to Blair Castle. Had it?

Her daily housekeeping over, she was busying herself in her bedchamber on the fifth morning after the battle (and had not once looked out towards her mountain) when Phemie came in, rather flustered.

"There's a wheen outlandish sojers below, Miss Bride; and the officer man is talking to the laird. 'Twas mair at first than a body could richtly make out, what he was wishing tae say, but they're convairsin' together the noo in a tongue I'm no acquaint wi'. But the officer seems a

douce sort of creature; aiblins we're no' to hae oor
thrapples slit."

An outlandish officer—unintelligible talk! Who could
they be? Government troops, presumably—it could not
surely be a French reinforcement, *now!*

She heard voices in the hall, and listened a moment
over the stairs. Her uncle's tones, slow, a little halting . . . what language *was* he talking? She went down.
At sight of her a stoutish, middle-aged man in a perfectly
unfamiliar uniform swung round, brought his heels
together in a way new to her and bowed with much
correctness.

"Ecce neptis mea!" said Uncle Walter to this strange
soldier, indicating her; and then, to Bride herself: "My
dear, this is Captain Zimmermann of the Hessian regiment, who is under orders to occupy this house with a
small detachment. And as we can neither of us understand each other's language, we are driven back on Latin;
and mine, I fear, is somewhat rusty."

"And I have none!" exclaimed Bride, dismayed. "What
does the Captain speak—German?"

Captain Zimmermann, seeming to understand this
query, said, with an amiable smile: "Che barle aussi un
beu le franzais, Matemoizelle."

And so Inchrannoch entered on its second enemy
occupation; and Uncle Walter Stewart, after a day or two
of it, said he could better bear to see at his board the
honest South German countenance of Captain Zimmermann than the visage of Campbell of Glenure; in short,
that he preferred the Hessians to the Argyll militia. It
had always been a source of annoyance to him that
Glenure, by his chance absence that March night, had
not been captured with the rest of his men, and when,
six years later, the Red Fox came by his sudden and
bloody end at Ballachulish, the only regret the laird of
Inchrannoch showed was caused by the fact that it was
an innocent Stewart who paid the penalty of the crime.

Whether the strain of conversing in Latin or in very

unfluent French was greater or less than that of carrying on communication entirely by dumb show Bride could not quite judge; but to this latter expedient was the kitchen driven with the rank and file. However, water, straw for bedding and large punctual meals were all that these warriors demanded, and, these wants duly satisfied, there was little call for more conversation. They proved amenable if noisy, being, in fact, very much what Phemie had diagnosed Captain Zimmermann to be, and it was not difficult to remain on good terms with them—which was important. There had been no atrocities in Atholl, and if the glens were sheltering fugitives, the Germans did not go out of their way to hunt for them. Rannoch housewives with husband, son or brother in the heather soon discovered that good cheer and a warm fireside, if such could be provided, was the best insurance for their own fugitive kin who had neither.

Captain Zimmermann had with him a subaltern, Lieutenant Schmidt, who constantly made eyes at Bride, but not possessing even the tottering French of his superior was debarred from oral converse. After they had been there about a week she was called upon to agree to her uncle's suggestion that an officer quartered at tragic Dalchosnie should be asked to supper one evening with their own couple; Captain Zimmermann had been strongly hinting that such a course would greatly please him. Mr. Stewart, discussing the matter with her, had sighed and said that it would relieve poor Mrs. MacDonald for an evening, and that anything to keep the Hessians contentedly within doors was good. For not very far along the loch, up Carie Glen, old Struan was hiding—poor old Struan, who had been sent home from Edinburgh after Prestonpans with such signal honour in General Cope's captured chariot. So Bride agreed, and this Captain von Schroeder was bidden to supper next evening.

CHAPTER XIII

(1)

It was fairly clear why Captain von Schroeder from Dalchosnie had angled for an invitation to sup at Inchrannoch House. He was full of small gallantries and pretty speeches; having more fluent English than Captain Zimmermann possessed French, he used his advantage to the full on Miss Stewart, not neglecting, however, to do justice to the meal as well. From time to time Bride answered, smiling pleasantly and mechanically. She had by now perfected a code of behaviour towards Hessian officers which left her thoughts free to roam elsewhere—but, Heaven knew, not in happier regions.

But the wished-for moment came at length when she could leave the four gentlemen to their wine. Captain von Schroeder leapt up and held the door for her with assiduity. "I tink we soon come after you, Mees Stewart!" he said, with a meaning glance. She was afraid they would, and she was weary of them, amiable as they were; however, she could not affront them by vanishing entirely, so she went into the drawing-room to await their entry with her uncle, intending meanwhile to resume some embroidery which she had left there. Yet, when she had lit the candles, she stood looking out of the window into the untranquil night.

The black branches of the fir-trees outside were tossing restlessly against a sky of shattered clouds and a scudding moon. They looked to Bride horribly like arms perpetually raised to fend off some perpetual menace. In spite of herself she shuddered a little. But there was nothing to fend off now; the worst had happened, for herself and for all she loved and reverenced. She hoped

that the moon would have shown her the beautiful stead-
fast peak to which, like the needle to the magnet, her
heart had turned again, but those mournful and agitated
boughs obscured it. That the wind was moaning outside
was clear, though in this room, behind the closed windows,
she scarcely heard it—in this room where there was a great
log fire, and the best walnut chairs with worked backs and
seats, and the harpsichord from the Low Countries, and
the full-length portrait of her grandfather in his long
Charles the Second wig, one hand holding a fowling-
piece, the other extended to his prim young wife, Inchrannoch House behind them, and Uncle Walter, unbeliev-
ably a small child of two, playing with a dog at their feet.
Bride kept her back turned on these comfortable, familiar
things and continued to stare out. Fifty miles away the
same wind was wailing over that blood-soaked expanse
which had indeed been made the plain of breaches, the
same moon looked down upon . . . what did she look down
upon now, sixteen days after the overthrow, on Culloden
Moor?

She heard someone come in—one of the servants, no
doubt, to see to the candles. But she had already lit them.
Fiona's nose was poked into her hand; mechanically, without turning, and still absorbed in her sad thoughts, Bride
stroked the rough, narrow head. The next thing was
Phemie's voice, lowered to a whisper, almost in her ear.

"Miss Bride, ye maun be coming ben to the kitchen!"

She turned listlessly. "Why, Phemie, has anything gone
wrong?"

There were signs of unwonted perturbation on Mrs.
Reid's dour visage. "I doot there'll be something wrang if
ye dinna come, for he swears he'll no' gang till he sees
ye!"

"But who is it?"

"It's ane ye ken—and he fra yon ill place, Drummossie
Moor. Forbye there's twa o' them."

"Phemie, for God's sake, their names!"

Gaunt Phemie stooped to her and clutched her wrists.

"I dinna ken the ither. But—noo, ma lambie-loo, dinna let a sound oot o' ye—the ane's yon gentleman o' the Macleans was here last summer."

It was hard to utter no sound, especially as Bride's heart was suddenly plunging so that it seemed to shake her whole body. The room went dim for a second, then was a-dazzle with lights.

"He wants to see me?" she asked in the tiniest of voices.

"Aye, and that noo!"

"I'll . . . come," said Bride, with a long breath. "But, Phemie, 'tis fearfully dangerous for him . . . three officers in the house . . . and the soldiers—where are they?"

"A' in the steading, pittin' awa' their victuals like coos in a spring field. They'll not stir for half an hour yet. And when the officers come frae their wine they'll not search for you, nor will the laird for a wee while. Come ben quickly!"

"It can't be, it can't be!" said Bride to herself as she left the drawing-room and crossed the hall. There was a passage thence to the kitchen; she had no recollection of going along it. The kitchen door was closed; Worrall was standing outside it. He opened it for her without a word and Bride went in.

Never had she seen that cheerful place so dark, for one half, save for the firelight, was unlit, and only a couple of rushlights stood on the table by the window, among the unwashed supper dishes. Even the glow from the hearth was obscured by a great drying-horse on which a blanket was spread to air. And . . . there was no one there!

Bride gazed round bewildered—was the whole thing a dream? Then out of the great recessed chimney-side, round the screen of blanket, stepped a tall, bearded man in a ragged plaid and philabeg, came straight up to her and took her hands.

"Bride Stewart, don't you know me?" he asked gently. "It is Ranald Maclean; and I want you to marry me."

Had it not been for his voice she would *not* have known him. And what he said was so startling that its meaning seemed to reach her ears only after a pause, as an echo does.

"Marry you!" she repeated in a faint, astonished voice. "Sir, how can I?"

"You can—the minister is here with me. But will you, will you? You know I love you madly, Bride; I wrote from Blair to tell you so the very day we withdrew. I had already spoken of the matter to your uncle, and he had given me leave to address you, but I could not do so until I heard that Girolac was mine after all. . . . And then came the defeat, and since then . . . I have been hiding where I could. But if you wish I will see your uncle again first."

"You know I love you madly!" He was actually saying that, he, Ranald Maclean, here in Inchrannoch kitchen . . . or was it in Eden? But what letter of his from Blair had she ever received? Then into the bliss and the bewilderment shot terror. She caught hold of the ragged plaid—there were prickles of whin in it. "See my uncle, no, no! There are three Hessian officers at wine with him—and a dozen soldiers out there in the steading. Did you not know the house was occupied by troops? Oh, it was madness, madness to come here!"

"Maybe," said Ranald Maclean—but not as if he thought it so. Recapturing Bride's hands, he looked down at her as if Hessians did not exist. "I have come to see you, and to marry you if you will have me, for by good fortune I fell in with Mr. Duncan Cameron, the Episcopal minister of Fortingall, whom I think you know, four days ago in Badenoch, and before we go on to skulk on Schiehallion or in Glen Sassunn . . ." He left the sentence unfinished and slid into the warm, caressing Gaelic. "O Bride, my heart's darling, I have had no thoughts of any woman but you since the day I first saw you, more than two years ago in this very house. You know it from my letter. 'Tis true that I have had no answer—but indeed there was little time for it—yet I have dared to hope! Say that I was right—say that you will marry me! I would not hurry you, Bride of the Gold, and yet . . ." He carried her hands to his lips and kissed them passionately.

How could there not be hurry, ringed as this kitchen was with soldiers! Yet—to determine her whole future life, here and now, to give herself for ever to a man who never before had said a word of love to her? Bride took her hands away from his clasp; he let them go. And then she wanted to put them back. . . .

"My dear young lady!" said a voice which she had last heard preaching in Innerchadden House, and another vagrant-like figure came round the airing-horse. "My dear young lady, I am sure Mr. Maclean would not wish to press you unduly. It may be that you are not prepared to marry him at all. But if you are you can be wedded very quickly; I have my Prayer Book in my pocket."

"But I cannot, I cannot," burst out Bride, "not without my uncle's knowledge, even though he has given his consent. I must see him first and tell him. . . . No, I cannot do that either, for the Hessians would find out somehow that you are here. Oh, you should go, both of you, quickly, quickly!"

"I'll go," said Ranald, very close to her, "when you are my wife, not before. That is, unless you want none of me. Can you say that, Bride?"

Say that, when he was all she wanted in the world! Had ever any woman a wooing like this? The letter she had never received; her uncle and guardian closeted with enemies; enemies outside, a mere stone's throw away, apt to come in at any moment! And could the briefest ceremony be got through quickly enough?

Mr. Cameron appeared to read her thoughts. He came nearer. "If you consent, Miss Stewart, we'll need a witness—and then, marriage service or no, you'll be man and wife by Scots law. But I know you would wish the Church's blessing, and you shall have it. . . . Provided there remains someone to watch this door." He went and engaged in a whispered colloquy with Worrall outside the door by which Bride had entered.

"If you are afraid, *m'eudail,* do not listen to me!" said her lover. But he had his arms round her now; she was where she had longed to be. What mattered his lost letter and hers that had never been written! With magical suddenness her little boat had come into harbour; was it likely that she would put to sea again!

She laid her head against the draggled plaid beneath which the heart she had thought stilled for ever was beating. "I am not afraid. I will marry you now . . . *Ranald* . . . if God gives us time."

Time was given. And indeed that part of the happenings in Eden went by so fast that it was more difficult than ever to realise what was taking place, as Bride and the man who was being made her husband stood side by side in front of the Rev. Duncan Cameron, with Worrall behind them. They were so close to the hearth-place that the airing-horse with its blanket—which Bride now guessed to have been put there on purpose by Mrs. MacRobbie—completely sheltered the chimney corner from the view of anyone entering by the passage door, which, moreover, Phemie was now guarding. Mrs. MacRobbie herself and Jeanie Macpherson were presumably standing sentry over that into the yard.

Mr. Cameron was rapid but not hurried, in the very abbreviated form of marriage which he used; and the big, solemn-faced old clock in the corner had not yet gathered its forces together to strike nine before Bride found herself saying after Mr. Cameron, her right hand fast in Ranald's, "I, Bride, take thee, Ranald—to my wedded husband—to have and to hold—from this day forward . . ." Then a ring warm from Ranald's finger was slid on to hers, and Mr. Cameron was joining their right hands and saying something of which only the last words came to her ears: "I pronounce that they be man and wife together, in the name of the Father, and of the Son, and of the Holy Ghost," and then Ranald bent to her and said gently: "Kneel, *m'eudail!*"

And when they were both on their knees on the kitchen floor the Reverend Duncan Cameron, with the fire-glow picking out the red and yellows of his unpriestly tartan and the metal-work on the butt of the pistol in his belt, lifted up his hand and began the blessing. "God the Father . . ."

But here the door leading to the yard was flung open, Mrs. MacRobbie came hastily through, gave a startled Gaelic exclamation at what she saw, and burst out: "Sirs, the soldiers are rising from their meat—ye'll not get clear this way now!"

It seemed to Bride afterwards that ever since she came into the kitchen some part of her had been preparing, unknown to her, for this crisis; and to her own surprise she was ready for it.

"You must go by the front of the house, then," she said quickly to the two men—her husband and the priest. "Jonas, send Phemie to find out if the gentlemen are still at their wine, and the dining-room door shut, or whether they have gone into the drawing-room." And as Worrall without a word stumped quickly out of the kitchen she added: "There's nothing for it but to run the gauntlet that way; but unless you should meet them face to face there is not very much risk."

But Ranald, who, from the way in which he was looking at her, did not seem to be troubling about risks, took her in his arms and gave her, his wife, her first kiss.

"I shall not be far away," he said very low. "One night soon I'll come again . . . and you'll let me in, Bride, will you not?"

"No, no, not while the Hessians are in the house!" she whispered back. "You must not come here on any account! I'll come to you . . . on Schiehallion, anywhere . . . send me a message . . ."

Phemie flew in. "The gentlemen are this verra meenit intil the drawing-room, and seein' ye wasna there the laird speered after ye, and I said ye were ben on a matter o' the household, and wad come verra shortly."

Bride nodded. "Now, Phemie, go again, and if they are safely in the drawing-room with the door shut, put out the light in the hall, while Worrall goes and stands outside the front door to see if all seems clear there." She cast a quick glance at Mrs. MacRobbie and the further door of the kitchen. "We will wait meanwhile in the passage, lest any of the soldiers should look into the kitchen—I thought I heard them just now out there."

"I told Jeanie," responded Mrs. MacRobbie emphatically, "to make them understand that no one should be coming in whatever!" And a distant burst of laughter seemed to show that in some manner or other Jeanie was carrying out her instructions.

Bride beckoned and the two men hastened after her. In the long, narrow passage which led from the kitchen to the other part of the house they waited silently for Phemie's second return. Bride's mind was bent so insistently on getting the two fugitives safely past the danger point in the hall that she hardly even heard Mr. Cameron's whisper: "You are a heroine, and a rare clever one, Mistress . . . *Maclean!*" but she was aware of Ranald's strong clasp of the hand which drew her against him—this man whom she hardly knew, and whose she was now for ever.

Once more Phemie came tiptoeing back. "Ye can gang noo," she announced briefly, and they moved forward in a body behind her. The stone-flagged passage was dimly lit, but the hall was now dark, with a smell of newly extinguished wick, and evidence in the shape of a cold draught that the front door was ajar. From the drawing-room on the left came male voices and laughter; and then, as they crept onwards, a sudden cessation of both which sent Bride's heart fluttering down into her shoes. But the next moment she heard the subdued tinkle of some chords on the old harpsichord and a tenor voice upraised itself in song. One of the Hessian officers—since it was certainly not Uncle Walter—had broken into some melody of his native land.

This was great good luck, for politeness must restrain anyone there from leaving the room while the music was in progress. The lamp in the hall need not have been extinguished; the absence of light made movement difficult. Together Phemie and Bride steered the two men lest they should knock into the newel-post of the stairs or stumble over some piece of furniture. Greyness showed the position of the outer door, which Worrall had now opened wider. "Nowt to be seen!" came his gruff whisper. Bride was once more pressed against the prickly plaid. "My little love, my wife, I shall soon see you again!"

"But not here, not here!" she whispered back. "Send me word and I'll come to you!" Straining upwards (how tall he was even when he stooped to her!) she returned his kiss. Mr. Cameron wrung her hand with a low "God bless you; may you be a happy wife!" and in a moment the two were through the door, swallowed up again in the night whence half an hour ago they had emerged . . . to change her whole life.

Bride sank trembling into a chair in the hall, and Phemie, who, all through this episode, had been so unlike her usual disapproving self, came and bent over her. Then a clamour burst out in the drawing-room louder than the Hessian's singing—Fiona's deep, angry bay.

"Heavens!" thought Bride, "I had forgotten that the dog was in there! She must have heard something!" The hope of a moment's respite to collect herself was shattered; she must go in at once and quiet the too-vigilant animal. "Worrall, come in and shut the door; and pray light the lamp again quickly, Phemie." There was still a danger for her to avert, and she was shaking with reaction. Giving her cheeks a feverish rub, lest she should be showing the pallor which she felt, Bride sent up a little prayer for help and entered the drawing-room.

In the face of Fiona's resounding demonstration the song had stopped, and Captain von Shroeder—for it appeared that he was the minstrel—was sitting at the harpsichord with rather a rueful smile, while Mr. Stewart was trying to quiet the deerhound, who, close to the window, was barking furiously, all her hackles up.

"Ah, there you are, my dear!" said her uncle, turning round. "I cannot think what has come to the dog; she seems to hear something outside. Best let her out, I think; she is deafening our guests."

"*Let her out!*" Thankful, at least, that this had not already been done, Bride came and caught the great dog by the collar. "Fiona, be quiet this instant!" A supernatural strength seemed to be given to her, for she managed to drag the reluctant and excited animal a little away from the window, fortunately closed and curtained, through which she seemed so anxious to bound. "Be quiet, there is nothing there!" And she smacked Fiona hard upon the muzzle.

Fiona was evidently equally surprised and hurt in her feelings; contrary to Bride's expectation she did stop barking, turned a reproachful eye upon her mistress, delivered one or two more protests in the direction of the window, and then, growling, betook herself with dignity to the furthest corner of the room and lay down. Her demeanour seemed to say, "If you prefer not to be protected from bad characters, then you shall not be protected!"

Bride plunged into apologies. "I fear she interrupted your song, sir. Pray overlook it, and continue."

"I am afraid, Mees Stewart," observed Captain von Shroeder, "dat it was joost mine sinking dat make ze dock park!" But he smiled quite good-humouredly as he said it.

"Best send Fiona out of the room, my dear," once more counselled Mr. Stewart.

But Bride intended to keep the deerhound, sobered though she was, under her own eye for a while. "She is quite quiet now, Uncle John.—Will you not continue your song, sir, to show me that you have forgiven my tiresome dog?"

"I tink, on ze contrary, dat if gnädiges Fräulein would zing to *us!*" replied the late executant; and Captain

Zimmermann, in his villainous French, added an entreaty to the same effect.

But Bride begged to be excused, saying—and not untruly—that she had a slight headache. It would be a great pleasure, however, to hear some German songs.

She did not really hear a note of any, when, after bows and polite speeches, her request was complied with—and raised no protest from sulky Fiona. How should she hear anything but the echoes of one voice, the voice which not half an hour ago had called her *my little love, my wife?* Yes, this was her wedding day; and she sat there (to all appearance just her usual little tranquil self) with her hands folded, in the low armless chair which Great Aunt Margaret Robertson had embroidered, and looked at her uncle, listening to the music with his hand over his eyes. And she was no longer Bride Stewart, but Bride Maclean —the wife of a man whom she hardly knew, who lay coldly to-night in some insecure nook on Schiehallion, and who to-morrow might be lying there colder still, with a bullet through his heart.

(2)

The new day, standing at her bedside, held out afresh to Bride's gaze this marvellous, half-frightening fact of her changed estate. And still her uncle did not know of it, for to tell him last night would probably have been to deprive him of his rest. But now Bride could not bear to feel that all the servants knew what he did not. Otherwise she might have waited a little longer.

Her uncle's habits were so regular that she knew almost to the minute what he would be doing before breakfast— at what stage of his toilet or of his private devotions he would have arrived. He will have finished his prayers by now, she reflected, when she rose from her own, into which such new and strange petitions had entered. She went and tapped at his door.

Mr. Stewart was sitting by the window, the open Bible

with his spectacles on it beside him, so she guessed that he had finished his chapter, which in the morning he always read to himself.

"Good morning, my dear child," he said, looking up. "Is there anything you want?"

"Uncle—dear Uncle—I have something to tell you," began Bride a little waveringly. "It will astonish you, I know. I only hope it will not displease you." She knelt down beside him, pale, yet with a kind of inner glow about her. "I want your blessing, Uncle Walter." And she laid her golden head upon his knee.

He put his hand fondly upon it. "Bless you, my dearest child, many times—light of my old life as you are!"

And instantly Bride wondered, self-reproachfully, whether Uncle Walter would ever call her that again. How could he, indeed, when she was, she supposed, going to be the light of someone else's life—if the English did not cut short that existence?

As she still did not speak the old man asked gently: "What is it that you have to tell me at this hour, my dear?"

Bride raised her head; but she looked down at her clasped hands, considering. He was old; he was rather frail; how could she best temper the shock which she was going to administer? She ought to have thought this out more carefully beforehand. She could not say baldly: "I was married last night!" The sight of her left hand suggested what she hoped was a better way.

She held it up; it was not quite steady. "Dear Uncle Walter, do you see this?"

He took her hand and looked at it. "A new ring, my dear—but a man's, surely? How did you come by it?"

"It was . . . given me by the owner . . . as a pledge."

"A pledge of what?" asked Mr. Stewart, rather sharply.

Of what, indeed? Of so much that a few words could hardly express it.

"Bride, do you mean that you have secretly contracted yourself to some man?"

She nodded, her eyes full of tears, but a smile at the corners of her mouth.

"Without consulting me—without asking my consent?" exclaimed Mr. Stewart in grave surprise. "Who is the man?"

"Uncle, I wished above all things to ask your consent, though I am sure you would not have withheld it. But I could not, without endangering his safety—indeed I could not! It all came to pass so suddenly—so very suddenly—last night after supper. The Hessian officers were at wine with you, and you could not well have left them without questions being asked——"

"Child, in God's name, *who was it?*"

The first plunge. "Mr. Ranald Maclean of Fasnapoll."

"Ranald Maclean! He is alive, then?"

"Alive and unhurt, I thank God!"

"And came here to visit you last night, with soldiers in the house!—But when I last spoke with him, as I told you——"

"Yes, I know, dear Uncle Walter, but it is different now. The French estate is declared to be his after all; and even when it was believed lost you would not have opposed his suit; you told me so, and him also."

"That is quite true. But if Mr. Maclean's circumstances are changed, why did he not communicate with you earlier? Or had he but just heard the news?"

"He did write to me, Uncle, the very day that Lord George Murray withdrew from Blair, but the letter never reached me."

The old man looked down at her searchingly. "And when he declared himself you found that you knew your own heart at once! You are sure that you love him, that you truly love him, Bride?"

"Should I be wearing his ring if I did not, Uncle?"

"No, child, I am certain that you would not! And certainly the young man himself must be sure of his own feelings if he could risk coming at such a time to make his declaration! He was alone, I imagine?"

"No, Uncle." For one moment she hesitated. To name Ranald's companion was to advance a step nearer to her final admission. "Mr. Duncan Cameron of Fortingall was with him; they had fallen in with each other and were skulking together."

"Good Mr. Cameron! I am thankful that he too has escaped with his life. And so, while I was entertaining the Hessian officers, you were having an interview with two fugitive gentlemen in the kitchen! Well, well! I am assuming that it was in the kitchen?"

"Yes, Uncle; the servants kept watch upon the soldiers outside, who were at their meat. We were not disturbed. But they had to leave by the front of the house, when you were all in the drawing-room; and it was at them that Fiona barked so madly."

"To come here at all was extremely hazardous on their part," said Mr. Stewart gravely. "Yet I suppose that it argues the strength of Mr. Maclean's attachment that he should run so great a risk to see you—though I do not know why the Reverend Mr. Cameron should have shared it. . . . And so you have pledged yourself to the young man! But, my poor little lass, you must know that it will be a long day before you can be joined in wedlock with a fugitive Jacobite who will likely have to flee the country for a while. You'll need patience and courage." He fingered her hand with the ring, looking at her tenderly, regretfully, musingly.

Bride waited a moment and then, with a prayer in her heart, took the second plunge.

"If Ranald has to fly the country, Uncle Walter, I shall go with him. I have the right now. Yesterday was my . . . I was. . . ."

"What are you trying to tell me, Bride?" asked her uncle, half sternly, half apprehensively.

"Dearest Uncle Walter . . . Mr. Cameron was here last night for a purpose. This ring is more than a pledge of betrothal! I am not merely contracted to Ranald Maclean; I am his wife!"

CHAPTER XIV

(1)

The first letter which she had ever received from him who five days ago had become her husband! Bride did not even know Ranald Maclean's handwriting. She heard Phemie say that there was a lad outside from "him," then she was opening the soiled and crumpled twist of paper—writing materials were not easily procured by those who had "taken to the heather"—with the most singular sensations. The note asked her whether she could come that afternoon to the Black Wood of Rannoch to speak with the sender. He indicated the place, not far from a track, and said that he would wait near it from noon onwards. The note, devoid of endearments, was merely signed "R."

And staring at that initial with a quickening heart, Bride wondered why she had never realised before that "R" was the most significant letter in the whole alphabet.

"What is that, my dear?" asked her uncle, looking up from his accounts.

She laid the piece of paper on the table by him. "The lad is waiting," she murmured.

Walter Stewart adjusted his spectacles and read. "Then you must go, Bride, on your pony. You will, naturally, take Worrall with you. And tell . . . your husband . . . that Inchrannoch is open to him directly it is safe for him to come here."

Bride put her arms round his neck without saying anything. But the old man was aware, as she bent over him, how fast her heart was beating.

It was not a propitious afternoon for the meeting of lovers. May though it was, a very cold wind was blowing down the loch, and in the far distance the Black Mount belied its name with snow and cloud, and the Watchers of Etive loomed threatening. The loch was hurling itself on the pebbles of its shore like the sea; and at this extreme western end, where there was a little straight strand, the waves, slate-coloured under the leaden sky, came in foaming and crested. The stunted alders which had foothold among the stones shuddered in the blast; yet among them the primroses were struggling into bloom. The folds of Bride's riding-habit were fluttered violently as she made her way against the wind on Mist, her grey garron; but she was not cold.

It had not been altogether easy to avoid the escort of Lieutenant Schmidt, for when he saw Miss Stewart dressed for riding he intimated, very respectfully, if mostly by gesture, his desire to accompany her. Bride suffered some moments of dismay, for if he had insisted she could not have carried out her visit to the Black Wood at all, but would have been forced to make an idle expedition elsewhere. But somehow her uncle, using the medium of the Latin tongue (for which reason she had been unable to guess his method of dissuasion), contrived to prevent it. Even so, as she trotted with Worrall along the windy lochside, she cast one or two nervous glances behind, and was not really happy until the six miles were covered and she and her escort, turning off to the left, were going softly along the track under the giant pines.

In this great sheltered wood—part of the vast original forest which had once covered so much of Scotland—the wind was stilled. Thought itself was almost stilled among the towering reddish columns, so old, so silent, and so beautiful. The pine needles muffled the horses' hoofs; not far off a hind disturbed at browsing bounded away up the slope.

Worrall broke the silence. "Yon's t'place, Miss Bride," he said, pointing to a sort of hollow, "wi' three oak trees an' a hollin. Yo'd best gan afoot, and Aw'll wait wi' t' nags a bit further on."

Bride dismounted, and gathering up her riding-skirt, made her way through the tussocks of bilberry and the dwarf arbutus. Now she could see all round the shallow depression, brown with last year's oak leaves, to which she was advancing; over it on one side the three big oak trees stretched out gaunt and crooked arms without a trace of leaf. There was no sign of any human being.

She stood still, with slowing heart-beats. He had been prevented from coming—he had been captured, killed! If that were so, life would hold no more for her than that drift of curled and faded leaves. But while she fought with the dawning premonition of disaster she heard quick steps behind, turned . . . and there was Ranald smiling at her, come from she knew not where. Next instant she was in his arms. He kissed her, gently at first, then not so gently.

"Oh my darling, my heart, my little spray of white rose . . . are you mine at last?"

A rose spray in a thunderstorm, Bride trembled a little under the vehemence of his passion. But certainly she could doubt his love no longer, though, indeed, there had not been much room for doubt that evening in the kitchen . . .

At last he swung off his ragged plaid—she noticed now that it was not of his own tartan—and going a little way down into the hollow for shelter from the wind, spread it for her over the dead leaves, and when she had seated herself threw himself down beside her and possessed himself of her hand. No longer bearded, as on the other night, he was, save for his shabby philabeg and coat, much more the Ranald Maclean of their first meeting. She gave him a smile which was at first a little tremulous, like the sun on an April day. But the spring sun has all the promise of summer in its rays. Her husband met that smile and then gazed down at the little ringed hand lying in his with a look so compounded of humility and longing, reverence and triumph, that Bride's eyes began to prickle with tears.

"I hope you are not cold, heart's darling?" he asked,

M

after a moment, rather unsteadily. "I would take you to my shelter, but that I'm not alone there."

"Is Mr. Duncan Cameron with you still?"

"No, the good man has gone away south, to some Lowland kin in Fife. There's one of your name—but from Appin—and a couple of Robertsons from Tummel Bridge, and they will all be there. Moreover, 'tis some distance off. . . . You did not come all this way alone, *mo chridhe?*"

She told him no, that Worrall had ridden with her, and was waiting on the track. He said that that was right; yet somehow, from his tone, she thought that he seemed disappointed.

They talked on, in the august silence of that forest which had seen so many hundred springs. And Bride learnt something, but not much (for he would not talk of it) of the dreadful overthrow on Culloden Moor, and how it came that he was wearing a MacLachlan plaid; having thrown away his own in the charge, and his clan being brigaded with the MacLachlans, he had caught up any afterwards. His claymore had been shattered by a bullet; he had given away his pistol to a weaponless fugitive. Yes, it was true that of the hundred and eighty Macleans there not more than half had come away alive. And yet he had been practically unscratched; it was still a miracle to him.

"But not so great a miracle as this," he ended softly, drawing her head very gently to his shoulder.

Presently he told her how many fugitives like himself were in this tract of country between Rannoch and Glen Lyon, always a haunt of flying or broken men, from the days when it had sheltered Wallace and Bruce themselves. Allan *Mór* Stewart of Innerchadden was there somewhere, and Stewart of Crossmount too, both neighbours of hers. In Glen Lyon there was a famous "sheltering bed" near Invervar; he had spent one night there himself—a place fourteen feet long and six feet wide, and nearly five feet high, with a spring of clear water at the end. In Glen Lyon, indeed, Menzies of Culdares, the chief proprietor, who had been out himself in the Fifteen, but pardoned, was very careful not to assist in hunting out fugitives, though he was nominally upon the side of the Government.

"So you see, my wife," Ranald's arm tightened a little, "a man is as safe here as he can reasonably hope to be. But I am not for staying here a day longer than is needful. Surely your Hessians will soon be leaving you?"

Bride looked down at her ringed hand. "Yes . . . my uncle heard from Captain Zimmermann that he expects orders to leave in about a week's time for Leith. They are all to sail home to Germany."

Ranald seized her hands. "You are sure! Then in a week I can come to Inchrannoch House, Bride—I can come and claim you!"

"You . . . will take me away?" she asked a little falteringly.

"No, no, not yet. But . . . you are not yet truly my wife, *Bhride an Oir!*" He pressed a long kiss on the back of her hand. "Tell Mr. Stewart that I will come secretly, some evening next week—when there is no moon, perhaps."

"Ranald, it will be too dangerous for you! O wait, wait!"

"There will be no danger once your Hessians are gone. Will you be ready for me, little pale flower by the loch?" He slipped his arm round her.

Bride leant her head against him. "Yes, Ranald. Yes, when you come. . . . And I am ready, too, to follow you anywhere; but I must think a little of Uncle Walter. He was saying yesterday that when the times are quieter, when the redcoats are no longer hunting for fugitives, you could take up your abode with us—in a few months' space, perhaps. Though, indeed, I am ready to go with you, Ranald, my darling . . . Yet I must remember too that my uncle is old and frail, and that I am all he has."

"We will not be unmindful of him. But you are all that I have, too, my little white love, and you do not surely think that I am willing to wait 'a few months,' even a few weeks, for you, now that you have let me put my great clumsy ring on your darling hand?"

There was no answer needed to that. "But I am afraid for you, coming to Inchrannoch," said Bride sighing. "It will soon be summer; let me come to you. Find a place, a cave—I am not a fine lady."

"No, you are a fairy, one of the *sidhe*," answered Ranald, holding her closer. "If I were to follow you into a cave on Schiehallion do you know what would happen? I should never come out again; you would take me down with you to the fairy place of feasting. The *dun* would be lit with this hair of yours. May I touch it?—If you knew how often I have dreamt of doing that . . . ay, silk is coarse to it! . . . And all my life there would pass like a day, but yours would go on for ever, till you snared another mortal.—No, I'll come to you in your earthly bower. But, to speak seriously, my darling, there are too many fugitives like myself on Schiehallion and up Glen Sassunn, or here in the Black Wood, and 'tis too early for a bridal night under the stars—nor is that way fitting for my wife. I will come to Inchrannoch on a night next week, should there be no obstacle. Will you be content, Bride, without a feast or wedding guests?"

Her head on her husband's breast, lulled by his voice, unalarmed by the touch of his hand, so gentle was it, on her hair, Bride closed her eyes and said softly, "Yes, Ranald, I shall be content." Yet, after a few seconds, she opened them and looked up at him uneasily. "O Ranald, the fairy *dun* would be safer! There should be a guard round Inchrannoch, or at least someone to watch. Worrall shall watch. If you were followed, or seen entering . . ."

"Who's to follow or to see me? The Hessians will be gone, and I'm not likely to announce my coming to all Bunrannoch!"

"But suppose new orders were sent for the Hessians to remain longer, and I could not warn you, and you should come nevertheless?"

His laugh was heartening. "Have I not come once

already when they were there, and they knew nothing of it—thanks to your wits, my darling? Think you I have neither tongue in my mouth nor eyes in my head? I should soon discover if they were there . . . Do not take that shining head of yours away; 'tis a long time till next week for a man who sleeps on fern with two snoring Robertsons for bedfellows!"

The "shining head" returned obediently to its resting-place. Never, in all her short acquaintance with this man who had married her, had Bride seen him so exhilarated nor known him talk so much. But when he had her leaning against him anew in the clasp of his strong arm Ranald Maclean fell quite silent, staring down through the wood to the ruffled loch, his mouth rather grimly set. And once he sighed.

(2)

"When the Hessians go"—synonym for the hour when Bride should put off her maiden snood, never to resume it, the hour which she longed for, and yet could not but dread. And it came at last, when a day or two later than was expected, Captain Zimmermann and Lieutenant Schmidt and their men departed. Many were the polite speeches of the two officers at their leave-taking, nor were the soldiers behindhand in expressing to Mrs. MacRobbie, as best they could, their appreciation of her cooking. And when Inchrannoch and its policies no longer echoed to the sound of the German tongue or the clatter of hoofs and the hissing of military ostlers, Phemie, duster in hand, came to Bride, who had gone upstairs to see the last of the foreign uniforms disappear under the fir trees.

"And noo will I be settin' the west bedchamber in order for ye, Mistress Maclean?" (It was the first time she had given Bride this title.) "Your man will be comin' here the noo, I'm thinkin'."

Yes, the Hessians were gone. "Oh, Phemie," began

Bride, turning from the window with appeal in her eyes—
for, after all, Phemie was a woman, and a widow to boot.
"It seems so strange . . . !"

"Strange!" echoed that widow woman. "I'd like fine tae
ken what's strange aboot it! It's no marryin' a man juist
tae say a wheen words afore a meenister in a kirk—or
in a kitchen! There's mair nor that tae bein' a marrit
woman! And a marrit woman ye are, though nae wife;
and best let Mr. Maclean mak' a wife o' ye while there's
nae sodgers aboot. Aiblins we'll see mair in Kinloch Rannoch yet."

But at that the girl seized hold of her mentor convulsively. "Phemie, Phemie, if you think that, then he must
not come here at all!"

"Come he will, and that's sure," said Mrs. Reid, dis-
engaging herself. "Ye may be thankfu' he hasna come
before yon outlandish bodies were awa. Sae I'll be reddin'
the west chamber and make it a' braw for yer weddin'
nicht."

Phemie was quite right; Ranald Maclean came to Inchrannoch that very evening. But a few hours went by ere
Bride was facing her husband across the supper table,
across the bowl of primroses on which the light from all
the pewter candlesticks fell with such a strange quality.
For outside it was not more than twilight, but the windows
must be closely curtained lest so much illumination should
shine too far, or some eye pry in. This was the marriage
feast—just the three of them, and every door fast shut
and bolted, save that of Bride's heart. Of what her uncle
and Ranald, meeting for the first time since that ceremony
in the kitchen, had said to each other before she appeared
in the drawing-room, she had small notion, but there was
no hint of anything but approval on Uncle Walter's brow
as he sat at the head of the table and dispensed viands
to which neither of the new-wedded pair did much justice.

As for bridal attire, Bride had made herself as fine as
she could for Ranald's sake, and her best hoop lent her

dignity and showed off that very green gown, petticoated
with daisies, in which she had danced . . . in another
world . . . at Lude House; for Lady Lude had afterwards insisted upon giving her the dress. It could not be
unlucky, for it had brought her happiness that night. And
Phemie had dressed and curled her hair as nearly like a
fine lady's as she could, close to her head; but Bride refused to have it powdered. She wore the brooch, the ear-
rings and the necklace of Scottish river-pearls which her
Aunt Rachel had left her, for of her drowned mother's little
store of jewellery she possessed nothing; only fishes now
could admire that in the dim light of the sea-bottom.

But the bridegroom, as he apologetically said, far from
having any wedding attire, could scarcely muster a decent
coat; he must sit at his nuptial feast in the outer clothes,
at least, in which he lay night after night in 'sheltering
bed' or cave, for no suit of Mr. Stewart's was big enough
for him. Yet, save that it moved her to a passion of pity
and tenderness, Bride scarcely noticed his incongruous
shabbiness, for when he looked across at her with that
smile in his deep-set grey eyes it would have been one
to her had he worn the finest satins of Versailles or the
veriest sorner's rags.

At the end, when he had drunk their healths, Mr.
Stewart solemnly gave them his blessing.

(3)

Ranald did not leave Inchrannoch next day, nor for
four days afterwards. In the tumble of war's after-tides
his ship and his love's had voyaged together to an enchanted islet, and anchoring there in the lagoon at its
heart, forgot for a little while the breakers outside.
Neither had dreamed it was possible to be so happy.

Then the sea broke through the sheltering reef. On the
fifth day a small party of the garrison of Blair Castle—
North British Fusiliers—appeared with scant warning in

Bunrannoch and camped on the level ground at the end of the loch. At Inchrannoch they heard the news at breakfast; Ranald had to leave instantly, making this time for the other side of the river, and the slopes of Beinn a Chuallaich; and Bride, with her heart almost torn from her breast, saw him once more obliged to take to an outlaw's existence.

But the Fusiliers did not stay very long, and when they were gone Ranald made his appearance once more. In deference to Bride's nervous entreaties he did not take up his abode for long together in the house. She was always in terror of a surprise. Sometimes he stayed a night and a day; sometimes he spent the day in some neighbouring cottage, at others in the open, but never far away.

June went by thus and half July. Much of Lochaber had been ravaged; the Jacobite colours from Culloden had long been burnt to ashes in Edinburgh; the London gaols were full of prisoners; yet the hunted Prince himself was still uncaptured. And Ranald was uncaptured too—even, it seemed, in less danger than formerly. But about the second week in July came rumours that Cumberland was coming south from Fort Augustus, leaving the Earl of Albemarle in command there, and that he would return, as he had gone north, through Perthshire. He was exceedingly unlikely to come out of his way to Kinloch Rannoch or to engage personally in hunting rebels, but the very mention of his possible nearness roused such exquisite fear in one who had never feared for herself, that Ranald yielded to her entreaties to leave the district altogether for a while and conceal himself elsewhere.

Reluctant though he was to quit Paradise, he had the more readily agreed to go, because he had latterly been wishing for some means of establishing communication again with M. Marcelin, the lawyer, in the matter of Girolac. If he did not take some steps—show indeed some sign of life—the heritage in dependence upon which he had married Bride might yet slip through his fingers. In addition, he felt that he ought soon to make an effort to journey to the West, to Isle Askay, to see how Norman was faring. But the other project was the more immediately important; moreover, it was said that the West was covered with a network of patrols searching for the Prince, and Bride implored her husband not to think of setting out yet for a region so dangerous. Afterwards, perhaps. But now he would merely betake himself to Dundee or some other East coast port and attempt to send a letter thence to France.

Clinging to him, trying to be brave, even cheerful, Bride promised that she would not be perturbed if she heard nothing from him for some weeks, possibly; that she would not even count the days till his return.

"As I cannot tell you myself when that return will be, little treasure of my heart," said Ranald laughing, "you cannot score off the days on a calendar. 'Tis I shall do that, *Bhride na Meala!*"

For he had given her a new name; he called her Bride of the Honey, and not only because, as he asserted, the colour of her hair was liker honey than gold.

(4)

The widow woman who kept the tiny hostelry at Fortingall, at the mouth of Glen Lyon, did not enquire too closely in these days who came to drink a hasty glass there or to exchange a few smothered words after dark with some other man equally gaunt, perhaps with a plaid or a cloak half obscuring his face. If she did not look at them, she argued, how could it be brought home to her that she knew them for fugitive Jacobite refugees from Schiehallion or the Black Wood? None the less she usually had a lad stationed about a mile away on the Aberfeldy road, in case the garrison at Castle Menzies should show undue signs of activity.

It was just the presence of that garrison at Castle Menzies, a couple of miles or so on the hither side of

Aberfeldy, which had deterred Ranald from taking the more usual and convenient route by Glengoulandie, the Strath of Appin and Aberfeldy. He judged it better to cross the hills by one of the little passes into Glen Lyon and, going round the head of Loch Tay and down Glen Quaich, to avoid Aberfeldy altogether. And now at evening he was resting himself in the little inn at Fortingall, not far from that very ancient kirkyard yew which some held to be the oldest thing in Scotland.

Ranald sat there, oblivious of the one or two others in the little hostelry, his chopin by his side, meditating on the past weeks with Bride and their magic, much more than on his chances of getting safely to Dundee, and the steps he should take there . . . though, indeed, a vision of vineyard-girdled Girolac rose up before him, wearing colours more attractive than ever before. Yes, it *was* Bride's hair, her spun gold hair, her locks of honey that his children would have when they came. Though all was lost in the Highlands save honour, there was yet an honourable refuge by the Gironde, and with her beside him it would not seem like banishment.

Ranald was so deep in these dreams that though he was aware that a man had sat himself down beside him at the rough table, he never looked in his direction. And then a voice whose harsh resonances he had not heard for many a day said close to him, "Good evening, Mr. Maclean of Askay! It is long since we met!" Turning his head, he found himself looking into the glinting eyes of Gregor Murray.

It was true; not once during the campaign in the south had they encountered each other; and the MacGregors had not been at Culloden. The two of them had never met since that scene in the garden at Lude House; and that might now have been played out on the other side of Lethe.

"Yes, it is a long time," answered Ranald, rather as one in a trance. "Here we are both now, I suppose, with our heads under the wood." He used the Gaelic phrase in which an outlaw is *fear 's a cheann fo'n choille.*

"Aye, mine is," answered Gregor shortly. "But you, from what I hear, you have mostly a roof over yours nowadays, and another man's roof too, who is not kin to you——"

Ranald faced round as though he had been stung; he was in no trance now.

"*Dhé!* what business is that of yours?"

"I am an older friend of the inmates of that house than you, Mr. Maclean. Unless you have made your peace with the English Government you run the risk of compromising them by your constant presence. If that has never struck you, then it is time that someone pointed it out!"

Ranald was already on his feet, seething with rage. "We will finish this conversation outside, if you please, Mr. Murray!" Indeed there was no smallest chance of privacy in the tiny low inn-parlour where already one or two had looked up at the couple from their drink or their talk.

Outside the evening star, faint as a sigh, hung sweetly in the lingering green behind the long ridge of Drummond Hill. Crest-high now on a wave of fury, Ranald turned on the MacGregor.

"I will tell you why I have the right to go, and shall continue to go to Inchrannoch House as much as I please, Mr. Gregor Murray! I know——"

"Right!" exclaimed Gregor in a suffocating voice. "*Right!* You, a stranger—an interloper—*right!* Mr. Stewart's kindness in giving you shelter——"

Ranald bore him down in his turn. "It is not Mr. Stewart who gives me shelter, and the right—aye, the *right* to enter Inchrannoch House whenever I wish! You are evidently not aware of my footing there. Bride Stewart of Inchrannoch is my wife!"

The dirk which he had drawn but never used in the shrubbery at Lude could scarcely have dealt a more piercing thrust. Gregor Murray fell back against the side of the inn, a hand to his throat, just as though he had been stabbed. For one moment it came to Ranald, borne on the full tide of mingled wrath and triumph, that the insult of the flung plaid-end was more than avenged.

But almost simultaneously with Gregor's collapse the woman of the inn burst out of the doorway. "Get you gone quickly, sirs! The lad's just come running in to say there is a sound of horses' hoofs a way back on the road; he doubts 'tis the *saighdearan dearg* from Castle Menzies. Best go, lest he is right!"

She vanished, calling warnings to those within. Ranald stood a moment. Gregor had turned his back on him; he seemed to have an arm over his face. Then Ranald left him and ran lightly down towards the wide space by the river, where every June the broom made a lake of golden fire over the forgotten trenches of the Roman legionaries, and where, with flames not yet quite extinct, its thousand bushes offered shelter.

But Gregor Murray, when at last he stirred, set his face not back to the pass and the shelter of the long glen, but eastwards towards Aberfeldy and the oncoming troopers. Treachery? But he did not see it so. Under the blow from which he was still gasping there was room for but one thought—revenge. And he came of the clan—the lawless, wronged and hunted clan—which once in a feud had not scrupled to set on the table before a woman, and she expecting a child, the head of her murdered brother, a piece of bread in the powerless jaws.

He walked at first like a drunken man, but he went on nevertheless, quickening at last to a run, but listening fiercely for some clatter of advancing riders. For unless he met with them soon Maclean would be over the river or gone to ground in Glen Lyon, and it would be too late.

But he listened in vain, for there were no redcoats out that night from Castle Menzies.

CHAPTER XV

(1)

BRIDE did try not to count the days; she did try not to
wonder too much how Ranald was faring. She hoped that
he would not be tempted to slip over in person to France
by the vessel—if he found one—which was to take his
letter, because, though by so doing he would be withdrawing himself from the constant danger of discovery in Scotland, he would be running into another, that of capture by
an English vessel on the way, since France and England
were at war.

Her thankfulness that he had removed himself from
Perthshire was redoubled when news came of the Duke
of Cumberland's personal visit to Sir Andrew Agnew at
Blair Castle on his way south. The presence of the
Butcher, even at twenty miles of distance, made her shiver.

By the first week in August she was beginning to expect
her husband back; by the second she was trusting that he
would not come yet, for rumours were going round the
countryside that on the thirteenth of the month the Earl
of Albemarle, in command at Fort Augustus since the
Duke of Cumberland's departure, would come south with
all his force, and it was expected that the troops would
march partly by Crieff and partly by Blair. Still more
fervently did Bride hope that Ranald would keep away
when, on this movement taking place, it became apparent
that Inchrannoch was once again to suffer an armed
occupation. A small party of Skelton's regiment who had
been detailed to go by way of Dalnacardoch and Trinafour, came and demanded quarters for a couple of nights
or so, and had to be received.

Their officers gave little trouble and behaved with

courtesy and consideration, so that when one of them, a certain Captain Dawson, asked Bride whether she would be good enough to allow one of her maidservants to mend a uniform coat of his in such need of repair that he could not wear it, his servant, a raw lad, being no hand whatever with the needle, she assented willingly—though Phemie snorted when she was told of it. Yet—and it was like her—finding later on a very soiled pair of white buckskin breeches thrown down in Captain Dawson's room, presumably for the servant in question to pipeclay, Mrs. Reid seized upon these also, announcing that what they wanted was the dirt removing, not covering up after the manner of a whited sepulchre, as the Book said; and that the filthy things should either be scrubbed or thrown away.

Eaten up with anxiety lest Ranald should at any moment walk into the midst of these unexpected intruders, Bride thought no more of Phemie's change of heart. Next afternoon, returning from a visit to her old pensioner up at Annat, she was surprised to observe an air of great quiet round Inchrannoch, and beyond words relieved when Worrall informed her that the English soldiers were gone—had left at half an hour's notice, for Perth or further south, he believed. The officers had desired their compliments to her; the Laird would tell her all about that.

"And Aw hope this is t' last we'n see o' sojers in this house—though to be sure t' best of 'em coom at t' end!"

"They were your fellow-countrymen, you see, Jonas!" suggested Bride, with a glimmer of her old elfin smile.

Upstairs Phemie, already furiously putting to rights one of the just vacated bedchambers, was echoing Worrall's wish. "Forbye," she admitted grudgingly, "they were no' sae ill, they southron officers, and I'm vexed that I let yon Captain man gang awa wi'oot his auld coat and breeks."

"Phemie! Why did you do that?"

"Because I clean forgot them, Miss Bride—and sma' blame to me, wi' a' the feery-fary there was this afternoon! Ye were well oot o't!"

"But why did not Captain Dawson's servant remember the uniform?"

"I doot," returned Phemie, sweeping hard, "if he minded o' onything but the clout on the lug that Jeanie Macpherson catched him when he tried tae kiss her!"

"But what shall we do? We cannot send the uniform after Captain Dawson."

"Och, dinna fash yersel', Miss Bride. Gin we hear nae mair of it yon red dud will make a braw tatie-bogle tae fricht awa' the birds next year."

And Bride, half smiling at this new version of the transmutation of sword into ploughshare, was just going out of the room when she stopped and gave an exclamation.

"Phemie, where *is* that uniform?"

"In nae place wheer ye can come at it," snapped Phemie, pinning up a bedcurtain and then thrusting violently under the bed with her broom. "Losh, the dirt a man brings intil a hoose!"

Bride went over to her. "Phemie, please fetch it at once! I have a notion that it may prove very useful some day, soon—a godsend. Phemie, do you hear me? Pray bring the coat to me immediately, and the breeches also— I'll need to see the size. Now be quick, Phemie!"

Phemie threw her broom against the wall and looked at her young mistress with the utmost disapproval. "What's got ye? I doot the colour of yon coat has gane tae yer heid!"

"I believe it has," admitted Bride with a laugh. Indeed, it wanted but little more and she would have been jumping up and down like a child under the stimulus of her sudden great idea.

(2)

Ranald had had no premonition, when he left Fortingall for Dundee, either that his journey thither would take so long or that he would have to wait at that pleasant, thriving port, carefully concealing his identity and his business for nearly three weeks before he could find an opportunity of sending his letter to France. However, in the end, he had the satisfaction of entrusting it to hands which were not less trustworthy because they were pretty clearly those of a smuggler.

On his way back to Perthshire in the latter half of August he was met by the news of the coming south of Albemarle and his regiments. This necessitated extreme care on his journey and sometimes the employment of devious routes, so that his return took even longer than his going. But by the time he reached Loch Tay-head he learnt the heartening news that the garrisons both of Castle Menzies and of Blair had marched south with the army, and that in Badenoch, Atholl and Rannoch there remained no troops at all save some detachments of Loudoun's Highlanders. Nevertheless, he decided to return exactly as he had come, by Glen Lyon and the track over from Innerwick to Dall on Loch Rannoch, a decision which (like most decisions) was not without its effect upon events.

It was with a joyful heart that he set out upon the ten miles up the lovely glen. After six weeks of exile he was going to look once more into those eyes which held the sea, to hold that honey-sweetness in his arms, and all the trees of Glen Lyon and the impetuous river itself, leaping, struggling, or flowing at ease, seemed to rejoice with him. Through sun and shade he went, under the crags of the narrow entrance, past the spot where the hunted Mac-Gregor of nearly two hundred years before had leapt the river at the risk of his neck, past the wishing-well, the Pool of the Sword and the high falls across the Lyon, with the ancient bridge below them.

At the foot of the high mound of Carnban, whereon the ruins of the castle of that Campbell of Glen Lyon, Red Duncan of the Hospitality, strove with weeds and saplings —that castle where the same hapless MacGregor, visiting his wife, Red Duncan's daughter, was finally captured, and which came to its own fate through the flame-tipped arrow of a Lochaber raider on the other side of the river—sat an old half-blind beggar with his boy. He asked for alms, and Ranald, pausing to put a coin into his outstretched palm, was surprised but not ill-pleased when the old man, peering up at him through filmed eyes, exclaimed in his native tongue, "The hand which gives me this is surely a lucky one, and the heart is light, and the feet go to a happy meeting!"

"Ay, honest man, you are right!" answered Ranald, smiling. "These feet carry a light heart to the happiest of all meetings!"

And he continued, thinking it a good omen, on the track which immediately turned and dipped, hiding the old beggar from him. Over there on the far side of the river was Dericambus, and a little farther on, so he had been told, at the march between Dericambus and Innerinian, began the Toiseachd, the lands of the MacGregors of Roro. Ranald suddenly thought of Gregor MacGregor, and wondered where he was. To-day, for the first time, he felt rather sorry for him.

Some six or seven miles further on, at Innerwick, he rested a little in the tiny smithy before addressing himself to the track over the heights to Rannoch side, and talked to the smith, whose acquaintance he had made when he came over that way the month before. Yes, it was good, said the latter, that the *saighdearan dearg* had gone from the Highlands, and now Sir Robert Menzies would be able to go back into his own castle, out of which he had been protestingly turned to make room for the garrison, for all that he had remained strictly neutral.

Just as he was leaving the little forge-lit place it occurred to Ranald to ask the smith who was the beggar he had seen under Red Duncan's Castle; he did not remember having seen him there six weeks ago. The smith said he did not know; a man who was having a garron shoed—though most rode them unshod—suggested with a smile that had the gentleman been on the other side of the Lyon, and further up the glen, it might almost be that

N

he had seen the *Bodach Odhar,* the grey goblin that
haunted Innerinian burn, but this being had not been
known to cross the river. Then another who had just come
in observed that it might very well be old Somhairle
from Roromore, he that used to be a kind of *seannachie*
to the Chief, for during the last month, perhaps because
Duncan MacGregor was greatly impoverished and in
hiding, this old bard had been observed by several people
to have taken up a daily station under Carnban. Ranald
thanked him and started up the hillside towards Rannoch.

The heather was flooding everywhere; he had it and
the mountain breeze, instead of the glen's green and
sheltered enchantments. When he got to the highest point
and was clear of Meall a Bhuic, he had before him, too,
all the length of Loch Rannoch and its spacious mountain
background to the north, yet even Ben Alder himself was
dwarfed by the great cloud masses, buttress upon buttress,
throne upon throne, which towered behind him in the
blue. It was still only afternoon. Ranald's desire, as he
came down the descent to the loch, was to make at once
for Inchrannoch. But though the district was said to be
entirely clear of redcoats, it might be better to take some
precautions first, perhaps even to wait until dark. Yes, he
would wait until dark, when Bride would have retired to
her room. Descending through the outskirts of the ancient
forest, which had seen their first real meeting as lovers—
married lovers—he was more and more gripped by the
romantic fancy that he should wish her to be the first to
greet him on this return of his, which would not be the
case if he knocked at the door of Inchrannoch in daylight.
Nevertheless, though romantically inclined, he would be
prudent as well; he would not traverse those open miles
along the lochside before dusk and immediately he was
down at Dall he would make enquiries at the little farm-
house, whence he had usually sent the farmer's son to
announce his coming to Bride.

The farmer at Dall confirmed the fact of the district
being clear of redcoats, and of there being, so far as he was

aware, no strangers of any kind at Inchrannoch now, though there had been English soldiers there. But did not Mr. Maclean know that there was a post of Loudoun's Highlanders at the head of the loch, on the River Gaoire, and another up at Dalnacardoch? Ranald frowned; this was like to prove very inconvenient for him when he set out for Askay, since both the western and northern gates from Rannoch would thus be controlled. That, however, was not a matter for immediate concern; he was now almost at the safe, warm end of a journey, with the dearest welcome in the world awaiting him, not setting out as yet upon another. And, in reply to a further question, he said that he did not intend to send a message to Mistress Maclean—for here, naturally, they knew the true state of the case. Perhaps that was as well, then, for Lachie had hurt his foot a day or two ago, and it would be difficult to find a trustworthy substitute for him.

The day died too tardily for Ranald's impatience; died also in a sunset over the end of the loch unexpectedly angry and ragged. He supped with the farmer and his family and thought, "The next meal I take, my darling will be sitting at the breakfast table with me and the old man, and Fiona will lie at our feet, and Mrs. Reid will come in with a fierce face on her and ask whether we have not finished." Already, during the brief snatches he had had of life there, in this strange half-gipsy existence, Inchrannoch was become more home to him than Fasna-poll after all the years. But that scene pictured with such pleasure was a long way off yet; first there would be the night, and that was his and Bride's alone.

At last it was dark enough to start. The loch was only a glimmer as he set out along its southern side. And the wind was rising fast. Just as well; footfalls were less easy to hear—not that there was anyone about to mark his progress. He only met one man, coming back from cutting peats, in all the six miles.

By half-past ten or so he was outside Inchrannoch. The house was entirely dark; he had expected that, he had even

hoped it. Bride alone should welcome him. Quieting the
watch-dog, who had begun to growl, but ceased at the
sound of his voice, which he had grown to know, Ranald
slipped round to the back of the house, and was soon
below the window of Bride's room and his, which looked
out on the river, new-born from the loch.

That window too was blank; she must be in bed. And
now, because the wind was still rising and, blowing eastwards over that ten-mile sheet of water, was felt in all its
strength at its extremity, so that between the gusts Ranald
could hear the Tummel fretting against the little boat
chained by the bank, he began to have a fear lest he might
not succeed in rousing her, if she also were asleep. But
no, she could not be asleep; something, surely, must tell
her that he, her lover and husband, was below waiting
for her to let him in! He stooped, gathered a handful of
earth, and threw it up.

There was a tinkling sound against the glass, a shower
fell back, but nothing happened. Ranald began to think
that he had been too romantical, for it was far more sentiment than prudence, this time, which had led him to come
after nightfall. Feeling about he made a collection of
small stones, telling himself the while that he must neither
alarm her nor break one of Mr. Stewart's windows. If
he were driven to it he could probably arouse Jonas
Worrall to let him in. But he did not want to.

The second volley made a good deal more noise. Ranald
waited a little and soon saw with joy a light glint behind
the window-curtains. Then they parted a trifle, the window opened and her darling voice, surprised, called down:
"Is there anyone there?—Who is it?"

"Bride, my dear heart, here I am!"

He heard her draw a swift breath, had a glimmer of her
nightshift.

"Will you come down and let me in?" he sent up in a
strong whisper.

"Yes, yes, at once . . . Oh, Ranald . . . !" She leant
out a little further into the windy dark, as though she

could reach down to him; then abruptly the curtains **fell** to and the window was blank again.

Magic, it almost seemed, transported Ranald in **the** twinkling of an eye to the front of the house. He heard the key grind, the big door opened a little way, he slipped through, and there she was, candle in hand, all white and gold, Bride, his wife, the first to welcome him, as he had desired.

CHAPTER XVI

(1)

HE had her crushed in his arms for a very long minute, while Fiona, who slept in the hall, sleepily rousing herself, came stretching, and wagging a slow tail, to welcome him too. And by the end of the minute he was saying something incoherent about how small his little love was—he had forgotten—adding with a laugh that he would carry her upstairs.

Half laughing herself, but half crying too, and both for sheer joy, Bride laid a warm little hand across his mouth. "You must be quiet, Ranald, or we shall have Jonas coming out to us with his ancient pistol! Lock the door, my dearest, and . . . I would truly rather walk up the stairs!"

He took one hand away and turned the heavy key, and then, his arm about his wife, they went up the staircase in the sleeping house. When they were in their room she slipped from his embrace to light more candles, asking him the while why he had not sent a message to announce his coming—had he not had time?

The sense of the pseudo-clandestine, and the spice which it lent to this encounter, was momentarily strong on Ranald as he watched Bride dispersing the shadows. But he knew that she would not share it and might even be horrified at his feeling it, she who was a very snowdrop for innocence and purity. So he answered, and with perfect truth, "I had plenty of time. But can't you guess that I wished for once to be my own messenger? Did I startle you, *m'eudail*, bombarding your window? I ought not to have brought you out of your bed for a whim. Get back there at once; you will be cold."

"I never was warmer," she assured him gaily. Nevertheless she obeyed, and sat up among the pillows in her nightcap, with the candleshine picking out the springy braiding of the twin ropes of gold upon her shoulders. "And did you send your letter successfully from Dundee?" she asked, as he sat down beside her on the edge of the bed. "You have been so long away that I almost wonder you recognise me!"

To that suggestion Ranald gave her a conclusive answer. And when he had stopped kissing the lips that dared make it he told her of his doings in the six weeks of his absence—not, however, including in the narrative the angry little encounter at Fortingall, pointless and to her, perhaps, distressing. And when he had finished Bride, looking at him with an expression which he found so distracting that he nearly started kissing her all over again, expressed a hope that Mr. Ranald Maclean would now stay for a while with his wedded wife.

"If Mr. Ranald Maclean consulted his own wishes he'd never do aught else," replied her husband, reaching across and pushing the dirk he had just taken off under the other pillow. "But I fear, wedded wife, that it behoves him, as he said before, to go to Askay. I must see how my brother Norman has fared and speak with him about Girolac—and tell him the most important news of all, which he cannot know, I think. You can guess what that is!"

"That news will keep yet," said Bride, a dimple appearing. "I'd not have you go an hour the sooner in order to tell your brother what kind of a hasty marriage you made! Oh, Ranald, when I went into the kitchen that night how little I thought. . . ." She bent forward and hid her face a moment against his shoulder.

"If you had not come, I believe I should have fetched you out of the room, Hessians or no Hessians!" said Ranald, tilting up her chin.

"I believe you would. You are much rasher than I thought you—once!" The little smile, half mocking, half tender, turned to a look wholly pensive. "That is why, before I allow you to go to the West, you must promise me to take special precautions. For, as I expect you know, there are two posts of Loudoun's Highlanders in the district now. . . . Do you mean, for instance, to travel wearing those clothes—to go in the tartan?"

"But, my darling, the Loudouners themselves wear the tartan! What would you have me wear?"

The mischievous little smile came back. "Ah, what? Well, I have been full of forethought, as a good wife should be. And so I have travelling attire all ready for you—if you'll condescend to wear it!"

But Ranald was now beginning to undo the silken braids so near his hand. This was of custom now since their wedding night. "If you were to weave me a mantle of this, *Bhride na Meala*," he said, not very practically, "I should probably be invisible. Is that what you propose for me?"

"I should never have thought, before I married you," observed Bride, "that you could talk such nonsense! Leave my poor hair alone and I will show you what I have for you. Yes, 'tis true that in a way it might make you invisible at need." And sliding out of bed again she flitted to a press.

"What do you think of that?" she asked triumphantly, as she turned round. She was holding up by the arms a flaunting scarlet uniform coat. "Here are the white breeches too, but I have not any gaiters or boots. Still, at a distance. . . . Try, Ranald, does the coat fit you?"

"How in the name of the Good Being did you come by these?" asked he, astounded.

"'Tis Phemie you must thank—though the notion of thus using them is mine." And she told him the tale. "Can you thole to become a *saighdear dearg* for a while, do you think? If not, you could perhaps carry the uniform with you, in case of need. But put the coat on; I think Captain Dawson and you are much of a size."

Smiling, Ranald hung his own shabby, much-enduring

coat on the footboard of the bed where his plaid was already heaped and did as she asked. "It is none too ill a fit," he pronounced. "I'll think about the matter in the morning. But, you little plotter, why has this Captain—what did you say his name was?—not discovered his loss?"

"Perhaps he has, but he is far away now, further than Perth, it may be. And as you see, it is an old coat. If he has missed this uniform yet, I doubt he will have troubled much about it." And she slipped back into bed.

Ranald flung the coat on to the chair at a little distance where Bride had already laid the breeches. "The disadvantage of that scarlet and white attire, useful as it might possibly prove if one actually met with soldiers, is that it is so conspicuous at a distance. Whereas the tartan——" He surveyed his own discoloured, faded philabeg, then, looking up, saw Bride gazing at him with the clearest love and pride in her eyes; going to the bed again he knelt down almost in the shadow of the overhanging curtains and pulled her to him.

"How long it is—six full weeks—that I have gone without seeing you thus, my fairy saint!" he murmured. "Witch, rather, witch of white magic! . . . Bride, do you love me, do you love me?"

Her arms went round his neck; she laid her cheek against his, and the loosened gold fell over his shirt. "So much that I do not know how I am to let you go to Askay, nor how I am to exist while you are gone!"

They stayed thus in silence for a moment, conscious of nothing in the world but each other. The wind was strong outside; it moaned in the chimney and gave a sudden rattle to the locked door. They did not hear it; but after a while Ranald gently disengaged Bride's arms, kissed both her wrists with deliberation and got to his feet. Exactly at that moment a dog somewhere in the policies of Inchrannoch began to bark furiously.

Bride sat up tensely in bed. "What's that?"

"Why, a dog barking," replied her husband, with composure, going round to the other side of the bed and feeling for the buckle of his kilt.

Bride was listening intently. "But . . . 'tis Grey Jock! What makes him——" And then in the house itself began another deeper note. "Ranald, stop, stop! That's Fiona! Wait—there must be some reason for it.—No, no, are you mad? Don't go to the window; I will!" She was out of bed like a flash and, first peering through the window curtains, disappeared behind them. Ranald heard the window opened. The barking outside had ceased; that below in the house had become a furious baying. Ranald had heard that note before, on the night of his marriage. . . . The window shut again, and there was Bride, clutching the curtains to behind her. One look at her face was enough for him.

"Soldiers?" he asked under his breath.

Unable for a moment to speak, his wife nodded.

"Many?"

"I . . . I looked out . . . both ways . . . and I think the house must be surrounded."

"Then I cannot leave by the window. I'll get out of this room and find some place—the garrets perhaps." He ran lightly across to the door, but before he could open it there came a sudden rush of heavy feet along the passage, a series of thumps calculated to rouse the soundest sleeper, and a voice with a strong Lowland accent shouting: "Open, open, in the King's name!"

Ranald stood a moment motionless, then he retreated noiselessly towards the bed, caught hold of Bride and whispered: "Is there any corner here where I can hide? If not, I may as well open the door."

"No, no!" Bride whispered back in an agony. "Not that—you shall not do that!"

"What then?"

"Here—quick! This closet—the door is near the bed— it may be overlooked." She pulled open a narrow door covered with wallpaper and so close to the head of the bed that the hangings half hid it. "It is deep; go right to

the end and I will say that there is no one here but
myself."

"Open, open, or we'll ding doun the dure!" came booming from without.

Bride pushed her husband in, seized his coat and plaid
from the bed and flung them in after him, latched the door
—there was no other fastening—caught up a shawl and
ran halfway to the assaulted door of the bedroom, which
was now quivering under the blows of a musket-end.

"What is it?" she called out in a shrill voice unlike her
own.

"Open the door, mistress," replied that stern voice, "and
we will tell you!"

It was like throwing Ranald to the wolves, but it had
to be done. She went to the door as to her own death, and
opened upon the dark passage full of faces. Nearest to
the door, a lantern in his hand, stood a hard-featured man
of uncertain age, a soldier, but without the tartan of the
rest, who addressed her, showing however a rough kind of
respect.

"Ye are Mistress Maclean, are ye no,' madam? I am
Sergeant Barclay of Lord Loudoun's Highlanders. I'm
gey sorry, but we maun come in—and ye ken why. Ye
hae a rebel in your chamber, and although he's your
husband, we maun do oor duty! Please to stand back
noo!"

But the little shawled figure still stood fast in the doorway. "You are quite mistaken. There is no one in the
room with me. You can see that for yourself." And she
thought very quickly: "They can tell if they but look that
only one person has lain in that bed . . . but is it of any
use? They are sure to find the closet in the end; I cannot
prevent them." It was taking every ounce of her self-
control to keep herself from rushing towards it and standing with outspread arms in front of it, screaming: "You
shall not go in there!" But that, as anyone might know,
would be of all acts the most fatal! So, after facing the
Lowland sergeant and his Highlanders for a second or

two longer, she wrapped the shawl she had caught up closer round her and retreated towards the bed. This was the end, then, the end of their brief tale of happiness. O God, if only Ranald had not come to her to-night!

The sergeant entered with two men at his heels; the rest stayed in the passage. He looked round the room and his sandy eyebrows lifted at the view of the three candles which, not half an hour ago, Bride had kindled with so glad a heart and so lavish a hand.

"It's nae gude pretendin' ye are yer lane here, Mistress Maclean! If ye were ye'd not be sae wasterfu' wi' lichts. Forbye we hae had information that yer husband wad be visitin' ye the nicht, and onless he was awa' before we came"—here, lifting the lantern, he briefly scrutinised the undisturbed portion of the bed—"whilk is maist improbable, he's aye here somewhere. And seeing I maun take him prisoner it micht be the better for ye," he added not unkindly, "if ye were tae leave the chamber afore we——"

At that point, abruptly, the sentence came to a stop. Sergeant Barclay's jaw dropped and he stood like Lot's wife. When Bride's eyes followed his her heart seemed to leave her body. There, over the back of a chair, hung Captain Dawson's buckskin breeches and on the seat of the chair, one arm touching the floor, was the forgotten scarlet coat, just as Ranald had flung it there.

As if fascinated, the sergeant approached.

"What in the deil's name is this?" he demanded, picking up the coat and turning towards Bride, who, by the side of the bed, was staring at it no less petrified. How could she have been so mad as to leave it there!

A curious smile, which she interpreted wrongly as one of triumph, was dawning on the soldier's face. "I'm thinkin' after all, Mistress Maclean, that oor information wasna ower correct!" he remarked, with a sly note in his voice. "A man ye hae here wi' ye indeed . . . but it seems it's nae yer ain!"

It took a moment for Bride to perceive his meaning. She

gave an exclamation of horror. "Sir, how could you think——" she began, with the utmost indignation.

"There's nae call tae do much thinkin', my lass!" observed the sergeant, the note now deepening to enjoyment; and one of his men sniggered. Bride sank down upon the bed and buried her face in her hands. The suggestion, made, too, before these alien Highlanders, was so appalling to her that she felt as if she had been suddenly stripped naked.

"Still and on," continued the sergeant, grinning. "I'd like fine tae ken where ye hae put this officer o' yours, for I jalouse ye'll scarce deny——" And he lifted up the accusing scarlet.

Out of the burning whirlwind of shame—undeserved though it was—which enveloped the girl, there spoke all at once a tiny voice. Was there not here a loophole, a chance for Ranald, between whom and discovery, perhaps death, there stood only the easily lifted latch of the closet door and her wits. What if she were to withhold the truth about the uniform, accept this unspeakably repugnant suggestion, say—what even then should she say?

It came to her. "The . . . the officer, not wishing to compromise me," she murmured, almost inaudibly, "he's . . . there's a closet to this room . . . he went in there when he heard you . . . so that he . . . so that I . . ."

Sitting on the edge of the bed, her hands writhing together in her lap, her loosened hair fallen round her shamed, bowed face, Bride was, without any need for acting on her part, the very picture of guilt surprised—at least, to the rough perceptions of this sergeant of Loudoun's Highlanders.

"There's a closet, you say?"

Some supreme breath of inspiration, as wise as it was daring, made Bride lift a hand and indicate the head of the bed. "Yes, there," she answered faintly. "But if you try to go in . . . he will be angry."

"Aye, that's certain!" agreed the sergeant, with a guffaw. "Weel, weel, tae think that an English officer—but, in

Gude's name, what officer?" he demanded in sudden suspicion. "There's been nane in Rannoch this week or mair!"

It was too true. Bride's heart seemed to give a twist in her breast. She could not, after all, carry through this horrible stratagem. Impossible to call up a regiment, a lover, out of space. Yet, driven to the wall, she made a last desperate but simple throw against her own honour—and succeeded.

"I shall not tell you his name . . . but there were officers here a while ago . . . of Lord Albemarle's. . . ." A pause, while she swallowed and pressed her hands tighter together. "When they left he said he would get leave . . . and come back. . . ."

"And he did?"

She nodded. Thus to be definite, to give that discarded coat a wearer—it choked her.

"Aweel, I'm sairtainly not blamin' him!" commented the sergeant, looking at her appreciatively. " 'Twill be ane of thae officers of Skelton's then." And he strolled to the head of the bed, pulled aside the hangings and gazed rather longingly at the little papered door thus fully disclosed.

"There's nae lock, I see. And there'll be nae bolt neither, I'm thinking?"

"I . . . I have forgotten." The words came out with a gasp. But now any display of emotion or embarrassment was interpreted in one way only by her audience.

Her eyes were glued upon the sergeant, upon his hands. If he put one out towards the latch of that undefended door, could she keep from screaming? At present his thumbs were stuck in his belt. Next she became convinced that he was going to call through the door; and even though Ranald was probably at the far end of the closet, he, if he answered at all, would certainly not answer in the rôle of an English officer.

But the sergeant neither tried the latch nor attempted to open communication with the occupant of the cupboard.

To Bride, holding her breath, it seemed impossible that he should not think it incumbent upon him to verify or disprove her statement. Afterwards she guessed that it must have been the very fact of her pointing out the closet which convinced him that she was speaking the truth; though she hardly realised how little wish also he had to draw down upon himself the wrath of an officer, even of another regiment, by discovering him in a humiliating situation, hiding half-clothed in a cupboard. For Sergeant Barclay knew that he would pay the penalty of this imprudent act by a rating now, and, very possibly, by trouble thereafter with his own commanding officer.

Unwillingly, like a dog relinquishing a bone, he came away from the closet door and stood beside the bed again. His eye ran over it once more; he bent and looked for a moment underneath. Then he raised himself and gave a hitch to his belt.

"Aweel, my lass," he observed, with a grin, "we'll be awa noo and leave ye to better company. But I hope yon braw lover o' yours doesna intend to gang to bed wi' ye wi' his boots on—for he hasna pit them off, that I can see!" Bursting into a long hoot of laughter, he then bestowed his valediction. "A gude, a verra gude nicht tae the baith of ye!"

A trampling and her door was shut. Bride sank face downwards across the bed. She had saved her husband—but not without cost. . . .

(2)

But had she saved him? After a moment or two a very disquieting idea seized her and she started up again. Her uncle—the servants! If that odious man took a fancy to question them before he left, all alike would be quite certain to deny the possibility of what she had just confessed to. Could she prevent her uncle, at any rate, from being questioned?

Bride flew along the passage. The men were descending the stairs; but outside her uncle's door on the further side stood a Highlander on guard and—O heavens!—the sergeant was just going purposefully in that direction. She rushed after him.

"Sir, sir, don't tell my uncle, I implore you! Oh, say you will not tell him!"

Sergeant Barclay's face as he turned it towards her, holding up the lantern, showed rather glum and thoughtful. But at her words it cleared surprisingly. Bride did not pause to wonder why, all her mind being set upon stopping him from entering Uncle Walter's room. She had just, as a matter of fact, unconsciously put the final and most convincing touch to her deception. It was so exactly the precaution which a girl in her guilty situation would have taken that Sergeant Barclay's half-doubts left him and he ceased to wonder whether he had been a fool not just to insist on looking into that closet—despite the possibility of unpleasant consequences. He smiled, and dismissing the sentry, laid hold of Bride's wrist.

"Nay, then, my bonny lass, I'll not go near your uncle . . . on one condition. Ye maun gie me a gude kiss—as gude as yon English callant will get, nae doot, when he comes oot of his closet! Will ye? It's a bargain, then!"

It was almost the worst part of this nightmare. Outside Uncle Walter's door the sergeant held and kissed her as though she were really what she had made herself out to be. Then, remarking with a chuckle that "the Captain" had good judgment, he plunged down the stairs after his men, whom she could hear talking down below—discussing her, no doubt.

Bride took the edge of her shawl and vigorously scrubbed her face with it; then, just about to knock at her uncle's door, she changed her mind, sped back into the bedchamber, locked the door, ran to the closet, and opening the door a crack, called: "Ranald, Ranald, they have left the room—but they are still in the house."

Opening the door a little wider she could make out her husband, looking very large. "They have not yet left the house, you say?" he whispered back.

"Not yet. You must not come out of this place . . . not for a long time, perhaps. Some might stay behind . . . or they might return to search again."

Her hands were seized. "*M' eudail*, how did you do it? I could only hear voices, not what was said. What did you tell them?"

"You shall . . . hear afterwards. Now I am going to latch the door again. Do not come out until I tell you that it is quite safe."

In the narrow space of the barely opened door Ranald caught her face between his hands and stooped his mouth to hers. "You are of the *sidhe*, as I have often said, so I suppose you put enchantment on them." He gave a low laugh, but Bride laid a finger on her lips and drawing back, shut the flimsy door on him again.

Once more Bride started for her uncle's room, but this time she encountered Mr. Stewart in his dressing-gown coming agitatedly along the passage towards hers. She caught his arm and silently indicated that he should return to his own; and when they were both inside and the door shut, said hastily: " 'Tis Ranald the soldiers are after, Uncle, but he's safe—so far!"

"Ranald here!" exclaimed the old man, horrified. "But when did he come?"

"About half-past ten o'clock. I let him in myself. He is still in the closet in my room."

"In the closet! How was it they did not find him?"

"I . . . used a stratagem. Dear Uncle Walter, will you not go back to bed?"

"And leave these Campbells to pillage my house, perhaps? Certainly not!" replied the old gentleman stoutly. To him, since Lord Loudoun was a Campbell, all his nineteen companies must necessarily be of the same detested clan. "Go back to your room, Bride; 'twill be best—God send they do not return thither—and Worrall or I will

o

tell you when the Loudouners are gone." And this time he started for the staircase.

But by the time Mr. Stewart got down into the hall it was empty. The search-party was drawn up in the dark outside, and the watchers round the house were hurrying to join it. Complete conviction had by now descended upon Sergeant Barclay that the man they hoped to capture would not come here to-night, nor was anywhere in the neighbourhood. The bonny lass of the house would have made quite sure of that before she admitted her English lover. He could almost find it in his heart to be sorry for the luckless rebel, cuckolded so soon after marriage. . . .

"Fall in, ye domned loiterers there!" he shouted from the doorstep. Then he became aware of Mr. Stewart behind him. "I'm sorry, sir, to hae pit ye aboot to nae purpose . . . and disturbit the young leddy your niece." The sergeant passed the back of his hand over his mouth to wipe away a smile. "Ye'll do weel to let her sleep in peace the lave o' the nicht."

Here his own wit overcame him, and he exploded into a guffaw; a ripple of mirth passed over his men too, though only some of them had the English. Next moment they were moving away from the house, leaving the laird of Inchrannoch frowning, and wondering in what the departing invader could have found a subject for his ill-bred mirth.

However, he gave it no more thought; a matter of much greater moment demanded attention. He shut the door and addressed the figure which had just appeared. "Worrall, go carefully all round the policies and make sure they have left no one behind to watch the place." He sank his voice. "We must get Mr. Maclean away before it is light, if possible."

Jonas Worrall, who, having been surprised in his sleep and tied down in his bed, was in a thoroughly bad temper, said shortly: "Get him away, sir? He's not here!"

"Indeed he is. Miss Bride—Mrs. Maclean—has just told me that he is hidden in the closet in her room. I do not know how she kept the soldiers from looking in there, but she did."

"T' brave, clivver lass!" ejaculated her bondslave.

Going upstairs again Mr. Stewart found his niece on the watch outside the bedroom door. "They have gone, my dear," he told her; "but I have bidden Worrall search carefully round the house. If all seems clear your husband had best get away before daylight; but if Worrall is not fully satisfied, Ranald must stay hidden here for a while."

"Yes, Uncle," said Bride, who looked rather wan. She kissed him suddenly. "You will go back to bed now, will you not?"

"And you too, my child. We must thank God, who has preserved Ranald through your agency. But I'll not keep you now. You must tell me the tale to-morrow." And off he went with his candle, seeming to Bride more bowed than he did in the daytime.

When she was back for the second time in her bedroom, although she had learnt that the search-party had drawn off, her legs began to shake under her a little. The first thing she did after locking the door was to take the hateful and yet saving English uniform and cram it out of sight. For it had been flooding in upon her with increasing force during the last few minutes, how little her husband would relish the method she had adopted to fool the sergeant of Loudoun's. But perhaps she need not tell him exactly what it had been—only in that case what should she say? He would certainly want to know why no one had even tried the closet door, and he could scarcely be got to believe that her mere assertion that the place was empty had afforded him this immunity. Besides, she had never made this assertion, and it would be a lie to tell him so.

She had hardly got the scarlet coat out of sight when she heard the closet door opening. Ranald's voice came softly: "Will the gaoler allow me to come out now?"

She ran to the head of the bed and was folded in his arms. "Yes, yes . . . but not out of the house yet. . . .

And indeed, Ranald, I'm not sure but that you would be safer if you stayed here awhile."

"I know one thing, and that is that I should be much happier," answered her husband, holding her close. "We must consider it, Bride of the Spells. You have yet to tell me what spell you put on them—facing them all by yourself! How many were there, my darling?"

"I do not know—most of them stayed in the passage. There were three came in."

"They were Highlanders of Loudoun's regiment, I suppose—all but the man in command, the man who talked with you. He was a Lowlander."

"How did you know that, if you could not hear what was said?" asked Bride, a trifle apprehensively.

"Wouldn't you know, *mo chridhe,* even through a door, when a man's voice lacks the lilt of the Gaelic?"

"Yes, I suppose so," answered Bride, leaning her head against him. Her husband had sat down on the edge of the bed and drawn her with him. And then she caught his free hand between hers. "O Ranald, Ranald, I can hardly believe that you are safe!"

"To tell truth, neither can I! And I have yet to hear how you routed them, my little heroine!"

The heroine stayed leaning against him a moment without answering. "Oh, my heart," she said, with a tiny sigh, "I am so tired! I will tell you in the morning . . . for you cannot leave to-night. I am sure it is not safe; you might run into the Loudouners; or there may be some of them on the watch."

"That depends somewhat upon what you told them, my darling," he said, catching her up in his arms and with one strong movement depositing her back in the bed. "Tired though you are—and I can see it, indeed—I fear I must learn that before I can decide what I had best do." He sat down again on the bed and bending, kissed her gently. "Just this, my dearest—did you tell them I had been here and was gone, or did you tell them I was never here? Whichever it was, God knows how you made them believe it, for they must have seen the closet door if they made the least attempt at search!"

"I . . . said something—no, I did not say it, it was what the sergeant thought himself—which . . . made him sure that you had never been here at all. And so he was satisfied, and after a while . . . went away." Dear heavens, how tired she was; too tired well to pick her way without stumbling or lying! And now she was sure, penetratingly sure, that he would be very angry with her for her ruse.

Ranald looked down at her lying against the pillows rather like a lily after storm.

"But what *was* it you said, Bride? That I was somewhere else?—Or had they not come to search for me after all?—Darling, if you would only tell me!"

There was no help for it; she must tell him. It was only making matters worse, rousing his entirely natural curiosity like this. Bride closed her eyes for an instant.

"I did not want to tell you, because I think you may dislike the lie which I—the stratagem which I used."

Her husband took up one of her hands to kiss it. "My little heart, I'm not a minister or a dominie!" he said, half laughing. "There are occasions when a lie is fully justified . . . and I think one of them is when a brave wife is shielding her husband from his enemies."

"Yes, that is what I felt," said Bride, taking a little courage. "It came about, at first, this lie, without my contriving . . . because there was one thing I overlooked when I hustled you into the closet." She smiled faintly. "I forgot that the English uniform had been left lying on a chair. It was very careless of me . . . but, Ranald, it was that, after all, which saved you."

"Which saved me?" queried Ranald, involuntarily glancing towards the chair where he now evidently remembered having left the uniform. "I do not understand. How could that save me?"

"Because the sergeant thought . . . Oh, don't you see what he thought, Ranald? I had only . . . not to gainsay him . . . and then he did not search any more."

Ranald got slowly off the bed, and as he looked down at her a tide of red mounted, slowly, too, from throat to forehead. It ebbed much more quickly, leaving him startlingly pale.

"Are you, my wife, telling me that you allowed it to be thought that it was not your husband, but another man—and that an English officer—whom you had admitted to your room to-night?"

His voice, that always pleasant voice, just now brimming with love and admiration, how could it be changed to this? It chilled Bride like the winter blast on Schiehallion—took her breath away so that she could not answer anything at all, but stared up at him half in terror. Her husband's face also seemed to be carved out of ice—a frozen face, with eyes of frost and fire. And the silence stretched on and on—until he repeated his question.

"*Is* that what you are telling me? I can hardly bring myself to believe it . . . I think I must have misunderstood you!"

She managed to shake her head. "You have not . . . misunderstood. It was to save you, Ranald—the only way!"

"You made yourself out a wanton—to save me! You know me so little that you did not comprehend that I would rather be taken, rather hang—rather hang ten times over—than that you—Good God!" And it was he who looked at her with horror now.

Bride raised herself in the bed and threw out imploring hands. "Ranald, Ranald, my darling, do not be so angry! I had not a moment for thought! It was the sergeant who first . . . and there were you only the other side of that door, with no key, nothing to stay him from going in! What was my reputation to me then?" And, as Ranald made a violent gesture, she added, with more spirit: "The sergeant was only a stranger, a Lowlander. No one in Rannoch would believe such a thing of me for an instant! . . . Ranald, the ruse was almost forced upon me!"

But her husband did not seem to be listening. He had thrown himself down in a chair; he was holding his head between his clenched fists and staring at the floor. Yet he must have heard, for he repeated her word.

"A ruse! You can view such a disgraceful admission as a ruse—you can hold your own honour and mine so cheap——"

"I did not hold it so cheap, Ranald," she broke in, agonised. "God knows I did not! But there was nothing else to be done. Was I to explain why the uniform was there, and to say, 'In that closet is my husband, for whom I designed to use it'?"

Ranald lifted a face altered beyond belief.

"Rather that than pretend before a roomful of Loudoun's mercenaries that you were false to him—and with one of the enemy!" He jumped up and stood by the bed again. "Bride, you *cannot* have done this thing!" he said almost pleadingly. "You are my stainless flower, my white rose; there is some misunderstanding . . . or else, since you are so young, you did not realise what you were doing?"

But Bride would not catch at that plank in threatened shipwreck. She was clasping her hands together so tightly that the nails went in; her voice came in jerks. "Yes, I did realise, Ranald. It was . . . most horrible to me to do it. But I was saving you. I *did* save you. It . . . it cost something, I know. I could not . . . help that."

"Cost something!" he repeated savagely. "God in heaven, I should think it did! And you, whom I thought so pure that I hardly liked to touch you, could not see that it cost too much! But if you could so easily acquiesce in such a vile deception, and not see the intolerable disgrace which you were putting on me as well—By God!" he exclaimed suddenly in a sharper voice, "was that why I heard laughter through the door?" He bent towards her. "Answer me! Was that why?"

And at her whispered: "I do not know, Ranald," he broke out, with a strange sound, equally terrible, whether it were sob or laughter, "And you, a newly-wed wife, supposed virtuous—nay, I don't doubt your virtue! But ... so easily to feign unvirtue—why, I have come back to a stranger, not to the Bride Stewart I married! Who and what are you, I wonder?"

Bride fell back on the pillow; she was in truth a white rose now. It was as though the ball of the world were lapsing fast through space, and they two with it. She must make one more effort to stay it; and indeed, though her heart seemed to be melting to nothing in her breast, she was conscious also of a sharp stab of resentment.

"Ranald . . . you speak as though I had done it, as though I *had* deceived you! I think you cannot know what you are saying!"

"It was you a while back, before the Loudouners, who did not know that!" he retorted in a tone like a whip-lash. "That's the best that can be said for you!" He was thrusting his arms into his coat; now he caught up his plaid.

"Oh, Ranald, what are you doing—where are you going?" cried she in the sharpest alarm.

"To kill this lie; to give myself up if need be. This night's work must be undone whatever it cost." He swung on his heel. "You'll not see me again until it is!"

Bride made an effort to spring out of bed. But she had to clutch at the hangings for support, and it was as though the curtain had come away in her hand. She heard the door shut with a bang, and fell back in a huddle among the bed-clothes.

CHAPTER XVII

JONAS WORRALL was grimly locking the front door of Inchrannoch House when he heard a man running down the stairs behind him. It could only be Miss Bride's husband. The ex-seaman was minded to utter a reproach about his oversight in having given the key but one turn in the lock —hence the easy and silent entrance of the Loudouners— when Mr. Maclean surely knew by now that double-locking was necessary! Though indeed even a properly secured door would not have kept the fellows out indefinitely. But when, by the light of his own solitary candle, he saw Ranald Maclean's face he suppressed this comment. If ever he beheld a man in the grip of black fury, that man was before him!

"Which way have the soldiers gone?"

"Aw suppose they'll be gone back to wheer they coom from—th'head of t'loch."

"That's no answer! I asked which way they took, the south side of the loch or the north? Did they cross the river?"

Worrall nodded, staring. Why was the Highlander in such a rage? "Ay, they went over t'river."

"Then the passage-boat will still be at the further side. But the boat of the house—did they use that, too? Don't stare like that, *amadain,* answer me! On which side is the small boat?"

"But yo'n surely not be takin' t'north side yo'sel, sir?" protested Worrall. "Yo'd likely run slap into t'sodgers!"

Ranald Maclean's eyes blazed, and he took a step forward as though to shake the speaker. "God, give me patience!" he exclaimed. "Answer my question!"

"For aught Aw know t' little boat's wheer she allus is." And Jonas Worrall spoke with visible resentment, for this was a method of address to which in the last twenty years he had grown unaccustomed.

And on that Miss Bride's husband rushed past him out of Inchrannoch; and a moment or two later the Lancastrian, still standing in ruffled amazement upon the doorstep, thought he heard in a lull of the wind the clank of the chain, which told him that Mr. Maclean was, most unaccountably, loosing the little skiff which the soldiers either had not discovered or had not thought it worth their while to use.

Ranald rowed himself across the Tummel like a man escaping from an enemy instead of a man pursuing one. He had, too, to tug hard, and was savagely glad of it. The wind was high now; half-way over he could hear Loch Rannoch roaring, and the river itself clapped against the bow of the skiff as in rivalry. But louder than all rang the burst of remembered laughter which he had heard through the closet door—laughter at his expense, laughter generated by the evidence that he, Ranald Maclean of Fasnapoll, had been deceived by his newly-wedded wife! Intolerable, intolerable . . . and most intolerable of all, that Bride had not known he would find it so!

Once on the further bank he scarcely stopped to secure the little boat, but started to run towards the loch. Arrived at the shore the wind met him full; it came driving straight over those desolate tracts between the western extremity of the loch and the mountains of Glencoe, and then, tipping the waves with white, straight over the entire expanse of water itself. Ranald knew that he would have it against him all the way—another obstacle to combat; he rejoiced obscurely at the prospect. . . . And the man who had laughed? Well, he and his mercenaries would laugh no longer when he overtook and had speech with them! An English prison, leading quite probably to the gallows and the quartering-block, would be the fruit of his action; the fury in his blood made small account of that. For his dishonour and hers, imaginary though it was, would be purged, and that vile laughter quenched for ever. And without question it was a better way to be captured—to march boldly into the midst of one's baffled pursuers and say: "Here I am; take me—for it *was* I in my wife's room, and no other!"—a better way than to be dragged like a housebreaker out of a cupboard.

And there was always the chance that in the darkness he could break away again after he had slain the lie and silenced the laughter. As he hurried along Ranald's brain almost unconsciously busied itself with devising plans for thus eluding capture.

Highlanders march fast, and Sergeant Barclay was mounted. It was not until he had gone between six and seven miles, some of them at a jog-trot, and was within about half a mile of Killichonan burn and village that Ranald knew, partly by hearing, partly by sight, that he was overtaking the little force—that he was indeed approaching it rapidly, for it had halted. He halted, too, and kept in shadow. And presently he guessed that the halt would be of some duration, for he saw motions which looked as if the Loudouners were loosening their accoutrements, as their shadowy figures vanished into a little wood which spread up the slope of the Sliosmin.

This unforeseen proceeding at once began to paint for the pursuer fresh vignettes—"plans" they could hardly be called—of the various courses which he might follow for delivering his message, and yet avoiding the consequences of his audacity. He wondered if he could possibly contrive to get speech with this sergeant alone. If so, escape thereafter might not be insuperably difficult. He let a little time elapse, ascended the slope outside the wood and began to reconnoitre the hillside.

It was already dawn. The high wind continued; the loch was tossing, the trees creaked and rustled, there was noise in the wood. All the better. Yet, when he had at last bethought himself of a project, Ranald had to be very cautious in his movements, for though he was a Highlander himself, it was with other Highlanders equally keen of hearing that he had to deal. Luckily the wind was blowing from them to him. The Loudouners had lain down, evidently to sleep for an hour or so, and, free now-adays from fear of surprise, had posted no sentry any-where with whom Ranald could open communications—unless indeed a man lying on his face at some distance from everyone else on the outskirts of the reposing force had originally been designated to keep watch. In any case, his isolated position was fortunate, and towards him Ranald crept on his hands and knees; then when the soldier, half asleep already, began to stir, he laid one hand on his shoulder, the other over his mouth and whispered something into his ear.

The Loudouner lay quite still; then, without a word and moving as cautiously as Ranald himself, he got to his feet and followed him out of the copse. If any of his com-rades observed him, none made either comment or move-ment.

Outside, in the grey light, Ranald cautiously amplified what he had just said.

"If the man in command of you—a sergeant, is he not? —will come alone and unarmed to the sheepfank up on the brae yonder, he will learn of the present whereabouts of the Jacobite he was seeking in Inchrannoch House to-night. For he was in the house all the while; the sergeant let himself be fooled by a lying tale of an English officer." Ranald looked at the other Highlander hard. "Fooled, do you hear? Ranald Maclean and no other was in that closet in his wife's bedchamber."

"But how do you know this, honest man?" queried the surprised Loudouner. "And who is it that wishes to give news of the man we were seeking, and why?"

"An enemy," answered Ranald, prepared for this. "A man the Maclean has injured. And that is why he desires to be secret—not to be seen of any—and why your sergeant must come alone to meet him."

"Come alone he will not. With some of us, maybe—but not alone!"

"Then he'll find no one there! You think it is a trap? It is not. If your sergeant comes alone and unarmed he will take no harm; on the contrary, he will learn something. If he fulfils those conditions he is as safe as if he had a whole company round him with muskets at the ready. See, I will swear it!"

It was not till that moment, as his hand went to pull out his dirk, that Ranald realised he had in his haste and anger come away without it. It was still under his pillow. All he had now in the way of a weapon, all the steel he had to swear upon, was his *sgian dubh,* the little black knife. He brought it out and kissed the blade.

On a Lowlander the gesture would have had small effect, but for one who wore the tartan that sacrosanct oath was enough. The Campbell intimated that he would inform the sergeant, and opined that there was at least a chance that the latter would appear at the rendezvous; Ranald, on his side, said that he would go and tell the informer to be ready at the place appointed. The other Highlander would have been a fool if he had not suspected that this informer might be no other than the man who was speaking to him, but he gave no hint of this suspicion, re-entered the wood and began picking his way between the recumbent forms of his comrades.

The convenient sheepfank, a mere stone enclosure, which Ranald had discovered, lay a good quarter-mile away, and considerably higher up the slope, running itself also uphill. The self-styled informer intended to crouch outside its upper wall, just looking over it, and thus to have a good view of happenings on the hillside below. Thus if, as was not by any means out of the question, the sergeant should respond to his invitation by bringing the whole of his little force to surround the place, Ranald would have time in which to take to his heels. As he waited there in that wan light behind the half-broken-down upper wall, his chin propped on one of its cold stones, while down below the loch showed fitfully between the restless branches, a curious and unpleasant thought suddenly pricked him. Was it possible that someone really had played this part with regard to him? What had brought these Loudouners all the way from the far end of the loch on this particular night? Had information of his presence at Inchrannoch been sent to them, and if so, by whom and when?—for it must have reached them before he had even started from Dall. The whole idea was intensely distasteful; but there was no time to turn it over, for a man in uniform was coming up the brae towards him; and the man was alone.

Sergeant Barclay, for it was he, came through the unbarred gap which was the entrance, and staying close inside the wall, looked round the empty enclosure. Ranald let him wait a minute, then he climbed over the upper wall and came towards him. When he was about ten feet away the redcoat pulled a pistol from his belt.

"Ye can e'en bide where you are, my man," he called out. "I've nae fancy for a nearer acquaintance wi' ye!"

So the sergeant had not fulfilled the condition of coming unarmed as well as alone! Then at least I am absolved from my oath, thought Ranald, and continued to advance. It was improbable that the soldier would shoot him out of hand before hearing what he had to say.

Sergeant Barclay levelled his pistol. "Bide where ye are, ye cateran! I can hear ye verra weel—if ye've the English."

Ranald held out his empty hands on either side of him. "Sure you are very timid, redcoat!" he said, half mockingly. "I cannot shout the secret to the whaups!"

"Aweel, ye may come a wheen nearer. I'm no a fearfu' man, but I'm no fule neither."

Ranald went a wheen nearer. Not eight feet separated them now, and he could see the sergeant's coarse red face, the small eyes with lashes as pale as a pig's. This man had heard Bride's avowal and had laughed at her—and him! His fury began to boil in Ranald again; he clamped it back.

"But a fool is just what I fear you are, Sergeant! You have been finely taken in, and by a mere girl, too! You believed what Mistress Maclean of Inchrannoch told you, that she had an English officer hidden in her bedchamber, when all the while it was her own husband, the very man you were hunting for! If you are not a fool, I know not who is!"

"Her husband! Wha tellt ye that tale?" retorted the sergeant scornfully. "Why, there were the officer's duds all ower the lassie's chamber. Forbye she owned tae it— 'twas a captain of Skelton's she had wi' her. But 'tis nae consairn o' mine who fathers Mistress Maclean's next bairn; I'm after him wha'll be giein' his name to it. So tell me wi'oot mair havers where Ranald Maclean is the noo—if ye ken it—or I'll pit a ball intil ye for bringing me here for naething."

Afterwards, thinking over these phrases which were like red-hot iron on bare flesh, Ranald wondered that he had been able to hold himself in yet a little longer. But he contrived to.

"I have not brought you here for nothing," he said, edging a little nearer. "I have come, as I said I would, to tell you where Ranald Maclean went after he had left the closet in his wife's room."

"Still harping on that, ye gomeral!" said the sergeant, irritated. Then a humorous thought occurred to him, and he suddenly grinned from ear to ear. "Ye canna mean that he was in there wi' the ither! The baith o' them kept domned quiet then! And when did Maclean come oot, then?—will ye tell me that? Was it when the lassie rinned after me tae beg me not to tell the auld man, and gie'd me a kiss for my pains?"

"You *kissed* her, you filthy Lowlander!" The words burst from Ranald like a projectile, and he was on the speaker with such a sudden and ferocious leap that Sergeant Barclay, armed though he was, and suspicious— at least, until he gave rein to his sense of humour—was completely taken by surprise. The pistol flew from his hand—luckily it could not have been cocked—and he went over backwards.

They came to the ground together, Ranald the uppermost. Only for a moment or two did he lose the advantage which youth and surpassing fury gave him, and during that moment Sergeant Barclay was too much occupied to shout for assistance. Afterwards he could not, for the Highlander was kneeling on his chest with both thumbs compressing his windpipe.

"If you let the whisper of a cry for help out of you," he said to the purpling face below him, "I'll put my *sgian* into you, as there's a God above us. If you lie quiet and listen to what I have to say, you shall go unharmed." He took away one hand and it reappeared with the wicked-looking little "black knife" in it. A trifle more air entered the sergeant's lungs, already considerably compressed by the heavy weight upon them. He could do nothing else but gasp and listen . . . and wonder whether the quarter of an hour were up, after which he had told the corporal and four men to come after him.

"You wanted to learn where Ranald Maclean was," went on his assailant. "He is here; this is his hand on your throat; and if he hangs for it he is going to make you believe the truth!" The point of the *sgian* touched the sergeant's neck, above his stock. "I was with my wife when you surprised the house. It was I, and no one else, hidden in the closet. The English uniform had been procured as a disguise for me, and, when you jumped to the foul conclusion you did, my wife, having no thought but to save me, acquiesced in it. And you will make known that fact to all the scum of Campbell hirelings whom you have with you, and you will swear to keep your own dirty tongue quiet . . . or you will be found some morning with a disability that will make you dumb for ever. Do you understand?" The knife-edge went sliding gently under his chin.

There was not much difficulty about understanding, nor much choice about swearing. The Lowlander gasped out

something compliant and the knife went away; the very
hard knees digging into Sergeant Barclay's diaphragm
also shifted a little. The infuriated Highlander—why, oh
why had that closet not been investigated—was going to
remove himself, which was all the sergeant personally
cared about now. . . .

But no; he was seized by the shoulders and rammed
against the ground even harder than before.

"You understand, but do you *believe* what I say?" That
menacing visage was right over his own. "Do you believe
it? *Answer* me!"

"Ay, I . . . believe it was you yourself in there . . .
curse ye!" gasped the sergeant. "I believe it . . . I'll not
say again 'twas . . . an English officer."

"You swear that?"

"I swear it!"

"Be sure then that if you break your oath I shall know
it; news travels fast in the Highlands! You have already
broken the conditions by coming here armed . . . or I
should not have had this satisfaction!" said Ranald
savagely, still sitting astride the soldier. "I could not have
touched you else. Remember that and do not dare to say
that a *Highlander* broke his word!"

And with that parting recommendation Ranald sprang
off the suffering sergeant to his own feet, was across the
sheepfank and over the wall in a score of seconds and running like a deer up the hillside. He felt a different man.

So, probably, did Sergeant Barclay.

CHAPTER XVIII

(1)

BRIDE recovered that night to find Phemie bending over her, slapping her hands and speaking to her in the admonitory tones she had so often heard in childhood. For one moment it almost seemed to her as if she were a little girl again, being scolded. . . .

"Come awa, noo, Miss Bride, come awa! Dinna tak on so . . . and for ony sakes let me get ye back decently into yer bed!"

Bride remembered. No, indeed she was not a child again . . . would that she were! "Phemie, he's gone, he's gone!"

"Aye, has he," observed Phemie in no very concerned voice, pulling up the bedclothes. "But ye ken, Miss Bride, Mr. Maclean had nae choice; he cudna bide here, they Cawmell bodies might hae come back. That's richt; let auld Phemie hap ye up!" And as she tucked in the blanket, she added reproachfully: "I'm thinkin' it looks gey ungrateful, gangin' intae a dwam like this, when the Lord has presairved yer man frae his enemies!"

"It . . . it was not the Lord!" answered Bride, a great sob coming into her throat, and she immediately turned her face to the pillow. But only a few slow tears soaked into it; she was too stricken and too desolate-hearted to cry. Even that Ranald had left was a much lesser calamity than the manner in which he had left.

Could he really have gone to undo what she had accomplished at such cost—to give himself up, after all her painful lying, without a thought of what his capture would mean to her? Surely her reputation was first of all her own concern? Besides, no one would believe that sergeant and his Loudouners. It had been an unspeakably dreadful moment, that of her false admission, but nothing to what it would have been to see Ranald dragged out from the closet. Yet, for saving him at the cost of her deepest modesty, he had said . . . no, no, if he had really said that (as her memory only too clearly assured her that he had) then he had been momentarily crazy, and was not responsible for his words . . . any more than for his actions. For certainly it was crazy to rush away with the intention of getting taken prisoner in order to convince the sergeant that it had really been he, and no other, hidden in the cupboard!

"What is this, my dear, that Worrall tells me?" asked her uncle at breakfast. "Do you know anything about it? He says that your husband enquired of him which way the soldiers had gone, and then went off in the same direction. Surely Worrall must have been mistaken!"

From behind the tea-urn Bride, so pale and extinguished that even her hair seemed to have dimmed in colour, answered: "I am afraid, Uncle Walter, that that is just what he did. I . . . I have prayed that he might not find them."

"But, my dear child, what led him to do such an extraordinary thing? Good God, he must have gone crazy!"

"I think, almost, that he had," said Ranald's wife, bending her head while a tear splashed on to her plate. "Yet it was my doing . . . I had better tell you all about it, dear Uncle."

Leaving her breakfast untouched, she came and, sitting close to him, told him what had occurred, though not even to him did she uncover the deepest wound of all, Ranald's actual words to her.

"Oh, Uncle Walter, was it so shameless of me to do it?" she cried, the tears running freely down her cheeks now. "The sergeant almost put the words into my mouth. It was hateful, hateful, *hateful;* I thought I should have died of shame. But it was to save Ranald . . . and what does it matter in any case? No one in Rannoch will believe it of me; and if the sergeant tells anybody, it is he they will laugh at, not——" She pulled herself up. "I mean, they will laugh presently when they learn how *he* was fooled."

All this was a good deal for an old man to digest with his breakfast, especially after a night of alarms and disturbances. Mr. Stewart scarcely seemed to know how to take it. "Most extraordinary behaviour in both of you!" he said at last, shaking his head. "Most extraordinary—highly unusual! I should never have expected such . . . such boldness in you, Bride. Not that I exactly blame you . . . yet I know not what your poor aunt would have said. But if it is true that your husband was intending to give himself up in order to prove to the sergeant that a trick had been played upon him—which does not seem over-sensible, though I see Ranald's point of view—then your very singular and unseemly lie will have gone for nothing."

Bride, wiping her eyes, sighed deeply. "Yes. But I have prayed so hard that he may not encounter the soldiers at all!" She spoke with almost the simplicity of a little child. "Or that if he does he may get away from them again."

"The first alternative would be the better," said Uncle Walter doubtfully. "Yet Ranald gives me the impression of a man very well able to take care of himself, and so we must hope that he does not pay the penalty of his regard for your reputation . . . and his own. For, of course, my dear child," added the old laird unhappily, "a man does not enjoy its being thought that his wife is unfaithful, even when she is not. 'Tis a very strange situation; I cannot say I ever heard the like—But get on with your breakfast, Bride; the thing is done, and we cannot undo it now."

Yes, poor Uncle Walter was unable to cope successfully with even the surface aspects of the night's happenings. What lay beneath them he did not know. And she—how could she really hope that Ranald would not pay the penalty of his rashness?

(2)

But it was not Ranald, after all, who paid it; it was Uncle Walter himself. Two days later, on Sunday, the 31st of August, he was arrested on the charge of having harboured a rebel, to wit, one Ranald Maclean of Fasnapoll, and despite Bride's prayers and entreaties, taken off to Perth.

The officer in charge of the small detachment sent to escort him thither—English, like his men—was apologetic and regretful, but he had to obey orders. He had not known, he said, that Mr. Stewart was so old a man; most certainly he should be conveyed to Perth in a carriage directly they reached Wade's road, and Miss Stewart might be assured that his captivity would probably only amount to confinement in a private house. It was merely that the authorities felt the need of keeping him under surveillance; he had long been suspected of harbouring fugitive rebels, but the fact was not proved against him until a report to that effect came in from the post at the head of Loch Rannoch.

"But the charge is not proved, sir!" objected Mr. Stewart, who had borne himself with self-command and dignity. "Neither Mr. Ranald Maclean nor any other 'rebel,' as you call him, has been surprised in this house. So I claim that what you term 'proof' is merely suspicion."

"No, sir," replied the Englishman, "'tis more than suspicion. I have not yet heard the full particulars, but I have been told that on last Thursday night—or rather, early on Friday morning—Ranald Maclean, under pretext of furnishing him with information, induced the sergeant in charge of the party of Loudoun's Highlanders which had previously searched this house to meet him alone on the hillside, and there violently assaulted him, asserting that he *had* been in hiding in Inchrannoch House, though the sergeant had failed to capture him. So it is, sir, to

Maclean's own words and actions—whatever may be the explanation of these—that you must look for the reason of your arrest."

"But Ranald Maclean—was *he* arrested?" broke in Bride breathlessly. "For he is my husband. Was he captured then on that hillside, or did he——"

"Your husband, madam!" exclaimed the officer, who had already stolen several appreciative looks at this Miss Stewart, as he supposed her to be. "No, he got clear away, and nothing has been heard of him since . . . worse luck!" he added under his breath.

But Bride had turned away to hide the tears of thankfulness which had sprung into her eyes. Oh, God was good—how could she thank Him? And she had another lesser cause for gratitude, too, in that she had not to blush before this officer from Perth, for he did not appear to know of her stratagem, to have heard why the sergeant had not captured "Maclean" at Inchrannoch. And— Ranald "clear away" after carrying out his audacious intention! It was like his courage and resource! She turned round again with a glow on her cheeks.

"You will allow me to accompany my uncle, sir, will you not? He is not in very good health; he will need me. And you see that it is I, not he, who should be taken to prison. It was I who sheltered my husband; Mr. Stewart actually knew nothing of his being here."

But as to this the officer seemed doubtful; he had, he said, no instructions in the matter. In any case, Mrs. Maclean could not be kept in custody; she would have to be lodged separately. And Mr. Stewart, putting his hand on his niece's shoulder, said something to her in Gaelic. It had an immediate effect, but the English captain was wrong in supposing that it was any ordinary dissuasion which was being offered. What Mr. Stewart had done was to remind Bride of the possibility of her husband's return after he had visited his brother in Askay. She surely would not wish him to find her gone to Perth, where he could not with safety put in an appearance. And as

Bride had an even more potent reason for hoping for Ranald's speedy return than her uncle knew, she said no more about accompanying him.

And so Bride stayed behind at Inchrannoch burdened with the knowledge that but for Ranald her uncle would not have been taken away. She urged Mr. Stewart to take Worrall with him, if it could be compassed, but he refused. She could not, said Uncle Walter, be left alone at Inchrannoch without a trustworthy man in the house; as for himself, he had no reason to suppose that he should be treated with neglect at Perth. And the manner of his removal did not indeed augur too ill, for he was allowed to take comforts with him. But Bride did feel bitterly remorseful that he, old and rather infirm as he was, should suffer on Ranald's account—and hers—and said so; to which Mr. Walter Stewart replied almost gaily that as he had been unable to do anything active for his Prince, he could at least show, even at the eleventh hour, that he was counted worthy of imprisonment in his cause.

So he went off with his escort in the rain, and Bride shut herself up in her room and cried. And yet, despite what it had involved for Uncle Walter, she could not help feeling a sort of pride that Ranald had made good his threat. And surely, now that he had vindicated his honour, he would in a little while, when it seemed safe, come back to Inchrannoch or send her a message to join him. She made a calculation of how long it would take him to reach Fasnapoll, to stay there, to return. She could not look to see him in less than a couple of weeks—unless, indeed, he had repented of his hasty and cruel words and was even now lurking in the neighbourhood in order to see her and tell her so. But she hoped he would not come to the house; it might be watched, for all she knew. He would be more likely to send a message telling her to meet him somewhere.

But no message came.

CHAPTER XIX

RANALD woke upon the mountain-side, wondering for a second or two what was this many-fingered canopy of sweet-scented green filigree which shut him in; and then among the bracken he remembered everything. And far from seeming more tolerable the memory of his last moments at Inchrannoch House took on a still more scorching aspect. The only consolation was the end of that scene of a few hours ago in the sheepfank, which was such a pleasurable oasis in the fiery desert that he stayed on it a while in memory. Small doubt but that he had made that sergeant of Loudoun's believe him!

But now that it was fully daylight and the battered soldier had recovered his wind, he was likely to be indulging thoughts of pursuit. Events were not calculated to have diminished his appetite for the capture of a quarry who was now also a personal assailant. Better for that assailant, perhaps, to go on at once.

Ranald raised himself and was just getting to his feet when he stiffened and subsided again. He had been here too long already! The hounds were out, on the opposite hillside! But he dared not raise his head far in order to watch them. He must lie hid like a hare in its form among the kind fern, than which he could have no better cover. Even in his flight last night, raging, triumphant and reckless as he had been, he had broken and trampled as few fronds as possible when he plunged into that friendly green sea.

In time the shouts from the hillside grew fainter, and then were heard no more. The Loudouners had not searched this slope at all, but they might yet do so. Ranald therefore lay an hour longer in his lair, then he rose up. There was no sign of human beings anywhere.

He had originally meant to make for the west along Loch
Rannoch and the River Gaoire, thence up past the lower
end of Loch Ossian to Loch Treighead, but after last night
it would be madness to return to Loch Rannoch side. He
must therefore make a circuit round the lower extremity
of Ericht, that lonely, high-set loch thrust like a long sword
into the mountains, and trust somehow to reach the other
end of Loch Ossian. It would mean striking into country
completely unknown to him, and, as he guessed, very wild
and desolate; yet, unless he lost himself among these
savage hills of Badenoch, he might still hope in a couple
of days to be making his way along Loch Eil to the coast,
to Askay and his brother's home under the headland, and
little Helen with the yellow hair. There his angry hurt
would be washed and soothed, though it could never be
made whole. Now it ached and shuddered, and all the
while, as he plunged on through the heather, his heart
was crying: "Bride, Bride, how could you do it—take up
mud to cast upon your white self . . . and on me?"

Midday and the Bealach Dhu, the Black Pass; he did
not then know its name. He suspected that only miscalcu-
lation on his part had brought him to this high and narrow
defile between two great lofty mountains, for it was to the
north-east that it pressed downwards, and Loch Ossian
must be to the west of him. Yet Ranald plodded dully on,
weary and hot, for the wind had completely dropped, the
day had become very sultry and the midges were out, re-
inforced by horse-flies eager for blood. But he was not
deeply conscious of his surroundings. Hammers in his
brain were now beating out that recurrent question to
Bride; but there was no Bride to give an answer.

So far he had not met a soul of whom to ask guidance,
and he was not therefore ill-pleased, when he was nearly
down the pass, to see coming up towards him a little party
of five men. They were armed, but were not, clearly,
soldiers; and Ranald told himself that he did not care if
they were. In fact, from the manner in which this little

group advanced up the mountain-side, it seemed as if they, too, were going with circumspection, one or other continually turning his head and looking about as they followed the faint, winding track. If Ranald continued downward upon this he must meet them. Telling himself that he had no reason for avoiding them he went on.

The travellers, who had evidently not seen him as soon as he had sighted them, halted. Three of them went a little off the path into the heather and turned their backs as if wishing to avoid recognition; but in the track, as if to bar it, stood two stalwart men—gillies, apparently—one in the Cameron tartan and the other in that of the Glengarry MacDonalds. Ranald quite expected them to stop him when he got down to them, yet they only looked him over very hard and then moved aside to let him pass. But he gave them good day, and asked where he should find himself if he continued downwards, when his real objective was Loch Treighead and the coast?

He learnt from the two men that he was between Ben Alder and Aonach Beag, the highest mountains in Badenoch; that in order to reach Loch Ossian he must, as he had surmised, retrace his steps to the top of the Bealach Dhu and make his way westwards down the stream, which eventually ran into Loch Ossian after some half-dozen miles of rough and trackless going. But if he continued as he was now the path would take him to a little loch, Loch Pattach, and there he could strike off on another which tended in a westerly direction. By this he could eventually gain the line of the River Spean; the rest would be easy. It was, in fact, a choice between a longer way with a track, or a shorter and trackless one, with the prospect of retracing his way up the pass into the bargain. Ranald had no great wish to gain Spean side, which was slightly too far north for his purpose, but it irked him to turn back. So he thanked the men and went on downwards, glancing as he passed at the three superiors of the party, one of whom was whisking away impatiently with a tuft of heather at the cloud of midges. Their identity was no business of his, nor was he wishful of intercourse with any human being. He carried away from the scrutiny of their backs the impression that two of them were in middle life and the other, he of the fly-whisk, young.

Hardly had he gone more than a few strides downwards before he heard a voice calling after him: "Sir, by your leave!"

Ranald stopped and turned. One of the two seniors was coming towards him. "If you are a true man, sir, as by your tartan you should be, tell us if you have come upon any Hanoverian troops to-day in Badenoch?"

Ranald stared a moment at the grizzled and weather-beaten speaker. For it was MacDonell of Lochgarry, who had commanded Glengarry's men in England and again after the chief's second son had been killed by mischance in Falkirk. And the sight of him brought back in one flash of time all that had been suffered and won, all that had been lost, before ever he himself had come to his own private triumph and disaster.

"I have seen none, sir, since about six o'clock this morning. But a detachment of Lord Loudoun's regiment is quartered at the upper end of Loch Rannoch and, I believe, at Dalnaspidal. You and the gentlemen with you are no doubt skulking, Mr. MacDonell?"

"You know me then?" asked Lochgarry. "You are yourself a MacLachlan, I take it—on your way back to Argyll, perhaps?"

Ranald was in the middle of explaining that, despite the plaid he was wearing, his name was Maclean, when the younger of the other two men, who had been whispering together, here broke away from the elder, and, throwing back the plaid which had muffled the lower part of his face, said in a voice which Ranald had never thought to hear again: "Don't tell me that it is Mr. Maclean of Fasnapoll—and Dunkirk—for if so we are old acquaintances!"

And that voice jolted Ranald out of his almost trance-like condition of wrath and misery as nothing else in the world could have done just then; yet for all that he stared unbelieving at this disreputable, red-bearded young man in an old black coat, soiled shirt and torn kilt. . . . But it was, it *was* the hunted Prince, and Ranald's amazed knee would have sought the heather had not the young man, gun in hand, stridden to him and stopped him.

"Not here, Mr. Maclean, not here!" he protested, half laughing. "Who knows what eyes may not be watching us from the tops of yonder hills!"

"But surely," said Ranald, finding at last a tongue stammering in its wonder and eagerness, "surely I may kiss your Royal Highness's hand? Oh, God, to know that you are still uncaptured!"

The Prince's hand, which had come into his, snatched itself away again before the kiss could reach it. "No, Mr. Maclean, not that neither—only a hearty grip as between good friends unexpectedly met upon a journey! And we go, I see, in opposite directions!"

"Your Royal Highness is actually venturing yourself into Badenoch? There are Highland troops——"

"What of that? Yon great fellow"—he waved a hand towards Ben Alder—"has sheltered the good Lochiel and Cluny Macpherson well enough from them; and here is Lochiel's brother, Dr. Archibald, whom you know, come to fetch me thither to join them. I'd have you know also that Mr. MacDonell of Lochgarry here has some fifty of his clan out as scouts—I wonder you have not happened upon any. . . . Moreover, I have been a great deal nearer to the redcoats—to Highland militia too, notably at Loch Nevis—when I was in the West."

"Will your Royal Highness at least allow me to turn back with you?" asked Ranald earnestly, devouring the Wanderer with his eyes. The long red beard was so strange, and the bare legs scored with scratches . . . his shirt was really dirty . . . yet he looked in good health.

"No, no," said the Prince, smiling. "Go on your ways, Mr. Maclean; you are for your own hearthstone in the West, as I guess, and have nothing, surely, to keep you in these parts. I have escort and guides enough." He flapped away at the swarm of white midges with his bit of heather. "But pray do not depart thinking how much more shabbily clad is your old friend of Dunkirk than he was that night; for even as I came by Corry Arder, Mr. Ranald MacDonell of Tullochcrom was good enough to bring me a new coat and a shirt and a pair of shoes; the shoes I'm wearing, for I was in sore need of them; but I am keeping the coat to make a fine appearance when I meet with Lochiel."

A lump came into Ranald's throat; not at the destitution, but at the gaiety with which it was carried.

"And is there no way in which I can serve your Royal Highness?" he asked, with disappointment in his voice.

Charles Edward shook his head. "No way, I thank you, save to have a care for your own safety, as every good Jacobite now should."

But here Dr. Cameron came up, touched him on the elbow, and said something in a low voice.

The Prince nodded. "Aye, that he might do if he will.— Mr. Maclean, I have heard from more than one source that there was a French ship put into Poolewe or Loch Broom a good while ago with some French volunteers, and that four or five of their number landed in search of me. Not one have we happened upon, yet I believe they must be still trying to find me—tho' two of them are said to have been captured. And as I have recently been for some little while in the neighbourhood of Achnacarry, 'tis likely they may be making for that spot. Are you travelling by way of Loch Arkaig, Mr. Maclean?"

"I can easily do so, your Royal Highness," answered Ranald. "You would have me search for these officers, and, if I meet with them, direct them to these parts—or bring them here myself?"

"Nay, not bring them; give them directions. You speak French, I know."

"But not too precise directions," broke in Lochgarry. "You must be careful to use your judgment, Mr. Maclean.

These officers might even not be French at all; at the best they might prove indiscreet."

"Too precise directions Mr. Maclean cannot give, my dear Lochgarry," said the Prince, laughing. "Who knows where in this country of Cluny's I shall be by the time the French officers enter it—if they ever do! None the less, I would urge caution upon you, Mr. Maclean; yet, since I hear that these officers carry despatches, I own I have a desire to see what is in them."

"And you wish me to search for them at Achnacarry, sir? But Lochiel's house is burnt, is it not?"

"It is; yet, as I can testify from recent experience, there are many excellent hiding-places within reach. Archie, describe to Mr. Maclean some of the spots round Achnacarry where 'tis possible the French officers may be awaiting me."

Ranald listened attentively to the instructions of Lochiel's doctor brother. So many and so secure from observation did these hiding-places sound, that it seemed to him he was little likely to come upon the Frenchmen if they had ensconced themselves in any of them. Something of the same sort apparently struck the Prince, for he cut short Dr. Cameron's directions with a laugh.

"I have no wish to cause you to spend days prowling round Achnacarry, Mr. Maclean! Do what you can in a short time, and, should you come upon these Frenchmen, and are satisfied with their *bona fides,* direct them to yonder mountain of Ben Alder. They will fall in with some trusty scout or other, who will bring them to me wherever I may be in his recesses, with Lochiel and Cluny. —and now, gentlemen, we had best be pushing on. Adieu, Mr. Maclean."

He held out his hand. Ranald seized it and kept it a moment fast prisoner. Having been forbidden, he did not bend his head to it, but he carried it half surreptitiously to his lips, and some of the surge of devotion and regret which went through him was in the kiss which, after all, he imprinted on its scratches and its sunburn.

Charles Edward smiled. "Au revoir, then, not adieu—till happier times!"

Two farewells, in stormy weather and in calm, before the great hazard and after it, when hope lived, though it had been bitterly wounded, and when the death-bed candles were all lit. As he watched the five men going away from him up through the endless heather in the brooding and almost sinister heat, Ranald Maclean knew that he should never see that gallant, defeated figure again.

He turned away at last from watching, and immediately his own tragedy swept down upon him anew, as if it had been waiting, like a hawk at hover, for this interlude to end. "Your own hearthstone . . . nothing to keep you in these parts," the Prince had said; and the irony was all the sharper that it had been so unconscious. He plunged forward again, accompanied by horseflies, as if the Furies, rather than these lesser winged pertinacities, were after him.

CHAPTER XX

HARD by the Water of Arkaig, whose current sparkled like tossing silver in the light of the early-risen moon, the blackened corpse of Cameron of Lochiel's burnt-out house stared grimly next evening at Ranald. He stood there thinking that Fasnapoll, at any rate, had not suffered this death, nor was Norman, like Lochiel, a wounded outlaw hiding in a mountain corrie. He had at least achieved that by going "out" instead of his brother. And an owl's cry in the distance seemed to offer him sardonic congratulations.

He was weary beyond words, because though the latter part of his long day's tramp—on Wade's road beside the Spean—had not been difficult, he had, since fording Lochy, spent hours climbing and beating round the Prince's recent hiding-places in the woods on the other side of the Water of Arkaig. He had found no trace of anyone, nor was there anyone in these ruins. Wrapping himself in his plaid he lay down to sleep, of choice, among the charred beams and fire-licked stones of what had not long ago been a happy home ringing with the laughter of young children. The desolation of the place suited his mood.

The morning stepped with a quiet and heartless gaiety over the tops of the young beeches which the Chief of Clan Cameron had been about to plant in an avenue when the call came last summer; in his search yesterday Ranald had noticed them, merely heeled into trenches . . . so to remain for ever. He rose early, went some way along the southern shore of beautiful Loch Arkaig and plunged down Glen Mallie, for he had now to go south if he wished to strike Loch Eil side, as he intended. By eleven o'clock, having crossed first the watershed into the head of Glen Loy, and then that from Glen Loy into Glen Suileag, he was tramping down the latter glen, up which in those early hope-flushed days, after the raising of the standard, the Prince had hastened towards his first astounding successes. But Ranald, now that he had abandoned all expectation of coming upon the French officers, had again become more or less oblivious of his surroundings. He was not in the sunny glen, but back in the candle-lit bedchamber at Inchrannoch, rent anew by his indignation, his horrified amazement and his anger—his just anger . . . for surely it was just?

Immersed as he was in his bitter dream, it was against his will that he became aware of other and more corporeal pangs. Yet the fact was that he had not eaten since early the previous afternoon, and, however sad and wroth and puzzled he might be, he nevertheless realised that it was necessary to procure a meal somehow, or he would not be able to continue his journey to the coast. In Glen Mallie and Glen Loy the terror and incendiarism which had made a waste of Achnacarry and its surroundings, had left nothing but burnt or deserted habitations, and here there seemed to be no habitations at all. Very soon he became sharply aware that the sight of smoke from some hearth fire, however humble, would quickly wean him from his inner preoccupation; indeed that the hope of such a sight had already so weaned him, for as he went his eyes were now on the alert to discover it.

But it was not until he was, so he reckoned, about a couple of miles from the mouth of Glen Suileag, and the valley itself had opened out a good deal, that he perceived a solitary little dwelling, which seemed to be inhabited, standing by a stream in a level piece of ground. It was a miserable place enough, a mere framework of wattle and sods, many of the latter green and growing, in which a cart-wheel, imbedded in the vegetation-clad roof, served as a chimney, with the axle hole for smoke vent. But the inhabitants could probably let him have some drammoch at any rate, and he might be able to induce them, since they were obviously very poor, to accept payment for it.

Q

As he came nearer two dirty tangle-haired children, a boy and a girl, who were playing on the threshold, bundled in, screaming out that there was a stranger coming; and there emerged from the low entrance an almost equally dirty old woman, followed by a younger one slightly cleaner. Yes, they would be pleased indeed to let the gentleman have some oatmeal—they had plenty—and they would cook it for him. Would he please to come within and eat?

Ranald, who guessed at the conditions prevailing inside the hut, would much have preferred to remain without and soak his oatmeal in the burn, but he could not deal such a wound to the sense of hospitality which even the neediest of his race so eminently possessed. He therefore braved the smoky interior and its parasitic population, and was soon rewarded for his courtesy and hardihood; for during the preparation of the porridge it emerged that he and these women—Camerons by birth, both of them, and both of them the widows of Kennedys—were at one in their Jacobitism. Moreover, he had not been there a further five minutes before the elder Mrs. Kennedy had told him that, curiously enough, two strangers had passed not very long before, going up Glen Suileag—she wondered the gentleman had not met them. By their speech they were outlandish strangers too, but not Sassenachs of any kind, having no Gaelic, apparently, but one ill-pronounced sentence: "Where shall we find the Prince?" As the two women did not know the answer to this question, nor would have given it to the strangers if they had, one of the outlandish men had uttered the word "Achnacarry"; and so the women had nodded and pointed up Glen Suileag, and the strangers had immediately proceeded in that direction.

The effect of this information on their guest was startling. He jumped up from his stool by the fire. "How long ago was this, good wife? I must go after these men at once—it is for the Prince's service!" And on hearing how short a time had elapsed since this encounter, he rushed out, saying that he would return and eat his porridge later.

These strangers could surely be no other than the two missing French officers, though what they were doing near Loch Eil Ranald failed to imagine. But they had asked for the Prince, for Achnacarry. Would he be able to overtake them? How odd it was that he had not met them as he came down the glen! They must have gone aside off the track, and he had passed them unperceiving.

He set forth rapidly, looking about him all the time. Just here by the hut there was no cover, but a little further on, half-way up the slopes on his right, there was flung a dark pelt of wood. They might be in that, though he did not know why they should be. But looking up as he went at the distant wood, and not unconscious of a wish that he had got the porridge inside him before he started off on this chase, Ranald suddenly heard in the silence a sound like a human voice, and immediately stopped. And not only did he hear a voice but, now that his attention had been diverted from the side of Druim Fada, he also saw something—a delicate spiral of blue smoke twirling up from a clump of birches a little way further on, upon his left hand, which he must already have passed half an hour ago, but which, between his painful thoughts and his search for a human habitation, he had not noticed.

At all events there must be someone in this thicket. He approached with caution, and as the makers of the fire seemed not very much to have troubled themselves about keeping a look-out, he was able to get near enough to have a good view of them through the slender, ringstraked stems before they were aware of his presence.

There were two men there. One was on the point of beating out the tiny fire, which appeared to have cooked a meal, the other, standing face to face with a birch stem, had, from the manner in which he was feeling his chin, just finished shaving. A glint of light from the tree showed that he had the amenity of a tiny mirror, hung on that unusual support. Ranald's eyes took in quickly the bright blue breeches, waistcoat and coat—the latter lined with white, and a far from immaculate white at that; but something queer about this coat caught and kept the eye a moment. The Highlander suddenly realised why. He was looking at the inside of the coat; it was a white uniform coat reversed, perhaps in order to attract less attention. His gaze swept for a moment to the other man and then came back again to the first. He did not need further to study either figure, for these were obviously the missing Frenchmen from Poolewe.

Yet one of them—out of the past shot suddenly a vision of a young man in uniform (but a different uniform) examining his face carefully in a mirror. *Could* it be, that of all King Louis' officers . . . ? Ranald gave a slight exclamation; the man by the fire looked up, saw him, and in the twinkling of an eye had whipped a pistol out of his belt.

"I am a friend!" called out Ranald hastily in French. "I have been searching for you!"

Razor in hand, the other swung round from the birch tree. Yes, it *was* the young officer of Dunkirk! He had kept his pledge then, if a little tardily! How astonishing! And as the other had lowered his pistol Mr. Maclean advanced into the birch grove.

"You have been looking for us, you say?" enquired the officer with the pistol. "My faith, I think it is time that someone did so!" He sounded distinctly aggrieved, and, indeed, now that Ranald was nearer, he saw that the Frenchman's attire bore traces of not a few misfortunes encountered from bog, scree or briar. In particular it seemed that the adventurer must recently have parted with his boots, for he was wearing—no doubt much to his discomfort—a pair of the true Highland brogues of skin, with apertures to let the water run easily out. This footgear, together with some strips of deerhide wound round his otherwise unprotected legs, went very oddly indeed with the once smart and vivid blue of his breeches and waistcoat, and the gold braid, now tarnished, which adorned his uniform.

"Who sent you to look for us?" he continued, in the tone he might have used to a man of inferior class to his own—which, indeed, he probably took the Highlander to be.

Ranald was not going to utter the name of that sender unnecessarily. He did not answer at all, but looked instead at his old acquaintance, the Vicomte de Lancize, as the latter came away from his improvised dressing-table, putting his razor in his pocket. His attire likewise had suffered from exposure to the elements and to mountainsides, but not to the same extent, and his boots still held together.

"Sir," said he now, politely in French, "you are very welcome, whoever you are, if you will give us some news and directions. Of travels in this land of yours we have already had more than sufficient; it was surely designed to lose one's way in!"

"Then," said Ranald with a smile, "I am happy, Monsieur de Lancize, to be able to offer you my assistance."

"You know me!" exclaimed the young Frenchman, much astonished. "In heaven's name, who are you then—one of the tribe called MacDonald, from whose country we have not long come? No, those are different patterns," he added, casting puzzled glances at Ranald's plaid and kilt, rather than at his face.

"No: I am not a MacDonald, I am a Maclean. We met one stormy night more than two years ago at Dunkirk. And I had another visitor, too, that evening, you may remember, monsieur, in my little lodging!"

Light, and further astonishment, broke in upon M. le Vicomte de Lancize.

"My kind host of the tempest—it cannot be! *Tudieu*, but it is! And you come a second time, Monsieur Maclean, to my assistance! You are doubly welcome!" He held out his hand with alacrity. "I am sure that you never met any persons more glad to see you," he reiterated, "than the Chevalier de Galand and I. Galand, let me make you acquainted with each other."

The Chevalier de Galand was a young man about the same age—at a guess, five- or six-and-twenty—but he had not Marie-Cyprien de Lancize's fine, clear features, nor was his expression, like that gentleman's, partly of mockery at the plight in which they found themselves, but—just now at any rate—half sullen. And this look of discontent sat oddly on a face of impertinent cast, with full eyes and a nose so short or so tiptilted that the nostrils were fully visible to anyone standing immediately in front of it. It was not, somehow, the physiognomy of an adventurer; yet here the Chevalier was, a volunteer, presumably, upon this quest; and no one surveying his general appearance could deny that he must have been through some at least of the hardships proper to an enterprise of the sort. Only, as was clear, he had ceased to find them amusing.

He bowed to the Highlander, without any perceptible lightening of gloom, and said nothing.

"I must have some converse with you, sir," said Ranald to M. de Lancize. "I can, I think, be of use to you—give you certain directions." But he did not say to where or whom. And the Chevalier de Galand, stooping to tie his brogue-thong, muttered that they had been given directions and to spare during the past weeks, all to little purpose.

"Take no notice of him!" advised M. de Lancize gaily, "but let us have news, if you please, of the Prince Charles Edouard. We are hoping to find him at the château of Achnacarry."

"Achnacarry is burnt down these three months," said Ranald. "And I am afraid that you will not find the Prince there now."

"Then where is he?" asked M. de Galand, fixing Ranald with those full eyes of his.

The Jacobite was immediately conscious that he was

not going to tell him—yet. It would, in fact, be flying directly in the face of his instructions if he were to divulge that secret to either of these officers without first satisfying himself that it was safe to do so. Yet he could not, without giving great offence, allow anything of this hesitation to appear. He deflected the conversation a little.

"If you will forgive me, gentlemen," he said with a smile, "I will ask you to allow me to postpone my answer to that question until I have broken my fast. The truth is that I have not eaten since yesterday afternoon, and am most damnably hungry. I was in fact just about to set to on some porridge at that hut a little way back where you made enquiries, when the good people told me that you had passed. I therefore left it and hastened after you."

"But, indeed, you must eat first!" instantly exclaimed the Vicomte. "And, since you say that the Prince is not at Achnacarry, we will collect our few possessions and bear you company to your breakfast. But you will forgive us if we wait outside while you eat it?"

Ranald acquiesced. The plan suited him excellently, for not only did it, as he intended, allow him time to reflect, but it afforded him some chance of getting M. de Lancize apart for a moment or two, perhaps even inside the hovel, and asking him about his companion. In fact, as he stamped out the fire and the two officers picked up their belongings, he had a hope that this Chevalier might decide not to accompany him back to the hut, but would wait in the birch thicket; but this, however, did not happen.

As they retraced their steps the Vicomte de Lancize gave Ranald a sketch of their adventures. It appeared that he and the Chevalier de Galand had formed part of a group of nearly a score of officers from the *compagnies franches de la marine,* whose much enduring uniform M. Maclean was now, he said, beholding, and to join which force he himself had obtained a temporary discharge from his own regiment. They had set sail in June from Dunkirk in the *Bien Trouvée,* owned by Pierre Anguier of that port, in order to find the Prince. The *Bien Trouvée* had searched the Outer Isles, but in vain; so five of the volunteers, leaving the vessel at the Isle of Uist, after fixing a rendezvous with her at the Orkneys, had come carrying despatches to the mainland in search of the royal fugitive. There they had separated into two groups. And M. de Lancize described with a good deal of humour their wanderings, their great difficulties with the Gaelic language, the gradual deterioration of their apparel, their sufferings from midges and "taons," their many mistakes about their route and the various places in which they had hoped to find the Prince; how they had erroneously come right down to Loch Eil supposing that the seigneur called Lochiel must have his château upon it, how he himself had lost his sword, scabbard and all, by sounding a bog with it in a thick mist, and what misgivings, amounting almost to terror, had assailed them when they first heard the wail of the bagpipes and could not see the players.

The more he heard, the more was Ranald amazed that these Frenchmen, clad in foreign uniforms and ignorant of the prevalent language, should have succeeded both in eluding capture for more than a couple of months, and in reaching their present whereabouts from the coast of Ross-shire.

"We were lucky," confessed M. de Lancize, when the Highlander gave vent to this opinion. "Luckier than our poor comrades, of whom I heard a rumour somewhere or other that they were prisoners in Fort Augustus—had given themselves up, I believe."

"Like sensible men!" muttered his companion. Ranald threw him a critical glance. So that was his spirit! M. de Galand certainly looked as if he were heartily sick of the whole business, whereas the Vicomte de Lancize—though he might indeed have merely been assuming the rôle of the traditionally light-hearted Gaul—seemed to be viewing the whole affair as an entertaining adventure.

Perhaps it was this look of Ranald's which stirred the Chevalier de Galand then to ply him with questions about the Prince's present whereabouts, questions which Ranald parried, for there was something in M. de Galand's manner of putting them which made the Highlander not precisely suspicious, but uneasy; and he remembered anew the need for caution which Lochgarry had impressed upon him. Yet that these were French officers come to seek the Prince there could be no question; and one of them he had met before in circumstances which admitted of no doubt of his *bona fides*.

But when Ranald, having left the two outside the hut, fell to at last upon his porridge, the uneasy feeling began to evaporate. Perhaps, as he told himself, it had been chiefly generated by an empty stomach. And then, while he questioned the two women about the possibility of procuring a guide for the two officers to Badenoch, a dim project already stirring unacknowledged at the back of his mind began to take on a more concrete form and an appeal of greater urgency. What if he himself were to turn back and put the two on their way to Ben Alder— whether he actually conducted them to the Prince or no? What if afterwards. . . . The words began to take form. "Bride, Bride, I was hasty . . . Bride, indeed, I never thought you aught but driven snow . . . I think so still . . . but you shocked me so, you horrified me! To take your own fair name and make of it a stepping-stone for my escape—how could you expect me to condone it! Nevertheless I *was* too hasty, too hard. Forgive me, *m'eudail!*" And she, who by this time must have realised how deeply she had outraged his feelings, and how justifiable was his anger, *she* would ask for forgiveness for the mad, the scandalous impulse to which she had given way. And he would stop her mouth with a kiss. . . .

Into this agreeable imaginary conversation penetrated the voice of Mrs. Kennedy the younger informing him that there was a very trusty man at the mouth of the glen, at Fassefern—in Mr. John Cameron of Fassefern's employment he had been—a decent man who had been "out" in the earlier part of the campaign, and whom only an accident had kept, it might be, from sharing the fate of so many of the clan at Culloden Moor.

Ranald absorbed this information and the rest of the porridge together. Would this guide be needed after all? Not if he himself turned back with the Frenchmen. He must make up his mind on that point quickly. And still his lacerated pride was in revolt. Saved in such a manner —a newly-wedded husband who owed his escape to his supposed identification with his young wife's paramour— a trick contrived by that wife herself! What would be said of him . . . and what would be said of her? What were folks saying in Rannoch even now? But surely they, who knew his "fairy saint," could not but know that she had lied!

In that dim, stuffy, smoky place, with the old woman squatting by the fire and watching him, Ranald's pride and his sense of what was fitting fought together against his love in such an uncertain contest that the issue was still in suspense when he got up to seek M. de Lancize and his companion. For he must in any case have a little further conversation with them; in particular he must discover, if he could, why this Chevalier de Galand seemed at the same time so eager to come at the Prince and so disgusted with the whole enterprise that he was envious of the comrades who had given themselves up. After that he would make his decision.

Telling Mrs. Kennedy that he would return and speak further about the matter of the guide, Ranald went out. He found the two Frenchmen variously employed on the further bank of the little burn. The Comte de Saxe's erstwhile aide-de-camp, leaning against a boulder, appeared to be amusing himself with the two wild, half-fascinated children. A considerable distance further up, where the stream was rather wider, M. de Galand, without his coat, belt or weapons, all of which were disposed by his side, was washing his doubtless tired and bruised feet in its waters.

On seeing Ranald emerge he at once called out to him in a peremptory manner, "Monsieur—Monsieur l'Ecossais, please to come here a moment!" And when Ranald, not too willingly, had complied, and had come within speaking distance of him, the burn still separating them, he withdrew one foot from the water and asked, without preamble:

"If you were sent by the Prince de Galles to find us, as I gather, why do you now propose to hand us over to some unknown man to conduct us thither?" For these two facts the Frenchman had elicited, somewhat prematurely and to Ranald's vexation, in the course of his recent questioning.

Ranald, who had intended to be the attacking party, was for a moment disconcerted. He looked down across the stream at the barefooted enquirer in surprise and some annoyance.

"My reasons, sir, as I think I mentioned, were private ones. I am on my way to the coast in the opposite direction. However," he added stiffly, suddenly disliking the admission, because it seemed to have a flavour of recantation about it, "I have just been considering whether I will not, after all, undertake to guide you myself—that is, if you really wish to make the journey."

The Chevalier de Galand, who had started to dry his foot with a tuft of bog-myrtle, looked up sharply.

"What is that? I think, *monsieur le montagnard,* that you do not know what you are saying?"

"On the contrary, I know very well," replied Ranald temperately. "I know also that you are fatigued by these weeks of wandering in difficult country, which have worn out your boots, as I observe. I am sure that I have no blame for a man who wishes himself . . . back in the vessel which brought him hither." In the interests of peace he substituted this phrase for "in the hands of the enemy," which he might quite justifiably have employed.

The Frenchman withdrew his other foot from the burn, but he did not apply his improvised towel. "In other words, monsieur, you call me a coward!"

"Nothing of the sort," replied the Highlander. "I am but echoing your own words."

"They were words you need not have fastened upon! And here is another thing I do not like; you know, or appear to know, where the Prince de Galles is hiding, yet you will not tell us!"

Ranald was getting angry. He was to have been the catechiser, not the catechised. "I will see that you are taken to him—or take you myself," he said shortly.

"Blindfolded, perhaps?" hazarded M. de Galand, with half a sneer. "I believe you expect us to show you credentials!"

"And would that expectation be so outrageous?"

By something resembling a snort M. de Galand intimated that it would. "This affair tends to become more and more ridiculous!" he exclaimed with heat. "Must we observe the formalities of ambassadors to a crowned head before we can obtain an audience of this prince who spends his time scrambling from one mountain-top to another? It will not be easy, since at one moment he is hiding on an island, at another——"

"I will ask you, Monsieur de Galand," said Ranald Maclean, with hardly suppressed passion, "to speak in more becoming terms of His Royal Highness the Regent of this kingdom!"

"Regent! *Oh là là, la triste régence!* Poor young man —for I pity him from my soul—he will do better to abandon the phantom 'regency' of this horrible land of bog and mist and settle down as the pensioner of France. 'Tis all he'll ever be, I fear!"

If, at the moment when Ranald had emerged from the hovel, the ragged boy and girl had not been so enthralled by that strange object, the Vicomte de Lancize's watch, and the young gentleman himself so amused by their wide-eyed awe as he dangled it before them, matters might not have fallen out as they did. For he would probably have left his boulder at once and joined the Highlander, instead of lingering by it, laughing at the urchins and trying to explain—in quite useless English— the purpose of this shiny, ticking thing.

But when, shattering and sudden, the shot rang out, he all but dropped the watch as he started forward. The children scattered wildly as, with an exclamation of dismay, he ran past them along the stream.

"In the name of God, Galand, what have you done?"

"Saved myself from a dagger thrust, probably," returned Maxence de Galand. He had got to one knee; the smoke was still curling from the pistol which he had just snatched up from the ground. And on the other side of the burn Ranald Maclean lay writhing in the heather with a ball in his thigh.

"I had not time even to get to my feet," indignantly explained the marksman, scrambling to them now. "He would have been on me like a tiger had I not forestalled him."

"But . . . but what did you differ about? I can scarcely believe that he would—you must have gone crazy!" Marie-Cyprien de Lancize jumped the little stream and stooped over the man lying on the other side.

"Monsieur Maclean, where are you hit? Good God, I hope it is not serious!"

Ranald, his head bowed forward, a hand tugging at the tough heather-stems, uttered between his teeth one short word—"*Bride!*"—and, as Marie-Cyprien touched him, fainted.

CHAPTER XXI

THE heather round was deepened in colour and even the serviceable water of the burn slightly tinged before the two conscience-smitten Frenchmen had finished their ministrations. The ball had struck the Highlander slantingly in the left thigh; fired at such comparatively close quarters it had done a good deal of damage; indeed, for all they knew, it had shattered the bone. Two things, luckily, it had not done; it had not even grazed the great artery, and it had not lodged in the limb—it had gone through, a fact which had, on the other hand, occasioned additional loss of blood, and there was a sad lack of material for staunching and binding. The women, whom the sound of the shot had brought out, produced some dirty rags which were rejected, but the two officers, by sacrificing their extra linen—a couple of shirts and some pocket-handkerchiefs—contrived to tie up the doubly-wounded limb.

Ranald came to before the operation was over. He said not a word; made no reply to M. de Lancize's expressions of remorse nor to the lamentations of the women, but lay there with his teeth set looking up at the sky above him, with but one thought standing out like a black pinnacle in the waves of pain and faintness which swept over him— that now he *could* not return to Bride. The power of choice had been shot away from him. It might even be that he should never see her again. . . .

By signs the two women intimated to the foreigners that they should carry the wounded man into their miserable dwelling, and the very much sobered adventurers, after having poured their last drops of brandy down his throat, deposited him there upon a bed consisting merely of a deerskin spread over some tufts of heather. On this they made him as comfortable as they could, and then, since he seemed to wish it, left him and went outside to confer upon the situation.

And here Marie-Cyprien de Lancize told Maxence de Galand what he thought of him and the pass to which he had brought the two of them, not to speak of his victim, with such complete lack of ambiguity that the Chevalier hotly suggested an adjournment to a convenient distance in order to put the question of his recent behaviour to the arbitrament of the sword.

"If the sun shone in this country more than once in five days," returned his comrade scornfully, "I should be tempted to think that you were suffering from a sunstroke! How, if you please, would the one of us killing the other help the survivor to find the Prince or even to reach France again? If you have a fancy for steel reflect that we may easily, both of us, receive one of those great ugly Highland daggers in our vitals, and that before another day has dawned! Some petticoated mountaineer has only to arrive upon the scene to be given an account of what has occurred by these women, whose speech we do not understand, and Mr. Maclean will be amply avenged! Luckily there seem to be no men in this desolate place."

Maxence de Galand hung his sulky head and kicked with his alien footgear at some peats lying near him. He acknowledged that he had been too hasty; but how was he to know what was going to happen in the case of a wild Highlander? The man had looked very threatening, had laid his hand upon his dagger, and moved forward; he himself had merely fired in self-defence, as anyone would have done.

"Laid his hand upon his dagger!" exclaimed the Vicomte. "But he had no dagger! You saw that as well as I did, afterwards."

"But I thought he had one," muttered the Chevalier angrily.

"Better to look closer before you shoot an unarmed man, especially when you have a stream between you into the bargain," counselled Marie-Cyprien. "And what was it that you said to provoke him so?"

But the culprit was saved a reply. The younger woman had come out of the hovel, and, approaching with justifiable nervousness, made signs to M. de Lancize that he should go in again.

It was difficult on entering to see anything at first. But from the corner where they had laid him came the voice of the wounded Highlander, curiously flattened, but not faint.

"Is that you, Monsieur de Lancize? I should like to speak to you."

Old Mrs. Kennedy, who was sitting beside him on some kind of rough stool, hitched herself off and bundled away.

"Sit down," continued the voice, and the Frenchman took the old woman's place, looking down anxiously at the man whom his comrade's hasty action had stretched there. The ill light did not hide from him the pallor under the tan which four months of lurking almost uninterruptedly in the open had set on Ranald Maclean's features, and those features themselves were altered and drawn. It was the most miserably unfortunate occurrence . . .

"Monsieur Maclean," began the young officer fervently, "there are really no words to express my profound regret——"

"Then do not search for them," broke in Ranald with a harsh little laugh. "Nor indeed have you personal cause for apology . . . unless your crazy companion was of your own choosing. However, it is not of myself that I wish to speak, but of how you are to obtain a guide to take you to the Prince."

"The Prince! We cannot continue our journey leaving you thus—our doing!"

"Had your friend shot me dead it would not, I imagine, have made the slightest difference to the papers you carry," observed Ranald dryly. "And I am not dead. You can do nothing for me by remaining here; you would only add two more mouths to diminish these poor people's store of oatmeal. If you can but prevail upon this man at the mouth of the glen to act as your guide for at least part of the way, my misfortune has no importance—except to myself. I have spoken with the younger of these women and she has agreed, when twilight comes on, to accompany you down the glen to Fassefern. There she will find this man they know of, and, if he consents to guide you, will pass on to him the instructions which I have given her. That is the best I can do." And having said this, Ranald shut his eyes.

"It is a great deal more than we deserve," answered Marie-Cyprien in a subdued manner. "Well, I will tell that imbecile comrade of mine, and we will await the coming of dusk." And as the Highlander gave no further sign he, after sitting there a little longer, got up and went quietly forth again.

But Ranald was neither asleep nor, at the moment, exhausted. The first shock had passed, and the physical pain had dulled. It was the mental torment which was beginning to rack him now. Here he must lie and lie; here, possibly, if the wound were to mortify, he must die, without ever seeing Bride again, without ever begging her forgiveness. Oh, if only, only he had turned back while he still had the chance! Now that chance was gone, perhaps for ever.

All through that long afternoon he lay either with his eyes shut or fixed almost unwaveringly on the low aperture which was the door. It was hot in the windowless hut, where the fire was never allowed to go entirely out; the deerskin smelt; shoots of agony went through him if he moved his leg in the slightest degree. And this was only the beginning. He would be in fever to-night, he knew; it was edging upon him already. All the more reason for doing what he had in mind while he yet could.

The sun was sending almost level rays sideways through the aperture when he asked the young woman for a drink of water, and then, raising himself with pain and difficulty on to one elbow, fished out a little pocket-book he had

R

with him. He put this on the beaten earth floor, wrote a few words in Gaelic on a leaf, and, lying back again, tore it out. The effort, mental and physical, exhausted him more than he had anticipated, and clutching the leaf he drifted off immediately into a region between swooning and sleep, where waves from both those unplumbed seas broke over his head, and then, receding, left him awake and perfectly conscious.

It was in this latter state that Cyprien de Lancize found him when he came in to take a remorseful farewell at dusk. It was practically dark now inside the hut, but the old woman had lit a torch of fir-root and stuck it in the customary projecting iron ring. The flame, spurting and leaping, fell strangely on the Highlander's face; it looked to the Frenchman considerably sunken already, and a real pang of apprehension seized him. What was going to become of the unfortunate Mr. Maclean, left helpless in this hovel?

The light had roused Ranald. He looked up, remembered what he had in his hand and beckoned to his visitor to stoop.

"Will you do me a favour?"

"You know, Mr. Maclean, that I will do anything in my power, and gladly!"

"Then . . . take this letter, and when you get into Badenoch . . . give it, if you possibly can . . . to some man who knows Loch Rannoch, and tell him . . . to take it to Inchrannoch House . . . at the far end of the loch, on the river . . ."

"You may rely on me to do my utmost!" replied Marie-Cyprien earnestly. Ranald folded together the little paper with hands that fumbled a trifle and held it up to him. The Frenchman, about to put it carefully into an inner pocket, hesitated. "There is no name on this, Mr. Maclean," he said almost apologetically. And as the wounded man gave a sound almost like a groan, he added, with some hesitation, "Will you allow me to write it? I have a pencil here."

Ranald nodded. The hut for a moment swung round, then steadied itself. "Write, 'Mrs. Maclean, Inchrannoch House,'" he said, and from the floor watched the pencil move. "We were only married in May," he went on, in an odd and rather breathless fashion . . . "married in the kitchen, with soldiers in the house . . . and I then off to hide in the heather again. . . . You'll understand that I wish to reassure my young wife . . . she's but a girl still. . . ."

Marie-Cyprien de Lancize bent down and laid a finger on the speaker's pulse. It was hammering. "God knows," he said with feeling, "that I wish with all my soul there were no need for you to reassure her! But she shall have this letter; I will find a messenger somehow. And when we return from our mission, Mr. Maclean, you may be sure that we shall do our best to learn how you fare. If these women will but keep the wounds clean and well washed with water from that brook—you must make them understand that, for I cannot." And after a moment he asked with concern, "Is there *no* place from which I could despatch a surgeon to you?"

Ranald shook his head. "Only Fort William—which would mean your arrest . . . and mine as well. I shall not want for what care these good women can give me . . . Many and many a man would have been thankful for as much after Culloden . . . Only, I implore you, Monsieur de Lancize, do your utmost to find a messenger for that letter to my wife!"

"I swear I will; it is the only reparation I can make for this most unfortunate occurrence!" He bent down and pressed Ranald's hot hand, for young Mrs. Kennedy, a plaid drawn about her head, was standing by the door ready to set out. Of the Chevalier de Galand there was no sign; he was keeping carefully out of view.

"Reparation," muttered Ranald to himself, seizing on the word. "This is reparation, perhaps . . . But it brings *her* no profit . . ."

"What did you say?"

"Nothing, nothing . . . Make haste, make haste!" The fir torch, nearly burnt down, gave a sudden flare. Ranald tried to raise himself. "Why, who's that woman by the door? I *can* ask her forgiveness then!" But he relapsed, his voice gone dead again. "No, no, it is not she . . . I beg your pardon—was I talking nonsense? I believe I have a trifle of fever. . . . As I say, Monsieur de Lancize"—he spoke now with the precision of a man picking his way among words which threatened to elude him—"as I say, Mrs. Ken . . . Kennedy will instruct this guide where to find the . . . the . . . you know whom I mean . . . I have given her details . . . I wish you God speed!"

But he spoke the farewell in Gaelic, not knowing that he used that tongue. The Vicomte Marie-Cyprien de Lancize, casting a last long, doubtful look at what he could see of him just before the torch light failed entirely, joined Mrs. Kennedy at the door of the hut and went out.

CHAPTER XXII

(1)

RECENT events had considerably strained the relations between the Vicomte de Lancize and the Chevalier de Galand, and both gentlemen were remarkably silent as they went that evening with the Highland woman down the glen towards Loch Eil. With her, of course, they could not converse at all, and it remained to be seen whether the man whom she was to find and if possible induce to accompany them to Badenoch could speak anything but Gaelic either. It was to be hoped that he had some English, which Marie-Cyprien could speak fluently, and his comrade a little. Yet even if he had not he could still act as a guide.

It was almost dark when Mrs. Kennedy returned to the spot where she had left them near the policies of Fassefern, the house almost on the loch itself, which belonged to John Cameron, the younger brother of Lochiel. She had with her a taciturn, bearded individual who proved, fortunately, to have some knowledge of the English language, pronouncing it, however, in a high sing-song very strange to foreign ears. He agreed to conduct them part of the way—as far, that was to say, as the head of Loch Treig, and to give them directions for the rest of their journey. He calculated that by setting off immediately (for they would do well to get past the neighbourhood of Fort William under cover of night) they would be at the further end of Glen Nevis by sunrise.

The word "Nevis" alarmed M. de Lancize, who in their previous progress along Loch Eil had had the square implacable shoulders of the great mountain always before his eyes, and had learnt its name. But Hugh Cameron assured him that he would not be called upon to climb it; he had been speaking of the Glen and not of the Ben. And he informed them that once they were past a place which he called . . . but neither of the Frenchmen could seize the name of Achriabhach . . . the open glen would soon cease and they would be among the mountains, and safe even if it were daylight.

Marie-Cyprien shrugged his shoulders under his reversed coat. No doubt. And the Chevalier de Galand, when this pronouncement was translated to him (for he seemed to find the Highlander's English quite unintelligible), swore vigorously, and declared that when he returned to France he should go and settle in the flattest district he could possibly find—in La Beauce, for instance.

(2)

It was daylight; more, the sun had risen. And it was as their guide had said; they were out of Glen Nevis, had scrambled over one waterfall, gone along a ledge-like path, and turning a corner, found themselves not long afterwards in a level space with a farmhouse facing the eternal thunder of another and much higher waterfall, a big one, racing down the side of that same ever-present mountain, which Marie-Cyprien had now learnt was the loftiest in the whole of the British Isles, a fact which he had no wish to dispute. All the latter part of the night they seemed to have been going under its bastions, first south-east, then, as now, almost due east; the stars had shown its horrid bulk. And it was still with them, and another nearly as great beside it, and another again; and on the right hand it was the same thing. Yet the young Frenchman stared fascinated and weary at the long cataract.

"In the name of God, let us remove ourselves from this racket!" said Galand crossly. "Imagine choosing to pitch a dwelling here!"

But Hugh Cameron was indicating that they should go

into the farmhouse for rest and refreshment; and afterwards it was decided that they should sleep awhile there
also, and not proceed until late afternoon.

It was about five o'clock when they set forth again,
following the stream, the track always rising under Ben
Nevis's rival and neighbour, Aonach Beag, and the
travellers having always to cross the many little tribu-
taries hurrying down from the heights on either side to
swell the stream which they were following. Only for
some quarter of a mile or so were they without the company of running water, for when they came to the watershed there was another stream coursing in the direction
which they were taking—the Amhainn Reidh, their guide
called it.

As they trudged along Marie-Cyprien found himself
thinking a good deal about Ranald Maclean, to whom
their recent meeting had proved so disastrous, and, with
a certain curiosity, about this young wife of his. He himself would certainly do his utmost to find a messenger to
take her the letter with which he was entrusted, but the
time for that was not yet, for they were, he gathered from
Hugh Cameron, many miles from the western end of
Loch Rannoch, which loch itself was a good ten miles or
more long, while Inchrannoch House was, so Mr. Maclean
had said, at its further, its eastern end, on the river which
flowed out of it. Marie-Cyprien had repeated these scant
details to himself in order to direct his messenger (when
he found him); but he could naturally only transmit them
if the man could speak English. Often and often in the
last weeks had he and his comrade found occasion to
curse that architectural calamity, the Tower of Babel.

But why, he wondered, had the unfortunate Mr.
Maclean—M. de Lancize easily deduced that it was only
the onset of fever which had forced the utterances from
him—why had he spoken of asking his wife's forgiveness?
Probably for the usual reason, that he had been deceiving
her and she had found him out. But that must always
remain a conjecture, for even if he had been dishonour-

able enough to read the unsealed letter committed to him, Marie-Cyprien strongly suspected that he would find it written in the heathenish language which, it seemed, was spoken even by educated Highlanders.

At last their stream and rough path brought the travellers down to the end of a long, grim funnel of a lake pressed between high mountains and trending northwards. This, Hugh Cameron informed them, was Loch Treig, and here he would part from them. They were to follow this strip of level shore until in about half a mile they came to a stream—it helped them little to be told its name, the Amhainn Chamabhreac—this they must cross, and after a little they would come on a rough path leading up and away from it, which made for a smaller lake, Loch Ossian, running north-east. If they followed round the southern shore of this loch they would find at its end a fold in the mountains down which ran a stream from the Bealach Dhu—that was to say, the Black Pass—a matter of five miles or so further on. But before they got to the Black Pass the big mountain they sought, Ben Alder, would itself be on their right hand, and from what the guide had been told they would most likely fall in with a scout somewhere on its sides, and so they would be taken without more trouble to . . . him whom God preserve!

"It appears to me that we ourselves shall have considerable need of the Divine preservation," remarked Marie-Cyprien, after communicating these instructions to the gloomy Galand. "If we lay our bones among the mountains our blood will certainly be upon the head of this obstinate fellow." For they had tried without success to induce Hugh Cameron to accompany them further.

Galand, who seemed dully resigned even to that fate, observed with some sense that at any rate they had better not engage upon any enterprise involving a "Black Pass" except in broad daylight. Cameron had indicated a fair-sized croft not far off, where they could get food—he himself had turned back without it—and Galand suggested spending the night there as well. And although the bed which they shared had undoubtedly other tenants as well, they were too weary to care very much.

(3)

"Corbleu! what a singularly unpleasant spot!" observed the Vicomte de Lancize, with distaste.

It was about eight o'clock next morning, and the two compatriots were standing at the end of Loch Ossian, to which, after about four miles of uphill walking from Loch Treig, they had come as directed. The place was certainly not attractive, at least upon this particular day, for Loch Ossian, being nearly thirteen hundred feet above sea-level, was not a little windswept, and the view southward over the beginning of the desolate Moor of Rannoch was discouraging in the extreme—patches of black bogwater, soulless grass that shivered in the wind, stones, curlews and advancing rain-clouds. The loch itself was level-shored and not large, but away over its further end were visible the gloomy heights which contained this ominously named Black Pass. However, there was nothing for it, and the two Frenchmen began to trudge forward along the loch side, carefully avoiding the dark, oozy peat-holes which gaped for the unwary foot.

And ahead Ben Alder—if it was Ben Alder—continued to clothe himself with cloud; sharp drops of rain began to flick at them in the wind. It was early yet, but they were both tired; they had covered more than thirty miles since leaving the hut in the glen. One of Galand's brogues showed signs of disintegration, and as for Cyprien de Lancize, he had his only remaining pocket-handkerchief stuffed into a boot. But they neither of them said anything; they went on. Somewhere—at least so they had been led to believe—somewhere in that jumble of mountain slopes they should find the Prince de Galles, and the object of their weeks of tramping and wandering would be fulfilled when they at last handed over the despatches, of which, for safety's sake, they each carried half.

Marie-Cyprien was thinking of all sorts of things as they trudged along: of his maritime experiences, none too pleasant, on board the *Bien Trouvée,* of those in the victory over the English at Fontenoy in the May of last year—a near thing that had been, too!—of a girl at Tournay who had pleased him, of whether his family had given him up for lost, and of what a sulky fellow Galand had become.

Quite suddenly the sulky fellow stopped. "I am not going along this lake of hell any longer!" he announced angrily, facing round upon his companion.

"And where, pray, *are* you going, *mon cher?*"

"You see that track along the hillside there," said Galand, pointing away from the loch to the south-east. "I believe that would be a much better way to come at this accursed Ben Alder."

"But, *juste ciel,* it is at right angles to our route to the Col Noir!"

"That is exactly why," replied his fellow-wanderer, with animation. "You remember that rough map we were shown by our host this morning, and the position of that very long lake behind this mountain with a name like a Jew? It is clear to me that if we can get round that massif on which the path runs and then turn north-westwards, we shall come to the end of the long lake and the other side of this Ben Alder. Like this." He whipped out a pocket-book and began to sketch. "The route in my opinion has two advantages; it may prove shorter, and by taking it we shall avoid altogether the Col Noir—towards which, moreover, I think you said there was no track after we have left the end of this lake here."

"Yes, that is true," said the Vicomte de Lancize, hesitating. The suggestion was certainly tempting, for the track along the hillside looked good and he remembered having noticed on the map the position of the long north-ward-trending lake behind these heights, and even its name, Ericht. "Very well," he said; "I agree," and the pilgrims turned their faces southwards and boldly set their feet upon the lower slopes of Carn Dearg.

The track was undoubtedly quite good—but there was so much of it! Two miles, four miles, six miles, and still there was no sign of the "massif" coming to an end. And all the while the couple were coming nearer to the Moor of Rannoch proper, four hundred square miles of forlorn and dangerous bogland, and getting glimpses of desolate lochans lost in the waste; now and again, as the mist lifted raggedly in one quarter or another, a vista of peaks and shoulders innumerable would show itself. It was true that they themselves were raised above the melancholy prospect of the moor as men walking along the cliffs are raised above the sea, but, like a sea in ill-humour, so did that forbidding expanse affect the mind.

At last the track along this species of scarp brought them, almost without their realising it, to a small, patchy river. It was the Gaoire, rushing in loops and pools through a bed strewn with stones straight into Loch Rannoch—though of its destination the travellers were at present unaware. They had missed the opening by which they might have turned off to Loch Ericht and were now a good deal too far south. Marie-Cyprien gave voice to this opinion.

"I wanted to turn off a while ago," retorted his compatriot angrily, "but you would not. God knows where we are now! I am sick to death of this fool's chase!"

"I cannot pretend that I am finding it delectable," returned his fellow-adventurer. He sat down and with grimaces drew off his boot. "As I thought!" Despite the protecting handkerchief, his heel was raw and bleeding. He got up again, and hopping down to a pool of the pebbly river, bathed the injury and discussed the situation.

But by the side of the river there was a distinct track, almost a road. If they followed it they might quite well come upon a hamlet or at least some person who would give them directions; perhaps even a house where they could get rest and shelter from the rain for a while, for they were both dog-tired. In fact, Maxence de Galand declared bluntly that he, at least, would not lament if he were captured by the English, for as a uniformed officer of a foreign power, his life would be perfectly safe, which it was not at the present, ranging this barbarous and waterlogged country without a guide, without provisions, without proper foot-gear even—"as well wear the sandals affected by the Holy Apostles as these objects!" he concluded, looking down with undisguised hatred at his dilapidated brogues.

"As to the guide," observed the Vicomte dryly, "you should not have put a ball into our first one—Mr. Maclean. Had you not done so, we might have been paying our respects to the Prince de Galles in yonder mountain fastness by this time!"

"Don't think it!" retorted Galand hotly. "Your Mr. Maclean would not have turned back with us—at least, it was not certain. Why should he? he said he was going to the coast."

"Perhaps because he has a . . . *enfin*, I don't know why, except from loyalty," replied Marie-Cyprien, suddenly deciding that he would not reveal that Galand's victim had a wife in these regions, but deciding also that the time was come to attempt to forward the letter to that lady.

Going very slowly now, they resumed their progress, and about half a mile further on fell in with two natives, one of whom could speak English. This man told them that they would soon come to a village by the name of Dunan, whence they might attain Loch Ericht by following up the stream, the Allt Chaldar, which came down there; or they might push on for four miles or so until they came to Camuserieht, where the River Ericht itself came down into Loch Rannoch, and follow it up.

"Loch Rannoch!" exclaimed the Vicomte. "Are we near Loch Rannoch?"

Indeed they were; and if, said their Highland informant, looking in a significant manner at their uniforms, they might not be wishing to meet with soldiers, it would be better to take the first of these routes for Loch Ericht, since there was a post of Campbells at the head of Loch Rannoch, and though they wore the tartan they were, he explained, in Government pay.

It was the first the two travellers had heard of this, no one having warned them of these hostile presences, since neither Ranald Maclean nor Hugh Cameron had ever supposed they would find themselves in this neighbourhood. "Soldiers!" repeated the Chevalier de Galand below his breath, and took on a musing look which his companion did not see . . . and for a very good reason. For Marie-Cyprien de Lancize was hunting furiously in the inner pocket where he had bestowed Ranald Maclean's little letter to his wife, turning over everything it contained, feeling in all his other pockets, although he was positive that he had never put it in any of those. And at last there could be no avoiding the shock of the unpleasant, the indeed rather disgraceful fact that he had lost it! Here was a possible messenger, but no longer any message! The young man swore at himself with vigour. Really he was as devoid of wits as his comrade, and had behaved nearly as ill towards Mr. Maclean. But when Galand, after watching this performance, asked the reason for it, Marie-Cyprien told him a lie.

Parting with the two Highlanders, the weary nomads started on once more, hoping that this village of Dunan would produce a meal. The rain had now ceased, but wherever they turned their eyes it was to see bulging clouds sitting in a most purposeful manner on the tops of the mountains, near or distant; and, at a lower level, stones and rocks distributed with the utmost profusion and impartiality over every slope or level, even over the river-bed, in a manner which suggested the use of some monstrous pepper-pot. And the warfare of the river with these obstacles had in itself a dispiriting sound. Hampered by his sore heel, M. de Saxe's ex-aide-de-camp began to contemplate exchanging his boots, if possible, at the

village ahead of them for the Highland brogues despised
by Galand, as more pliable. Then somehow his thoughts
leapt nimbly by way of contrast to a certain very elegant
pair of red-heeled shoes, which he had admired upon their
fair owner's feet the last time he was in Paris. Yes, he
had certainly rather be in Madame de Coucy's boudoir
at this moment, even though he was tired of her, and
tepid love-making was never to his taste. He had not got
tired nearly so soon of Madame de Jaligny, ugly as she
was.

These memories, though detached rather than fond,
must have had power to remove the Vicomte de Lancize
a considerable distance from his present surroundings, for
he had perceived nothing of what was threatening them
until Galand suddenly gripped his arm.

"Look behind you!"

Marie-Cyprien turned quickly. A body of Highlanders
in blue and green tartan, with two mounted officers in
scarlet coats, were advancing rapidly along the rough road
in their rear. Where they had sprung from only the mist
knew.

"*Ciel*, this is the end!" thought Marie-Cyprien, with an
angry bound of the heart. After all their tribulations,
when they were nearly at their goal! There was nowhere
to run to, and not a trace of shelter here; both Galand
and he were tired out, and he was lame into the bargain.
Nevertheless, he tugged out his pistol—his sword being in
the custody of that Ross-shire bog—and hobbled as fast
as he could towards a boulder which he espied ahead by
the side of the road, resolved to set his back against it
and make what resistance he could.

Not such were the actions of the Chevalier Maxence de
Galand. "You are a fool, Lancize!" he called out in a
high voice after his companion. "This is the best thing
that could have happened to us!" And he deliberately
walked back towards the oncoming force.

In the end both gestures, the resigned and the defiant,
came to much the same thing; it was, in fact, somewhat

galling to be left so long with one's back against a large, cold stone waiting to be made prisoner. For the two officers were so busy questioning Galand that at first they gave themselves little concern about his less submissive companion. One of them did indeed give a glance his way and said a word or two to his men—not, however, to urge them on after the quarry, who waited against the boulder, increasingly annoyed at this cavalier disregard, and half resolved to send a bullet into the midst of the group to show that he was not so negligible after all. Had he had the full use of his legs he believed that he would have done it, but with this hampering heel it would have been senseless.

After a minute or so one of the officers spurred his horse towards him, half a dozen kilted followers trotting after.

"I understand that you are a French officer," he called out in English. "You will therefore be treated as a prisoner of war. Give up your pistol, sir, and surrender yourself as your comrade has done."

But that was just what Marie-Cyprien could not stomach doing. He was a Latin, and his native logic indicated to him that there was no conceivable advantage to be gained by shooting this officer—on the contrary; yet he felt that in order to differentiate himself from the white-livered Galand he would like at least to shoot *at* him—deprive him of his three-cornered hat, for instance. So he did not answer, but brought his pistol to full cock.

He never got a chance to fire it, which was certainly as well for him; but he did get the chance of a rough-and-tumble resistance, for three Highlanders were upon him in a moment and pulled him down. The distinction was therefore his of limping into the village of Dunan with his arms secured to his sides and an appearance so generally dishevelled as to remove him several degrees further from the usual conception of a smart officer of Dauphin-Dragons or even one of the *compagnies franches de la marine*. M. de Galand meanwhile walked free; but he studiously avoided his companion's glance.

In a small house in Dunan village they were both systematically searched, even though M. de Galand had apparently already given up his half of the despatches which they carried. Marie-Cyprien's boots—that very popular hiding-place—when removed disclosed nothing save evidence of the plight of their owner's heel, but the papers were soon ripped out of the lining of his coat. Since they were in cipher their actual falling into the hands of the English was not a very great matter; the loss to Prince Charles Edward by their non-delivery the bearers were unable to estimate, since they had small idea of their contents.

What caused the Vicomte de Lancize, however, a good deal of anxiety was the assumption which he feared the two officers would make that the Prince, for whom these papers were presumably intended, was somewhere in the neighbourhood; he could only hope that Galand had had the good sense not to admit this. But Galand would not look at him, and he was afraid to speak to him in French lest the officers should understand. On his own account, therefore, he hastily treated his captors to a story of having received directions to go the length of Loch Rannoch until they met a guide who was to conduct them still further, to what point he did not know. And since he was, naturally, entirely ignorant of the geography of Perthshire it was as well that he did not attempt to be more specific. After this it appeared that the two prisoners were to be taken to the temporary barracks which had been erected at the nearer end of the loch, until orders were received as to their final destination. To his surprise and gratification Marie-Cyprien was lent one of the officers' horses in consideration of his flayed heel; but Galand had to go on foot.

The temporary possession of a steed naturally encouraged in the Vicomte's mind the idea of giving his captors the slip after all; but at present, though his own arms were free, the horse was controlled by the Highlanders who led it on either side. About two miles from

Dunan the party crossed the Gaoire on a rough, temporary bridge and came to some makeshift quarters, a couple of cottages and a hastily-put-up building made of tree-trunks. The captive saw that he would now be separated from his horse before he had had any chance of utilising it, and indeed signs were soon made to him to dismount.

Over his shoulder, just before he reluctantly quitted the saddle, he observed that the mounted officer had already alighted and had gone into the foremost of the cottages, perhaps to arrange quarters for the prisoners. With no definite plan in his head Marie-Cyprien yet conceived that it might be of ultimate advantage to pretend to be a great deal lamer than he actually was; so on arriving at the ground he made a very wry face and, no one staying him, limped to a sawn-off end of pine-trunk left by the builders and sank down upon it. Galand was standing moodily between two of his kilted escort; the rest, the dismounted officer also having disappeared, began to talk together in a very unmilitary fashion. One of them led the other officer's horse up to the beast which Marie-Cyprien had ridden and left the two side by side, nosing at each other—evidently either so quiet by nature or so pleased to be near their stables that nobody troubled to hold them or even to hitch up their bridles to a post or nail. And the Vicomte observing this was visited by a sudden wild idea. It was worth trying, anyhow. But he must obviously go off with both horses. . . .

Next moment, before even a cry could be raised, the lame French prisoner was off his log, across the few yards which separated him from the horses, had flung himself on to the back of the nearer, made it rear so that it knocked over the Highlander who had seized the reins of the other, and was off with both of them towards the loch, now visible not far ahead. So astounded were the soldiers at the audacity of the action and its extreme suddenness that it was several seconds before they woke to the realisation of what had happened. And one or two cried aloud that he must be some kind of a wizard. But this M. de Lancize was not; only, by training, a cavalry officer.

He knew from the shouts and the one or two wild shots fired that the kilted soldiery were pursuing him to the best of their ability, but they were, naturally, soon outdistanced. The pace he got out of both horses was most gratifying; unaccustomed to being ridden postillion fashion, they were even a trifle unmanageable for a moment or two; then they settled down to a steady gallop. Naturally the fugitive did not want both of them; the second was a nuisance; but if he abandoned it too soon it would be utilised for pursuit. He wondered if they had any more at the post; probably not ready saddled, anyhow. If he loosed the second horse it might even return to its stable, and he had a momentary regret for the loss of his sword, with which he might have hamstrung the animal—no, no, *par Dieu,* he could not have done that to the poor beast! Had he even a switch, however, he might flog it off the track among the trees or up a glen. But he could not stop to cut one for this purpose.

Here, as he tore along beside the big loch whose further side was veiled in mist, came a hamlet on his right hand. Even if the inhabitants did not try to stop him, they would probably give news of him; he did not know that this was Camghouran, a Cameron colony, to which no wearer of a Campbell tartan need look for assistance. With his led horse's nose scarcely a head behind that of his own steed, he dashed through a scattering group of children and went on.

After a while the Black Wood of Rannoch began to loom ahead. Marie-Cyprien skirted it for a while, then slackened his pace, turned in among the giant pines and ashes, loosed the second horse, kicked it hard and saw it canter off, shaking its head, among the ancient trees. Should he hide in here? It seemed the beginning of an extensive forest, thick with stubby bushes of juniper and great cushions of moss and bilberry. . . . No, not in this weather! A roof of some kind was really becoming a necessity. Perhaps further on—for he guessed that he was not more than half-way along the loch—he could find a hut or some kind of shelter.

Returning to the track by the lochside, there being no other, the fugitive proceeded, but at a less breakneck pace, since his steed was a trifle blown and there were still no sounds of pursuit. How fortunate that horses were, apparently, scarce in the Highlands! Marie-Cyprien wondered if those petticoated individuals who had captured him could track by hoof-marks like the Red Indians of North America. If so, they might follow the other horse's traces. A Red Indian, however, he believed, would probably be able to tell which of the two animals was riderless, so it was possible that Highlanders, who were in his eyes very little removed from Peaux-Rouges, had this savage faculty also.

At last the end of the long grey sheet of water was beginning to come into view. It seemed to terminate in a kind of beach. Was he to ride round this, or continue straight past the end of the lake towards the open-looking country ahead? But one could not go fleeing on like this for ever! M. de Lancize had begun to realise afresh how hungry he was and how weary, and that his heel was hurting like fire. . . . And then he suddenly remembered, what he had never once given a thought to since the encounter with the foe, that Ranald Maclean's wife lived in a house at the far end of Loch Rannoch, on the banks of the river which issued from it—the directions which he had intended to give to his messenger recurring aptly to his memory. If he could but find this house Madame Maclean would surely grant him shelter, even though it were of the most temporary; and he could in return give her news—not very happy news, it was true—of her husband. Why not try to find it? And if he were recaptured there, *eh bien,* he was recaptured, but in the meantime he might possibly enjoy a night in a proper bed with sheets.

But to reach the river coming out of the lake and the

house thereon he must, he saw, follow round the extremity of the lake until he came to the stream in question, and he could not do it on this horse, for he would certainly be betrayed by its presence.

By the little beach, therefore, Marie-Cyprien dismounted, and picking up stones, threw them mercilessly after the luckless animal, which made off at once away from the loch. The chimneys of a house were visible in that direction, but they could not be Maclean's. Looking back he could discern nothing coming along the lake side, nevertheless he thought that he could catch the distant beat of hoofs. The grey loch was lipping morosely at its tract of foreshore; a stretch of boggy land faced him if he turned his back upon it, and disheartening hills half shrouded in mist were everywhere. No, he was hanged if he would spend the night in the open or in a cattle-byre either! There, surely, was the river, and quite near it, a house behind sheltering fir-trees! Marie-Cyprien began to run haltingly towards this dwelling, convinced that he had not been mistaken about those hoof-beats. How his heel hurt—no need to feign lameness now! And yet there was every need of hurry. . . .

CHAPTER XXIII

THE work of a house must go on no matter how keen
the heart-break within its walls; and the work in question serves at least to distract the mind. Two days after
Mr. Stewart's removal to Perth the preparations for the
great semi-annual wash at Inchrannoch House came to a
head, and that extensive purification began, under
Phemie's superintendence and with Bride's co-operation.
All the sheets and other household linen, and personal
linen too, which had been accumulating for months in the
attics, were brought down, and the whole personnel of
Inchrannoch, with the exception of Worrall, attacked it
vigorously amid a maelstrom of soap-suds, lye, steam, and
the slap and swish of water.

The day, which had begun by being fine, with a good
drying wind, had tailed off into rain; the many clothes-
lines in the open did not therefore yield up their fruitage
as quickly as they should have done, and it was waste of
time to hang out fresh articles. Nevertheless, the wash
proceeded with undiminished vigour; outside the wash-
house there was a kind of open pent-house on whose floor
were already rising several mounds of newly-wrung sheets
fresh from the tub, ready to be hung out if to-morrow
should prove favourable, when, if there were sun, it would
be possible to do some bleaching as well.

Mrs. MacRobbie had retired from the fray in order to
cook. Jeanie MacPherson and the girl from the village
who was helping her chattered in subdued tones at their
joint tub, Phemie worked in grim silence, and Bride—
Bride had a little while ago discovered a pocket handkerchief of Ranald's and was washing that slowly, by itself,
in mind far removed from this wet, steamy, busy scene.
In spirit she was following her husband, along mountain-

sides, through heather, by streams, down to a beach where a boat waited to take him to his island home, and there saying: "Ranald, if you do not come back to me, I must come to you. . . ." and on that finding him her Ranald again, not that cruel and ungrateful stranger who had flung out of their bedroom five nights ago.

And just then, with the most astonishing suddenness, another stranger ran hobbling round the side of the house and was among them in the steam and the piles of wet linen—a dishevelled, handsome, foreign-looking young man in a dilapidated blue uniform, who glanced hastily round and then addressed Bride in a stiff, carefully-moving English, with hurry beating at the back of his words:

"Madam, would you have the goodness to allow me to hide somewhere? I am a French officer, and the soldiers from the end of the lake chase me!"

The amazed Bride withdrew her hands from the suds. "But, sir, this is the first place where they will search for you. They have already——" She broke off; *were* those hoof-beats that she heard? "Quick, quick then! the sheets!"

M. de Lancize looked round too, bewildered. There was certainly in one corner of this half open-air laundry a solid pile of damp sheets—was the young lady designating those as a hiding-place? Surely not; rather the still larger heap of unwashed ones at the other side. He made for this mound, but the fair laundress rushed after him.

"No, sir—they might well look here, but scarcely among those!" It was the wet pile which she indicated.

A second or two later she and Phemie were removing the topmost sheets from the mound, tugging and pushing aside the heavy, damp, twisted bundles of linen until they had made among them a hollow large enough to hold a man of moderate size if he lay crouched up. They then pointed to this hollow.

The fugitive hesitated, as well he might.

"*Mes bottes, madame!*" he exclaimed apologetically,

looking down at those bespattered and disgraceful objects.

"What do they matter?" returned this bright-haired young lady, and Marie-Cyprien felt her little wet hands giving him a push. "Quick—I hear someone in the house!" So without more ado M. de Saxe's erstwhile aide-de-camp stooped and crawled into the moist, hard cavity provided for him, disposing himself as best he could and thinking, as another sheet was placed entirely over him, that the soiled but dry linen would have felt far less inhospitable. Then came the piling above him, on top of this sheet, of more and more of these chilly weights. The young man wondered if he ran any risk of stifling. This was really rather a damnable sort of hiding-place, and ludicrous into the bargain! Had he been a student of Shakespeare, which he was not, he might have been visited with memories of the third act of *The Merry Wives of Windsor*.

Bride had her arms back in the wash-tub, the picture of housewifely industry, by the time that Worrall, with a man in uniform behind him, appeared in the back doorway, coming out of the house.

"Miss Bride, here's an officer coom lookin' for a Frenchman!" His voice expressed justifiable indignation. "Aw axed him what i' God's name we'd be doin' wi' Frenchmen here!"

A Highland officer of heated appearance pushed past him. "Are you the mistress of the house, madam? Two French officers were captured some hours ago near Dunan, and one gave us the slip from the barracks at the Gaoire, going off with a couple of horses, too. We have reason to think he has taken refuge here."

Bride withdrew her hands and wiped them. "You are welcome to search the house, sir, as much as you like," she replied, with dignity. "If a French officer has gained admittance I am ignorant of it, for, as you see, I have been occupied this long while past out here in the laundry."

Evidences of this prolonged industry were certainly not to seek. The officer looked round, and Bride feared for a

moment that he was going to question the girls—being a
Highlander, and probably indeed a Campbell, he would
certainly have the Gaelic to do it with. "Go and fetch
some more water," she said hastily, distrusting not their
loyalty but their discretion, hoping, too, that they would
have the sense not to return. With a clattering of pails
the damsels reluctantly withdrew.

Meanwhile the lieutenant of Loudoun's had gone and
kicked at the big heap of soiled linen, but not as if he
thought it concealed his quarry. With a grunt he then
walked to the other heap, and moved aside a sheet. Finding it, perhaps, unpleasantly damp and heavy he desisted,
looked round, was apparently going to give an order for
the demolition of the pile, seemed to think better of it,
and was just turning away when, to the horror of the
two women, he suddenly drew his sword, inserted the toe
of his boot as a lever about half-way down the mound,
and thrust the blade some way into the crevice thus
formed.

Behind his back Phemie carried both her hands to her
mouth to suppress a cry. Bride stood very still, but her
cheeks paled abruptly to nearly the hue of the sheets.

The officer withdrew his sword, sheathed it, went, without looking at her, back to the door and called:

"Corporal! Go with this man to the stables and see if
the horse is there or hidden elsewhere; come back and
report to me. I must be satisfied of that before I search
the house. Take the corporal to the stable!" he said
sharply to Worrall.

Directly they were gone the invader, turning to Bride,
observed suddenly: "This is Inchrannoch House, is it
not?"

"Yes," she answered gravely.

"Then you are the young lady whom Sergeant Barclay
found last Thursday night with an English officer hidden
in her room!"

Bride made no reply.

The lieutenant laughed. "And now it seems you have

a French one to console you! Your taste in lovers is wide, madam!"

Bride flushed the brightest, most lovely red—the red of anger. "How dare you suggest such a thing, sir! It was my husband who was hidden there—as is known now." For she remembered the officer from Perth who had arrested Uncle Walter. As far away as that they knew the truth, so it was safe to admit it.

"So you say," said the lieutenant, still grinning. "Oh yes, I know that the Highlander who got Sergeant Barclay alone and nearly strangled the poor fellow early next morning gave himself out to be your husband. And the sergeant believed it. But everybody is not so simple. No man in his senses, having been saved thus, would risk capture immediately afterwards merely in order to prove that it was he who had been concealed!"

Bride had turned white now. But her little head was back and her eyes were fairly ablaze.

"Then who do you suppose, sir, did meet your sergeant and tell him the truth, if it was not my husband?"

"Faith, I can't tell you—but I don't doubt you could supply the name if you would. Someone—as the Highlander who saw him can testify who did not wear the Maclean tartan—is not your husband a Maclean? Some other lover, perhaps, solicitous about your good name!" He sniggered.

Bride fell back, appalled. Was it possible that a gentleman of Clan Diarmaid, as she supposed him to be . . . ! Thank God that Worrall was out of hearing.

Phemie, however, was not. Unable to contain herself, she had snatched up a piece of soap in one hand and a wet cloth in the other; and thus equipped advanced upon the speaker from her wash-tub.

"I'se advise ye gie yer foul tongue a wash wi' this!" she said threateningly, "though I doot if soap wad clean it! Sae yon's the way ye talk tae weemen when there's nae man handy tae teach ye manners! Ye dirty Cawmell, for twa pins I'd pit ye in the wash-tub!"

Tall, gaunt and muscular, Mrs. Reid looked very much like doing it. Bride caught her arm. "Oh, Phemie, hush! This gentleman" (she stressed the word) "does not know what he is saying; he is angry about this French officer he is after." And Worrall and the corporal becoming visible again at that moment, she said to the lieutenant:

"If you will go and search the house now 'twill be the greatest kindness you can do me!"

Since it was hardly to be supposed that the officer was alarmed by Phemie's threat, it must have been either Bride's patent aversion or the return of his corporal with the news that he could not find the horse anywhere, which put a term to his offensive surmises. He gave the man an order and said to Bride, with just a trace of shame in his manner: "You will come with me, if you please, madam. I shall need every place unlocking."

Bride gave him a steady look. "No, that I will not do—accompany you. My servant will unlock for you any door you wish; she knows where the keys are. Do not put any obstacles in this officer's way, Phemie; and remember that his manners are no concern of ours."

Phemie flung down the cloth and soap, wiped her hands on her apron and marched into the house without so much as looking at the lieutenant. He followed her; the corporal followed him; Worrall brought up the rear. Directly they were out of sight Bride sank down on a chair near the long trestle table and, her elbows on its soapy wetness, hid her face in her hands.

A step, a quick stumping step, and a gentle touch on her shoulder.

"What ails ye, Miss Bride? He'st find nobry—for theer's nobry t' find!"

Bride got up, passing the back of her hand across her eyes, and gave a half-hysterical little laugh. "But, Jonas, that's just it! There *is* someone—the French officer is here . . . only I think . . . I hope . . . that they will not find him now."

Worrall looked at her as if he thought her crazed.

"Here? In God's name, lass, wheer?"

She indicated the pile of washed sheets in the far corner. "Under those. But we had best not go near them until *they* are gone. Then we must hide him somewhere else."

Jonas Worrall stared from her to the white mound as if he could not believe his ears or his eyes. "Under a' them! But, lass, he's likely smoort by now!"

"I . . . I hope not!" said Bride, struggling with an unmirthful mirth. "We tried to arrange the sheets so that he could breathe . . . but 'tis true they are very heavy. No, Jonas, don't go near him! The soldiers might come out at any moment!"

Her servitor hesitated, looking from her to the corner. "Little use saving him from t' sodgers if theer's nowt to do wi' him after but bury him! What a place to choose, lass! Eh well, I suppose if he'd felt himsel smooring he'd 'a coom out."

"Yes. On the contrary, he has been very quiet, even when the officer drove his sword in among the sheets."

"He stoock his sword in! Then likely——"

"No, indeed, I do not think so!" said Bride, suppressing, however, a slight shiver. "I wish I could make sure that all is well with him, but I dare not do so yet.—Oh, Jonas, how can we get them gone quickly? They may be another hour searching in the house for what they will never find there! Go and see what they are doing; try to hasten them so that we can get the poor Frenchman out!"

"To try hastenin' 'em, Miss Bride, is just t' way to keep 'em longer," observed Worrall; but he went in, nevertheless.

A moment or two afterwards Bride, in spite of what she had said, approached the heap of sheets. She made pretence to feel the state of the top one, and then, bending her head, said: "Sir, are you—can you stay a while longer?"

There was no answer. Her heart contracted. "Monsieur, cannot you hear me? Is all well with you?"

It was immensely relieving to hear a muffled male voice ascending through the damp bundles. *"Oui, oui, ne vous tourmentez pas—je le supporterai jusqu'à ce que ces messieurs soient partis!"*

Bride waited for no more, but drawing a long breath hastened back towards the kitchen door and, possibly just because she had broken one intention, straightway broke another. She went in through the kitchen—which she could never enter now without remembering that the hearth, where Mrs. MacRobbie was at this moment stirring something, was the altar which had witnessed her strange marriage—into the hall, where two Loudouners were keeping guard over the entrance door. For she felt suddenly ashamed that because she had been so atrociously insulted she should neglect her duty to poor Uncle Walter—in not making sure, as he would have wished, that none of the "Campbells" went off with anything of value.

Then she heard the officer's voice at the head of the stairs. "He has brought in the horse, you say—found it at the gates of Innerchadden House? Then 'tis not much use searching here any longer; we are on the wrong track. Corporal, get the men together and we'll be off."

He came running down the stairs, his hand on his claymore. At sight of him Bride turned her back on him and went into the dining-room. He checked a moment, then followed her.

"Madam," he said, with evidences of discomfort in his manner, "will you allow me to apologise for my words? They were indeed unpardonable. I desire to say that I do believe that you passed off your husband as an English officer . . . and I offer my congratulations on your presence of mind."

Bride did not want his congratulations, but she was glad of the apology. She bent her head a second. "I should like to know, sir, what has wrought this change of opinion?" she asked in a very cold voice.

"Madam, the fact that in our search upstairs we came

upon an English uniform. Had there been a real wearer he would certainly not have gone away without it; and so again I make my apologies and take my leave. My men have done no damage." He bowed himself out of the room.

Bride watched from the window the little detachment ride off, one of the men with a second horse, splashed and wearied-looking, beside him. She would wait another three or four minutes and then inform the fugitive that he could come out from what must have proved a very moist and cramping retreat. Would she then have to hide him further? She heartily hoped not. He could surely now go on to his destination, whatever that was. She could not indeed imagine what a French officer was doing in these parts at all.

There seemed to be some commotion in the kitchen as she approached it a few minutes later, Mrs. MacRobbie scolding in high-pitched Gaelic. "You foolish girl, what ails you? In the name of the Good Being be silent! You'll have the Campbells back again!"

"What is it?" asked Bride, entering quickly. "Jeanie, do not shriek like that!"

"Miss Bride, Miss Bride," half sobbed the handmaid, pointing out of the door, "go and look! It is dead he will be, for sure . . . and the sheets all to be washed again! Oh, King of Virtues, the cruel fear it put on me!"

"Be quiet, girl!" said her young mistress vehemently. But she ran out herself into the washing place with a horrid apprehension at her heart. Her eyes went at once to the mound of sheets and were greeted as instantly by one particular pool spreading among the other little pools and streamlets which had gradually formed at the base of that damp heap . . . for its hue was a pale red. She gave a little cry, as Worrall, exclaiming: "This is not for thee, lass," went very quickly past her into the pent-house, followed by Phemie.

Bride steadied herself by holding on to the edge of a wash-tub while the two at the far corner dragged off the wet bundles and stooped over what was, perhaps—horrible thought!—a tomb. Yet since the moment when that sword had gone into the sheets she had spoken to the Frenchman and he had answered.

They were getting him out. Ashamed of her cowardice, Bride nevertheless shut her eyes for a moment. What would she see when she opened them—a limp, trailing body in a blue uniform?

No. What she saw was a young foreign officer standing upon his own feet between Phemie and Jonas Worrall, the latter of whom supported him. One of his arms was round Worrall's neck, the other Phemie was hastily swathing in what looked like a pillow-case. He was exceedingly pale, and in some way the wet components of his hiding-place had half dragged off his once white wig, so that his own short brown hair showed beneath. Bride ran forward.

"Monsieur, you are hurt—it is your arm then?—Oh, I hope not much!" His own tongue no doubt came easiest to the damaged adventurer at that juncture, for, with an attempt at a bow, he replied in it: *"Ce n'est qu'une espèce de saignée au bras, mademoiselle. . . . Permettez-moi de vous remercier mille fois de ce que vous venez de faire pour moi!"*

"Indeed I am deeply thankful——" began Bride, divided between relief and anxiety, but Phemie, holding the pillow-case round the injured arm, broke in: "Ye'd best come intil the hoose, young man, instead of standin' here making speeches that naebody can understand!" And between them she and Worrall took him without more ado through the door, steered him into the kitchen and sat him down in a wooden chair while Bride flew for brandy.

CHAPTER XXIV

I

IF the Vicomte Marie-Cyprien-Benoît-Philippe d'Ornières de Lancize had been quite sound in body, it is possible that he might have found himself disposed that night, for safety's sake, in the famous closet where Ranald had taken refuge—since Bride, unable to bear the memories of that room, was once more occupying her own maiden bed-chamber. Even as it was, Worrall urged his mistress to bestow him in that dark and windowless nook, but was smartly reproached by her for inhumanity. A compromise was therefore effected by making up a trestle-bed in one of the long-disused back rooms of Inchrannoch House, so full already of lumber and discarded furniture that, once a sheet or plaid thrown over the bed, a careless search would have failed to pick it out, much less to discover its occupant. But to install the French officer openly in the laird's own bedroom, as Miss Bride seemed to wish, was, declared Phemie and Worrall together, downright crazy.

So the fugitive awoke next morning, after a moderately feverish night, to stare with puzzled eyes at the massive ebony-black press of bog-oak behind which his lowly couch was situated, at the medley of decrepit chairs and tables, and in especial at the partly moth-eaten stag's head with a broken antler, propped against the wall in a corner already tenanted by a couple of holed warming-pans and a shattered hour-glass. By the evening he actively disliked the way in which this ostracised beast looked at him from its eyeless sockets.

During the day his wants had been supplied and the cut in his arm newly dressed and bandaged either by the harsh, middle-aged woman or the man with a wooden leg

whom he had already seen—not, to his disappointment, by
that charming, quick-witted young girl who had saved him
from his pursuers, although her hands had been covered
with soap-suds. She had not even come to see him, and
Marie-Cyprien felt slightly aggrieved at this lack of
interest. Why, then, had she provided him with that exceedingly damp and uncomfortable hiding-place, and, presumably, told lies on his behalf? His own recollection of
his exit from the wet linen was a trifle hazy, but he retained the impression that the nymph had seemed concerned about his state.

Next morning, when she brought his breakfast, he forced
his reluctant nurse into conversation.

"This is Inchrannoch House, is it not, madame?"

"Aye, is it." After a moment's reflection the young
Frenchman concluded that this curious phrase signified
"Yes."

"You must pardon my ignorance," he proceeded deprecatingly, "but to whom does it belong?"

Phemie stared at him. "Ye dinna ken that? Why, tae
Mr. Walter Stewart, tae be sure!"

"I beg your pardon," said the invalid mildly. A moment
of puzzledom succeeded. "I thought the name was Maclean?" he murmured.

"Aweel, it isna Maclean," declared Phemie, with
truculence, dumping the tray on to a chair. "The Stewarts
of Inchrannoch—Stewarts of the royal line they are—hae
been at Inchrannoch syne the days of King James IV."

No measure of time being conveyed by this statement
to her hearer he merely observed "Indeed!" and then said
half-questioningly: "I have not yet had the honour of seeing the master of the house himself?"

"That's an honour ye're no likely to hae. The laird was
taen aff to prison in Perth last Lord's Day."

"I am very sorry to hear that! For his Jacobitism, no
doubt?"

" 'Twas sairtainly no' for thievin'!" returned Phemie
dryly.

Why was this woman so short with him, wondered Marie-Cyprien. He was accustomed to smiles from her sex. After a moment or two he began again undeterred:

"The young lady I saw, who so courageously hid me, is Mr. Stewart's daughter, I suppose?"

"Then ye suppose wrang," replied Phemie, propelling chair and tray within his reach. "She's his niece, is Miss Bride. Eat your breakfast afore 'tis stane cauld, sir!"

"Bride!" An unusual name, surely! So attractive a demoiselle would doubtless become a bride before long, too.

"I hope I shall soon have the opportunity of thanking Mademoiselle Bride for what she did for me," observed the invalid tentatively.

"Nae doot ye'll hae the opportunity when ye leave yer bed."

"I assure you, madame, that I am ready to leave it as soon as possible," declared its occupant, adding to himself: "For it is none too comfortable!"

But Phemie took no more notice of this declaration than a nurse of some impracticable or fractious observation of a child, but, being already at the door, shot through it out of the lumber-room.

Marie-Cyprien pulled himself up in bed. "I have a very good mind to rise at once," he muttered. "A very good mind indeed!" he repeated defiantly as his arm gave an unpleasant twinge. But, look where he would amid the confusion, he could see no sign of his clothes; and so, without any very sincere reluctance, subsided again and fell to upon his breakfast.

About noon the next day M. de Lancize was lying dozing when he heard the door open and two lowered female voices the other side of it. He kept his eyes shut, but was aware that his austere attendant had creaked over to the side of his bed and retired again; he even caught the whispered words: "He's asleep, Miss Bride, if ye want a keek at him."

"Miss Bride" at last! Should he open his eyes? No, for

T

if he did she might disappear again. He contrived, never-theless, himself to "keek" at his fair preserver as she came round the corner of the black press. And, *dieux*, she *was* fair!

"The arm's daein' fine," observed the elder woman in a whisper. "I'll hae him oot o' this the morn, I'm thinkin'."

Would she, indeed! Out of this welter of decrepit furni-ture and mouldering stags' skulls, yes, *et très volontiers* —but out of the house, no! Not until he had seen more of "Miss Bride." Marie-Cyprien was debating whether to open his eyes and address her now when, glancing round, she said herself, in a little soft voice: "I am afraid that he cannot be very comfortable here, Phemie."

"Comfortable?" queried Phemie, throwing back her head. "What call has he tae be comfortable? Isna he lucky tae be a free man the day? And what call either," she went on, "had he tae be rinnin' tae this hoose at a', that's had its fill o' steeryfykes already wi' searchings and red coats and they sleugs o' Campbells——"

"Hush!" said the girl, holding up a finger. "You'll wake him. Come away!"

They retired behind the bog-oak barrier, but "Miss Bride" must have asked further about his wound, for he heard the harsh whisper in reply: "Ach, a bit scratch like yon! A Scot wad hae thocht naething——" But at that the outraged young man could not suppress a movement, and as a result the door hastily opened and closed again. His visitors were gone.

And that evening he evinced so decided an intention of leaving his bed for awhile and going downstairs—an inten-tion in no way combated by Mrs. Euphemia Reid—that Worrall was summoned to assist him in his toilet—and to shave him. Marie-Cyprien had no intention of appearing before his nymph of the soap-suds otherwise than trim.

"You'll not be fit to get away for a day or two yet, I'm afeared," said the improvised valet at the conclusion of his good offices, studying the young Frenchman's appearance; but what precise brand of regret was in his tone Marie-

Cyprien was unable to determine.

"But I must not put the young lady of the house to inconvenience for longer than I can help!" he disingenuously returned. "Especially as she is left here, is she not, without any of her family?"

"Aye," replied Worrall; "more's t' pity! But Aw'd have ye know, sir," he continued, with an air of vindicating the proprieties, "that Miss Bride's a married woman. Her husband's nobbut a week gone from t'house. T'sojers was after him."

"Married!" exclaimed his hearer in astonishment. "The . . . the young lady who hid me—she is a married woman?"

"To be sure," replied Worrall unemotionally. "She's Mrs. Maclean now. She was wedded in this very house to Mr. Ranald Maclean of Askay, when he was skulking, as t' Scotch calls it, after t' battle near Inverness."

Marie-Cyprien sat down again, with a good deal of suddenness, on the chair he had just vacated. It was not that the idea of his nymph's being the Mrs. Maclean he sought had never occurred to him, but that it had subsequently been dispelled by the repressive woman's persistently calling her "Miss Bride" and her repudiation of the name Maclean in connection with the house. So, after all . . . and he no longer had the letter with which he had been charged!

"A pretty fool I shall look," he reflected as he followed the wooden leg slowly down the stairs, "a pretty fool, when I say, 'Your husband, who has met with an accident some way from here, gave me a letter for you, which I regret to say I have lost!'" Then, naturally, would follow searching questions as to the nature of the "accident," for which, if not he himself, his companion had been responsible. It might have passed as some effort at atonement if he could at least have produced the missive which the injured man had sent; in fact, thought the Frenchman as he attained the level of the hall, it would have been possible to make it appear that he (who was, moreover, entirely guiltless in the matter of the shooting) had been on his way to Inchrannoch House of set purpose to deliver the letter when he was captured and chased. . . . But, without the letter, how could he pretend that?— Unless, of course, he stated that his captors had taken it from him?

He had not made up his mind what to do, except that he would not blurt out his bad news immediately, when he was ushered into the drawing-room.

The heroine of the pile of sheets—Maclean's wife—was seated in the window, sewing. As she looked up Marie-Cyprien saw the colour rise under her skin—the clearest and fairest skin he had ever set eyes on. Her hair, too, was of a colour he had never met, save perhaps in dreams. He had not yet had time to realise that. . . .

"May I at last thank my gentle preserver?" he asked, and bowed his best bow over the little mittened hand.

By the time he sought his bed that night M. de Lancize more than suspected that he had acquired a fresh wound in quite another region than his arm. "Yes, it begins," he decided, as he got back into the trestle-bed. *"Je suis bel et bien épris d'elle!* Fair hair has always been fatal to me!" But even his considerable experience could not determine, at this early stage, how long the cardiac disturbance was likely to last.

What a little darling she was, and how delightful, to him at least, had been the innocent intimacy of the meal shared with her this evening, endued as it was with a considerable spice of adventure, since he might at any moment have been haled out from it and carried off! He had always preferred married women—though it was hard to believe that Madame Bride was a wife. She seemed to him a wholly delicious blend of grave and gay. Her expression might be pensive now, even sad, but he did not think it her habitual look. She was distressed because her uncle was in captivity, her newly made husband a proscript. Since, however, she was not yet aware of the latter's present unfortunate plight, it would obviously be cruel to enlighten her—yet. It was his business, if only in gratitude, to bring a smile to that adorable little mouth. With all the respect and delicacy at his command Marie-Cyprien had set about working this transformation . . . and it had been an entrancing smile when it came.

His last words to his young hostess before he retired to the company of the stag's head and the warming-pans had been that he hoped to relieve her of his compromising presence, if not the following day, then the day after that. In reality, he had small intention of doing this if he could avoid it. For what was the use now of continuing the search for the Prince Charles Edouard? There were no despatches to deliver even if he succeeded in tracking down the royal fugitive, who might not now be in these parts at all! No, he would stay in this house a while longer. Nothing was easier than to retard the progress of a healing wound; at the cost of a little preliminary pain he could offer to the eyes of either of his attendants tangible evidence that his arm was not doing so well as it had promised. Before blowing out the candle he made a derisive face at his broken-tined enemy in the corner.

At the other side of the house Bride's slow tears were soaking into her pillow. Another day, and no news, no news. . . .

(2)

But Bride was not the only person who had reckoned up that tale of days. She was about to make the tea for breakfast next morning when the door opened, and Mrs. MacRobbie's voice—not Phemie's—said somewhat apologetically: "Here's a gentleman come with news, Miss Bride," and Bride looked up to behold Gregor Murray.

The caddy-spoon dropped from her fingers, scattering tea-leaves on the cloth. "News!" she said faintly. "News of——"

Gregor did not answer for a moment; he was drinking

her in with his dark, hollow eyes—more hollow even than of old. Then he came forward. "Your servant was mistaken, madam," he said quite gently. "I have no news, good or bad. I came to ask for them."

"No news!" repeated Bride, with heart-break in her voice; and putting her hand for a moment over her eyes she sat down in the nearest chair.

Gregor walked round the breakfast-table. "I am sorry to come empty-handed, when there are two of whom you wish to hear tidings—your uncle and the man you married. Ah yes, I know how you allowed a stranger whom you had scarcely seen to trap you into a hole-and-corner marriage in your own kitchen——"

On fire in an instant, Bride jumped up. "Trap! There was nothing of trap about it! Was it for this that you came, Mr. Murray—to insult me! You should remember that my uncle is no longer here!"

"How could you think that I should insult you? It was precisely because I had just heard that Mr. Stewart had been arrested that I came to Inchrannoch—because you ought not to be alone here."

"But I am not alone," answered the girl. "I have the maidservants, and Worrall too.—I was not allowed to accompany my uncle to Perth," she added.

"Do you know where . . . your husband is?" asked Gregor, looking at her hard.

Bride shook her head.

"Perhaps he will come back here, when it is safe for him?"

"I do not know; I have no news."

"May I," proceeded Gregor, with a smile, but not a very pleasant one, "offer my congratulations on your quick wit in saving him from the search-party in the way you did?"

Bride suddenly coloured. "How did you hear of that? Someone here must have told you! Who was it—Mrs. MacRobbie? I did not wish it spoken of!"

Now Gregor Murray, having entered cautiously by the back regions (for was he not "a man with his head under the wood"?) had indeed extracted a good deal of information out of Mrs. MacRobbie, but he did not acknowledge his debt. He merely replied: "Do you not know that you are the heroine of all the country-side—that as far away as Fortingall they speak of your wonderful address! Why, I heard the tale in Glen Lyon, where I have been skulking. It is likely that Miss Stew—Mistress Maclean of Inchrannoch will go down in song and story as the wife who saved her husband by feigning that he was her lover . . . though that is not indeed a subterfuge which every husband would relish!"

His tone indicated pretty plainly what he thought of a husband who did.

Bride flushed still deeper. "The subterfuge was entirely of my devising, Mr. Murray. My husband knew nothing whatever of it at the time. Afterwards he——" She stopped, realising that the completest defence of Ranald against contempt was the revelation that he had parted from her in such furious anger at what she had done that he had intended to go and give himself up in denial of it. But to tell Gregor Murray, of all people, what she had only brought herself with great difficulty to mention to her uncle—no!

She was saved from the necessity. Gregor was close beside her by the breakfast-table, and had her hands in his. "Bride"—his voice was hoarse—"Bride, there's no need to finish; I know it. Maclean went off in wrath—against *you!* Oh, Bride of the Gold, Bride of my heart, if I had been in his place you would not have found me so ungrateful, even though a MacGregor's honour is a hundred times dearer to him than any Maclean's could be to him! You know you could never do wrong in my eyes! Do I not guess that it wellnigh slew you to tell that lie, of all lies, for his sake! Oh, my sorrow, my sorrow, why did you marry him, why did you let him steal a march on me? You have always known that you were the light of heaven to me! . . . No, I will not frighten you again, but at least let me kiss this hand of yours. Little white love, you must let me be of some service to you! I cannot thole the thought of you, all alone and unprotected here!"

"Pray, Mr. Murray!" Bride was less angry than agitated, and felt a little stab of pity, too, for him, inconsiderate and unruly though he had always been. "What is the use of saying these things to me? I beg you to desist—and see, the kettle yonder is about to boil over! I must... What is the matter?"

For whether the mention of the kettle were the cause or no, Gregor's eyes, hot and devouring, had suddenly shifted from her face to a lower level. A most extraordinary change passed over his whole aspect. Stiffening, he dropped her hand; and when he turned his gaze upon her again it could only be described as a glare.

"Who is in the house with you?" he demanded like a blow. "Who is going to drink out of that?" He pointed dramatically at the second cup and plate upon the table. "Are your servants taking meals with you?"

"Certainly not," replied Bride, with dignity, very much wishing, nevertheless, that Phemie had not insisted upon laying the table for two. "Did not Mrs. MacRobbie tell you, since she holds her tongue so ill, that we have here a fugitive French officer—he who escaped on Tuesday from the Highland company at the end of the loch?"

"So you are not alone after all!" said Gregor, slowly and unpleasantly. "You *have* a protector . . . from heaven knows where . . . and a Frenchman!"

Any ground that his real distress might have won him was instantly lost again.

"Do not, I beg of you, be absurd, Mr. Murray!" exclaimed Bride indignantly. "You must recognise that in this case it is I who am giving protection. Moreover, the Vicomte de Lancize has been wounded and obliged to keep his bed until yesterday. And in any case . . ."

She broke off. As if in response to a cue on the stage, the door-handle was turning. "Is it permitted to enter?" asked a foreign voice at the door.

Bride faced round and took a few steps in that direction. "Come in, pray, monsieur, and let me present you to Mr.

Gregor Murray, who is paying me an early visit. Mr. Murray, this is Monsieur le Vicomte de Lancize, come to Scotland upon the Prince's business." It was a good deal her displeasure with Gregor which had suddenly given her command of the situation. How dared he call her to task like this!

For some reason best known to himself Marie-Cyprien de Lancize was this morning wearing his white uniform as its designer had intended it to be worn, and though its pristine hue was now abated to a dingy cream, and though his left arm was still disposed beneath it in a sling, it yet made a certain effect over the bright blue waistcoat and breeches. Having kissed his young hostess's hand, he bowed pleasantly to the frowning Highlander, who did little more than acknowledge the greeting.

"Mr. Murray, like yourself, monsieur, is in hiding," announced Bride, "but he was so kind as to come to Inchrannoch to enquire how I did with neither husband nor uncle here."

"You have small need, madame, of any man's arm or wits," the Frenchman assured her. "Have you heard, sir, by what means she hid me from my pursuers?"

"No, sir," replied Gregor, looking hard at him. "But whom, may I ask, did she give *you* out to be?"

Not quite understanding the idiom—and the insinuation not at all—Marie-Cyprien wondered why the little châtelaine seemed to blench at that. He was beginning a description of his hiding-place when Mrs. Euphemia Reid was suddenly among them.

"I'm waiting this lang while tae bring in the parritch, Miss Bride," she announced warningly; and then, casting an eye on this morning's unbidden guest, asked: "Will I set anither place for this gentleman—'tis Mr. Murray frae Roro, I'm thinkin'?"

"Certainly, set another place," answered Bride, without hesitation. The tradition of Highland hospitality left her no alternative, and in any case Gregor was a Jacobite and suffering for his loyalty. He could always excuse himself from staying to breakfast, and take his leave; she hoped he would.

But Mr. MacGregor Murray did nothing of the sort, and in a few minutes the two young men were seated on either side of their hostess. The Highlander, thought M. de Lancize, seemed uncommonly glad of a meal. What a smouldering, fiery glance the man had, even when eating his porridge! There might be a reason for that, however, for surely nobody, not even a Scot, could absorb that concoction without effort! For his part, he only attempted the feat from politeness.

But *la belle petite* was annoyed about something, that was clear. He had not seen that sparkle in her eyes before, nor heard just that note in her soft voice. So clear an evidence of spirit made her doubly attractive.

The talk centred for awhile round Mr. Stewart's imprisonment. Madame Bride was able to tell this black-avised friend of hers that, from his recent letter, Uncle Walter was well, and not at all harshly treated, being, in fact, confined in a private house. Then this Mr. Murray rather brutally asked whether his arrest had to do with her husband's visits to Inchrannoch; and the poor little wife, dropping her eyes, was forced to avow that she feared it had. He had been held responsible for the presence under his roof of a proscribed rebel. And on that Marie-Cyprien himself was inspired to ask how the soldiers had known that M. Maclean was there; had there perhaps been treachery, or merely indiscretion?

His remark provoked a storm-gust. *"Treachery!"* burst from Mr. Murray's indignant lips. His glance was like a dagger. "You forget, I think, monsieur, to what country you have come! There are no traitors in the Highlands!"

"Pardieu, what a magnificent claim to be able to make!" retorted the Frenchman. He took up his tea-cup. "If this were wine, I would drink to the Highlands, so singular and so blest. . . . And yet," he added rather maliciously after a moment, "your Montrose" (he gave the name

its French value) "was he not betrayed in the Highlands, and by a Highlander?"

The angry gaze was not abated. "You seem well
acquainted with Scottish history, monsieur!"

"If I were, I hope it would not be a crime?" answered
Marie-Cyprien lightly, helping himself to another bannock.
"Yet in truth I know very little of it, and always so many
kings of the same name confuse me. But the story of your
Marquis de Montrose I read as a boy."

"Some day," said Gregor Murray, with emphasis, "all
the world will read with admiration the story of a Prince
who wandered for months in the Highlands with a price of
£30,000 on his head which not a Highlander, however
needy, would claim!"

"*D'accord!*" agreed M. de Lancize heartily. "*Ma foi,
c'est magnifique!* I did not know it was so great a sum."

"Ah!" said Bride Maclean under her breath, "if one only
knew where the Prince wanders at this moment!"

Marie-Cyprien threw a look at her. He could have told
her, approximately, and told this fiery visitor of hers, too.
He did not, however, intend to do so.

"I also wonder that," he murmured.

But the Highland guest was not going to let his ignorance pass unchallenged. "Yet you, sir," he remarked
aggressively, an elbow on the table, "have come to Scotland—at least, so I was given to understand—on the
Prince's business! You must have some notion of his
whereabouts, else why are you here?"

"I am here, monsieur," replied Marie-Cyprien, "because
I had the ill-luck to be captured—and subsequently injured
—earlier in the week."

Frowning, Mr. MacGregor waved this away. "That is not
what I meant! What brought you to these parts at all?"

But for the presence of a lady, M. de Lancize would
certainly have shown more openly his annoyance at this
cross-questioning. "Not the hope of earning £30,000, if
that is what you suggest, sir," he said, smiling, but not
altogether pleasantly. And conceiving that a complete

reversal of fact might be a safeguard to him in other ways, he went on: "You mean, where did I expect to find the Prince Charles Edouard? I think that I may with discretion reveal that I was on my way to the country of the chief called Lochiel when I was captured."

"Oh, I thought——" began young Mrs. Maclean, and then was silent.

The romancer at once half regretted his announcement, possibly too rash in face of what the officer who pursued him might have told her. However, he could rescind it again when this unattractive Highlander departed, as it was to be hoped he shortly would.

But the Highlander pursued his enquiries. "To Lochaber? You are on the point, then, of resuming your journey?"

"Confound his impertinence!" said Marie-Cyprien to himself. Aloud he observed, blandly and sorrowfully: "Alas, there would be no purpose in my doing so. The papers which I and my companion were to have delivered were taken from us on our capture. If I succeeded in finding His Royal Highness, my presence would only be an embarrassment to him. No; directly this slight wound permits," he glanced at his beslinged arm, "I make my way as best I can back to France."

In the moody gaze of Mr. Gregor Murray he could almost read the question, "And how soon will that be?" but fortunately it did not come to utterance. Indeed, to his gratification the Highlander, removing that brooding stare, announced to Madame Bride that he must be leaving. *He* would not endanger her, he said meaningly, by lingering under her roof; and in any case, the pine-tree as shelter and the heather as bed were good enough for him. Marie-Cyprien, disliking him more and more, privately decided that they were too good.

When they had all risen Mr. MacGregor Murray approached their young hostess and lowered his voice.

"Before I leave, madam," Marie-Cyprien heard him say, "can you not give me some notion of the direction in which

. . . your husband . . . went that night? For if I knew it I might be able to obtain news of him and send it to you —since all these ten days you have had none?"

The child wife, standing at the head of the table and, as Marie-Cyprien saw, red and pale by turns, stammered out: "He . . . he took the same direction as the soldiers of the search-party themselves . . . he crossed the river."

Gregor shrugged his shoulders. "And that is all you know? 'Tis not much to go upon. But it is clear that Mr. Maclean never fell in with them, else we should have heard of his recapture. Do you not think that after all he is still skulking in the neighbourhood, but will not even send a messenger to Inchrannoch for fear of being traced?"

Still that embarrassment on little Madame Bride's part! It chained the Frenchman's attention so closely that he was able to disregard his own prickings of conscience, just then becoming tiresomely active. He had already firmly stifled the impulse of good manners which bade him withdraw a little further off from a private conversation; he was too deeply interested in it.

"No, no," at last said Madame Maclean, drawing her finger to and fro on the table-cloth, "I do not think that at all. I think . . . I think that my husband has carried out the intention which he had before he was surprised, of returning to Isle Askay in order to see his brother and his family . . . and has had no opportunity of sending me a message to say so. If no misfortune has befallen him, he must be there by this time; so pray do not, Mr. Murray, put yourself to any trouble in the matter."

Again it was odd, reflected the spectator, how much wiser was he than either of his companions! He could have informed them exactly how far Mr. Ranald Maclean had got on that ill-fated journey to his brother's home. . . . He would have to tell the little wife eventually, of course; but not in front of this somewhat sinister gentleman. And he would dearly have liked to discover the cause of the curious constraint which the mention of her husband seemed to bring upon the child. Ought she not to be delighted that this person should wish to obtain news of him for her?

"Gone to Askay!" repeated the latter after a moment, and with what might have been a note of disappointment. "Ah, then I am not likely to be able to serve you in that way. But if there is any other in which I can be of use, send a messenger over to the smithy at Innerwick in Glen Lyon, and he will be told where to find me."

Little Madame Bride thanked the speaker—who nodded curtly to the Frenchman—and moved with him to the door; she even went with him into the hall.

During the brief space in which she was out of the room the key of the riddle shot as down a lightning shaft into the receptive hands of M. de Lancize. Of course, the girl had discovered—since her husband's departure, perhaps— the (to Marie-Cyprien's mind) easily guessed at delinquency for which he had in the Frenchman's very hearing murmured of reparation and forgiveness. To a wife so recently married, the shock of the discovery had been so great that she was plainly not desirous of her husband's return . . . not yet awhile, at least.

It was with a distinct rush of interest and relief that M. de Lancize received this specious enlightenment, not pausing, not desiring indeed, to scan its probability too closely. It quite absolved him, for a while, at any rate, from telling his young hostess about the unfortunate events in Glen Suileag; it even caused him to congratulate himself upon the involuntary loss of Maclean's letter, and it made instantly manifest to him that the good progress of his wound *was* going to be checked. In fact, when Bride came slowly back from the hall she was distressed to find her convalescent sitting sideways in a chair with his elbow on the breakfast table and a hand over his eyes. At her step he instantly rose, but not before she had had time to see, as his hand fell, that his face had been twisted as though with pain. But to her anxious query the heroic young man replied that it was nothing—merely a momentary twinge.

CHAPTER XXV

Two days more and still no news! It was now nearly a fortnight since Ranald had left Inchrannoch. Some ill must have befallen him, for unless he intended never to see her again (and that Bride could not bring herself to believe), he surely could not be so cruel as deliberately to refrain from writing. Yet Askay was a long way off . . . She remembered the day when he had first spoken of the island and his brother, and little Helen, whom since she had hoped to see and embrace . . . And he had told her how there on the shore of Camus a' Chaisteil the child's fair hair had brought hers to his mind, save that hers was so much more beautiful. To-night, back in the little bedchamber which had been hers all her life until he came, she was wondering whether her husband would ever take pleasure in her hair again.

It hung now in its supple twin braids over her nightrail. Bride had just risen from saying her prayers, and her eyes were wet. For if one were not to be wholly selfish one must remember how many others were in distress of mind or body, drinking much more deeply than she the cup of defeat. She had prayed to-night for those who had still to go to the scaffold, for the kin of those who had already gone, like the "Manchester rebels" and Lords Balmerino and Kilmarnock; and now she went and pulled aside the window curtains and looked out towards her dear mountain. But it was a dark and wet night; she could see nothing at all, and hear nothing but the steady patter of the rain. If Ranald were at home in Isle Askay he was not, at least, lying out upon the heather in a downpour. But oh, if only he were here in Inchrannoch . . . and then that other disastrous night would be forgiven by both of them, and blotted out for ever, and he would

293

remain a while peacefully in this old house, which now, surely, had had its fill of alarms and military visitations, and would be disturbed no more.

But he was not here. She must still have patience, though by nature, as she knew, she was not over-gifted with that virtue, and remember that there were other women—many, many others—whose husbands could never come back to them . . .

She dropped the window curtain, and, opening a drawer, took out all she had of Ranald save the ring on her finger —the sheathed dirk which he had left behind him in his hasty departure. It was hardly a comfort to her, for it reminded her too poignantly of the circumstances of that going, and, moreover, she wondered how he had fared without it. Nevertheless she pressed a kiss on the handle which had known the touch of his fingers, put back the great knife and slipped into her bed between the green and mulberry curtains, the candle still alight by her side.

She was not sleepy, and the events of the past days persisted in marshalling themselves before her again, dominated by the figure of the young man whom she was somewhat unwillingly sheltering. M. de Lancize had been so brave about the wound which had taken such an unfortunate turn for the worse, so charming to her, so considerate (in some ways) but so inordinately desirous of her company. And she had other things to do during the day but sit and talk to him and be looked at in the way she supposed every Frenchman looked at any young woman who was not positively ugly. Yesterday he had kept his bed again for a while, but to-day he had absolutely refused to do so, saying that he had now no traces of fever and that on the morrow the state of his injury would permit him to tear himself away from Inchrannoch House . . . or so he feared. Bride hoped with fervency that he would carry out this intention, for this evening in the drawing-room, leaning over the harpsichord on which at his request she had been playing, he had delicately but unmistakably hinted that a kiss would complete the cure of his hurt more effectually than anything else in the world; to which overture she had responded by getting up and leaving the room.

It was true that he had come after her and apologised so penitently that she had been almost tempted to forgive him. But she could not; in such circumstances as hers his action was unpardonable, and her manner must have told him so. She had not returned to the drawing-room.

Bride had been asleep some time when she became aware that the sound, whatever it was, had an existence outside the territory of dreams. Half awake, she thought drowsily that it must be caused by the loose ivy branch beating against the smaller window. But surely Worrall had fastened it up a couple of days ago? Besides, there was no wind to-night.

The realisation of this fact brought her wide awake to another—that the noise which had penetrated her sleep was made by someone knocking softly but persistently upon her door. *Tap, tap, tap,* pause; *tap, tap, tap* . . . How long had this been going on? It must be Phemie, or just possibly Worrall, wanting her. But why? . . . O God, could it possibly be that Ranald was here? No, no, she must not allow herself to think that! Yet, once the candle lit, she sprang out of bed, snatched up a shawl and ran barefoot to the door, her heart thumping as though to choke her. For though she told herself firmly that it was not Ranald who knocked, she knew, nevertheless, that it was not impossible that she might find him there upon her threshold. And at least it might be someone to tell her that he was near.

Bracing herself against disappointment Bride shot back the bolt and opened the door—to give a sharp exclamation and draw away. For the beams of her candle and of another standing on the floor at his feet had shown her the Vicomte de Lancize, in his shirt and breeches, supporting his injured left arm with the other hand, and looking at her with an expression half apologetic, half imploring. Bride followed her natural impulse and attempted to shut the door.

But it would not shut; M. de Lancize must have put his foot in the way. And through the crack came his voice, low and agitated. "Mademoiselle . . . Madame, for pity's sake, do not shut me out! My wound has reopened—it bleeds. I need assistance . . . and I do not know where your servants sleep!"

Not a little alarmed, Bride immediately opened the door again. And she saw that her midnight visitor was indeed speaking the truth, for there was fresh blood on the bandages round his half-bared arm—bandages upon which she now set eyes for the first time—and the light of the Frenchman's candle, striking up from below as hers was further withdrawn, seemed to lend a strange ghastliness to his pallor.

"Wait there, then," she said breathlessly, "and I will find some linen with which to tie it up!" She went quickly over to her dressing-table and began hurriedly to search, thinking 'I will call Phemie, but first I must do what I can myself.' Of what she ought to do she was quite ignorant, and she had never seen the wound; but the gory evidence on the bandages surely demanded instant attention. For all she knew M. de Lancize might be in imminent danger. Finding nothing more suitable she brought out some pocket handkerchiefs to take to the sufferer; and then discovered that he had meanwhile slipped quietly into the room, and was standing, candle in hand, inside. The door, however, was still ajar.

"I thought you would see better here, madame," he said as she hesitated. His candle suddenly flickered. "Ah, the draught!" He set it down upon a convenient chest of drawers and softly closed the door. Bride did not relish that, but she told herself that with a man in such need as he was it was no time for prudery.

"You are unaccustomed to the sight of blood, is it not?" observed her visitor gently. "Give me the linen, madame, and I will do my best."

"I will help you," answered Bride, her heart beating faster than usual, not because of the blood, but because of the shut door . . . and of that episode after supper this evening. She brought the handkerchiefs, spread out a couple on the chest of drawers where he had set his candle, and, not looking at him, began with unsteady fingers to fold one into the semblance of a bandage; then realised that it would be inadequate and that she had better knot two together.

But as she was about to take up the second the young Frenchman laid his hand on it, for somehow he had moved a little nearer—and said in quite a different tone:

"Before you touch this foolish wound of mine, Madame Bride, you must cure the one more grievous that you have made yourself. That is sound surgery, is it not? You must show me, I mean, that you forgive me for my speech downstairs in the salon!"

Bride felt a prickle run over her. Was it conceivable that this business of his arm was a mere blind, a pretence? No, that was fresh, bright blood on the linen. "I think," she said, with some difficulty, "that I will call Phemie to rebandage your arm, monsieur. She will do it much better than I." And she made a movement to pass him.

Instantly the Vicomte receded before her and stood in front of the door. "Ah no!" he said with a smile. "No one else comes until you have forgiven me! My wound must wait."

Bride lifted her head and looked at him steadily. "If you are a gentleman, Monsieur de Lancize, you will leave my room at once! It is past midnight."

"But that is to go away without what I have come for," he answered, still lightly, still smiling, but with his eyes running all over her in her night attire. "A gentleman must always intensely desire pardon for any fault he has committed against a lady . . . *n'est-ce pas?* and you were so displeased with me this evening that I could not sleep . . . *Ma foi,* was there ever anyone so hard-hearted! And meanwhile, my poor arm! Suppose I should faint here, at your feet?" . . . And as she still stood facing him like a little statue, her shawl now clutched tightly round her, he said in a much more serious tone, "Bride, enchanting Bride, cannot you see that I am crazy for you? It is not my fault that I am here! You are a sorceress . . . you have drawn me into your bower with that so lovely hair of yours. Is it any wonder that my arm begins to bleed when my heart is bleeding too? . . . Let me have a kiss or two and I will go. No one shall find me here, I promise you—I am discretion itself . . . and so we will fasten the door." He turned and shot the bolt.

It was quite clear now how he had planned and what he had come for. If she screamed no one would hear her; the servants all slept too far away, and the door was shut. There was only one hope. In a second Bride was back at her little dressing-table, her hand in the still open drawer from where she had taken her handkerchiefs for that fictitious urgency. It emerged clutching the *biodag*, while with the other she tugged off the sheath. The foot and a half of steel came sweetly out as though it knew her need, and the touch of the hilt, joined to her own intense anger, almost killed her fear.

"If you do not open that door and go at once," she said, and her voice scarcely trembled, "I shall use this dirk— my husband's dirk! I had rather die than that you should touch me!"

The invader remained looking at her admiringly—as one looks at a picture which pleases. Candlelight—night-gown—braided hair—steel—and a darling little white face into which he would kiss back the roses. It titillated his sense of humour to see the little châtelaine of Inch-rannoch as a heroine of Racine or Corneille. And when she added, in a voice throbbing with horror, "To do this . . . in my husband's absence—after I have given you shelter—to pretend, to take advantage of your injury . . ." he interposed in half-diverted tones, "Ah, *belle Lucrèce,* but what of a little revenge on your part? Has not your husband himself given you cause for it?"

But from her look he could see that she did not even know what he meant. Was the child then of such an unheard-of simplicity? And why did she continue to gaze at him like that—why should she so absurdly clutch that useless if formidable weapon which he could have wrenched from her before she could as much as scratch either of them? What a puritanical little country wench she was! Surely, since her husband had deceived her, a girl of the spirit and contrivance which had sent away those pursuing soldiers empty-handed should not be averse to paying him out in his own coin! These scruples only required removing. Perhaps after the first kiss . . . and he advanced, humming under his breath, "*Jeune fillette, profitez du temps!*"

She could not get any further away from him. The candlelight ran up and down the blade of the dirk as it wavered slightly in her hold. *Ciel*, what portentous daggers these Highlanders used! That little hand could never wield it effectively. Yet all at once Marie-Cyprien came to a stop, the gay little air dying on his lips, for another explanation of this extreme reluctance had occurred to him. Could it mean that he himself was personally distasteful to her—insuperably distasteful? Was that it? For he prided himself that he had never yet had to take a woman, gentle or simple, against her will.

It was while he paused to consider for a second or two this disconcerting idea, that without warning, the thing happened to him which he was afterwards to remember with an astonishment and incredulity that never lessened. Quite suddenly, and at first extraneously, as a man perceives a scene on the stage immediately the curtain has risen upon it, Marie de Lancize had a vision of himself and what he was actually doing—a searing vision which ripped away in an instant the amused self-satisfaction with which he had been regarding this adventure in gallantry and the ruse which he had employed to pursue it, so that he saw both himself and them for what they were. . . .

Bewildered, all his self-confidence torn from him, he stood a moment staring uncomfortably at Bride Maclean, gazing as fixedly at him in the candlelight. He had called her sorceress—but he had not meant *this!* Then, shrugging his shoulders in an attempt to recover himself, he turned and went back to the door.

"I . . . I perceive that I am unwelcome, madame," he said hoarsely, snatching at any plea to cover his retreat. "If I had guessed it . . ." His fingers sought the bolt. "I shall be gone by the morning . . . Your woman—shall I find her and send her to you?"

And as Bride, unable to speak, shook her head, Marie-Cyprien d'Ornières de Lancize, that young man *à bonnes fortunes,* opened the door and went out defeated.

CHAPTER XXVI

To have weathered Prestonpans, Falkirk, Culloden itself, without serious injury and then to be laid low by a shot from the pistol of an ally; to have loved a woman, and to have given up for loyalty's sake the chance of winning her; to have found that the sacrifice was not called for; to have won and married her as by a miracle, in an hour . . . and then after half a dozen meetings to have deserted her because she had saved his life by a means which displeased him; to know as he did with unshakable conviction that she was crystal pure and steel true . . . and then with cruel words to fling out of the house where she had endured shame for him . . . And all that brutality of his irrevocable now, unredeemable; that was the thread of fire on which the long feverish hours of Ranald's first days and nights were strung. For now—although the bone of his thigh had escaped the bullet—he *could* not get back to Inchrannoch.

But later it sometimes wore so incredible an air, that behaviour of his, that, lying on the floor on the deerskins in perpetual twilight, he was tempted to believe it a tale whispered to him in delirium. But every day, as his head grew clearer, so did the knowledge that it was true.

The cabin in Glen Suileag was miserably uncomfortable, the two women, though solicitous enough, almost entirely unskilled, the children fretful and noisy. The wounded man could not hope for medical attention lest it should be bought at the price of capture; there was no spare linen for dressings or bandages. But old Mrs. Kennedy had the traditional knowledge, come down from the fiercer times of clan fights and forays, of a bright-coloured moss of healing property, and knew where to find it. And whether because of its efficacy, or because his injury was less serious than the fever and weakness which it brought in its train seemed to portend, Ranald did not succumb; in a week he was out of danger, in ten days more or less convalescent, though still tied to the heather and deerskin couch by the unhealed wound.

It was the eleventh evening after the Frenchman's pistol-shot—though Ranald had a little lost count of the days—and he was alone in the half-dark hut. The two women had gone to dig peats, but occasional screams and scraps of dispute outside testified to the presence of the two small children. And no captive beast in a cage ever ranged more drearily to and fro than did Ranald's mind over the past. Now he was outside Holyrood House, looking up at Arthur's Seat on a fine October morning, now back at Fasnapoll, now trudging half frozen with the army over the Cumberland fells, now writing his letter in the little kirk at Blair, now walking with old Mr. Fraser among the laden vines at Girolac, now in the sempstress's parlour in Manchester with Malcolm Robertson. . . . Poor Malcolm! He had far better merited to win Bride—*he* would never have said to her . . . Ranald groaned aloud. It was surely the fever, distorting the past as water refracts falsely, which had scored those words into his brain —he had never really flung them at his "fairy saint"! And for the hundredth time he shuddered away this evening from the memory.

He had been haunted to an extraordinary degree in these past days of pain and fever by the verses of the Young Gentleman of the Temple which he had come upon at Blair. Day and night they jingled in his head: *And from my tomb an almond tree shall spring, bright with slim leaves, but never fruit nor flower; one only voice . . . hadst thou but sooner come . . . too long delaying, he prepar'd the tomb . . . now in the blessed sun no more to live. . . .* And once, half dreaming, half delirious, he had thought that the minister was sitting by him saying: "You would have done better to read a sermon, Mr.

Maclean, as I counselled you."

But Bride, Bride would never put an end to herself because he had deserted her, nor would she pine away. Little as he really knew her, he guessed at stronger stuff in her than that—what had Struan said once about a lion's heart?—but, just because she was no pliable and clinging girl, he must for ever have slain in her the love she had so wonderfully shown him when she entrusted herself to him without warning or preparation in the kitchen at Inchrannoch. And how had he repaid that trust?

He had tried, indeed, to undo his madness, but how was he to measure the chance of her having received the letter he had sent? The Vicomte de Lancize might not have been able to find a messenger, might himself have been captured. But, since the improvement in his condition of which Ranald was conscious during the last couple of days, he had resolved to go back somehow to Perthshire the moment his wound permitted. Yet since that was a long journey, difficult and dangerous for a disabled man who was also a proscript, it was very possible that he should never get there after all . . . and she would never know that if he had broken her heart he had broken his own as well.

And if he did ever reach her, he could never hope to find his Bride again. She would be changed to him . . . she must be. He was not now even like Ovid's tardy lover, since, favoured by fortune, he had not come too late. No, he had left too soon!

The light faded more and more, yet some reflection from the embers of a sunset which the prostrate Ranald could not see, crept through the place in the side of the wigwam where the sods had fallen off the wattle. Ranald began to doze; then roused as he heard the unusual sound of a man's voice outside. There followed a pattering of bare feet; the small boy, Dougal, who was no longer shy of him, stood beside him signifying that there was a gentleman come to see him.

"Bid him come in," said Ranald, wildly perplexed as to who this could be. But the visitor had not waited for an invitation; his figure was already stooping and darkening the doorway.

"Is Mr. Maclean there? 'Tis so pestilentially dark that I cannot see. Have you no torch, boy?"

"There is a fir root in the corner there, sir," said Ranald from the floor. The voice told him nothing of identity. "Give it to the gentleman, Dougal.—If you would be so kind as to light it, sir?"

The gentleman was kind enough, pushing the natural torch, dug from the peat moss, into the half-dead peats. And when he rose with it in his hand the smoky flare showed Ranald the dark wolf visage of Gregor Murray.

His pulse quickened violently. Gregor looked about until he had found the iron ring in which to set the light. Then he signed to the child to go out, and coming nearer looked down at the man on the deerskins.

"Well, Ranald Maclean, so you have met with an accident! I am very sorry to hear it."

"That is uncommon good of you, Mr. Murray," replied Ranald, returning his look, from which the emotion he mentioned was conspicuously absent, though others were not.

"*Dhé!* I am sorry because we cannot finish what was interrupted that night in the shrubbery at Lude House. At Fortingall we were unlucky also."

"It is an ancient quarrel now," muttered Ranald rather wearily. He had other wrongs . . . and of his own making . . . to occupy him now, God knew!

"A little more than a year old! Is that ancient?" Gregor pulled forward the rough stool and sat down on it: "Your illness has perhaps injured your memory; I will try to remedy that. It cannot be, Mr. Maclean, that you have really lost all recollection of a plaid-end that was thrown in your face before a good many people!"

Ranald reddened and stirred. "No, Mr. MacGregor, I do not forget insults so readily, least of all when they are causeless ones. But since that day so much has happened——"

"Aye, so much has!" broke in Gregor with intense meaning. "Since that day you have stolen a jewel . . . and thrown it away!"

This time Ranald turned white; his hands clenched. "*How dare you!*"

Gregor looked down at him contemptuously. "Are you set, pray, like a god, above reproof? You do not much resemble one at this moment!"

"If you do not like my looks, Mr. Murray MacGregor, you can take yourself off again! Your departure will not grieve me!"

"Take myself off after having been to so much trouble to find you? Surely not!" said Gregor mockingly.

"How *did* you find me?"

Gregor smiled. "I have been successful, that is all that matters."

"You speak of resuming the encounter we had at Lude House. For my part," said Ranald between his teeth, "I wish for nothing better. But, seeing that I am not at present in a condition to meet you——"

"Which is your misfortune, not my fault," interrupted Gregor. He was not smiling now, and the fingers of his right hand were running in a somewhat significant manner over the interlaced pattern on the handle of his dirk.

There was a second or two's silence, for Ranald was not quite sure . . . So he asked.

"Do you mean by that speech that you are contemplating killing me in cold blood?"

"That is how a thief is killed, is it not, if he is caught? And there is nothing to prevent my following that excellent custom, if I choose."

"Nothing whatever," answered Ranald coolly. "Only the fact that I am not a thief, and that it would therefore be murder, since I have no means of defending myself."

"Your misfortune, as I said before. I am not answerable for it. And so," said Gregor with a gloomy gusto, "I can kill you as one kills a sheep—and with as little remorse. But I think I will not do it to-day."

"You are generous indeed!" said Ranald bitterly. He threw up his left hand—the further from his visitor—in what looked like a careless movement, to bring it nearer to the little black knife beneath his pillow, which was all he had between him and death. Not that it could avail him anything in the end—save that that end would not be quite a sheep's finish. "And why do you abstain from murder to-day?" he demanded.

Gregor gave a short laugh. "Does one drink down the best wine at a draught? I have had enough trouble to come at this choice vintage—enough trouble in vain, too. So I will turn it over on my palate a while longer."

Ranald tried to raise himself on to his elbow. "What do you mean by 'enough trouble in vain'? Is it possible that it was *you* who gave——"

"Who sent Lord Loudoun's men to Inchrannoch that night? Aye, why not? Thief-taking is the law's business, and they the only arm of it within striking distance. I knew you would be harking back to your stolen property; I had but to have Glen Lyon watched . . . You remember, I see, the old *seannachie!* 'Tis true that Castle Menzies should have done the business for me that night at Fortingall, had not the alarm been false. The third time is aye the lucky one; you'll hardly escape me now when the hour strikes." For a moment a fire gleamed in Gregor's eyes which was almost madness, and he hitched his dirk until it lay over his thigh; but he did not draw it. "And once you are out of my path, beggarly islander that you are, I shall have her whom you stole—I shall have her by one means or another! She shall marry me to save her good name—when you are carrion. The English have already removed Mr. Stewart to Perth— you don't know that, I suppose—in consequence of his having sheltered you . . . Yes, there'll soon be another marriage at Inchrannoch—in the kitchen again maybe.

Or perhaps after I have carried her off to Roro . . . And indeed," finished Gregor negligently, rising from the stool as he spoke, " 'twas plain enough from your wife's manner the other day, when your name was mentioned, that she has small wish ever to see you again!"

"*What!*" The prostrate man gave himself a painful jerk, trying vainly to catch at the other's plaid, as he moved out of reach. "My wife's manner . . . you have seen her—spoken with her? At Inchrannoch—or where? And when, when? MacGregor, if you are not quite dead to human pity, tell me of her! How does she? what does she know, what——"

But Gregor was already at the door of the hut. "I saw her six days ago, but 'twas not easy to have speech with her, so much was she taken up with some young spark of a French officer who was installed at Inchrannoch. I fancy you have better cause for jealousy now, Ranald Maclean, than with that imaginary English captain of hers! This one is flesh and blood, and handsome at that!"

"A French officer!" exclaimed Ranald astounded. "Then it must be one of the two——"

But Gregor had vanished, and when Ranald shouted angrily after him his cries went unanswered.

With a groan he threw an arm over his eyes. If one of the French officers were at Inchrannoch—and Gregor Murray, half crazed though he was with malice, could hardly have invented this—then Bride must not only know of his whereabouts, but have received his brief plea for forgiveness. For, since Gregor spoke of him as "handsome," the Frenchman was undoubtedly M. de Lancize, who carried the letter. His enemy's allegation of undue interest in him on Bride's part had passed over Ranald unheeded—a slander designed to torture him, but without power to move, it was so palpably false. But that Bride might in some way have shown, even involuntarily, that the idea of his return was unwelcome . . . O God in Heaven, could that be true? It might be; it might be: he had done enough to merit it! And he could not question further the man who had planted this poisoned dart, for, having planted it, he had gone instantly away, no doubt of design.

"I had rather he *had* stabbed me!" groaned Ranald, twisting himself to hide his face on the hot, dirty deer-skin.

CHAPTER XXVII

(1)

"Aweel, I'm glad tae see ye're awake, Miss Bride," observed Phemie, bursting in at an earlier hour than usual the morning after the midnight invasion of that little chamber. "Because Worrall's just after finding the French gentleman downstairs dressed and ready tae leave the hoose, saying he maun be awa wi'oot mair delay. But he's gey wishful, it seems, ye sud read this bit letter first. I'm thinkin' 'twill only be tae thank ye for havin' gi'en him shelter, and his thanks wad read as well when he was awa—and time eno' he was—but no, Worrall says naething will content him but that ye sud read it before he leaves the hoose. Sae here it is. Bide a wee till I pu' yon curtain!"

Bride sat up in the bed in which she had lain indeed, but not slept. However, Phemie, who was not over-observant, and in any case did not approve of anything that savoured of "cockering," made no comment on her wilted appearance, but having thrust a folded paper into her hand, vigorously drew aside the curtain and let in the morning.

Bride shut her eyes a moment, feeling sick. Her impulse was to hand the note back to Phemie unread. She wanted no attempts at self-exoneration. Yet, if she sent it down unopened, M. de Lancize might really delay his departure until it was read. Anything was better than seeing him again, so she unfolded the missive and found it to be couched in French, of which tongue, as the writer knew, she had a good knowledge.

Madame, said the foreign handwriting, *there is no*

309

apology that I can offer for my unpardonable conduct, nor can I suppose that any plea would earn your forgiveness. I make none, therefore: and what I am about to write can only add, I fear, to the contempt and loathing with which you must regard me. Nevertheless, I cannot leave without informing you of facts which it was my duty to have told you at the first opportunity—and which I must leave you to divine why I withheld.

There followed a paragraph which Bride read at first uncomprehending—read and reread, till its meaning came in like a flood . . .

"Losh, what ails ye?" asked Phemie, turning round at the exclamation which fell little short of a scream.

"There's news," said Bride, white as her sheets and half out of bed, "news of him, my husband! I must rise at once! Run down instantly, Phemie, and ask M. de Lancize at all costs to delay his departure until I have spoken with him."

"Why, what has he tae do wi' Mr. Maclean?"

"A great deal—almost everything . . . And I never knew! Phemie, my husband is lying hurt—badly hurt—and M. de Lancize knows where he is! Oh, bring me my clothes quickly!"

"Kens where he is! Did the Monshere aiblins learn it in the nicht?" asked Mrs. Reid, not without justification.

"Never mind how he learnt it!" retorted Bride, catching up the letter again as she suddenly realised that she had not read it all. For overleaf, after that amazing paragraph of confession, came another:

Any further details which may be required concerning Mr. Maclean's whereabouts I will furnish, Madame, to anyone you may send, or to yourself, in the presence of this person, should your desire to hear them be stronger than the repugnance which you must feel for the sight of me. It is on this account that I am delaying my departure until this letter can be conveyed to you. But if you are satisfied without a personal interview you will escape the necessity of setting eyes on me again.

There was no signature.

Bride poured water into a basin. "Phemie, for God's sake go down and tell him not to leave yet! Go at once!"

Phemie, who disliked being hustled, went to the door with the sarcastic rejoinder, "Ye're no' suggesting, I hope, that I sud bring the Monshere up here?"

The girl raised a dripping face and stood a moment without moving.

"No, not that!" And when the door had shut she fell on her knees by the side of the bed.

(2)

The Vicomte Marie-Cyprien de Lancize stood at the dining-room window of Inchrannoch House and looked out, between the fir trees, at the tip of Schiehallion's cone. Behind him, at the other side of the room, he could hear what was almost an altercation in low-voiced progress between Bride Maclean and her wooden-legged servitor. She was all for setting out in person to her husband; the man seemed to be opposing it.

To the mind of the young officer, whose conduct had put him outside the pale with regard to his hostess, the severance of even ordinary relations with her seemed to have removed him to some other sphere of existence; he was now a ghost, a thing disembodied, a mere voice. Since she had come in accompanied (as he had himself suggested) by a third person, even her eager questions had been put, not to a man who a few hours ago had been on the verge of offering her the ultimate outrage, but merely to some stranger who happened to be possessed of information which was all the world to her. That she knew it to be information deliberately withheld until this eleventh hour no spectator could have guessed. Marie-Cyprien sup-

w

posed that she must have made it appear to this trusted
servant of hers that the informant had only just realised
the identity of the man whom he had left lying in Glen
Suileag—and this not in order to shield her treacherous
guest, but because she did not wish to touch upon the
reason for that unpardonable silence.

All that Marie-Cyprien could tell her was told now,
and he awaited dismissal. He did not know whither he
should betake himself when he left the roof whose hospitality he had so shamefully abused. His arm was still in
a sling, and not much the better for the display of gore
which he had brought about last night. However, all he
wanted was to be gone; once away from this house he
might in time recover his self-respect, even though it were
in an English prison. Some day he would be able to smile
at the memory of his present frame of mind. Even so, if
ever he were to have this girl in his power again, were
it to-morrow or years hence, he knew that he would not
be able to touch her. He had learnt last night that in some
people—Bride Maclean was one of them—purity and
innocence are not mere negative virtues, they are active
powers. He had not yet got over the shock of that disconcerting revelation.

He heard the man Worrall illogically urging that it was
no use his attempting to find the way to this glen, and
yet that he must accompany his young mistress—she
should not go without him. Then they must have a guide,
replied she. Various names were suggested; there seemed
to be a difficulty about the bearer of each . . . and none,
at any rate, would know the exact spot where the injured
man lay in the little cabin.

And then Marie-Cyprien heard the gruff tones of the
wooden-legged one, a little lowered, yet quite audible,
urging that the "Monshere" himself was the man to guide
them, and that it was the least he could do, seeing that it
was his friend who shot Mr. Maclean; but that he would
have to put on some other clothes than that crazy uniform
of his, if he were not to have the soldiers after them.

("You need not trouble yourself about that point, my good fellow," thought the 'Monshere' to himself. "There's no man on earth whom your mistress is less likely to accept as a guide.")

And yet . . . and yet . . . he must make the offer, though it would be refused. It was, as this Worrall had said, the least he could do. He turned, and found himself stammering—he who was usually so cool and self-possessed: "Madame . . . he is right . . . if you wish, if you permit . . . I will guide you there."

And in Madame Bride's face, despite the faint flush which had risen as he addressed her, he saw, to his astonishment, that she was going to accept. Her anxiety to reach her husband was then so great that it outweighed all the repugnance and the distrust which she must feel for *him!* Cyprien de Lancize was balanced between humility and a kind of elation. He came forward a step or two.

"I swear to you, madame, that I will not fail you in any way," he said submissively and earnestly. And then, slipping with even greater earnestness into his native tongue, "*Vous pouvez disposer de ma vie; je jure de vous honorer comme une sœur . . . et puis vous aurez aussi, n'est-ce pas, la compagnie de ce respectable serviteur?*"

The shining head was bent; and, speaking with some difficulty, the girl said quietly, "I thank you, Monsieur de Lancize. I accept your offer."

Marie-Cyprien found that he could not speak at all, but he made some sound and a little gesture like a bow, strangely awkward—for him.

"Aw must say it agen, Miss Bride," put in Worrall with a certain vehemence, " 'tis noan needful for thee to gan trawncing off to t'west in this fashion; him and me——"

"I have told you, Worrall, that I am going," said the little châtelaine with quiet firmness. "Pray let there be no more arguments! Find some clothes of my uncle's for M. de Lancize, for I think he will agree that to wear his uniform would be dangerous for us all. Then you must

look to Mally's shoes and my pony's, and try to borrow
another horse. If you cannot, you and M. de Lancize
must ride Mally in turns. Mist does not go very fast,
and in some places, I suppose, we shall not be able to
ride at all."

"In a good many, I fear, madame," said Marie-
Cyprien.

"Yo'st be a deal safer-like in these here, monshere,"
said Worrall a little later, stumping moodily into Marie-
Cyprien's lair, and laying on the trestle-bed a coat and
breeches of an unbecoming elderly colour.

"Shall I?" asked the Frenchman, with a small sardonic
smile. It was a moot point. His papers proving him a
foreign officer were gone, taken from him when he had
been searched after capture, and now his protective, if
conspicuous uniform was to go also. To be found in enemy
country in civilian attire was to invite unwelcome treatment as a spy. Hostilities, however, were long over; and
had he not told Madame Maclean that his life was at her
disposal?

(3)

Ere that same evening it was to occur to M. le Vicomte
de Lancize that Mrs. Bride Maclean might show small
scruple in taking him at his word in this matter, if need
arose; that she would even dispose of her wooden-legged
follower's life with the same equanimity . . . if one might
judge from the small regard she showed for their several
disabilities, as they all wended their way westward that
afternoon between the slopes of the Sliosmin and the loch.

For, after all, M. de Lancize was still partially incapacitated—though he had precious little desire now to call
attention to his injured arm—and the man Worrall was
permanently one-legged. Yet the same middle-aged mare
(for no other horse could be procured) must serve them
as steed, accommodating both on her back at the same

time, or in turns, Madame Bride's sole idea was, evidently, to push on as quickly as possible, and she contrived to communicate this spirit pretty successfully to the grey pony, even if its paces were not of the swiftest.

A pretty pair of knights-errant we are, thought Marie-Cyprien, as, clad in the discarded snuff-coloured suit of Mr. Walter Stewart's, the old-fashioned cut of which afflicted him more acutely than its shabbiness, with the man Worrall sitting sideways behind, his wooden leg jutting out like a bowsprit, he jogged along on Mally the mare behind that grey garron and its impatient little rider. This Highland Lucretia was on fire to reach her wounded husband, so much was abundantly clear: and since one could not assign this zeal purely to feminine regard for male suffering—seeing how little consideration she was showing for the two partially-crippled males in her company—it must be either that she had forgiven that husband's betrayal of her, or else that he never *had* proved false.

But upon that point the young Frenchman was already coming to the conclusion that he had made a wrong deduction. For whatever delinquency Ranald Maclean desired his wife's pardon, it was not for *that*.

"I could wish it were, for then she might not be in such a hurry!" he thought ruefully, as the pony once more shot ahead, and the man Worrall behind him beat upon the mare's flanks and observed impatiently: "Cannot yo' get t' mare to gan a bit faster, monshere? Aw'd 'a doon better to ride i' froont after all; Aw've two hands annyhow. Happen we'st change places next toime."

However, there was not to be a next time. Before they reached Killichonan poor Mally was so tired by her double burden that it had become for her a question of carrying one rider only. That one, of course, must generally be Worrall, although in fact he was almost as quick over level ground as a two-footed man. The arrangement caused constant argument, for the ex-sailor at least remembered that the Monshere was not long out of bed, and still bore an imperfectly healed wound, and wished him to take spells of equal length in the saddle. Slowed down by Mally's fatigue to a walking pace, the garron's rider allowed her escort to argue out the point between them; all that she cared about, evidently, was speed, and the shortest route to Glen Suileag.

She might almost have been endowed with that troubling possession, the second sight.

The travellers had selected the track round the northern shore of the loch, in order to avoid as much as possible the vicinity of the military post already familiar to one of them, but even so they must pass not far from it to reach the road along the River Gaoire. Should they encounter any of Marie-Cyprien's captors, his fate, in spite of his change of attire, would be in the balance; should they meet the officer who had searched Inchrannoch House it would be certain, for he would recognise the young lady of the house and the wooden-legged servant at once, and they, too, would probably be arrested. So they had timed their start to reach the end of the loch by the hour the light was beginning to fail; now that they were going more slowly it had more than failed, and it was as much as they could do to make their way to the hamlet of Dunan (where they intended to spend the night) without straying off the rough road. But they had the luck not to meet any Loudouners, and they did arrive safely at Dunan—a spot which again Marie-Cyprien knew only too well.

Next morning early they set out upon that stone-strewn valley which in the rain had seemed so utterly repellent to M. de Lancize. But it was a fine morning now, and the breeze, keen and steady, blowing down from the heights of Rannoch Moor, was invigorating to a pedestrian for whom the effort to find another horse at Dunan had proved fruitless.

When they came to the track leaving the Gaoire for Loch Ossian Marie-Cyprien took the lead. Neither Bride nor Worrall had ever been further than Dunan in their

lives. Having started very early and the going proving
not too bad, the little party had left the end of Loch
Ossian behind them and got down to Loch Treighead by
midday; and here they rested themselves and their two
steeds at the farmhouse. With the sun upon it that trough
of a loch also looked very different; and very different too,
as Marie-Cyprien reflected, were the companions for
whom he had exchanged the sulky Maxence de Galand
and the unloquacious Hugh Cameron.

Not, indeed, that this little company was given to
chatter. Worrall was far from talkative; if he did not
entirely disapprove of the expedition, he certainly dis-
approved of his young mistress's making part of it. And
as for Madame Bride herself, her thoughts were clearly
elsewhere—in Glen Suileag. Marie-Cyprien, effacing himself as much as possible, had never yet directly addressed
her since they started.

Before they went on again, therefore, it was Worrall
whom he warned that the worst part of their journey lay
before them that afternoon, and that as it was ten rough
miles to Steall, the farm by the great waterfall under Ben
Nevis which they must reach if they wished for decent
shelter that night, he was of opinion that, with a lady in
the party, it would be better to delay their start until morning. Worrall went over to deliver this opinion to his little
mistress, sitting by the hearth; and Marie-Cyprien, from
near the doorway, could see her vehemently shaking her
head. So he departed for the stable; was it wonderful that
a young wife whom his culpable silence had kept all this
time from her wounded husband should be without consideration for the fact that he, with his arm still in a sling
and a heel now threatening to chafe again, had walked
most of the fourteen miles, nearly all uphill, from Dunan?
(Nevertheless, he had really not allowed that fact to weigh
with him when he gave his opinion about waiting until
morning.)

So they set forth again due west, between that great
array of the peaks of Mamore on one side, and of the

peers of Ben Nevis on the other. The sun was still high,
but not as high as though it had been mid-August instead
of mid-September, and the hour was not far distant when
not sunset, indeed, but one or other of the massive
shoulders which hedged them in would steal his rays from
them. But that hour was not yet, and the first part of the
way proved not too discouraging. Armed with a stout
staff which he had procured, Marie-Cyprien went first on
foot, then came Bride on her garron, while Worrall riding
Mally brought up the rear.

Soon the path, which had been mounting all the time,
took a sudden little dip downwards, dwindling at the same
moment to a mere thread, only wide enough for a goat,
among weather-worn and slippery outcrops of granite.
It became necessary to dismount and lead the horses, even
the garron, the surer-footed of the two, seeming nervous.
Marie-Cyprien, realising this, stopped at the top of the
descent.

"I think, Madame," he said formally, "that you would
do better to dismount and allow me to lead your pony."

Disregarding the hand which he half offered, Bride, with
a murmured word of thanks, slipped nimbly off Mist, and
he preceded her down, holding the pony by the bridle.
Worrall, too, had got off, and the young Frenchman wondered how he would fare, with his wooden leg, among the
stones of the descent. Glancing back once he saw that
he had wisely left the mare to her own devices and that
Madame Bride was offering to help him. They all got
down, however, without accident.

So it was not really the scramble itself which brought
about the mishap. Neither Marie-Cyprien, apologetically
offering his hand, stirrup-wise, for Bride to mount, nor
Bride herself, just about to place her foot in it, actually
saw it occur; they merely heard an exclamation, turned,
and saw Worrall picking himself out of the heather. He
got to his knees, then subsided again, cursing in an under-
tone.

The two others hurried back to him, Marie-Cyprien at

least feeling certain of what he should see. It was so; quite a foot of the sailor's wooden leg was snapped off; there was the splintered end, all fresh and clean.

"Oh, Jonas!" exclaimed Bride in horror, "how did you do it?"

"Leg went down a rabbit-hole amoon these yirth-bobs. Aw had holt o' t' owd mare's reins agen, and afore Aw could get me leg out she poo'd me ower, dang her!"

And thus—since Worrall could not now walk at all, nor even stand without a prop—had the staid Mally, in conjunction with the housing arrangements of the coney tribe, rendered his company much more of a hindrance than an advantage to a young lady whose one idea was speed. There was unfortunately no gainsaying that conclusion. They would have to leave him behind.

But he was with his young mistress not only as a retainer, but in another capacity as well. Seated in the treacherous "yirth-bobs," or heather, muttering under his breath the full-blooded curses of his seafaring days, Jonas Worrall faced this latter problem with a somewhat embarrassing frankness. Bride, kneeling beside him, had shown her clear if reluctant intention of proceeding without him; they would, she said, convey him to shelter— there was a croft up the braeside—leave him a share of their provisions, and, if possible, find him out on their return.

"Tho' meanst to gan on alone wi' *him,* lass?" he demanded gruffly, jerking a thumb towards the third member of the party, as he stood there with a somewhat clouded brow, holding the two steeds.

"You know I must lose no time," answered Bride gently, and without any sign of resenting his tone.

But the Frenchman at least felt the need of some reassuring gesture. "Monsieur Worrall," he said earnestly, "it will be a great privilege for me to make myself entirely responsible for the safety of Madame Maclean. And how should harm come to her in her own country, where, as I am told, always the inhabitants are so honourable? But if it come, I am a dead man first! Give me, therefore, if you please, that pistol with which to protect her; for as you know, I have no weapon."

But Worrall made no attempt to comply. Still seated among the heather, the broken stump protruding in front of him, he glowered up under his bushy brows and observed squarely: "Ay, there's no danger loike to coom to Mrs. Maclean fro' any Highlander. It's thysel Aw don't trust, yoong man; and if she believes them foine speeches o' thine, she's got a sight less sense than Aw've allus gi'en her credit for!"

It was Marie-Cyprien who coloured and bit his lip. "Why, my good fellow, what have you against me?" (Could this serving man *know?* It was most unlikely.)

"Tho' 'rt a Frenchman; that's eno' for me wheer a lass is concerned!" growled Worrall.

"Jonas!" interjected his "lass" rather breathlessly.

"I suppose," remarked the Vicomte de Lancize, with some haughtiness, "that you have never heard of the Chevalier Bayard, the model of chivalry?" (Quite obviously Mr. Worrall had not.) "Eh bien, *he* was a Frenchman. And with me madame will be as safe as if——"

Madame herself broke in. "Dear Jonas, *I* am going to trust this gentleman. That should be enough for you, as I think . . . I hope . . . it is enough for him."

And, turning her head, she looked gravely and rather sweetly at him whom she had so little cause to trust. The hood of her cloak had fallen back. It came suddenly to Marie-Cyprien that she had the air of Our Lady when she was very young, before the Annunciation. . . . She did not hold out her hand, but her look carried all the significance of that gesture and more. And, quite instinctively this time, without any thought of producing an effect upon the surly watchdog at his feet, he caught up a fold of the dark cloak and kissed it. He was really moved.

But if Worrall was impressed at all by this spontaneous action, it was not in the right direction, for he scowled.

Nevertheless, he slowly extricated the long, clumsy pistol from his belt and unfastened the powder-horn. "'Tis main owd-fashioned," he grunted; "th' only one the domned sojers have left us. I'd liefer give it to Miss Bride, but she'd not know how to use it."

Marie-Cyprien received in silence the firearm and its ammunition. It appeared to him of an antiquity almost pristine, the butt-end of more value as a weapon, probably, than the muzzle. Then, after a little further consultation between Madame Bride and her retainer, he helped the latter to his feet—or rather foot—and thence to the mare's back; and began to lead Mally in the direction of the croft which they had seen on the mountain-side, whence already a man was coming towards them. Bride remained on the track, ready, however, to come up should Gaelic be required to explain matters.

Fortunately this particular Highlander knew some English, was willing to receive the incapacitated traveller, and even undertook to make a temporary repair to his wooden leg; and, when Worrall had hopped within, Marie de Lancize rode down again alone to that little cloaked figure waiting by the garron, and they started on together for Glen Suileag.

CHAPTER XXVIII

NEVERTHELESS the young Frenchman did not find this situation either embarrassing or piquant. A disturbing reflection, a still more disturbing query was already occupying his mind to the exclusion of any thoughts of gallantry, in either of its meanings. With this delay, it would be as much as he could compass to bring his charge to Steall before dark; and if he failed to do so, how, at this season of the year, would a gently nurtured girl come through a night in the open among these inhospitable mountains?

Since setting out Marie-Cyprien had made no attempt whatever to bridge the gulf which his own indefensible behaviour had set between him and his young hostess; yet now, as the two of them journeyed alone, the very roughness of the way, the assistance which she must inevitably accept from him, could not but narrow it a little. It was narrowed still more by the tacit consciousness that the two of them were leagued together against the menace of the mountains round them, those great lowering beasts profoundly indifferent to the little creatures struggling along their flanks, yet ready, if chance offered, to enclose and overwhelm them. When the sun had withdrawn the heights became more formidable still. The coldness of the air made it clear that the invisible summits of these kinsmen of Ben Nevis were crowned with snow. Yet Madame Bride, living amidst mountains, did not seem alarmed, even when the daylight began gradually to fail. Indeed her escort was full of admiration for the quiet courage with which she faced the various difficulties of the route; it was on a level with that which had enabled her, after what had passed between them to trust herself to him in these lonely wilds. He noticed, too, that the further they went the more she seemed endued with something more than courage—a kind of grave radiance. Yet all their surroundings were coldly hostile, the track only just possible to follow, and both of them weary, before they made out the lights of the farm-house at Steall and heard the roar of the waterfall behind it.

Marie-Cyprien drew a breath of profound relief. Evidently St. Joseph, to whom, on parting with Worrall, he had put up a petition, conceiving him to be a saint with an interest in travellers, had heard him; they had attained the hoped-for shelter in time. And though he had already settled that, in the event of encounters, he should pretend to be merely a servant, and thus avoid, perhaps, the display of his French accent—not that it would sound more alien in Highland ears than a perfect English pronunciation—he now announced, as they were approaching the dimly seen farm-house, that it had better be he who should first approach it and ask for hospitality. From his experience of twelve days ago he was aware that Mac-Sorley, the farmer, could speak English, and (since Hugh Cameron had chosen it for his and Galand's resting-place) must have Jacobite leanings. Even if MacSorley were to recognise him, it would not, therefore, greatly matter.

The waterfall roared louder now, but it did not drown other and quite different sounds which assailed their ears as they drew nearer to the solitary dwelling. And Marie-Cyprien at least was visited by uneasiness. Were they going to find, after all, that there was no room for them—or rather for *her?*

He had to knock hard upon the door before anyone opened it, and then it was a girl who knew no English. After a little delay MacSorley himself appeared, not too steady upon his feet, his English, though coherent, issuing from his mouth with unreadiness.

"Two beds for the night? No, no, the house is full—gentlemen from Fort William. I am sorry, honest man, but we cannot take you in."

"But I have a lady with me!" insisted the applicant. "You cannot possibly turn her away on a cold night like this! Where is she to sleep among these mountains? I am only a servant, but you must give my mistress a bed somewhere! She can pay!"

MacSorley frowned and mumbled that it was not a question of payment. And what, he asked half suspiciously, was a lady doing so late in the glen? As he put the question a burst of laughter and scraps of the chorus of a song surged out of his kitchen.

"We are late," explained Marie-Cyprien, "because the lady's other servant met with an accident. But——"

Behind *him* a clear little voice spoke out of the gloom, and there was the lady herself, holding the weary grey pony. To her few gentle words in Gaelic MacSorley, with a change in his manner, replied in the same tongue.

Bride turned to her companion. "What are we to do? He says there is not a bed to spare. There are three travellers here from Fort William, Englishmen. He and his wife have given up their bed to two of them, and the third is in the only other room—a very small one. I must sleep in the kitchen, or in an outhouse."

"That, madame, you will certainly not do!" replied Marie-Cyprien, with decision and in French. "Let us go in, and I will make this third traveller give up his room to you." He offered his hand with a determined air, the farmer standing back as one not quite certain what he is about. And Bride at least knew that he must have been deeply fuddled for his reception of her to be so little consonant with the traditional hospitality of the Highlands and the arrival of a benighted woman.

She hesitated a moment. "But—have you not said, monsieur, that you are my servant?" she asked softly. "Because if so, this traveller would not listen to you. And . . . how noisy they are in there! Is there not a barn or an outhouse? Truly I could sleep in the hay."

Highly unsuitable as this would be, her harassed escort

did for a moment consider whether it would not be preferable to attracting the attention of Englishmen from Fort William. But—a dirty shelter with the probable company of cattle or horses—no! St. Joseph was really carrying matters too far! He was about to condemn this proposal with vigour when out of the kitchen there suddenly rolled a stout red-faced gentleman, conformable, whether he were one or no, to Marie-Cyprien's idea of an English squire.

"What's this, Mr. What's-your-name?" he demanded of his Highland host in a jovial, wine-cheered voice. "New arrivals? The more the merrier!" He peered past MacSorley. "A lady too, I declare! Come in, madam, come in, young sir! Good God, don't keep her out there in the cold, man! There's supper enough for all—and a pleasure to have one of the fair sex to share it with us." Thereupon he made large shepherding gestures towards Mr. MacSorley's kitchen.

"It is absolutely necessary, then, that I should come in with you," whispered Marie-Cyprien rapidly into Bride's ear. "I shall not be your servant now, but . . . some kind of a relative. Courage; I will answer for it that no harm befalls you! We can leave the horses for a moment; they will certainly not run away!" And with her hand on his arm he led her past the self-constituted host straight into the warm kitchen, where at a long table spread with food and drink sat the two other travellers. For a second or so they stared owlishly at the new-comers, then, perceiving a lady, got slowly to their feet. And one of the two was a young and tipsy redcoat officer.

Grand Dieu! Had they walked into a trap instead of into shelter? Marie-Cyprien felt the little hand on his arm jerk slightly; his own heart gave a jump. But he must keep his head. Provided that the farmer still did not recognise him and proclaim the fact! That probably depended upon the exact stage of intoxication at which he had arrived, hanging about there in the doorway.

"Come, come," said the hearty Englishman, close behind, "a place for the lady! Will you not remove your cloak, madam?"

"My sister," said Marie-Cyprien—and paused, frowning—then resumed quickly, in his most carefully pronounced English, "She will prefer, I think, to sit by the fire." For by the big hearth was a woman, Mrs. Mac-Sorley, probably, busy with a pot. He led Bride in that direction.

"Your sister!" exclaimed the Englishman. "But—eshcuse me, madam—she don't look foreign. And you are, ain't you, sir? . . . Eshcuse me!" he added again, as one half conscious of a breach of manners.

Now it is a fact that the Vicomte de Lancize had never meant to claim this improbable-seeming blood relationship; he had intended merely to refer to one by marriage. But the English word for *belle-sœur,* if he had ever known it, had eluded his memory. Annoyed, he murmured: "No, no, not my sister, my——" But the term would not come.

To his relief and admiration his new relative supplied it. "This gentleman means 'sister-in-law,' " she explained shyly.

"But you are *not* a native of this country, sir, are you now?" pursued the elder of the two at the table—drily, for all that he was far from sober.

"Nevertheless, my brother may have married one, may he not?" retorted the young Frenchman pleasantly, placing a stool for Bride by the fire. "No, sir, I am not of these islands; I am—an Italian." For to be French was hardly safe.

"Well, I'm damned!" observed the pseudo-squire, staring at him. "An Italian! Who would think of meeting an Italian in these outlandish parts! And with a Scotch lady, too! For I take it——"

But here, to Marie-Cyprien's intense relief, the harsh-looking individual at the table curtly bade the speaker desist and come and finish his whisky, nasty as it was; and with surprising docility his companion obeyed.

Rid of this interrogatory M. de Lancize, after giving

Bride into the charge of the woman, whispered that he was going out to see to the horses, since on their proper and immediate care depended their own chances of getting away early next morning. Yet as he proceeded to the door he heard the young officer, who was clearly the least sober of the three, proclaiming his very low opinion of Italians in general—dirty Papists all of them, the people who harboured the Pretender and his jackanapes of a son. Marie-Cyprien took care not to seem to hear this. He did not appear to have made a very good exchange of nationality.

But at least he found in the rough outhouse—a mere peat and heather affair—a man who was willing to undertake the care of the horses; and he hurried back to find his "sister-in-law" with a bowl of broth upon her knee and the woman attending on her. He was also relieved to observe that the three men, absorbed in their potations, were not paying any attention to her; this was good, notwithstanding the noise and the atmosphere of tobacco-smoke in which these were conducted. He sat himself down at the end of the table with one eye on them, one upon her. What a pretty picture she made, despite her evident fatigue, as she sat there, the bowl of soup upon her knee, the firelight playing on her *chevelure de fée!* He almost wished that she did not—prayed at least that the idea would not occur so forcibly to the three topers as to call forth vinous compliments. The next question was, Where was she going to sleep? "The cares, but not the privileges, of a husband appear to have become mine now," he reflected as he embarked thankfully on the broth which Mrs. MacSorley put before him.

Before another half-hour had passed "the Italian gentleman" had attained his object. The two elder men—the other, whose social status Marie-Cyprien could not even make a guess at, was quiet, almost morose, in his cups—eventually, and by means of many bibulous repetitions, made it clear to the young officer (who turned out to be

x

an ensign of Houghton's regiment from Fort William) that he was to give up his room to the fair traveller. Perhaps the soldier was too drunk to understand on whose behalf he was thus being ejected from what he pathetically protested was only a cupboard after all, only a damned poky little cupboard, for while his effects were bundled out by Mrs. MacSorley he, too incapacitated to interfere, lamented, even with tears, that he had ever come to Scotland to be treated so scurvily.

"Be sure to lock your door, madame!" advised Marie-Cyprien in a low voice as Mrs. MacSorley finally bore off Bride from the kitchen.

The ensign soon subsiding on to the table, the two other convivialists removed and deposited him on the settle near the fire, where he sank into a stertorous repose. But they, though not in much better case, continued an interminable and repetitive conversation; at least, it seemed interminable to the young Frenchman, who was very tired and only longing to stretch himself out on the table with the plaid which he had unrolled from his saddle-bow. They were lucky enough to have a bed, those two; why did they not go to it? At last they did stumble out, and he was free from the danger of awkward questions, some of which he had already avoided only by pretending not to understand them—questions about his pretty sister-in-law and where he was taking her to, and why; and some very disconcerting topographical queries relating to Italy, a country upon which he had never set eyes. But now he could have some peace and badly-needed sleep.

Despite the plaid the kitchen table was uncommonly hard; his arm, too, was paining him. The firelight was still bright, annoyingly bright. It cast fantastic shadows on the kitchen walls and ceiling; the flames seemed to whisper among the peats like persons talking. How long had he lain here? Was he asleep or awake? Surely the fire could not, unaided, have cast that gigantic shadow, like a man's, nor have given body to that hoarse, sleepy voice muttering angrily something about a bed, a bed, not a ——

plank? The owner of this voice *knew* that he had a bed! Where the devil was it? He wasn't going to be fobbed off with a plank by any Papistical foreigner; by the Lord, he wasn't!

Marie de Lancize was off the table like an eel, added his shadow for a moment to that of this ornament of Houghton's regiment, then slid out of the kitchen and—noiselessly, having already discarded his boots—groped his way to the door which he knew to be Madame Bride's. Had she been able to fasten it? But he would not alarm her by awaking her to ascertain this; he could easily keep this drunken sot away.

He did not have to. By the light coming from the kitchen he watched with a sardonic amusement the antics of the sot as he felt over the wall in totally wrong places for the door of his ravished apartment. After two or three minutes of vain exploration, including the opening of the outer door and a puzzled and disgusted recognition of the cold to which he had thus exposed himself, the ensign went back shivering and cursing to the warm kitchen.

But it was by no means certain that he would not renew the search for his rightful bedchamber. There was only one thing to be done. In order to fetch his plaid Marie-Cyprien also stole back into the kitchen. He found the young drunkard sitting up on the settle. "I thought I had a bedroom!" he was muttering, with surprising clarity of speech. "Damme, I am sure I had a bedroom!"

"Yes, my friend, but you have it no longer!" murmured Marie-Cyprien between his teeth. "And if you come again to look for it, I'll wring your neck!"

Lying across Madame Bride's door it was impossible, of course, not to think of his rôle, so fundamentally changed from that of two nights ago. Had it not been infernally draughty here on the stone floor he could have smiled at himself. And there was another factor damping to humour—the thought of rats. The self-constituted sentry already fancied that he heard them squeaking and scuttling somewhere. He had been told that they attacked the faces of sleepers, and he was very far from indifferent to the present admirable shape of his nose. So he raised himself wearily from his recumbent position and sat upright, his back against the doorpost. There, with nodding head and frequent slipping and recoveries and starts he slept, in a fashion, until in the early dawn he woke, very cold and cramped; when nature, ignoring the possibility of ravage by rodents, coaxed him down to a more comfortable if still chilly position, and to dreams of sleeping under the spray of the great waterfall outside.

CHAPTER XXIX

(1)

M. LE VICOMTE DE LANCIZE had observed rightly; despite her anxiety, Bride was nearer to happiness than she had been for fifteen long days. No longer did she feel as if she were living in a frozen, sunless desert. The ice had melted, the desert was clothed with green at one breath of an appeal for forgiveness, though it had reached her from so far, and through the mouth of so false a messenger. Ranald *had* uttered that word, for M. de Lancize had heard it, and that was enough. He was sorry: he had written to her—though she could never read the letter now. Those two great facts were all she needed to know —they were the strands in the golden cord pulling her to him. As for her escort on that journey, his company was the price she had to pay to reach Ranald. And though M. de Lancize's conduct might have been unpardonably treacherous, she would, if necessary, have gone with *An Dòlas Mór*, the Big Sorrow himself, to Glen Suileag now. So, since she did believe that the young Frenchman was sincere in his penitence, and since after all he was the only link she had with her husband, she was able without much effort to regard him merely in the latter light. Her thoughts were really little engaged with him at all; when at times she realised how little, she was astonished.

Yet, engrossed and tired as she was, Bride did reflect for a moment, when she lay down on the rather austere bed designed for the dispossessed young officer of Houghton's, that M. de Lancize had that day proved extremely considerate and resourceful, that she had not disliked being alone with him on this afternoon's pilgrimage as much as she should have expected. She fell asleep thinking that by the same time to-morrow she should be with Ranald, her husband, all misunderstandings cleared away. Only, in what state should she find him?

Once in the early dawn she woke fancying she had heard a strange movement outside her door. But that door was securely fastened from within and she went to sleep again unalarmed.

Mrs. MacSorley roused her about half-past six, reporting that the Italian gentleman, her brother-in-law, was anxious to start in good time as they had a long day before them. If the young lady wished, she would bring her breakfast to the bedroom, for the English officer was still asleep in the kitchen.

There was that about Mrs. MacSorley which suggested all sorts of questions seething in her mind. Bride was sure that she believed M. de Lancize and her to be eloping, and wondered, too, that neither she nor her husband appeared to have recognised him, which was probably as well. No doubt Uncle Walter's clothes accounted for this. The suggestion about breakfast she gratefully accepted, hence she and her escort did not actually meet until she went out to the spot where he was holding Mally and the garron outside the door, against a scenic background of mountain-sides swathed in mist and an audible one of the never-ceasing thunder of the fall.

"I hope, madame, that you slept?" he enquired.

"Very well, thank you, monsieur. And you—you had a hard bed, I fear, on that table?" For Bride had heard overnight of that proposed couch.

Her "brother-in-law" looked at her for a second with a spark of something resembling suppressed amusement in his eyes . . . only how could it be that? "I had all the sleep I needed, madame, I thank you," he answered politely.

Before leaving the farm-house Mrs. Ranald Maclean's guide had been remembering with some uneasiness—chiefly on account of the horses—an awkward place which they would soon have to negotiate. And, after having covered little more than a mile, they arrived at this spot, where, the path having risen and turned, they found themselves hugging the very sides of the great mountain towering above them, with a sheer drop below to the tumbling stream, their steps to pick and another waterfall to cross. Round this gully, too, the wind came swooping disconcertingly.

It was not a dangerous place for a man or woman with a steady head; it had not in the least troubled Marie-Cyprien when he traversed it before, but he was anxious on his companion's account and on the mare Mally's as well, for she was not over-sure-footed. They were obliged to let the horses take their own way on the narrow path in front of them, and the mare suddenly appeared to the anxious eyes of her rider to be as fat as a barrel—while the rocky wall on the right hand gave no quarter to obesity. Bride followed the mare, and Marie-Cyprien brought up the rear close behind the young lady, ready to snatch at her if necessary. It occurred to him that possibly the presence of that young birch-tree a little way ahead, maintaining itself on the very verge of the track, might be a consolation to her, with its suggestion of some slight barrier against a fall. Beyond the tree the path soon began to slope downwards again, and, twisting itself and becoming wider, turned once more westwards.

The little cavalcade passed the tree and engaged on the downward slope. A particularly sudden and violent gust of wind rushed round the turn, and something white fluttered past Marie-Cyprien. The girl in front stopped and half turned. "My pocket-handkerchief!—No matter, monsieur, it has gone!"

But the young man, turning completely, saw that it had, on the contrary, been carried by the blast as far as the solitary birch-tree, and had lodged, flattened, about four feet up against the stem. "I will get it," he said, and ran back. Just as he was about to put out his hand to take the piece of cambric the wind impishly released its pressure, the fugitive slid down the birch-trunk, was caught in an opposing gust and sailed downwards over the edge of the path, Marie-Cyprien making a hasty and ill-advised grab at it as it went. The result was that but for the close presence of the birch-tree he would probably have followed it altogether.

Reflecting on the incident afterwards, not without a feeling of humiliation, he came to the conclusion that he must either have trodden on a loose stone or that a small portion of the edge of the path had given way. At the moment his chief impression was of the convulsive, dragging clutch he made at the tree, and, a second or two later, when he was in safety, and had relinquished his embrace, of the sickening wrench which he had given to his injured arm in saving himself.

He got somehow down the path to the white-faced Bride, backed against the little ferns of the rock wall.

"I am afraid that your handkerchief is lost . . . I am sorry. . . ." He hardly knew what he was saying; but he realised that he must be as pale as she. And she would think it was from fear; yet he must submit to that misapprehension, for he could not possibly bring himself to tell her . . . after the other night's business—that it was merely the pain in his arm . . .

"Oh, Monsieur de Lancize, it is I who am sorry! If you had—it was my fault!"

"Let us go on," he said rather abruptly, feeling that if his head were to continue swimming like this, he might yet end by staggering over the edge.

Perhaps Madame Bride read that possibility in his face, for she obeyed on the instant, hastening down the remainder of the narrow part of the path. Directly she was on the wider portion, at the turn, instead of waiting for him to do it, she went after the slowly proceeding mare and pony, caught their reins and brought them to a stand-still.

Marie-Cyprien followed, very close to the rock. "Madame," he said when he reached her, "I apologise for alarming you. And you must not think——"

But he did not make clear what she was not to think, but suddenly flung his sound arm across Mally's saddle-bow to steady himself, hearing at the same time someone give a kind of groan. And immediately, or so it seemed, he was then sitting on a projection of rock, leaning his head on his hand. When he raised it there, a few paces away, was the mare turning an enquiring head, and kneeling beside him Madame Bride with a little travelling-cup in her hand full of water.

"I fear you hurt your arm severely," she said gravely, "—and through my carelessness. Will you not drink this? 'Tis from the waterfall here."

It was, he decided, worth the pain and faintness to encounter her gaze as it was then. And he had not been driven, in order to save himself from being suspected of the white feather, to mention the real cause of his semi-collapse. Clever as she was courageous, she had guessed it! Marie-Cyprien thanked her with a smile, took the little cup and drank off its spring-cold contents.

The wind had already done them an ill service; rain was to do them the next. It began not long after this, the fine, thick, lightly-driving rain than which there is nothing wetter. For a while they went on enveloped in the plaids from their saddles; then Mrs. Maclean, to her escort's great relief, was induced to consent to their seeking shelter in a disused quarry which they happened to be passing. Here in a species of shallow cave they sat for what seemed hours and watched the mountain-sides opposite withdrawing themselves into that veil of spun water. They ate some provisions, and Marie-Cyprien even found himself conversing without awkwardness—about his family, in particular about a sister who was a nun, which had seemed a safe topic. . . .

At last the rain, contrary to their expectations, stopped altogether, and the travellers emerged from their retreat and remounted. But they had not gone another three miles—being now in the green and open part of that splendid glen—when they realised that the worst misfortune of all lay in front of them. For about a quarter of a mile ahead was a body of men with spades and picks, repairing the track. Most of them had their coats off, but from the couple who had retained them it was clear even at that distance that they who were engaged in this commendable and pacific operation were soldiers from Fort William.

From Marie-Cyprien's lips there issued a justifiable oath, followed by a half-hearted apology. What were they to do? Wait until the road-menders had finished and withdrawn? But that might be hours hence. Moreover, they themselves must have been seen, and such a proceeding might arouse suspicions. So, since there was no possibility of going round them, they must ride boldly on through the midst of these toilers. Marie de Lancize was exceedingly reluctant to do it, but he was beginning to think that his little fellow-pilgrim would handle the situation better than he. There were two unpleasant possibilities— that the redcoats might stop them altogether or that they might utter rough pleasantries about Madame Bride which he dared not resent, for the moment he claimed to be any kind of lawful protector his tongue would bewray him, as it had done last night. These men, moreover, were presumably of that English regiment which was graced by the possession of the drunken ensign at the farm-house.

Bride Maclean must have been reflecting much as he, for she turned to him a face which he thought had paled a trifle, and herself suggested that he should pretend to be a Highland servant understanding no English, and that if he had to address her it should be in French, which with luck the soldiers might mistake for Erse. And Marie-Cyprien, assenting but hoping that none of the fatigue-party had served abroad, dropped behind to a distance as short as was consonant with his new status.

The road-menders ceased work, straightened themselves up and stared as, without any visible hesitation, Mist's rider advanced towards them. And Marie-Cyprien was not too far off to hear their remarks. They were not of the kind he had feared.

"Stand aside and let the lady pass . . . Bill, take that pick out of the young lady's way! . . . Best let me lead your pony, ma'am—there's a bit of a place here we han't filled up yet."

Ciel! was it as easy as that? Madame Bride had said nothing that he could hear, but no doubt she had smiled. Following behind, little noticed by "Bill" and his comrades, who were too much taken up with the lady, Marie-Cyprien heard the pony's rider thank the corporal of the party, as he loosed her bridle and carried his hand to the salute. It came to him that it would make an excellent impression if he rewarded this man for his civility—gave him something in which to drink the lady's health, the English never being averse (so he understood) to this exercise. Only he was afraid to utter the phrase which should accompany the gift. With nothing more than a smile, therefore, he bent from the saddle in passing and slipped into the corporal's hand a coin hastily extracted from his breeches pocket—and had not ridden half a dozen yards before he could have shot himself for his stupidity in not looking at it first. It was an even chance that he had presented the soldier not with an English shilling, but with a French livre, for, as he remembered too late, he had a little French money in that pocket.

Badly shaken, Marie-Cyprien rode on after his charge. He had probably wrecked the miracle which she by some means or other had accomplished. Yet he dared neither look back nor suggest to her that she should urge her pony to a canter. He was afraid even to tell her what he had—perhaps—done.

This state of self-reproach and apprehension lasted for about a mile, when little Madame Bride, slackening her pace to allow her "servant" to come up with her, observed softly:

"I cannot think that *those* redcoats massacred our wounded in cold blood!"

"It is indeed unlikely," agreed her escort. Well, either his largesse had been coin of the realm after all, or the corporal had pocketed it unexamined, as it had been given. And falling back a little he passed his handkerchief over a beaded brow.

(2)

The dreary expanse of Corpach Moss, windswept and cloud-canopied, seemed endless when they came to it in the late afternoon, with the high-shouldered mass of Ben Nevis growing in some sinister fashion larger and more menacing the further they receded from it. And the Moss became more endless still when it was discovered that the grey pony had cast a shoe.

It was the last straw. Marie-Cyprien grimly dismounted, changed the saddles, put Bride on Mally and plodded alongside leading the limping garron. The going here, fortunately, was soft; but he seemed to remember that the track along Loch Eil-side was stony. It was to be hoped that at the hamlet of Corpach, which they would eventually reach, they might find a smithy.

They did, a very small one; and the forge-fire was out, and the smith unwilling to relight it for the sake of one shoe. Between the time spent in prevailing upon him to do so, in getting it to the proper heat, and in hunting for the right size of nails, the daylight was fast fading as the two rode out of Corpach towards the Narrows, where Loch Linnhe finally bent round and became Loch Eil. Along the grey, heron-haunted waters they went in silence, with a lurid rift of light straight ahead in the west behind the sharp Glenfinnan peaks a dozen miles away.

Somewhere beneath those mountains, thought the young officer suddenly, is surely where the Prince Charles Edouard set up his standard more than a year ago? Where was that unfortunate now? Still hidden on that unamiable mountain, or in the hands of a party of exultant

English soldiers? There was no agency, human or spiritual, to convey to the Frenchman or to the still more interested Highland girl the information that this very thirteenth of September was the day when the Prince, leaving his retreat on Ben Alder, had started towards the western coast, and that in exactly a week's time he should sail away from Scotland for ever.

Dusk was coming down rapidly when, half-way along the loch, the riders neared the spreading mouth of Glen Suileag, which, for all its width, was far from level, being encumbered at the entrance with a jumble of low hillocks. Marie-Cyprien was all for asking for shelter for the night at Fassefern House, which he knew to lie on the other side of the stream, though he could not actually see it, nor the lights of any other of the little dwellings in its neighbourhood; but Bride was determined to push on. So very few miles now divided her husband and her; surely there was still enough daylight to find their way up the glen; if need be, she would go on foot! It was impossible to resist the mixture of appeal and resolution, and so against both his better judgment and his own personal wishes, the young Frenchman had to yield. Dearly would he himself have liked to lie in a decent bed to-night; and as for Madame Bride, he knew what the sleeping arrangements of the Kennedys' hut were like—how could she spend the night on a filthy deer-skin? Moreover, it would certainly be more seemly to seek some roof before it became any later; but his charge seemed now to have cast the conventionalities to the winds. At any rate, that showed that she trusted him. And whose fault was it that she should feel such need of haste, to make up for time lost? Not by any means for the first time during this odyssey did that thought come to shut Marie-Cyprien's protesting lips.

But the light was failing with startling rapidity as they cautiously plunged over or between the wave-like hillocks, where the path was sometimes almost impossible to make out, so that they had twice to turn back a short space to recover it. They met no one; all the small habitations were, as Marie-Cyprien remembered, on the other side of the stream, except one partially ruined hut in a cleared but now half-overgrown patch of hazels.

And at last, inevitably, came the moment when it was no good disguising the fact that they could go no further; nor, now, could they find their way back and across the stream to Fassefern. They were already leading their steeds; Marie de Lancize turned, gave vent to this truth and met with no reply in the dusk but a sigh.

And how was he going to contrive any shelter on a far from warm September night for this devoted young wife? He could not make a tent out of their two plaids. He stood gazing down at what he could see of her face in its frame of hood; she looked so small and young and tired, the garron's bridle in her hand. Yet, Dieu, how *entêtée* she could show herself! But for that they would not be stuck here now. . . . Then he remembered the ruined cabin they had passed some five minutes ago; part of the roof had seemed whole. He suggested returning to it; and to this, sadly and meekly, Mrs. Ranald Maclean agreed.

This little erection had not been burned like some which Marie-Cyprien had seen further up the glen, but had merely fallen into decay. Looked up at from inside, one end at least of the roof appeared intact. The Vicomte fastened up the horses and then, stumbling over hidden obstacles, ensnaring himself in brambles, collected sufficient dead bracken to counteract the asperity and dampness of the earth floor, heaped this in the sound corner of the hut and spread a plaid over it. He had long ere this abandoned all attempts at avoiding the use of his left arm.

After that, standing together in the broken doorway of the place—for there was no possible seat of any kind, and it was lighter there than within—the benighted pilgrims ate some cold provisions . . . the strangest meal. By the time they had finished they could scarcely distinguish each other's features. Never had the Vicomte Marie de Lancize, late of Dauphin-Dragons, found himself in so bizarre a situation with a lady (though he was not in-experienced in situations) and he was certain that his fair companion had never been within a hundred miles of circumstances so unusual. Yet she gave no sign of em-barrassment. Marie-Cyprien believed that all her emotions were swallowed up in her deep disappointment at being so near her goal yet failing to reach it before nightfall, and he was sorry for her, even though he con-sidered that her reunion with Maclean could quite well wait until to-morrow . . . and that the interval might just as well have been spent under more civilised conditions.

The uncomfortable and frigid meal being finished, he obtained a momentary glow from his tinder-box and shed it over the couch in the corner so that she might know her way to it. A more lasting illumination was impossible.

"You will do your best to sleep, madame, will you not?" he counselled in the most fraternal-sounding manner. "With both plaids and that bracken I think you will not be too uncomfortable."

"Both plaids!" exclaimed Bride. "No, indeed, mon-sieur, nothing will induce me to accept both. One will be enough, with my cloak. But you, where do you——"

She stopped half-way to the question, and for the first time there was something of embarrassment in her voice.

But with cheerful tact her companion replied: "I must lie, madame, where I can have an eye upon the horses." He could here have revenged himself in half a dozen ways, as by asking her whether he was likely to share the same roof—the same piece of roof—with her; by announcing that he could scarcely be more uncomfortable than propped against her doorpost, as last night. But he re-frained, for after all it was not he who had wrongs to avenge—well he knew it! So, having agreed to accept the plaid and proposed that they should set out again as early as possible, he struck a light once more to show her the way to her couch, and leaving her in the unrelieved gloom went forth into the extraordinary stillness of the September night, in which the sudden blowing out of

Mally's nostrils sounded almost like an explosion, and the clink of the garron's hoof against a hidden stone might have been caused by the pick of some energetic miner.

Calling himself an imbecile if ever there was one, the disciple of Bayard chose as little uncomfortable a spot as possible in the lee of the hut, and rolled himself tightly in the plaid. It was not, of course, the first time that he had slept in the open in these latitudes, but he had never yet spent the night outside a shelter when he might have been inside it. It was cold, but he might at least thank Heaven that it was not raining, and did not, in fact, seem to have rained in this glen at all to-day. Yet the ground felt by no means dry. Rheumatism would be his portion, or at least a cold in the head. If it came on to rain, was he still to lie out here? Pondering this contingency, he at last fell asleep.

And despite sundry writhings and turnings he succeeded in sleeping until the sky above him was flecked with pinkish clouds, the prelude, possibly, to a fine day. He felt for his watch; it had stopped, and he could not tell what time it was. Yawning and stretching, he roused himself, and was suddenly rent with a sneeze loud enough, surely, to wake the fair sleeper within. Unrolling himself from the plaid Marie-Cyprien rose, went to the doorway, and softly called her name.

There was no answer, and as he felt almost sure that so explosive a sneeze must have awakened her if she were really there, it occurred to him to wonder whether his charge, so eager to reach her husband, had perhaps given him the slip during his own slumber, and was already proceeding up the glen on foot. Of this he must make sure, so he tiptoed into the forlorn little building, the interior of which he now for the first time saw clearly.

No, she was there in her corner, fast asleep, lying on the bracken with the red and green tartan drawn over her; lying like a tired child in the abandonment of slumber, the hood fallen away from her face and a long loop of sheer gold strayed out among the fern; her lashes down, motionless; one hand under her cheek—a child asleep.

But she was not a child; she was a grown woman and a wedded one. And he was the man who three nights ago had bent all his energies, even to the point of outraging hospitality, to secure the pleasure of looking upon her thus . . . but who had found that what he contemplated doing was impossible and always would be. Yet, as he stood there and looked down at her, a hot wave of the blood seemed for a moment a little to sap that conviction. Marie de Lancize stood a few seconds longer breathing rather fast, then turned abruptly and went out of the cabin. Best get the horses ready immediately.

But when he went to the clump of hazels where he had tethered them, the young man found that of his two companions of the opposite sex, though the human lady had not given him the slip, the mare Mally amazingly had. Hard as it was to believe his eyes, the grey pony was there alone.

Marie-Cyprien cursed the truant animal and her progenitors—and himself. He must have fastened her insecurely—unless, indeed, she had been stolen. But, provided that were not so, she would not have strayed far, sluggish beast that she was, so sluggish that he was surprised as well as mortified to discover that she had had sufficient energy and determination to wrench herself free and go off. And now, was he at once to pursue the runaway? No, not until Madame Bride was awake, for she would be alarmed if she found him gone, and he had no means of writing a note to reassure her.

Should he waken her, then? That seemed a shame, as it must still be quite early. Efforts to track the errant mare's hoof-marks proved quite unavailing. If only the grey garron, disconsolately twitching off hazel shoots and dropping them, could tell him something! He walked up and down, not too warm, in the morning damps, and all the time the pull was on him to steal into the hut again to look at little Madame Bride asleep. He knew it was wiser to abstain. Yes, she *was* guarded by her own purity and

Y

innocence, he was perfectly conscious of that, but all the same. . . . It was different when she was awake. . . . He decided to wake her and tell her what had happened to the mare, and standing in the doorway, but not where he could see her, he called her name rather loudly.

After a moment her voice answered, plainly alarmed; so he supposed that there must have been in his own more urgency than he was aware of.

"Is anything the matter, Monsieur de Lancize?"

"No, madame—at least, only a small mishap. When you are ready to receive me I will tell you what it is."

In a moment or two she appeared in the doorway, still a little rosy with sleep, but with no signs of disorder in her dress, the hood of her cloak held together under her chin to hide from him, he supposed, any dishevelment of her hair . . . but, as he told himself with a gleam of exultation, it was too late for that—and he informed her of Mally's most unexpected behaviour, and of how he proposed, now that she herself was awake, to go after the stray.

"I am sure that she will not have gone far, madame. You will not be alarmed at being left for a quarter of an hour or so?"

Bride shook her head with a little smile. "*I* have nothing to fear."

"Then wait here, if you will be so good. Here is some oat-cake, and when I return I will see if I can find water. I promise you, madame, not to go far; if I cannot find the mare we must make shift without her, and fortunately there is still your pony. But I am ashamed of my bad picketing; I fear you can have small opinion of me as a cavalry officer!"

It was the first time he had ventured upon anything like a pleasantry, since it was the first time that he had felt a little self-respect returning to him. For after all he *had* resisted the temptation to go in and look at her again!

Directly her escort had departed Bride went out in

search of water to wash her face, but the stream was too far away. After wandering round a little she returned to shelter, took a comb and mirror out of her little *nécessaire*, removed her cloak and shook down her disordered hair. She was not thinking of her appearance in the eyes of M. de Lancize, but in Ranald's. She had slept ill at first, not only from the discomfort of her unusual bed and its surroundings, but also from dreaming of all kinds of mishaps; but at least she could be neat. She put the little mirror on the ground and knelt above it. The comb went through and through; she put it down, shook back the golden flood and had just seized it in both hands preparatory to twisting it up when she abruptly let it fall again and stood up with a cry. Down the glen, and from no very great distance, had travelled the sound of a shot—of two shots close together.

Bride stood horror-struck. What had happened—in God's name what had happened? M. de Lancize—had he met with soldiers? Had they shot him? Those reports *must* have to do with him! Snatching up her cloak, her hair all unbound, Bride began to run in the direction he had taken, that path mounting and falling among the hillocks which admitted of no distant view at all. If he were captured—wounded—what should she do? It would be her fault, her fault entirely!

Once she checked in her running, but only for a moment. If there were soldiers they might stop her from going up the glen; or, even if they did not, she would scarcely dare to go lest they might follow her and discover Ranald. Then she was ashamed of having listened to that whisper, and started on again. She must know what had happened to her companion; she was not so ungrateful as *that*, not so unforgiving!

CHAPTER XXX

(1)

LIE here to be slaughtered—lie here while that treacherous cateran plotted against Bride, while Bride herself was left at Inchrannoch without a protector? No!

It was true, as Ranald knew, that he could not save himself if it came to a personal conflict with Gregor Murray, but he could surely crawl some distance away from the cabin and lie hid in the glen? The two women would never betray his retreat, once he had told them that the visitor was no friend of his, but his deadliest foe. A day ago he had actually contrived to stand for a moment or two, with the aid of a stick and by putting all his weight on his uninjured leg. The effort had wrenched at the wound and he had not intended to repeat it for a while: but now he would have to do so.

Where Gregor had gone to, from what spot he would come again, Ranald had no idea, nor, very naturally, had the children who alone had witnessed his arrival and departure. He had perhaps found a temporary habitation in some deserted and half-burnt-out crofter's house at a distance. But, wherever his enemy was, Ranald was determined that he should not have his life for the asking, and marry Bride afterwards. It was this latter thought which was flooding his limbs with a sort of crazy strength, his brain with a crazy determination.

Ah, God, if only he could be transported, as on an eagle's back, to the house which he had left so madly, so unjustifiably, that night! An eagle, with one beat of its mighty pinions, could traverse the airy space between two mountain-peaks in little more than the time of an eyelid's lifting; Ranald had himself witnessed that marvel. But

for him, crippled, weak from fever, why, if he succeeded
in evading Gregor, it would take weeks to crawl back to
Rannoch. Besides his enemy, there were the Hanoverian
soldiers to reckon with. If there were only some means of
transport, however rude . . . if he only had a horse, however old and slow! He would contrive to stay in the saddle
somehow.

Directly the women had given the children their meagre
supper and bidden them be quiet, he began to talk to
them, and told them what had happened and what he had
decided to do in the first instance—hide somewhere else in
the glen. Horrified both at his revelation and at this determination they could not, since his life was at stake,
attempt to stay him. But when Ranald mentioned a horse
it was as though he had spoken of procuring an elephant.
To come by a horse was out of the question; no one in
this part of the glen had ever possessed one, and even
had they done so it would have been carried off long ago
by the *saighdearan dearg*.

Yet Ranald persisted. Ever since the picture of himself riding, however painfully, eastwards had come into
his mind, he had felt convinced that a horse could somehow be procured. The only question was, how soon? He
asked whether the man, Hugh Cameron, at the mouth of
the glen, who had acted as guide to the two French officers
could not lay his hands on one somewhere? All that night
he dreamed of riding—riding a horse that moved like a
snail . . . that refused to move at all . . . that sank in
bogs or slipped on stony tracks. And when, in his dreams,
he reached a house which was not Inchrannoch, someone
who was not Bride opened the door—the real Bride was
gone for ever. And he knew who had sent her away—
himself.

Mairi Kennedy, when, very early next morning, she
bandaged his wound more tightly at his behest, plainly
suspected that the fever was lying hold of him again. So
that when her old mother-in-law came in with some peats
from the heap outside mumbling the word *each*—for there

was a horse grazing out there, she could not think why—
young Mrs. Kennedy uttered a shrill exclamation and sat
back on her heels looking at her patient in a half-terrified
wonder.

"I knew it, I knew it!" cried Ranald exultantly. "I
knew there would be a horse for me! Catch it at once
and bring it here! Pray God it will not go from you! But
where can it have come from?"

"I do not think it will go from us," said the old woman.
"Quiet enough it seems, and not a young horse, cropping
the grass a little way off and the bridle trailing. Mairi and
the children can catch it if you wish, *Raonuill Mhic
Ghilleathain!*"

"Surely you have the two sights!" broke from the
younger woman slowly and with awe.

"If I have, 'tis the first time in my life! But go quickly;
give me first the staff I had yesterday. Yes, you can lend
me your arm, Mairi; but waste no time, or the horse may
be gone!"

Effort it was indeed, and painful effort; but Ranald
struggled off the deer-skin, got by young Mrs. Kennedy's
aid to an upright position, and, while she ran out to secure
the strange horse, tottered, sweating, the few paces to the
low doorway. With difficulty, too, he stooped to pass out.
It was like bursting from a tomb. For there was the broad
green glen waiting in an utter stillness for sunrise—and,
in the midst of all that bewildering light and space, Mairi
Kennedy in her rags tugging along by the bridle a brown
mare which, indeed, seemed quiet enough, though reluctant to leave the scrap of grazing which she had found
by the burn. After what Ranald had been told, a chariot
of fire arriving for him in this remote place would hardly
have seemed more of a miracle. Staring at the mare being
pulled towards him he almost feared, indeed, that she
would dissolve into mist.

Moreover—or was the fever creeping upon him again?
—the beast was familiar! Surely he had seen before that
one white stocking and that oddly shaped white star; yes,

and that mark of an old cut on the near foreleg! He had seen this very mare being groomed in the yard at Inchrannoch during those few halcyon days which he had passed there immediately after he had made Bride his own. He leant back heavily against the sod-covered wall of the hut, turning so pale that the old woman, who was watching him, cried out in warning to her daughter-in-law.

A horse from Inchrannoch grazing riderless here in Glen Suileag! What in God's name could it mean? Only that someone from Inchrannoch must be near. But who? Old Mr. Stewart, so MacGregor had said, had been arrested. But perhaps that was a lie. Yet, in any case, where *was* the unknown rider?

"Which way was the horse straying, do you think?" he asked the old woman. For a traveller from Inchrannoch might have entered Glen Suileag from either end, though the southern was the more probable. Mrs. Kennedy answered that when she had first seen the mare her head had been pointing up the glen. So the animal had probably, though not certainly, come up from Loch Eil side.

Then and there Ranald made his farewells. The poor care of these two women, the best that they could give, had probably saved his life; they had fed and sheltered him when they had barely food for themselves, or bedding, or even a whole roof. Yet had it not been that he was able to urge the children's need he would never, he knew, have succeeded in inducing them to take a penny of recompense. With that plea he did succeed, even then only just skirting giving them offence.

Mounting was a problem which excluded the question of what he was going to do when he was in the saddle . . . if he could stay there at all. Yet, once he was up, despite pain and a passing access of giddiness, the sense of moving by predestined means to a predestined end began immediately to sweep him along like a bark moving to harbour on the flood. The means of transport had been miraculously provided for him; he would reach Bride now or die in the attempt . . . and he knew that he should not die. So purposeful an air encompassed him, so erect did he hold himself, he who could not walk a step save with a support, and had but a week ago been too weak to feed himself, that the two women left standing at the door shook their heads and said to each other: "He is fey!"

For with just that strange, half-fevered confidence were the fey possessed, and enabled often thereby to do extraordinary deeds: but in the end. . . .

(2)

It was true, reflected the Vicomte de Lancize, as he hurried away in the early morning stillness; Madame Bride had nothing to fear, or he would not have left her, even to retrieve the mare. (In fact, had she but known it, the period of slight danger—very slight, but still perceptible—was past.) The picture of her lying asleep among the fern in that broken hovel accompanied him for a little way; then he dismissed it for more practical matters. Where could that confounded mare have taken herself to? Had she been stolen? Highlanders, he knew, had a great reputation for annexing cattle. Really, as far as he himself was concerned, the equestrian side of this enterprise had been ludicrous from the moment of setting off—first half a horse, then the aid of a stirrup, then, it was true, a mount which he was no longer obliged to share with a wooden-legged man—and now no mount at all! And all the while the mare might be grazing quietly round the other side of one of these hillocks which so tiresomely obscured the view up the valley. Or, of course, she might have taken the other direction and gone back to Loch Eil. He really did not know why he was assuming that she had strayed up the glen rather than down.

After a while Marie-Cyprien stopped and swore. It was waste of time to go over the ground twice like this. He would be obliged to return, and on foot escort the grey garron and its rider. Well, that was no great hardship; but if the accursed Mally had really been stolen, how was M. le mari, when he was fit to move, to be conveyed from that abominable hut? For he would certainly not be able to walk; Galand's bullet had created too much damage. . . . The thought of his ex-comrade had not visited Marie-Cyprien's mind for some time; now he wondered for a moment how he was faring. It was more than possible that he himself would sooner or later join him in captivity, although it was encouraging to reflect that these three days of wayfaring had not brought him into as much hazard in that respect as might have been anticipated.

Although Marie-Cyprien was now beginning to despair of finding the stray, he suddenly perceived that if he mounted one more hummock he could very likely get a clear view up the glen. But this being a higher mound than usual, he went round the side of it, over the reddening little cranberry plants, and was immediately rewarded by the vista he had hoped for—and by something more. There about a quarter of a mile away, down on the level, was the fugitive Mally slowly returning to him—but, to his petrifaction, with the addition of a rider, a man wearing a plaid, a man being carried by the mare rather than riding her; a bearded man, he seemed to be, and one whom quite naturally Marie-Cyprien did not know . . . that was to say. . . .

Dieu! was it conceivable that that phlegmatic animal had of her own volition gone up Glen Suileag, stopped at the right hut, and spirited M. Maclean away on her back? No, it was not conceivable! And yet, as the two came nearer. . . .

"By all that's impossible, it *is* M. le mari! It must be witchcraft . . . though it is true that the hut cannot be much more than a couple of miles away. But I should have thought that his condition—and certainly he appears to be hanging on to the beast's mane. I must go and meet him! No, I'm hanged if I will—unless he shows signs of actually falling off. I shall wait for him here and direct him to that happy reunion which I, Cyprien de Lancize, have helped to bring about when it was so much to my interest at least to have delayed it! Yes, I will wait on this monticule, like a guardian angel!"

And he sat down on the cranberries and watched the slowly oncoming horse and rider with the greatest interest. Little Madame Bride—he supposed she would be happy now! Would she tell her husband of that affair the other night? But, first and foremost, how was she going to get him back to Inchrannoch, or to the West, to this island of his? For to the watcher sitting on the hillock it was more obvious every moment, as the mare brought her rider nearer, that he was not yet capable of a prolonged excursion anywhere.

And then suddenly the Frenchman no longer found himself contemplating Ranald Maclean's leisurely advance along the floor of the glen, but staring rather fixedly at a spot on the higher ground away to his own right, a sort of shoulder commanding, just as he did, a view of the horseman below, and, in fact, considerably nearer to the latter than he was himself. Here stood a couple of rowan-trees, the outposts of a small wood of mixed growth, from which they were separated by a short tract of bracken. Out of this wood into the bracken there had stepped all at once the figure of a man with a gun over his shoulder. And this man, at sight of the rider below, had first stopped dead and then quickly swung down the weapon—Marie-Cyprien could just make out that it was a musket, not a fowling-piece—dropped on to one knee and was now hastily loading it.

Marie-Cyprien drew in his breath sharply and his face darkened. He did not like these preparations. What was this man's purpose? He was not in uniform; could he be, not indeed a soldier, but some government agent or sympathiser about to seize a chance of killing a man whom, presumably, he knew to be a proscribed rebel? That at any rate, for little Madame Bride's sake, he, her admirer, could not sit by and see done. Yet the only method of preventing it was this ancient pistol, about whose carrying powers he felt doubtful. Still keeping his eyes upon the man by the wood up there he put his hand to his belt.

The unknown marksman, who had never looked round, rammed home the charge. Marie-Cyprien took a glance at his own already loaded firearm, and with some difficulty cocked it. The man with the musket got up and moved forward, crouching a little, into the tall bracken. "Ten thousand devils!" thought the observer. "What am I to do if he is going to lie in the fern where I cannot see him?" No, he was only creeping forward to a spot nearer to the edge of the slope—he was choosing the two mountain-ash trees themselves for his post.

Down below Mally came steadily on with her burden. Marie-Cyprien, his teeth set, changed his position and steadied the long barrel of the pistol across his injured left arm. He had the man covered at all events. His own thoughts were hopping about like peas in a pan. "It is just conceivable that he has seen a stag on the other side of the valley . . . a pretty business it will be in that case if I shoot the hunter . . . I doubt if this old blunderbuss will carry as far . . . possibly it will burst. . . . I must not be too hasty, like that triple fool Galand . . . better merely wing him. If he has any companions near, it will be devilish awkward for me afterwards . . . I must wait as long as possible, therefore, to make sure . . . By God, it *is* Maclean he's after!"

For, half leaning against one of the rowan stems, which hid him, presumably, from the rider's view, the marksman raised his musket to his shoulder . . . and it became quite clear what was his quarry.

He had not time to look along the barrel before Marie-Cyprien fired. Yet, as the assassin staggered, his finger convulsively pressed the trigger, and the almost simultaneous shots echoed and echoed through the quiet glen as he went down choking and coughing into the fern. Away below Ranald Maclean pulled up, startled, and the Frenchman, the smoking pistol still in his hand, ran like a deer down the hummock and along the level towards him, calling his name.

"I have given that fellow his quietus, I think!" he shouted in French, when he was within distance. "But in a moment I will go and make sure. Who was he?"

Mally's rider, one hand twisted in her mane, did not answer that question. He seemed considerably dazed. After staring hard at the apparition in snuff-colour he got out: "Monsieur de Lancize! But what are you doing here? Is it possible that you are come from——"

"Yes, from Inchrannoch," finished Marie-Cyprien. "To find you—your wife and I. Madame Maclean is there— at the end of the valley—waiting. I came on to look for this mare . . . which was fortunate, *hein?*" He held up the old pistol, which had done such execution.

But he saw instantly that Maclean did not realise how nearly he had escaped death, and by whose intervention. His mind had seized on only the one thing.

"*My wife!* Here in Glen Suileag! You are mocking me!"

"Go and see for yourself! You cannot miss the way. But I will come with you and lead the mare.—No, first I will look at the gentleman up there with the musket. He may be preparing for another shot . . . at us both."

He turned and ran up the steeper slope towards the rowan-trees. The bracken was aslant and broken, but Gregor MacGregor, who had threshed about there in a brief agony, was quiet now, with scarce enough breath left to bubble the bloody slaver on his lips. He was shot through the throat. Only into his already glazing eyes, as the young Frenchman bent over him, there sprang a brief gleam of defiance, and he tried to raise a hand; then the gleam went out, the hand sank, and he was gone to join those many dead of his fierce, hunted, vindictive race, who had drawn their last breaths much as he.

Marie-Cyprien took off his hat, crossed himself and hurriedly muttered a prayer, his mind busy with the astonishment with which he had just recognised his fellow guest of a few days ago at Inchrannoch. It was a private feud then, which had ended thus . . . and might so easily have ended otherwise for Ranald Maclean. "I think

Madame Bride should give me full pardon now," he reflected, as he covered the dead man's face with a corner of the plaid which had once been dashed into Ranald's. "I have played the guardian angel to some purpose, it seems, and purged that idiotic act of Maxence de Galand's as well. . . . And here is a weapon more effective than mine!" French, and practical, he collected the fallen musket, powder and balls preparatory to hastening back to the rider below.

But Ranald Maclean, whom he had thought barely capable of sticking on a horse, and lazy Mally herself, only too glad to go softly, had been moving on at a fast walk, and were just disappearing round the hillock whence the saving shot had been fired. No need for his good offices, for the path could not be mistaken. Maclean would find his wife unaided and, no doubt, prefer it so.

His own rôle being over, Marie-Cyprien d'Ornières de Lancize sat down under the rowan-trees but a few paces from *le loup mort* (as he thought of him) and pondered rather wearily on the best route to take back to the coast and a now extremely problematic *Bien Trouvée*—which vessel, in fact, did he but know it, had been captured weeks ago by His Majesty's ship *Glasgow*. Not very satisfactory three months, these! He had failed in his mission to Prince Charles Edward Stuart; in his *aventure galante* with the most attractive girl whom he had seen for twelve months, and had had the devil of an unamusing time among hills, bogs and mists—with the immediate prospect of entering upon a second period precisely similar. And he feared that he had left no very favourable memory of himself in the mind of little Madame Bride . . . except of course that he had behaved during the last two days and nights in the most exemplary manner imaginable. Bayard himself could not have bettered his conduct. Yet she would never know of his expiatory semi-vigil outside her door at Steall, nor had she even heard that devastating sneeze of his early this morning, evidence of his chivalry and its cost.

And he had undoubtedly saved her husband's life as well. Bayard's counterpart threw himself on his back, his hands under his head, and looked up at the morning sky between the ash-boughs. Here he was, back in the identical valley where the half-witted Galand had made such a mess of things. "Perhaps it is my fate," he thought, "to go circling round these execrable mountains for ever, like a man bewitched. I shall end by becoming a Scotch man, the founder of the Clan MacLancize. If Madame Bride could only have founded it with me I might not have objected. Alas, that is impossible . . . and without her this climate and this language would be insupportable." He yawned, rolled over, and in two minutes, lying almost as still as the dead assassin in the fern behind him, was enjoying some of the arrears of sleep due to him from the last two nights of heroic discomfort.

(3)

To Ranald himself, now, it seemed that he must be fey. How could Bride be here in Glen Suileag? Who had told him a thing so incredible? And yet he believed it. He believed that it was she who in some manner had caused the mare to be sent up the glen to him—for she had behind her the magic of the *sidhe*. Whether he was in the ordinary world or out of it, embodied or disembodied, he hardly knew, as he urged Mally along the winding and uneven track between the tangled hummocks where the risen sun was making silver of the gossamers. . . .

. . . And gold of the flying hair of a girl running towards him, reaching him with a cry as the mare stopped of her own accord, a girl there by his saddle, gazing up at him with the most lovely look of wonder and tenderness, putting her warm hands upon his that clutched the mane, and saying his name over and over again. The syllables were like honey in his ears; never had it sounded so. At her touch Ranald loosed his hold, bent from the saddle quite easily and strongly, and clasped her as she stood on tiptoe; and then Bride's arms came round his neck and her lips met his.

And at that—since nothing in life could be so piercingly sweet—he was sure that he was out of the body . . . and yet not so sure . . .

He had meant that his first words should be "Have you forgiven, Bride?" but the phrase, almost the thought behind it, was gone, swept out of mind on this deep tide of ecstasy. And yet he knew he was forgiven, without the asking; and in spirit he knelt before her. But she was speaking now, saying—what was it? Something about a shot—soldiers—something about Monsieur de Lancize?

Gazing down at the anxiety in those marvellous eyes of hers, he tried not to resent the effort he must make to reply, and shatter this crystal, this holy moment which held them reunited. And indeed he answered as a man new-landed in the country of his heart might dismiss the storms of his voyage thither:

"Soldiers? There are none, blessing of my life! The Frenchman? Someone fired at me, he said. . . . He shot the man. . . . What matter? Nothing matters now!"

Yes, Ovid was wrong, or else Malcolm; poor Malcolm had not the story right, nor that versifier at Blair, for the tardy, the cruel lover was not come too late! Here was Bride alive, more desirable, more magical than ever, his own, his very soul, her darling head bowed suddenly against his knee, the fairy locks streaming down the stirrup leather. And when she lifted it and, smiling at him through tears, began to lead the mare along the path, he took it as an omen—forgetting that it was autumn and not spring, the Highlands, not the country of the South— he took it as an omen that the early sunlight shone nowhere on the pink of almond blossom, but only on the clustering embers high-hung on the rowans, the small, faintly yellowing birch-leaves and the dark and changeless nobility of the pines.

AUTHOR'S NOTE

ALTHOUGH it took place in a house about seven
miles from "Inchrannoch," the episode related in
Chapter XIII is true, and its heroine was also
a Stewart.

It is likewise a matter of history that the *Bien
Trouvée* set on shore five French officers at the
time named, and two of them actually had an
interview with the Prince near Achnacarry, he
going, as a precaution, under the name of
Drummond.

Full details of the Dunkirk preparations and
fiasco can be read in Colin's *Louis XV et les
Jacobites*.

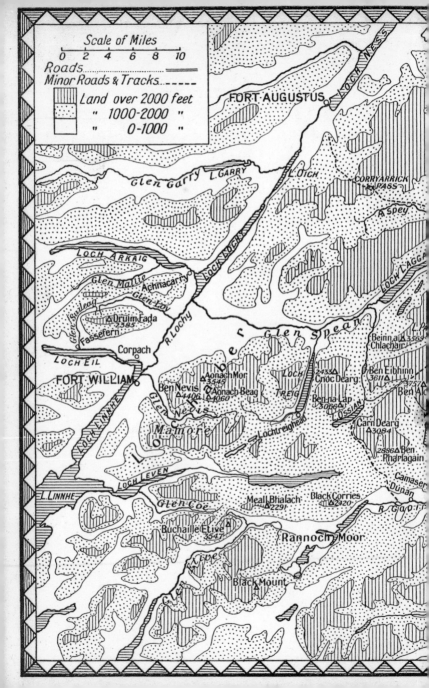